TROPICAL DOWNS

TROPICAL DOWNS

*A Novel of Peril and Misadventure
in Search of the Elusive Automatic Bet*

MARK CRAMER

DRF Press
New York

Published by
Daily Racing Form Press
100 Broadway, 7th Floor
New York, NY 10005

ISBN: 978-1-932910-74-2
Library of Congress Control Number: 2008937097

Cover and jacket designed by Chris Donofry
Text design by Neuwirth and Associates

Printed in the United States of America

In memory of Dick Carter (Tom Ainslie),
Art Kaufman (Lee Tomlinson),
and Dick Mitchell,
generous human beings
and maestros of the art of calculated risk.

S omebody asked me, "Bukowski, if you taught a course in writing what would you ask them to do?" I answered, "I'd send them all to the racetrack and force them to bet $5 on each race." . . . The human race is very good at treachery and cheating and modifying a position. What people who want to be writers need is to be put in an area that they cannot maneuver out of by weak and dirty play."

—CHARLES BUKOWSKI,
"Upon the Mathematics of the Breath and the Way,"
from *All's Normal Here: A Charles Bukowski Primer*

ACKNOWLEDGMENTS

The author would like to thank the following individuals: Martha Arraya, Brad Free, Alan Kennedy, Don Menaguale, and Ken Webster, whose critical readings of the manuscript were indispensable; Walter Solon Romero, who introduced me to his deep understanding of the spirit of Bolivia, and so many other Bolivians who contributed their wisdom; Steven Crist of *Daily Racing Form*, who has taken publishing risks (unusual in today's business); Dean Keppler and Chris Donofry of DRF Press and copy editors Jay Boggis and Robin Foster, who with exemplary skill and care handled all the complexities of putting out the book; professional researchers Drs. Kevin Maki and John Sember, as well as various *C&X Report* readers who contributed valuable racing research; Nick Kling, one of the great public handicappers, who allowed me to portray him in a fictional way that probably does not pay him the tribute he deserves; and Ed Bain, whose example as a practitioner of the automatic bet proved to me that it can be done.

Calvinism versus Hedonism

The inscription on my gravestone will read: *He searched for the automatic bet.* The Grim Reaper could not have kept a more rigorous betting ledger than I have, and from these records I am forced to recognize that the profits I have earned from horseplaying, when seen in terms of dollars per hour, are not worth bragging about. When facing my maker, I have an airtight excuse. Intrinsic to the activity of comprehensive handicapping is a Calvinistic work ethic. The daily toil of studying past performances, watching replays, analyzing statistics, doing research, and keeping records begins at the obscene hour when the first horses are working out before sunrise and ends when our favorite jazz clubs are closing their doors for the night.

Within this work regimen, where does the passion fit in? What happens to the immense thrill of a stretch drive in which our 10–1 longshot is fighting for the lead? This is the great contradiction. Horse betting is a hedonistic activity that requires a Calvinistic work ethic. Many sages would argue that the contradiction is irreconcilable.

One day I decided there must be a way to minimize the Calvinism and maximize the hedonism. I would throw all that study time onto the front end of the process, do extensive research, come up with worthy automatic bets, and then let the investments roll on their own with no further intervention. I would be able to partake of the excitement without paying the extraordinary dues associated with the investment of time, which ulti-mately is a greater obstacle than the investment of money.

Conventional racing wisdom has always been clear: There's no such thing as a winning system. With time, all systems must break down. Samples of 20,000 races show that all the usual primary handicapping fac-tors will show a loss. Anyone can engage in number crunching and throw categories such as class droppers or top speed-fig horses into the mix and come up with the usual garbage in, garbage out. And it gets worse when you pile on positive factors, as if more meant better. I can give you the horse with the fastest speed rating, the best early pace figures, the most recent peaking efforts, and the highest class competency, and you will have the type of horse whose low-payoff victories will not occur often enough to compensate for his disappointing losses.

I have been convinced of the need for more artistic combinations of factors: not primary factors but contrarian ones. What the experts call secondary factors will emerge as dominant under certain conditions, and if I could only define those conditions, then I'd have my automatic bet. I'll pronounce the "S" word: my "system."

My belief in nonlinear thinking was incentive enough for me to pro-ceed with the research. But then came an additional motivation. I had the opportunity to live abroad where great adventures beckoned. Specifically, there was a poorly paid but immensely exciting job as a journalist in Bolivia, a country that has remained outside the tourist circuit and therefore guarded its authenticity. Bolivia is in the tropical Andes, the region with the world's greatest biodiversity. You can literally walk from one climate zone to another, among 13 distinct life zones that include the cordille-ras (more than 1,000 peaks above 17,000 feet), the mysterious, fern-laden cloud forest, and the Amazonian tributary region with more species of plant, insect, bird, and mammal per acre than anywhere on earth. Botanists and zoologists still discover "new" animal and plant species. With dense mountain ranges and impenetrable cloud forests, a considerable part of underpopulated Bolivia is accessible only on foot. No wonder backpackers come across the ruins of ancient cultures, hidden in the hinterlands.

I hesitated. I had to consider my usual sources of supplementary income, freelance writing, language teaching, and most poetic: horse betting. There was no horse racing in Bolivia, and this was just prior to the period of Internet wagering. Even if I had been seduced abroad by a Bolivian beauty queen who doubled as a professor of theoretical physics, I would have had to reject the offer if it meant abandoning my love affair with racing. At the time, I already had one automatic bet that was bringing in regular profits. With the help of friends who agreed to fax me the past performances of my specialty races and put in my action, and with the understanding that I could travel back to the USA at least twice a year for extended horse betting (Saratoga, Santa Anita, Canterbury, Laurel), I decided, with my wife, to embark on the Bolivia adventure.

Aside from the betting action, my plan was to do what I call artisan research. I would receive regular infusions of *Daily Racing Form*, which I would use for pen-and-paper research, churning out reasonably large samples to prove or disprove my hypotheses. I could not compete with the numbers crunchers, some of whom admitted to me that large and apparently sophisticated databases nevertheless excluded most of the types of nuances I wanted to research because they were *not designed to re-create the way specific past performances looked for each horse in the field on the day any particular race was run*. By missing against-the-grain nuances, the databases produced Wonder Bread results. I carved out samples the way the artisan baker produces a crusty loaf of bread.

I would submit my findings, whenever possible, to reputable independent research artisans, who would subject them to separate samples for either negation or validation. The isolation of Bolivia would free my mind from the usual subjective static.

What happened after our arrival (wife, son, and myself) was completely unexpected. Bolivia was going through turbulent times, and as a reporter I had a chance to be in the middle of it. Not only was I able to cover international soccer, but my publisher had me doing investigative reporting on anything from illegal logging in lower forests to corruption in high places. I met people from all sectors of society and found myself in the middle of major historical events. One of my front-page investigations was picked up by prime time TV. Others were reprinted in various newspapers.

From all the drama, a double story emerged, one in which American horse racing and literally "high" adventure in Bolivia became entwined.

I resolved to portray this adventure in a novel, taking up the challenge of integrating all of my racing research into the story. Any images of autobiography are only contextual and not in the main character himself. Other characters, derived from diverse slices of humanity, are redesigned into composites that make them entirely fictional, though no less authentic, with the plot developing around their idiosyncrasies. Yes, people and events are changed so that this can be a story, but nothing within is farfetched—unbelievable as this may seem. The scene of a friendly softball game between Cuban and American embassy personnel, for example, could have been stricken from the story as pure invention, and yet it re-creates a real event.

Most important for readers who happen to play the horses, each and every piece of handicapping research is presented either to the letter of the law whenever possible, or in the spirit of the law if the concept is proven to be correct but parameters are only partly mechanical. Some names of horses have been changed for chronological and aesthetic reasons. Statistics may be abbreviated so as to not puncture holes in the story, but the parameters and outcomes of those statistics are rigorously respected.

In real life, I traveled regularly to racing venues, so the action in the novel often shifts to American racetracks and the regions where they are found. Anyone who has lived abroad knows that with the "distance" of a completely different culture and setting, travelers are able to view their own cultures from a special angle. In my case, the distance helped ease me beyond the boundaries of the numbers-crunching culture and come up with research that leads to smart bets.

Some skeptics confuse automatic bets with permanent bets. No investment is permanently sustainable. Sure-fire business paradigms evolve, change, and even dissolve. Some of the most profoundly beautiful love affairs end in separation. Even renewable solar energy will one day become a bad bet when the sun dies out. And during the final flickers, red-blooded statistical horseplayers will still try to get in another automatic wager.

None of this racing research would have come out quite the same were it not for a Bolivian context that was unrelated to racing, so if you're only interested in who's going to win tomorrow's race, this story may go beyond what you are seeking. For me there were hidden connections between the out-of-racing experience and the next day's wager. The more vulnerable I would feel in this risky and very foreign context, the more I learned to consider racing as a refuge. Here is a story of eternal return, an adventurous departure from racing and then a return at a surprisingly different level.

INTRODUCTION

This is a two-lane road that has spiraled up to a mountain pass, 16,000 feet above sea level, far above the tree line. I see tufts of boggy grass and minute butterflies, purple and yellow, cold brooks leading to lagoons of maximum transparency. I'm surrounded by glistening white glaciers. There's a rich blue lagoon in the direction where I plan to go climbing. It reflects a sky whose deep blue is unknown at lower altitudes.

Before I climb, I piece together the circumstances that got me to this forgotten corner of the world. Everything points to the fact that I have left Maryland and am living here against my will.

"You made me live in Laurel," Sonia had argued, "just so you could be in bicycling distance of a dumpy racetrack." Even when Sonia was not dancing or getting around on Rollerblades, an immense self-assurance emanated from her size 5 frame. Sonia's voice retained its youth and playfulness long after she had matured. The visual source of her agile authority was found in her deep, dark eyes. I looked beyond the flare of her long winking eyelashes, in search of a bend in her spirit.

"You loved the cherry blossoms in spring. You said that the autumn leaves were even brighter there than in New England. Those were your words," I reminded her.

"You could have chosen beautiful tracks like Santa Anita or Keeneland," she countered. "I've just spent five years in a place where there's no chance to grow."

"You worked in the literacy program, didn't you? You told me that was fulfilling."

Sonia had once dumped a promising banking career in order to follow me to Europe. I felt I'd saved her life from the overwhelming stress of Wells Fargo Bank. She felt as if the Trust Officer growing within her for nine years had been rudely aborted just before coming to term.

Even before we'd married, she'd dropped some hints about her real avocation. She had mentioned that in another life, she could have chosen to be a nun.

At the time, such words only made her more seductive. I imagined her flowing dark hair under a mysterious veil. On the outside agile and sensual, on the inside there was a hidden messianic lode in the tradition of Pope John XXIII.

In recent years more obvious hints trickled in. She had grilled me with annoying Socratic questioning about the social relevancy of my horse racing. Her rhetorical style was far from the combativeness of Brenda, my ex, who would badger me about my confining my life to things involving "play": playing the horses, playing jazz.

Sonia was firm but mellow.

"You're good at what you do," she would assure me, "but I've seen much bigger bottom lines at Wells Fargo. If you put the same effort into medical research or economics, you'd have discovered a cure for cancer or created a food distribution system to eliminate world hunger."

Normally, she would grudgingly admit that there was a human benefit, mind expansion, in the immense puzzle-solving challenge of horse race handicapping. But as years went by, faster than the horses I was betting, Sonia's need to serve a social purpose coalesced into a thick mist hanging over our household. One day, it all condensed.

"Matt, I've been talking with the Marianelas. They require a five-year commitment for mission work. There's an opportunity right now. I know we hardly have time to organize a change, but the project is happening right now."

The Marianelas are do-good missionaries who get themselves in trouble in places around the world that no one ever heard of. Their headquarters are in upstate New York, and that sounded good to me, having gotten my start in Saratoga. With my jazz piano future fading in the face of more talented competition, gigs in places like Albany or Burlington were more realistic than Manhattan or D.C. I had never gotten over my inexplicable block against playing in the keys of F and A-flat. In places like Schenectady or Troy, I would be important enough to choose the key.

"Go for it," I said, relieved that the uncertainty factor would be eliminated.

"But this means we'll have to move."

"No problem," I said. "The takeout is lower in New York State."

"I'm talking about Bolivia."

I had seen Argentine and Chilean shippers win at Santa Anita. Peruvian, Panamanian, and Venezuelan racecourses popped up in the news from time to time. Uruguayan breeders were a best-kept secret. But I'd never heard of a Bolivian racetrack, and not even a Bolivian horse. Nor had I heard of pari-mutuel llama racing in Bolivia.

That was back in the mid-1990s, before Internet betting. Sonia had languished in Laurel for five years, and now it was symmetrical payback time.

"We can take our fax machine," she said. "Your racing friends can fax you the past performances." Little did I suspect that online past performances would soon become ubiquitous.

If I were a normal player, that would necessitate supporting the whole fax paper industry. But, in fact, I only needed the maiden turf races. At the time, that was my exclusive play. Bet the high-rated Tomlinson turf pedigree horses switching from dirt to turf for the first time against proven losers on the grass or horses bred to hate the turf. No other method in my horseplaying existence had provided a higher return on investment. At that time, handicappers were judging turf maidens on their dirt form, and I was getting 20–1 on horses that should have been 2–1.

Friends like Art could fax me the turf maiden races from New York, Bill from Louisiana, and Vince from L.A. Vince had been a SoCal bookie, until multi-card simulcasting had ruined his business. He then opened an eclectic book store that featured horse racing in the front and pornography in the back. I could depend on Vince for putting in my action. He suffered from a syndrome that could be considered the converse of pathological liar. He was incapable of telling a lie. His bluntness had led to the breakup of three marriages. He'd say things like, "Honey, you look lousy this morning."

He was one of the very few adult human beings who had never learned to blast out the adjective "beautiful" when being shown a newborn baby. Vince would call 'em as he saw 'em. When our Deedee was born, Vince was one of the first to visit Sonia at the hospital. When Deedee was brought into the room by the nurse, Vince took a long look.

"She looks scary, Sonia. Weird."

Nothing fazes Sonia, and you can't put her on the defensive. Other mothers would have made a mental note to exclude Vince from all subsequent dinner parties.

"I'm relieved, Vince," she responded. "If someone like you, who considers pornography as pure beauty, had said that Deedee was beautiful, I'd have been horrified."

Vince's Zorro-like good looks got him into office jobs while Vince's clumsy honesty usually got him booted out. He was skilled at accounting but not with the subtleties of office politics. So he drifted into the bookie profession, where he could operate totally on his own. I could trust Vince with my bankroll. He was ultracompetent and incapable of telling a lie.

With Vince, I could get in my bets and trust his accounting. Playing the horses would be the easy part of being in Bolivia.

Sonia had explained to me that we would be living in La Paz, at 12,000 feet above sea level. I recalled that I'd once driven up to 9,000 feet on the way to Tahoe and was hit by a sudden desire to fall asleep and never again wake up. I had gotten out of the car, and then had to sit on a rock and bend my head between my legs to prevent a major fainting incident. Sonia was dutifully concerned about my adapting to the altitude.

"No problem," I assured her, unable to smother the machismo that seethed within. If Vince had been there at that moment, he'd have told her that I was bullshitting about the altitude.

In fact, I was perversely challenged by the idea of adapting to a territory where you need nearly two breaths to inhale the same amount of oxygen you'd get in one breath at sea level.

But I was not so thrilled about Sonia's new project: working with the Landless Peasants Movement. In those pre-Google times, I had to make a trip to the library to find out that the Marianelas go to these impoverished places and rather than giving out handouts, they enfranchise people, helping them to create collective economies couched in spiritual solidarity. On several occasions, Marianelas got gang-raped and murdered when their "base communities" had threatened the power of local landowners or oil companies.

Over dinner that evening, our discussion continued.

"What about my music, Sonia?"

"You can play in Bolivia. La Paz is a big city. There are music clubs, salsa clubs, even jazz clubs. You'll find work. You won't have to make nearly as much. The apartment comes free with my volunteer work, and the cost of living in Bolivia is a fraction of what it is in the USA. There's an English-language newspaper. When the editor sees your résumé he's bound to hire you as a music critic. You'll fit in fine. You even *look* Latin."

The description was not quite true. Yes, my old man was from Colombia, and I'd learned Spanish from him. True, I had the dark straight hair of a Latin, and my complexion could have earned me the label of "Hispanic." I was built like a Latin: not as short as Maradona but when I shot a lay-up, the basket seemed way up there. But I had never been to my father's country of birth nor lived south of the border, and my old man preached assimilation. I'd picked up an ear for music from my American mother, Gershwin and Ellington, and my mannerisms and gestures marked me as a gringo.

I relished the adventure of hustling up an income in a strange land, and I figured I could complement whatever I earned freelance with winnings from the races. But I was not convinced about Sonia's safety.

"The landowners have their paramilitary goons," I groaned. "Remember the Marianela nuns who were killed in El Salvador? Maybe you could forget the Landless Peasants and get involved with Mother Teresa-type work. You'd have the whole world on your side. Besides, what the hell do you know about farming?"

"They're taking me on because of my administrative skills. Death squads won't attack an office in La Paz. Besides, ever since they imprisoned their last dictator, Bolivian people have no tolerance for political violence."

Since that seminal discussion, our life has certainly changed. It took me six months to adjust to the altitude, by gradually extending the length of my walks, then beginning with light jogging until I built up the stamina that comes when the challenged body learns to manufacture extra red blood cells. I now do serious running around a makeshift soccer field, carrying stones as I accumulate laps, to scare off the menacing stray dogs. I've gotten used to climbing, as well, and I can now feel entirely comfortable at 17,000 feet.

I am heading up to a stone-silent 17,000-foot ridge that will allow me a face-to-face view of one of the roughest mountain glaciers in the world: the unclimbable Wila Mankilisani. I have tickets for a flight the following morning to Miami, with connections to New York and Albany, with my ultimate goal, Saratoga.

I am up here in the mountains to clean my mind, to prepare myself for three weeks at the greatest American racetrack. I want to expunge the tribulations of my daily life and establish a tabula rasa for the Saratoga past performances.

What better place than the totally silent ridge looking into the deep gorges where rivers wind down, taking in tall waterfalls, gaining momentum, eventually leading to the Amazonian rainforest. I can now gawk in total silence at the white robes that soften jagged peaks. I can empty the tainted contents of my mind.

ONE

The Long Way to Saratoga

White silence. That was the simple goal of hiking up to a perch where I could sit and contemplate the splendid Wila Mankilisani glacier.

From the minibus drop-off at La Cumbre, it only took me fifty minutes to get there. I thought I knew the territory with my eyes closed. I'd climbed four different peaks in and around the same area. I had two goat-cheese sandwiches with tomato in my backpack, along with a bag of potato chips, two chocolate bars, and a quart of water, all I'd need since I'd planned to swing back down to the highway two hours later and hail a minibus back down into La Paz.

Early August was the heart of winter in the Andes, which meant that it was the dry season. You never needed to consult a weather report. In mid-afternoon La Paz, it reached about 65 degrees in the sun but remained in the 40s or brisk 50s in the shade. With nothing to hold it in, the heat dissipated to the frost point at sundown. Two hundred meters higher, a rare bout of precipitation would touch the ground as white flakes, taking away the rough edge of the shanty town. Unless you lived there, you could appreciate the white blanket over the garbage dump at the edge of an open sewer.

Back down in the hole of La Paz, you'd wake up and see a white halo around the city. By 10 A.M., the halo would disappear under the glaring sun. Up in the mountains, the day temperature was warm in the sun and frigid in the shade, explaining why the snow never melted in some spots. It would fall below zero at night, but I wasn't planning on camping out.

I was a Peeping Tom, leering at Wila in her pure white gown. I sat on a pile of loose shale. A sharp ridge at my back shielded me from the unfiltered sun. The message here was unmistakable. I should avoid the hype surrounding Saratoga and look for nuances in the past performances, uncover pattern matches that no one else might perceive. The only thing in common between one Saratoga meet and another was the radical departure from any generalized annual pattern. I needed to find the rarer patterns, a trainer who wins coming from Rockingham, a small, low-percentage Kentucky stable that wins with one big longshot each year at Saratoga, certain Maryland turf trainers who have prepped back home for a weekday Saratoga win at 1⅜ on the grass.

Suddenly I spotted an imperfection. There was a trail on Wila's skirt, probably a thin llama track winding around like a sharp ribbon, descending then into a canyon that would lead to Chacaltaya, site of the highest ski run in the world and also an early indicator of the ravages of global warming. Chacaltaya's glacier was steadily receding, and might be gone in a few years. Wila's glacier seemed intact, but the llama track at her base suggested that the mystery beneath her veil might unravel.

I was now mentally prepared to confront Saratoga. Rather than retrace my steps back to the highway, I decided to scale a steep ridge with good shale shard traction, pass even closer to Wila, and then double back down to the Cumbre road, descending from the other side of the jutting peak that had acted as my sunshield.

Two jagged peaks to the right of Wila would be my guide. I had climbed both of them, and they had become my trusty landmarks. I looked down at the shards under my feet, not for more than a few minutes, and when I looked back up, my twin peaks had vanished in a sudden mist. The fog was an aberration from the normal weather pattern. This was the dry season, and the clouds were unexpected invaders, usually reserving their incursions for nighttime.

The momentary anomaly triggered serious questions about Saratoga.

What if the usual handicapping paradigms were suddenly shrouded in new and unknown phenomena?

Without my usual visible landmarks, I turned right, and down, not realizing that I had needed to progress another 30 or 40 degrees to the right before descending.

I landed in an eerie valley. With no llama paths visible, I suspected that I might have been the first human being to set foot here. I spotted two long-necked white birds with extended twiggy legs, wading in a bog. From their black-tipped feathers, I recognized them as Andean flamingos. None had ever been sighted in this region.

This should have been a great aesthetic moment, but I was lost. I didn't even have a camera to prove that I had spotted the flamingos. Instead of appearing in *Nature* magazine, I was more likely to end up in the *National Enquirer:* AMERICAN HIKER, DISAPPEARED IN THE ANDES, RESURFACES ON MARS.

Matt Bosch, second-division jazz musician, stumbled upon an unknown corner of the world, into a niche that serves as a portal to outer space.

I had been dumb enough not to tote a camera, but why hadn't I at least slipped my daughter's toy compass into my backpack?

I had no choice but to climb back up the same way I'd come down. This second climb of the day was not as easy as the first. I resolved to slow down for the early fractions so I wouldn't die in the uphill stretch. In brief moments of mental clarity, I realized that a mild panic was giving me the added energy to get to the top. Inevitably the adrenaline would dissipate and the energy sap. When I got there, the mist had thickened, and I could not even spot the trail I had come from. The sensuous Wila had disappeared.

I took another path downwards, roughly in the direction of the highway, with no idea whether I was on the proper downward spoke of a grand invisible wheel.

With no warning, a patch of light appeared, for no more than five seconds, allowing me to identify the floor of the valley. I spotted an indigenous woman with the typical bloated *pollera* skirt, woven shawl in patterns dominated by red and purple, and the typical black bowler hat of the Aymara. I had just emerged from a black-and-white *Wuthering Heights* into a Technicolor ethnological documentary.

The shepherdess was accompanied by six llamas and a son, about four years old. The boy-pastor had puffy red-brown cheeks and straight black hair. No schools around here for the kid. With the subsiding of my panic-produced adrenalin, great relief set in. With relief came a major bout of fatigue.

My Spanish served no purpose. I had intended to study the Aymara language but had put it off. It was a strange tongue with untranslatable words and insider jokes whose humor would not catch on with the Leno or Letterman crowds. I was aware enough of the Aymara lexicon to know that they would have a single word meaning "safety at the end of the valley."

"Cumbre," I said, pointing in different directions as if to ask her which path would take me to safety. She pointed into the valley, into a dark mist of near zero visibility. If I were to venture into that tunnel of mist, I could imagine finding more Andean flamingos before I found the highway. At the other end of the cloud chamber was a distant galaxy.

I had another option. I faced a ridge, one that I had once climbed. I knew that the highway was far below on the other side of the ridge. This would be my third climb of the day. But at least it was a known landmark. The mist was thickening, and the cold humidity had pointed claws. I had no time to rest. I was ill prepared to stay overnight. I was supposed to take a plane the next day, with Saratoga as my ultimate destination. What should have been a two-hour prance in the hills was turning into a supreme test of endurance, a challenge to the whole notion of hope.

I would be climbing from about 16,400 to 17,000 feet. That doesn't seem like a whole lot, about the distance of two vertical football fields, but I was only able to take 10 steps at a time before needing to stop and rest. During my first rest, I grasped for the image of Sonia. She would be the surge of hope that could strengthen the endurance factor. But I had no control over my thoughts, and interrupting petite Sonia dancing the *cueca*, swaying with erotic elegance, was the image of Marianela nuns being raped and murdered by death squads in El Salvador in punishment for their having defended the landless peasants.

I zapped the image. With each rest stop, I would now think of big scores at the races. I conjured up a Richard Matlow first-time starter with

Ortega aboard, slow works, no-win jockey, and I had the horse for a 9–1 return.

Ten more steps. Rest stop. Woodcote, 45–1 at Hollywood Park, and I had him. It was so easy to filter out all the losers. Horseplayers are skilled at forgetting their failures.

Nine more steps. I couldn't handle the tenth. I looked up. The mist was thickening. I couldn't even see the top. A $70 winner at the Cal-Neva tournament in Reno, with my partner Mike Holmes. Had more than a hundred on him. A McAnally horse, bred in Brazil. Lightly-raced versus proven losers at the nonwinners-of-one allowance level. My climbs were shortening, the rest stops were lengthening.

Eight more steps. Couldn't do step nine. I sagged onto a long rock. Hit the trifecta at Laurel when they still had that big turf festival on a Saturday in September and you could play the Euro shippers automatically. A Maurice Zilber horse finished on top at 14–1, and I also played him for the win.

I was not ready to lift myself off my rocky bench so I went over the whole harness season at Rosecroft. Then I got up to do another eight steps, and plop on another rock. The sixth step was long and rubbery. This time the ground came up to me.

With the shortening strides and the lengthening rest stops, I'd need a Pick 6 or a Pick 9 to inspire me to the top. My Pick 6 hits were too modest for latent energy. I was on my own.

Eventually I made it to the peak of the ridge, only to discover that visibility was zero. The descent to the highway was too craggy and booby-trapped to do it blindly.

My last chance: take the gusty ridge, which my memory told me went due north, eventually descending to the vicinity of La Cumbre. I ate my last chocolate bar, savoring each bite. Hours ago I had donned my final reserve level of clothing. It was only 4 P.M. (I'd started at 10 A.M.), but in the absence of sunlight and with the whipping of the gusts, the wind-chill index plunged below 32. I wore a Julie Krone tee shirt, a flannel shirt over that, an alpaca sweater over that, and a down windbreaker with hood as my fourth layer.

The wind-gutted ridge eventually descended, just as it should have.

I was taking a whipping from both sides, as if the wind were a tag team. I came upon a lagoon where I had once picnicked. The path was made up of hairpin turns, and I soon lost my sense of direction. Why hadn't I taken my daughter's toy compass? I called myself dumb, but that was an understatement.

I began to think the unthinkable, in two parts.

Part I: Having to spend the night near La Cumbre, building a shale hut stone by stone to avoid the mortal threat of hypothermia.

Part II: Missing my 7 A.M. flight to Saratoga.

The possibility of death in Part I was not quite as alarming as missing my flight to Saratoga in Part II.

Through the dark cloudiness to my left, a sudden opening, a magical patch of light that included the sun. Instantly I knew that I was walking northeast, which was the right direction. Seconds later, the opening clamped shut, and the sun was erased.

It was as if a second canister of adrenaline had burst open. I now jogged down the incline, with joy in my tank, nearly crashing into a parked four-wheel drive. The La Cumbre road had to be near. Inside, a romantic couple held hands, perhaps two adulterers, enjoying the rare tranquility of this inspiring but pitiless place where their legal mates could never find them.

I interrupted their reverie, asking to be driven to the asphalt road. The man gladly obliged. We arrived before I could finish humming "Viva Mi Patria Bolivia," imagining Sonia dancing the syncopated rhythms of the *cueca*.

I flagged down a passing bus. Never was the smell of peasant humanity in a Bolivian bus more heartwarming. In the final hairpin turn into the mainly indigenous suburb of Villa Fátima, the sun appeared, as if it had never really been absent. The August blue sky was once again cloudless, as it should have been all along.

I got off the bus, bought myself an *empanada* at an outdoor stand, and flagged down a radio taxi for La Paz. Suddenly it was hot. I removed the windbreaker. I slipped out of the alpaca sweater. I had gone to Wila Mankilisani to clean my mind for Saratoga. I had learned a valuable lesson. I would have to be poised for the unexpected, ready to improvise.

When I arrived at the doorstep of our eighth-floor apartment in the Sopocachi neighborhood, Sonia hugged me with mixed emotions: relief that I was there (since I should have arrived five hours earlier) and nunlike reproach, that I had stupidly risked my life.

"Don't talk about risks," I said. "You're working with those crazy Marianelas."

I asked her to promise me that she would not rub elbows with the landless peasants in the Santa Cruz hotlands, at least while I was gone. I reminded her that their movement needed her office skills in La Paz.

Next morning, I took a taxi up to the highest airport in the world, the only airport where planes fly downward after taking off.

I was off to Saratoga.

TWO

Klinging

A bsence makes the heart grow fonder. As we landed in Miami, I was
already missing Sonia. But at this moment in my life, Saratoga
was my other woman. She had been good to me in the past, but she was
known for spurning even those who loved her the most.

Another uncertainty hung over my arrival. Vince, my Southern
California action supplier, had suggested that I get together with a guy
named Panama Slim, an L.A. real estate magnate. Vince explained that
Slim could have been the Donald Trump of L.A. But while Trump cultivated celebrityhood, Slim, à la Howard Hughes, avoided all contact with
the media.

"Wherever you turn, you bump into a Panama Slim building, especially in West L.A."

Panama Slim was Vince's landlord. Slim was a rarity in the business,
a hands-on landlord. He would personally inspect the premises of his
multitude of renters. Vince called him a control freak. A few weeks back,
Slim, who had weighed in at 11 pounds at birth and sucked the nipples of
his mother like a trained torturer, had inspected Vince's store.

"I was worried he might object to the porno section, but he didn't
blink. In passing, just small talk, he mentioned he'd be away for a week
on business in Bolivia, and that was the second time in my 45 years of life
that I'd heard anyone mention Bolivia. You were the first. So naturally I

told him I had a friend who was now living in Bolivia. First he asked if you were dependable. I thought the question was strange, but of course I said yes. You know me. I can't hide the truth. Then he said he'd like to meet you. I told him I'd talk to you."

Vince's honest authenticity inspired people to share information with him. Evidently Panama Slim was negotiating with entrepreneurs in the Bolivian lowlands to build a racetrack. I imagined there could be some sort of gig in it for me, and with racing involved, how could I not be curious?

They had once raced in the eternal-spring valley city of Cochabamba, but the 9,000-foot altitude was simply too much for the horses. The highest U.S. track is near Santa Fe, at 7,000 feet, and even Arapahoe, at 5,200 feet, is a difficult racecourse for incoming shippers. One of my favorite angles involves horses vanning down to a sea-level track from Arapahoe, provided they showed their previous work at Arapahoe within two days of the race.

Racing failed to thrive in Cochabamba, and marketing problems shared the blame with the uncomfortable altitude. At near sea level, Santa Cruz was horse friendly. People gambled on local card games, cock fights, and even motorcycle drag races. The Santa Cruz region had replaced La Paz as Bolivia's business center, and money passed freely from hand to hand, disposable income that could easily find its way into pari-mutuel pools. Agribusiness and banking were big. Once you got out of the city, the Santa Cruz hinterlands were Bolivia's version of Manifest Destiny, with pioneers and adventurers drawn there in hopes of getting rich. I would learn the details from Panama Slim.

Miami should have been a simple transition. But something was coming over me. Carrying only a backpack, I found myself yearning to haul some bulky luggage, envying people with the heaviest loads. It was uncharacteristic. I'd spent the decade avoiding heavy objects ever since I'd worked on a janitorial staff and had had to bump and roll refrigerators up staircases. It was a small frame lifting a big frame, and I did it, but not without discomfort.

My ex-wife had had a penchant for home improvement, and she would start things that I had to finish. The finish might include disposing of heavy boxes of refuse, or changing the position of oversized furniture.

That was not the reason for my petitioning divorce, but it certainly didn't help the marriage. In a moment of epiphany, I had resolved to avoid all unpleasant physical labor connected to human maintenance. I even made that clear before I married Sonia. As it was, 80 percent of life is spent on maintenance, and I was committed to improving the quality of the maintenance time. I'd paid my dues.

Now, here in Miami, I was experiencing my Arapahoe-shipper angle in the flesh, and was bursting with pent-up energy. I found myself volunteering to lift an old lady's bulky suitcase from the carousel to the trolley.

My bloodstream was brimming with the extra red corpuscles that the body manufactures to compensate for the low air pressure and resulting lack of oxygen at obscenely high altitudes.

Considering my newly obtained superpowers, I discarded the rent-a-car idea, and resolved to buy a used bicycle for my energizing commute between the Glens Falls summer cottage of my Aunt Ada and Saratoga. My 88-year-old aunt, ruggedly individualistic, would not consider the possibility of a nursing home and continued to maintain this cottage as well as her regular home, a wobbly Victorian structure near downtown Albany.

Getting a bicycle was both an aesthetic and a strategic decision. I had found that bicycle commuting to Laurel Race Course had sharpened my mind for the intense decision-making tasks of in-the-trenches horse betting.

The first two afternoons of Saratoga racing proved that the anomaly of August fog in the Andes had carried over into the races. I hadn't the mistiest notion of how to pick a winner. The usual methods, based on small-track shippers and Saratoga trainer specialists, were not working. The turf course, which once favored closers, was now an ally of front-runners, but turf horses that had never raced in front were suddenly changing their styles and leading the pack.

Saratoga, my mistress, was spurning me.

For me, dying in the Andes is not as bad as losing at Saratoga, so I decided to take out a compass and find my way.

My compass was the racing column of Nick Kling. Kling, a farmer, a poet, and a nice guy, was one of those few public handicappers who actually cared about the folks who read his picks. He wanted them to win. Their happiness was linked to his success.

As a result, Kling was a rarity among public handicappers. He measured his results. Forced to pick a winner for every single race no matter how undecipherable, and two days prior to the scratches that might change the complexion of a race, Kling resolved to show a flat-bet profit at the end of each meet. Most of the time, he achieved his goal. If you've never bet two bucks, a flat-bet profit is the outcome of wagering an equal amount of money on each horse (flat bet), and your bottom line at the end of the meet is positive.

Betting to win randomly results in a loss of about 25 cents for each dollar, based on the tax, called the takeout, levied by the broker (the track) in the form of deductions from winning payouts, which amounted to around 15 percent at the time. But pin-the-tail-on-the-program random betting performs even worse than the track takeout as a result of a little-understood fact: Random betting picks more overvalued horses than undervalued ones.

By using Kling's picks as a foundation, I would gain 25 points in my return on investment! Given that significant percentage improvement, all I would have to do is filter out particular Kling picks that had a reason to lose, based on scenarios that Nick could not have anticipated 48 hours in advance. Nick picks a come-from-behinder because three front-runners figure to burn each other out. Nick grimaces when two of those front-runners scratch out of the race, and the remaining pacesetter can control the lead. Nick's come-from-behinder now has no chance, but he has to live with his pick. I don't.

Nick doesn't hang out in the press box. He's not a joiner. But when you meet him one-on-one, he wants to hear what you have to say.

On the morning of the third day of races, I located Nick on the backside, in front of the Barclay Tagg stable.

"Hey, Nick, I'm glad I found you."

"Matt, you're home again."

As we shook hands, I reminded myself to say nothing about my Nick-picking strategy. Never tell a friend that you are playing his horses, or subconsciously he might become overcautious. He might balk at picking longshots that he'd otherwise embrace.

We had coffee in the greasy-spoon backside kitchen. I filled him in on Bolivia, the Marianelas, and Panama Slim. Nick clicked open his brief-case, reached in, and extracted a few copies of his most recent poems. I expected I'd enjoy them, recalling the flashes of lyricism in his racing columns.

"So you're meeting Panama Slim," Nick said. "Don't let him walk over you."

"What do ya mean?" I asked.

"You'll find out."

I ended the day with a profit, thanks to a $16.60 winner in the fifth race, and helped by the fact that I'd excluded a Kling pick in the third race, following a negative rider change. (Nick had picked the horse because his last two wins were with Migliore aboard, but "the Mig" was off his mounts for the day and the new rider was a no-win journeyman.)

I was supposed to meet Panama Slim at 6:30 at Mangino's Ristorante. The worst I could do was get a free meal, real New York Italian food. Ever since the seventh race, I was thinking in terms of eggplant parmigiana.

I was oblivious to the post-race traffic. I used the road shoulder like the passing lane in the stretch of a harness track. From my angle the aroma of pine trees outperformed the exhaust fumes. I got there at 6:25, only to find not a single nearby post for locking my bicycle. Everything in the infrastructure is made for the automobile. Nothing for the bicy-cle. Life has been programmed so there will be no alternative to driving. The guys in the kitchen told me that my bike would be safe in the back between the trash bins.

By 6:35 I was rushing into the restaurant as if my eggplant parmigiana might not wait for me.

OVER THE PHONE, Panama Slim had told me he'd be wearing a Santa Anita baseball cap. I picked him out at the bar. As his name suggested, it was the bar sitting at Panama Slim and not the other way around. His head was a size too large for his already bulky frame. He was a Cadillac with a 747 engine bulging from under the hood. This was probably the first time that the tough black-shirted bartender had ever felt intimidated.

"Well, Matt, it's about time I found you. You come recommended."

As he spoke, he waved his baseball cap as if it were an instrument for conducting an orchestra.

"You can be 'Our Man in Bolivia.' You know, like 'Our Man in Havana.' We'll need you as our point man. You know racing. You know Spanish. You know Bolivia."

His words hit the surface like shoveled coal. It was a deep voice, but too gravelly to make the talk-show-host circuit. The green shine in his eyes was magnified in the dim light. He had dark, bushy hair, with an occasional silver strand functioning like steel reinforcement. I could tell his thick cigar was a Cohiba because he left the yellow wrap-around label on it, near the tip, as if to broadcast, *I smoke this illegal cigar, and what do you intend to do about it?* I noticed the No Smoking sign on a corkboard behind the bar. Slim acted as if he'd been granted immunity from the law, and no one around him dared to challenge. He let the fire die out naturally and then stashed the half-smoked Lancero in a silver container.

This was pre-Google time, and I wondered how he could have learned about me. Had I been from a traditional culture, I would have balked at doing business with the blunt Panama Slim. But I needed a raise in my income, and what better path to financial independence than racing! Playing a piano gig at Thelonius Bar on Calle 20 de Octubre in La Paz netted me a couple of dollars an hour. *Bolivian Times* paid me a Bolivian-level salary for writing music reviews and covering international soccer games. Even if I'd landed a straight job in Bolivia, the salary would not cover for an American lifestyle. I had a wife who was into volunteerism. In exchange for her work, they paid our rent, and that was it.

On the way from the Andes to Saratoga I had experienced the illusion of being a free man. Now I was clinging to Kling and tethered to Panama Slim.

For Panama Slim everything is literal. "Point man" meant that there were 10 points on the contract between Slim's West Hollywood real estate company and the Santa Cruz group, headed by Manuel Arce. All I had to do was get Arce's signature on the 10 points.

I ordered eggplant parmigiana. Panama Slim intervened.

"Hell, Matt, this place is famous for its fish. You can't order eggplant, can you?"

And then, turning to the waiter:

"Give this man the best fish dish on your menu."

I had asked for red wine.

"You can't have a red with fish. Give us a bottle of your best white wine."

Panama Slim felt that he could buy me out by giving me what I didn't want to have. He hadn't flunked his business psychology course because he'd successfully intimidated the professor.

Slim was frank, Slim was even naive. It may have been the effect of the whiskeys he'd downed at the bar.

He had grown up in the Canal Zone of Panama, an enclave known for its racism. He never forgave Carter for handing the canal over to Panama. It was "our canal," he said. "We built it."

The fish was good, the wine was surprisingly full and pungent, and I decided to dig in, enjoy the meal, ask for the best dessert on the menu, sip a rich Italian espresso, and then tell Panama Slim that I could not take the gig.

I certainly wanted to see a racetrack in Bolivia, but I had made it a point during my life to avoid working for people I would not like to see in my living room. I understood the business potential. In effect, they were outsourcing racing. Running a racetrack is a labor-intensive activity. Racing was one of the last labor-intensive businesses to remain in the USA. As it is, the industry would not survive without the importation of Mexican and Central American labor.

Slim also held the offshore card. The Santa Cruz Chamber of Commerce had influence. It was a combination of Wild West and modern capitalism. They could wrangle tax breaks and even get offshore benefits written into the law. Not far from the Bolivian lowlands there were thriving racing industries in Argentina, Brazil, and Chile. Bolivia was at the center of a triangle formed by those three countries.

A racetrack in Bolivia, with all its potential spinoffs, with a local monopoly, and integrated with Argentina, Brazil, and Chile was a mortal lock. The land itself figured to quadruple in value once the track was up and standing magnificently in the tropics.

Still, I had decided to turn down Panama Slim's offer after I'd downed the tiramisu.

He preempted me. He made an offer I couldn't turn down.

"You're the point man. We're offering you $10,000 per point. The contract has 10 points. Get Arce's signature on the 10 points, and you make one hundred thou." Slim was literal. He left nothing to the imagination.

Seizing a moment of strength, he turned the tables and made it seem as if I were an applicant instead of a consultant in demand.

"We gotta know that you don't discriminate," he said.

Panama Slim had suggested, between the lines, that he felt some cultures were superior to others. Now he was telling me he opposed discrimination.

"What do you mean?" I said.

"I mean, this Arce fellow is not a nice guy. I mean that I hope you have nothing against people who are not nice guys."

I had the urge to tell him that if I ate dinner with *him*, then he had all the evidence he needed that I could work with people who were not nice guys. Slim had once evicted a tenant with no court order, his two hired hands taking out the IKEA desk and dumping it on the Santa Monica sidewalk, where its bolts were loosened with the thud. The tenant was a young poet. The tenant could have called the cops. Slim would have been arrested. The kid saw the tattooed biceps of Slim's two assistants. His idol Bukowski would have put up some resistance, but the tenant decided that it was in his interest to let bygones be bygones.

Once again, Slim preempted me.

"I know you think that I'm not a kindly person, but this is business. Nice guys are the people who give you tips when you play the piano. We're offering much more than tips. After you meet Arce, you'll appreciate *me* as the nice guy."

Slim flashed a contract at me. I scanned for the 10 points and verified the hundred thousand. I signed. We shook hands. Or rather, his squared claw hand crushed my piano fingers. I wheeled over to the

Saratoga half-mile harness track for the late races, locking the bike on a rail fence in the parking lot. I found my buddy Stan Grabowski, former harness driver, masters in American literature, soccer coach, nice guy.

No need to handicap. I could play my preferred harness race system, the CCC:

1. *Class.* Horse must show at least a thousand dollar earnings per race (easily scanned from the performance box at the upper right-hand side of the past performances), for this year's and last year's races combined, with all the other horses in the field earning less than a thou per race. You can play as many as two qualifying horses in a field. (If there are three or more earnings qualifiers in a field, pass the race. At tracks with higher purses, you can use $2,000 per race as the cut-off point. Exclude horses going off at above 19–1.)

2. *Competitiveness.* Horse must have more wins than places or shows.

3. *Current form.* Horse must show at least one win or two places in its last four races.

4. No layoff horses.

All the information is available in the performance box at the upper right-hand corner of the past performances. I'd once tested the system for a whole summer at the Quebec City harness oval, and it came out with an 18 percent profit. It had also proved profitable at Rosecroft for earlier runs.

In the fifth race, I had two qualifiers, the 4 and the 8, the latter marooned on the outside. The 4 horse was 9–2 and the 8 was 6–1. I played them both to win and boxed them in the exacta. Stan's a better harness handicapper than I am, but he'll back my horses out of pure friendship. This time he convinced me to play the trifecta sandwich, in case my horses finished first and third in the exacta.

All the inside horses left sluggishly, allowing the 8 horse to glide into a perfect racing spot. He caught the leader, my 4 horse, who dropped back to third at the wire. We both collected on the 8 horse in the win hole, and the tri came back at 160–1.

Stan's solidarity and exuberant optimism restored my confidence in the human race. We cashed another one later on the card. Two hits were all we needed for a rewarding evening.

On the way to Stan's car, the glorious night humidity hung in stark contrast to arid La Paz. I craved to bottle the warmth and take it back to La Paz. Stan offered to park my bicycle on the rack on top of his old Buick (a battered version of Panama Slim's inflated Batmobile) and drive me home. But the pine-cone mountain aromas of summer in upstate New York were too splendid to resist. I decided to wheel home. My headlight was working, and I had a flashing red tail light. I rode back over Route 9 to Ada's house, wondering how I could have moved to a place above the tree line.

THE SARATOGA MEETING had its ups and downs. After having successfully excluded 10 of Nick Kling's top picks, I excluded an eleventh one, and that horse won and paid $22.00. In the later days of the meet, my exclusions became more refined. Nick's return on investment was plus 5 percent. I was up 9 percent.

I met with Panama Slim several times at the racetrack. He gave me a portfolio of papers, a list of talking points, and further instructions. I picked out a few faint traces of humanity in his gravelly voice, but he was still Panama Slim.

On the last day of the meet, with a profit assured, I decided to press the Nick Kling button to the limit. I decided to raise my bet on one of Kling's picks. Looking back at my records, Kling horses that "figured" less in the past performances were the ones that paid more. A Kling pick that got hammered by the bettors was far less interesting, even if it won.

On this card, Kling had picked a Michael Dickinson horse that was coming back after a 15-month layoff. River Reader had once been a top turf horse but horseplayers know that any horse that takes a lengthy vacation has a physical impairment. The logic is clear. Such horses need to work themselves back into form.

This was before Michael Dickinson was recognized as the great horseman he is. He had a small stable and few "experts" realized that his turf horses were making money for the players who backed them regularly. Kling's logic was contrarian. The fact that an accomplished trainer like Dickinson had laid the horse off for so long meant that patience and loving care had nurtured the horse back into form. Had Dickinson been using this race as a mere "prep," why would he have shipped River Reader up to Saratoga on the last day of the meet?

In fact, River Reader had regular workouts spaced every five days, and, more important, his record on the main Saratoga turf course was two wins in three starts. Yet, thanks to the layoff, he was 12–1.

The race was a mile and three-eighths. River Reader stayed along the rail in the early going, in midpack of the 11-horse field. By the time they entered the final turn, you could see that River Reader could hardly contain his pent-up energy, but had nowhere to go.

The unresolved polemic among turf race followers is whether it's better for a rider to wait for room at the rail and therefore save ground, or take the horse wide on the turn in order to profit from the horse's willingness to accelerate. Gomez usually waits along the rail. Three-fourths of the time, he finds an opening. In the remaining 25 percent of the races, he gets blocked and constrained and finds room too late to outgallop the closers on the outside.

Gomez waited and waited. Then, the tiring leader drifted out, as often happens, and the gifted rider rolled his RR over the inside track. River Reader drew off in the final yards. Following the race, Gomez noted that "the Red Sea opened for me," but in fact, it had been a skillful ride for a deserving trainer.

My Saratoga meet was over. Thanks to Nick Kling, I had won some money. But not nearly enough to even consider saying no to Panama Slim.

AFTER THE RACES, I invited Nick to Mangino's. I ordered eggplant parmigiana and drank red wine. I congratulated Nick on once more ending a meet with a flat-bet profit, and it was now possible to explain my Klinging, Nick-picking betting strategy. Nick was happy to hear about it, but fatigued. The meet had taken everything out of him, and his bosses at the *Troy Record* did not understand enough about racing to appreciate his feat.

On the River Reader pick, he explained that he had chosen the horse based on a pattern match. He'd remembered that at the previous Saratoga meet, in the waning days, Dickinson had won with a turf horse going a mile and three-eighths following a 13-month layoff. Today we call this decision making "thin slicing." Nick had extracted one slice of important information from a complex loaf of factors and had decided that this was *the* deciding factor of the race. This was a neat balance between objective science and pure inspiration.

There are players who win a Pick 6 or two, or triumph in an intense horse betting tournament, and then coast on the glory until they burn out. But few are able to sustain the intellectual passion. Nick Kling is one of the few.

While Nick Kling accomplished miracles, Panama Slim made money. Nick Kling retreated to his farmhouse to write poetry. Panama Slim went back to the bar for another whiskey, signing up yet another soldier for his worldwide enterprise.

THREE

Arce

You pronounce it *arsay*.

I had not done my homework on Panama Slim. Having been told that Manuel Arce was not a nice guy, it seemed prudent to do some research leading up to my flight to Santa Cruz, even if I learned nothing in advance about his taste for eggplant.

Sonia helped me, using the computers at the Marianela office. From time to time, I took a glimpse at her, not letting her know that I was gawking. She had both the height (5'1") and the agility to be a jockey, but she was built more like a woman who would hang out in dance clubs than turf clubs. The Marianela influence was now transforming Sonia's features. She wore a colorful Aymara shawl, and I feared it might be the first step leading to secular nunhood, if anything like that existed.

She used to apply eye makeup around her already large and transparent eyes. That was part of the past. Now just a hint of lipstick. She now used bras that were a size too small in order to guide attention away from the middle and upwards through her eyes and into her mind. In order to highlight her philosophical bent, she wore necklaces or bracelets featuring La Pachamama (Mother Earth), symbol of the Landless Peasants Movement.

Sonia found no conclusive evidence on Manuel Arce outside of the typical Chamber of Commerce hype. She found a speech in the *Presencia* archives in which Arce had criticized the feudal backwardness of the La Paz elite, predicting that the forward-thinking Santa Cruz capitalists would inevitably shift the focal point of whatever existed of a Bolivian economy to the lowland region.

There were certain contradictions between the stereotypes of lowland Bolivians (*Cambas*) and highland Bolivians (*Kollas*). Cambas like Arce were free-market neoliberals. Kollas were rooted in archaic indigenous traditions and steeped in the informal economy. Cambas spoke fast, danced, and partied. Kollas spoke slowly and went to sleep early at night. Cambas, according to the Kollas, were superficial. Kollas, according to the Cambas, were slow-witted. The Cambas liked beauty pageants while the Kollas celebrated by paralyzing the country with massive street demonstrations.

Arce was a Camba nationalist, in the mold of Northern Italian national fronts. That was all we knew about him. There were two rival nationalist groups, and he headed one of them. The Arce family included poets and drug lords, painters and rubber barons, sociologists and market ideologues.

Sonia begged me to be careful. I hadn't even told her about Panama Slim's unflattering evaluation of the Arce personality. Why create worries based on hearsay?

Later I learned that Sonia too was withholding information on the subject. She was aware of the potential for goon-initiated violence in the lowland region, related to landowner opposition against the Landless Peasants Movement, but she did not want me worrying about her safety.

I had two days of meetings with Arce, with a bizarre adventure sandwiched in between. He picked me up at the airport in his cream-colored BMW: tinted windows, a dashboard that looked like the cockpit of a 747, luxurious cream-leather seats.

There was no evidence to back up Panama Slim's evaluation of Arce. He was in his early fifties, fit and spry, slightly graying, a well-trimmed mustache, hand-knit *guayabera* shirt untucked. It was the portrait of a Spanish creole gentleman. Surprisingly, he drove on his own. You see tinted glass, and you have someone with something to hide. Maybe he hides his mistress inside, or he's being coy so as to not draw attention from his rivals for power.

Unlike cramped and hilly La Paz, Santa Cruz is flat and spread out. The city has "rings." Arce's ranch was in the third and outermost ring. Santa Cruz was founded in 1561 by the Spaniards to supply the colonies with rice, fruit, sugar, and cotton. Today it's a major producer of export cash crops, mainly soybeans, destined as animal feed in Europe. In fact, tropical agriculture on its extended plains has eclipsed the city's reputation as a focal point for drug trafficking. The city itself is modern, but not without traces of frontier architecture. The valley is clear, but the jungle is never far off, as represented by the sloths that hang out in the trees of the city's main plaza. Poor critters have no escape when teargas envelopes the plaza during a protest demonstration.

The roads from the airport were lined with palm trees, banana trees, and wooden vendors' stands painted in primary colors, with shelves of fruit and snacks. You could see the unobtrusive downtown skyline in the distance, with the generic cathedral spire in the center.

Arce's ranch was a tropical version of the Versailles gardens. First you had to get through the security gate. There were two checkpoints. Then you saw the orange-roof-tiled white stucco complex with a patio inside, dominated by a swimming pool, with surrounding arcades. This was the Spanish style, inherited from the Moors, with the pool replacing the Moorish blue-tiled *alberca*.

I was tense. First, I was not used to cavorting in this culture, and would have preferred to be taken to a hotel for the night. Instead, I was shown to my room, a spacious suite with modern Danish furniture. Second, I could not remove the $100,000 from my mind, based on the 10 "points" in the contract.

The early evening meal was lavish, but a little too carnivorous for my taste. The central plate was the *rodizio*, grilled meats that represented the entire "farm in the zoo." Cold beer was the drink of preference, thanks to the 90 degree heat. I went along with the crowd, which included several of Arce's business partners. His wife, a former beauty queen who was aging with grace, sat at a separate table reserved for the wives of his partners. Arce made constant eye contact with one of his partners' wives. A possible affair. I identified the woman as the wife of Mendoza. The dark-haired squat Mendoza peered over at Arce and me, and the spite in his eyes that should have been meant for Arce seemed to deflect upon me.

Sundry children were under the care of several maids. All the maids had the indigenous features of highland Aymaras or valley Quechuas.

The talk had nothing to do with business, except for a flurry of questions about American racing. This may have been their intentional strategy to put me at ease. What were the advantages and disadvantages of a mile track, as opposed to a mile and an eighth? Would it be a good idea to have a swimming pool for the horses on the backside? Should they create a replica of tropical Hialeah?

The business potential seemed even better now than I had imagined when discussing it with Panama Slim. Cheap labor was abundant, and the tropical aromas in the air meant that the Hialeah design would be seductive. Once the project got past the signing of the 10 points, I intended to push for special features that might draw people to the track, such as a free child-care center. I longed for a job where I'd be at the track and have something to say about the way it was run. This was the proverbial opportunity of a lifetime.

Who cared if I wasn't working with exemplary human beings. For me it was a moment of potential euphoria, except that Mendoza couldn't wipe the scorn off his face. Maybe he didn't understand how a jazz pianist and horse bettor, with little knowledge of the business world, could be in line for a piece of the cake.

Before dessert, we went inside to a large living room containing a piano. Like Panama Slim, Arce knew things about me that would have required research. He asked me to play a song for his audience. I chose a piece with some degree of Latin crossover: "Watermelon Man."

Polite applause, and then Arce lifted his glass and called for silence. He had an announcement to make.

"Matt, we are proud to say that we have read the 10 points in your contract and have decided to approve them. We only have a few wrinkles to iron out, but not in the contract. It's perfect."

He promised a pungent liqueur.

There had been no negotiation, no give and take, not even the chance to argue the pros and cons. It was all far too easy. I imagined what I'd do with the hundred thousand. Twenty thou for a betting bankroll, and finally I would be unburdened by scared money. Another twenty thou to buy off the ex-wife, put aside in a trust account where she could withdraw her child-support payments. In return I would receive a waiver from her, excusing me from all subsequent payments. The final sixty thousand would be handed to Sonia. I didn't care what she did with it. She could invest in the stock market (precisely what she would have done in her prior life with the investment crowd). She could put a down payment on an apartment. She could donate it all to the Marianelas. As long as I had my twenty thou horse-betting bankroll, I was well and fine. They say that betting 4 percent of bankroll is a safe strategy for money management. That would mean bets of $800. I'd never been above $200, and I usually got weak knees if my bet reached a hundred.

We never did get to the liqueur. That night, already in my pajamas and dozing off from the potent combination of beer and heat, I heard a hesitant knock on my door. At first I was frightened. Sonia's word "goon" had been sifting through my mind at that moment. Mendoza didn't like me. He could be sending over a hit man. I came to my senses and asked, "Who is it?"

"Mr. Arce has sent your liqueur."

It was a feminine voice with a resonant twist on the "queur" that dissipated like a petal in the breeze.

I opened the door, to the sight of a stunning *morena*, a well-stacked woman of smooth olive complexion, a seductive smile, and beautiful dark eyes with just a touch of a slant, suggesting Okinawan origin. That was only a guess, based on a paragraph from one of the travel books I'd read before arriving in Bolivia. Evidently in 1954, Okinawan farmers had been uprooted and dropped in sparsely inhabited eastern Santa Cruz with no drinking water and 50 hectares of useless jungle land for each family. Her long flowing black hair seemed right out of a Gauguin painting, but lowland mestizo Bolivians could also be mistaken for Polynesians.

She had nothing in her dainty hand but elegantly polished nails, mild pink. No aperitif.

"Mr. Arce has sent your after-dinner treat. May I come in?"

Her voice was as soft and caressing as Sonia's, but the contrast was in the overtones. Sonia's was a haunting flute while my visitor's greeting was a melodic viola.

Had I been a quick thinker, I would have explained that I was very tired after a day of travel and wining and dining. But there are certain moments in one's life when "yes" is the automatic answer, when the vocal cords move more quickly than the neurons.

She entered and sat down on the sofa, baring her firm but tender legs up to her thighs.

"May I make myself comfortable?" she asked, beginning to remove her shawl. I couldn't see much cloth under her transparent pink shawl. The faint lighting shone on soft, bronzed flesh with delicate curves in all the right places. She adjusted herself in the sofa with subtle movements that suggested she was a trained model, but her waist was a tad too fleshy to qualify as Miss Anorexia.

"I'm sorry," I said. "I am not used to paying for entertainment."

"That's okay. I come as compliments of Mr. Arce."

I glanced quickly at the ceiling and around the walls. I suspected hidden cameras. Perhaps this was Arce's way of exercising his control over me. I still didn't have any signed document in my hands.

I am not a Calvinist. And even if I were, it would have been difficult to resist this seductress. I don't go out of my way to become unfaithful to Sonia, but if a woman gets dumped in my lap, it is hard to resist. Lately, Sonia, under the Marianela influence, had shown enough faith to cover for the two of us. Part of me was very ready for this piece of modern art. But I sensed a setup. The hundred thou was more important than a night of forbidden flesh.

"I think you should leave," I said.

"You haven't even asked my name," she said, in near perfect English.

"What's your name?"

"I'm Muñeca."

"Doll," I translated. "What kind of name is that? You'd better leave."

"Mr. Arce would feel insulted," she said, in the sweetest way, curling up in the sofa and flashing more leg and beyond.

She was wearing red, yellow, and green panties, the color of the Bolivian flag.

"Look, Muñeca, I've had a long day. Why don't you let me invite you to lunch tomorrow."

I opened the door. On her way out, she brushed against me, advertising her curves in the most tangible way.

"Please let me stay. Mr. Arce would never pardon me for leaving you. I could sleep on the sofa."

I'm a sucker for a sob story. I led her back in.

"I gotta turn off the lights," I said, not wanting to mention the phrase "hidden camera," in case Arce had planted surveillance devices. I took her hand and guided her to the large bathroom, seating her on the edge of the bathtub. I sat on the closed toilet. It was reasonably safe to assume that there were no hidden bugs or cameras in this bathroom of earthy mosaic tiles.

I asked her how she got into this spot. She explained that she had been Miss Santa Cruz. She had been defeated in the quest for Miss Bolivia by candidates who danced ballet instead of *cumbia*, who contributed money to the pageant, who came from the leisure class rather than her origins as the daughter of moderately successful creole-mestizo farmers.

"You look Okinawan," I said.

"That would be a coincidence. I understand there's some Croatian roots on my mother's side of the family."

She now worked as an escort, she said, with no apologies. She had a luxurious apartment in Santa Cruz. She had been able to refine her once schoolgirl English thanks to conversing with so many international clients. She met diplomats, soccer players, and cocaine kingpins. She was able to support herself along with her seven sisters and brothers and her parents. She dug her hand into her Hermès leather purse and produced a business card, which she handed to me delicately. I stuck it in my wallet without inspecting it.

"You're working for Arce," she said. "That means we have something in common."

"Do we have job security?" I asked.

"Mr. Arce has a complex life. Some people are jealous of him. He makes enemies."

Even with her scant dress, Muñeca transmitted a whole lot of self-assurance. In business dress she would be capable of walking into a boardroom and controlling the meeting. She steered clear of personal comments referring to Arce but she did whisper that she had heard in her immense grapevine of all kinds of glowing predictions for the racetrack business.

I would have liked to pry out more information about Arce, but her soft moist lips would tighten with the mention of his name. I needed a few hours of sleep in order to be on my guard with Arce for our second and last day together.

I sent her to my bedroom, and I slept on the sofa. The *surazo* winds were blowing. The temperature had suddenly dropped. Minutes later she came out, asking me if she could borrow a shirt. I gave her my Julie Krone tee shirt.

The next morning, I whispered, "No talking." We took turns in the shower, and she left for the door. I shook her hand.

"Don't lose my card," she whispered. "You will find that you need me."

RIGHT AFTER BREAKFAST, I was taken by a servant to a sand-colored four-wheel drive. A driver was waiting for me in the front seat. He told me to take a seat in the back and that Arce would be with us in a moment. Arce waved good-bye to his wife and took a seat next to me in the backseat. Not a mention of Muñeca.

In 30 minutes, we stopped on the shoulder of the road. We got out. The driver stretched his legs.

"This is it," Arce said. "This is the property where we will build the racetrack!"

Something was terribly wrong with the scene.

"But there are people living on this land," I said. "They're farming."

I saw corn growing, and bananas growing, and soybeans growing. I saw wooden huts, tarpaper roofing, tin roofing, stray pigs, vegetable gardens, barefoot little children running around with nothing on below the waist, outhouses, thin streams of stinky waste waters.

"This is my land," Arce said. "I have the documents to prove it. The people you see are squatters."

"Can you get a court order to evict them?" I asked, stupidly.

Arce flashed the court order. He took out a cigarette lighter and burned the document.

"Those people are part of the Landless Peasants Movement. Those fuckers don't give a holy shit about the law."

Arce was sounding more like Panama Slim and less like a Spanish Creole aristocrat.

"Fifteen years ago, I could have phoned the army, and those people would have been evicted in two hours. Bolivia has changed. The Kollas want to bring us back into the Middle Ages. They hold our economic growth hostage. They would abolish the wheel if they had the chance, and then do everything on foot."

So this was the wrinkle that Arce had been talking about. For the first time I was staring at the people Sonia was defending. For the first time I learned that Sonia and I were in opposite camps.

"What shall we do?" Arce asked. "I have *friends* who could come in at night and remove these squatters before sunrise."

Stalling for time, willing to postpone the hundred thou, I suggested a conference call to Panama Slim.

"He doesn't want to know anything about this. That's what he said. You're the point man. Once we remove these people, I sign the contract, and Panama Slim pays you whatever he promised you. Then we will have new work for you, consulting on the design and management of the race-track, and recruiting American trainers."

No wonder everything had seemed so easy. Panama Slim had not sent me to get signatures. He had sent me to do his dirty work, or at least order it done, so that he would be exempt from legal responsibility.

"You have all this open land in the region," I said. "Just give these people another piece of land."

"They already had another piece of land, and they were tricked into leaving that land. They don't trust us about any new piece of land. And where are we going to get this new piece of land you propose? Here in Santa Cruz, the gringos have a reputation of being naive. Some say that's a cliché but you are validating the cliché."

"There's only one way," I said. "Diplomacy. You can negotiate. Find solutions through negotiation."

"Fine," Arce said. "We will pursue negotiation. But it will be in our style."

"What do you mean?" I asked.

"Never mind. It won't be worse than what you Americans practiced with your eminent-domain laws and the routing of the redskins."

"That was a hundred fifty years ago," I protested.

"You still have your eminent-domain laws," Arce noted. "And when did you ever see squatters tolerated in America?"

Arce had me boxed in. He put his hairy arm around me.

"Look, my friend. All I am asking for now is your empathy. We are not cruel people. But we cannot let this country waste away with medieval agrarianism."

I had mixed feelings about Arce. I wanted to believe that he was a reasonable man. There were a hundred thousand dollars hanging over me, nudging me into a position of "tolerance."

Later that afternoon, following a lavish roast-pork restaurant lunch that excluded all talk of business, Arce drove me to the airport in his BMW.

We said good-bye in the typical Bolivian style, a handshake, an embrace, and a second handshake. I could not forget Arce's last words.

"If it weren't for the fucking Marianelas, we wouldn't be held hostage by a bunch of serfs."

The word "hostage" rang in my ear.

Once on the plane, I mind-juggled with the events of my two days in Santa Cruz. I had always been an open book with Sonia. Now I wondered how much of this story would be good for her ears.

FOUR

Bad Bets

S onia and I joke about landing in JFK. The airport at El Alto shows a plaque with the name John F. Kennedy Airport. Most people have never noticed the plaque. For them it's the El Alto Airport. The airport lies at 13,000 feet above sea level, on the high plane (*altiplano*) above La Paz. Less atmosphere density at this altitude means less friction. For the same reason that a golf ball will fly for a longer distance, airplanes need a longer runway. This is the highest commercial airport in the world, and thus, when approaching El Alto, you will hear the announcement: "The pilot has announced that we are now beginning our landing ascent."

Depending on how you see it, El Alto is either the hotbed of well-organized indigenous protest movements or a former squatters' suburb that has developed into a sprawling shantytown of half-finished earthy red-brick structures, nearly a million inhabitants, mainly migrants from rural areas. The plane sets down, and you are landing over a spreading quilt of coarse uncertainty.

I could not miss Sonia's profile in the crowd of people meeting the arriving flight at "JFK." If there had been an Olympics event for most graceful movements in a busy airport crowd, Sonia would have won the gold. Her dainty feet touched the ground in a way that would leave no tracks. She cuddled close to me, effortlessly, the way it used to be before she'd been detoured by the Marianelas.

We stooped down to squeeze into a waiting van, Sonia going first. I guessed that she might have been one of a select few in the history of La Paz to have never bumped their heads against the top of the minibus doorframe. Her soft, thin neck curved ever so slightly, just enough so that not a single dark strand of her flowing hair made contact with the doorframe. She was a tough act to follow. I was agile on a bicycle or at a keyboard, but in unrehearsed movements I was just another klutz. This time I made it in there without knocking off my Brooklyn Dodgers cap.

They call La Paz "the Hole." You go straight down to get there. The bus bumped out of El Alto and spiraled down the only freeway of Bolivia, past precarious hillside slums prone to rainy season landslides, into the Hole. The freeway ended, and the road partly leveled out, heading directly toward the pastel downtown high-rises. We got out on Avenida 6 de Agosto, before the road would snake down again into a second hole: the lower, warmer, more affluent section of La Paz. We took the elevator to our eighth-floor apartment. Our high-rise perch offered us a view of the twin-peaked 21,000-foot Illimani by day, and a sea of lights by night, when La Paz would look like an inverted planetarium.

We made love that night with an intensity that had been missing since Sonia's infatuation with the Marianelas. Blossom Dearie crooned in the background. I told Sonia what I could say without lying, and withheld any information that I would have had to bend. She heard about Arce's tropical Versailles, but not about Muñeca's red-yellow-and-green panties, about Arce being willing to sign the contract as soon as a few wrinkles were ironed out, but not about the surreal view of the squatters farming what should have been the backstretch and training track.

Sonia wanted more information. I responded with questions of my own, like why the landless peasants do not accept alternative jobs somewhere else.

"It seems like a needless conflict," I prodded.

"These people have been kicked around again and again. They trust no one in the elites. They trust the Marianelas because we establish base communities founded on the Gospel. We open it up to participatory democracy. They express the Gospel in their own terms, mixing it with the simple philosophy of La Pachamama. We don't impose a European version of Catholicism."

I reminded her that centuries ago the Inquisition had already been imposed on the natives. I suggested that the Marianelas might get these peasants killed, and get some of their own killed along the way.

I was hoping for a miracle. Sonia would hear my reasoning from thoughtful angles and come to believe that there could be an alternative for her squatters. She could then use her growing influence among the Marianelas to find new plots of land for the landless peasants, perhaps hillier places that would not be conducive for a racetrack. Now that Sonia was doing the Marianelas' grant proposals and budgeting all their money, I was betting on her gaining enough influence to find a third way for the landless peasants and to liberate the racetrack land, and with it, the hundred thousand for us.

Sonia changed the tune. She reminded me that Deedee would finally be joining us.

Everything is upside down up in the Southern Hemisphere. Toilets flush in the opposite direction, and the school year begins in February. We were looking at a Montessori school, a strategic choice where she'd have some English mixed into the curriculum. Following the Maryland school year, Deedee had gone to a bilingual camp in Maryland to help her transition. We were buying some time before her transition, just to make sure the Marianela mission would pan out. For the time being she was just fine with her uncle and aunt in Maryland.

The Arce affair released an ominous cloud over Deedee's potential arrival, but I couldn't get myself to perturb Sonia's peace of mind. She was thriving with the Marianelas. I would give myself one more chance to resolve the Arce-Slim business before upsetting Sonia's new lifestyle.

IN THE MORNING I woke up to the faxed past performances of the sixth race at Belmont, a maiden turf event. A new pattern was developing. In the heyday of my system, I'd rarely find more than two or three horses in a field to qualify by the Tomlinson turf-sire ratings. Perfect for exactas and trifectas. I could usually eliminate more than half the field, horses that had been entered on the turf in spite of their poor Tomlinson turf pedigree, and other horses that had already shown they were proven losers on the grass. The Tomlinson Ratings were now even trustier when integrated with a newer product on the market, Mike Helm's sire rankings.

However, increasingly, trainers were subscribing to either Tomlinson or Helm. Several trainer acquaintances had even consulted me about whether or not their horse would do well on the grass. On my previous trip to Canterbury, trainer Eddie Nuss had stopped me on the backside at the workout stand in order to ask if a particular horse of his would be suited for the turf. He flashed the past performances, and I jotted down the sire and damsire. I took out the Tomlinson booklet from my back pocket and then noted to Nuss that the sire had a 120 rating with the damsire rating at 140. The stats usually required at least 200s to use a horse on the turf.

"I'd better stick to dirt," Nuss lamented.

That was a couple of years ago. Now, most trainers believed in these turf pedigree rankings. The result was ominous for my system. Fewer no-win grass-pedigree horses were being entered on the turf, and that meant that more potential turf winners could be found in most fields. It was increasingly difficult to eliminate can't-win horses. On the PPs faxed by Art, I found seven horses in the nine-horse field that would qualify by Tomlinson and Helm. Only two horses were easy throwouts. My system was melting away even faster than the glaciers above La Paz. Knowing when to get on a system is relatively simple. Much more perplexing is the decision on when to get off.

Not all was lost. Observing the actual breakdown of a successful system was like watching the implosion of a far-off star. The scientist discovers that nothing is permanent, and then studies what leads to a breakdown. My turf-sire system was losing its shine, but it had been enormously successful. In my search for the automatic bet, I would learn that "automatic" does not mean "permanent," and that each "system" would have its unique half-life.

It was not so easy for me to get off the Panama Slim–Arce deal. I was so near to collecting. Squatting in my way were the landless peasants. I considered using half my hundred thou to buy them another piece of land. Without letting her know that the squatters were blocking my path, I reasoned with Sonia that her farmers could be given another terrain. Sonia reminded me that it was far more complex than moving pieces on a chessboard.

"What other land?" she asked. "A property that they'd be kicked off of within two years? Or one as coarse as cowhide that can't even absorb a drop of water? They've been shuffled around so much. They trust no one. And you can't buy them off, especially with their base community creating deep roots."

They didn't want charity. They wanted solidarity. The Marianelas provided this solidarity. Arce's final message at the airport was confirmed with a vague threatening overtone: "Our problem is exacerbated by those Marianelas."

I crumpled the fax of Belmont's sixth race and tossed it into the cane wastebasket. I walked Sonia to her modernist office building and then continued up the El Prado boulevard to the post office at the center of town. Pedestrian traffic was thick. Trucks and buses belched. The motor traffic made the Beltway at rush hour seem like Freedom's Door. Less than 5 percent of La Paz inhabitants owned automobiles and yet motor vehicles, few of them private, mostly taxis, minivans, and decrepit buses, occupied 85 percent of all street space.

El Prado, the only main avenue in La Paz, is situated on the skirts of a gorge. On either side of El Prado, the streets run upwards. The parallel gorge contains what is left of the Choqueyapu River, now a sewer, mostly under vault covering, to minimize the stench. When the floods and land-slides arrive in February, the mud flows down from the hills. The whole mess is supposed to end up in the river. But with the river covered up, it coalesces around El Prado.

Past the post office, I turned left, in the direction of the Military Institute of Geography, in search of a contour map. It was past 10 A.M., so they'd be open. I was considering another escape to the glacier of Wila Mankilisani, in order to reflect on a new strategy that would get me out of this holy mess. Remembering my near-fatal hike to Wila, this time I would carry a contour map that would identify every nook and cranny, and I'd pick up a compass at the Huyustus bazaar.

My time was limited. Arce would discover that Sonia worked for the Marianelas. He would put two and two together and assume I was a spy. Or the Marianelas would discover that I worked for Arce, and they would conclude that I was Arce's spy. I was sandwiched in a box canyon.

Something shook. At first I thought it was a pickpocket. Pickpockets do this. They ruffle you at shoulder level so you cannot feel the agile hand in your pocket. I discovered that my arms were being grasped by two heavyset men in business suits. They sported designer sunglasses that reflected the nearby high-rises. Before I knew it, I was in the backseat of a four-wheel drive with tinted glass windows, flanked on either side by my abductors. The driver was the first to interrupt my futile protests.

"Sir, you told Mr. Arce you wanted a diplomatic solution. This is it."

"Since when is kidnapping a diplomatic solution?"

"This is complex diplomacy, sir."

The Suzuki wound down the hairpin turns of the Kantutani highway into the lower South Zone, the warmer level of La Paz, where much of the elite had their splendid residences. The road flattened out, parallel to the former Choqueyapu River, now a smelly open sewer having collected the refuse from the hillsides surrounding the city. The people in the South Zone opposed the type of tax hikes that could have provided sewers for the hillside dwellers in the north. What comes around goes around, and the South Zone inhabitants were obligated to contend with the waste waters from the north. We entered a dirt driveway, through a fruit orchard, past a garden, arriving at a two-story country manor. The stench had disappeared. The patio was surrounded by kantuta trees, brimming with upside-down red flowers.

Arce was seated on a white garden chair on a stone slab patio, nursing a drink. His slightly graying mustache and sideburns were trimmed neatly, as if they were an extension of his garden. Only his brown hair, tinged with gray strands, was slightly wild, with aristocratic flair. There was a remarkable transparency in his green eyes, as if they opened into a well of wisdom. I could not help but remember that Panama Slim also had green eyes and gray strands in his hair, but the comparison ended there. Arce was the authentic "Slim." Panama Slim would wave his arms when speaking, as if he were conducting the finale of the *1812 Overture*.

Arce communicated with more delicate strokes, like a first violinist. Slim's eyes bulged from their sockets. Arce only needed a faint sparkle of the iris to gain confidence or authority.

One of my escorts pulled out the garden chair, as if he were my waiter.

"What can I offer you, Matt?"

"An explanation."

"First we must socialize. That's the rule of Bolivian business."

"Have you ever heard of invitations?"

"If I'd sent you an invitation, your wife might have received it."

"My wife isn't nosy. She doesn't read my faxes. She doesn't butt into my affairs."

"But she butts into ours."

"Have your staff prepare me a double margarita."

"You're starting early, Mr. Bosch."

"It's already 7 P.M. in the Ukraine."

I took a sip of the margarita and waited for my kidnapper-benefactor to speak.

"You asked me to work on a diplomatic solution, based on negotiation. I have found one," Arce said, as if he were a father reassuring a son, just before the son went off to war. "It will sound bizarre at first, but you must hear me patiently, and you will see it is our only alternative to bloodshed."

It was a grand scheme to say the least. I would be kidnapped, of my own accord. Arce called it a vacation. Unwittingly I had just been involved in a rehearsal.

"You would be treated with dignity. We could send you to Chile to play the horses, or even to McLaughlin, Nevada, to a race-book hotel. You can decide. All expenses paid. If you wish, we could send Muñeca with you."

Arce sipped, savored, and saluted the surroundings.

"I am a lover of gardens," he explained. "I like to do things aesthetically. I'm cultivated. Not like your friend Panama Slim. He wanted your wife to be kidnapped. He's not a nice guy. But . . . his method might be more effective."

Finding it impossible to digest the onrush of veiled threats and new twists, I avoided groping for an inevitably ineffective response. Panama Slim's 10 points had been a smokescreen. In fact, there was a good chance that he had known, before he hired me, that Sonia worked for the Marianelas, and that his real intention was to use me as a wedge against the landless peasants settlement. As Kling had noted, Panama Slim was a control freak. If he didn't like eggplant, then you couldn't eat eggplant.

Sooner or later Arce expected me to grasp that no one gets a hundred thou for a simple signature and that I would be responsible for forcing Sonia to exert some influence upon the Marianelas, so that she would eventually convince them to abandon this base community and move their brethren elsewhere. Panama Slim must have argued for immediate eviction. The cooler Arce flashed historical cultural reasons for holding off. Those two partners had no ideological differences. It was a question of diverging tactics.

"Arce, for a consummate gardener, you should have more patience. You knew all along that my wife worked for the Marianelas. You knew I would see fit to pressure Sonia, but surely you also knew that I'd need more time to win her over to an alternate solution for the squatters."

"Yes, my friend. You seem to know me well. That was my intention. To give you more time. But your friend Panama Slim is the impatient one. It looks as if I am merely his instrument."

"I'll talk to him."

"Go try. I will bring you the phone. I assure you he has a harder head than those statues on Mount Rushmore."

We had seemed so close to the deal, but it had been a well-designed illusion.

"I could walk away from this if I wanted," I said.

"Too late, my friend. With your wife handling the accounts for the Marianelas, either she, you, or God forbid, your daughter, are now bargaining chips. Mind you, I would never agree to perturbing a child. But I am one of many partners. For people like Mendoza, a kidnapping represents a diplomatic solution because it *impulses* negotiation, and he would not be in favor of the kidnapping 'lite' that we're conceiving." (I didn't bother to correct his false cognate "to impulse." I knew what he meant.) "So this is a way of speeding up the negotiation process. Isn't that what you wanted? Or would you give the okay for my friends to move in tonight and evacuate your wife's peasant friends from our land?"

"There's only so much juice you can squeeze from the same lemon, Arce. I checked the law. Your land was unused. By Bolivian law, unused farmland reverts to anyone who can make that land productive."

"Whose side are you on, Mr. Bosch? You Americans would never tolerate such a law in your own land, would you?"

Without realizing it, I had reached the bottom of my glass. Drinks get to you quicker at high altitude. But I called for another. Arce hogged the podium.

"I would wish to have your good fortune, to be flown to a horse race betting venue, accompanied by a lovely lady if you wish, with a free bankroll at my disposal. If you accept, we would inform the Marianelas, by way of a third party, of your disappearance, and warn them that you would be eliminated if they or your wife talked to the police. This is the new way of doing business in Bolivia, using language instead of violence. Even the peasants might care about the fate of Matt Bosch if they knew he was the husband of a Marianela. But mainly these theatrics will put pressure on the Marianelas themselves.

"We would offer the peasants a new piece of land, somewhere in the hills. It would have to be cleared. We would supply the tractors. Even then we would have to deal with the ecology freaks.

"We would remind the Marianelas in a subtle way of the *tragedy* that befell the nuns and Archbishop Romero in El Salvador, and impress upon them that here in Bolivia we were being quite reasonable."

Arce made it seem oh so plausible, with the margaritas as effective catalyzers. I could come up with no alternative reality. What had to happen was happening. There was no butterfly effect. It was pure determinism, the determinism of power and wealth.

"Of course, all of this would be easier if your wife were kidnapped instead of you. That's what Panama Slim wants. But we Bolivians have a greater respect for women than you Americans."

"And if Sonia and I returned to the United States?"

"Too late, Mr. Bosch. You are perfect bargaining chips. You are the perfect bridge to the Marianelas. We will never find a better tactic. Do you think that you have been wined and dined in Saratoga and Santa Cruz for nothing? We have invested too much in you to send you packing."

I groped for alternatives. If I escaped on my own, Sonia would become the obvious target. If Sonia and I returned to the States, who said they wouldn't pursue us there? If I simply refused to be "kidnapped," sooner or later, Sonia would be taken hostage. I could spill it all to Sonia, but then she would become an accomplice to a false kidnapping scheme. I could inform the Bolivian police, but cops can be bought and owned. Arce would not be operating in the open if he did not know their price.

"I'm sure you have a direct line to the military police chief. You could have had the peasants removed," I said.

"Yes, indeed," Arce responded. "And then the neighborhood committees in El Alto would call for a national strike, blockade roads, and paralyze the country. The coca growers would join in. The teachers union and the miners union would follow. That's where the real power is in Bolivia. We are weaker than you think. But we have creativity as our weapon. In this case, a painless, hedonistic kidnapping."

I reflected on why this racetrack was so important to Arce. Yes, the labor costs were low, and he'd have a gambling monopoly in Bolivia. Yes, he could get kickbacks by offering his region as a tax haven for American investors like Panama Slim. Yes, there were simulcast opportunities and potentially an international market. But was this enough?

One other advantage crossed my mind, but I didn't dare mention it to Arce. With increasing bank regulations, drug-money laundering was becoming virtually impossible. Two Santa Cruz bankers were already languishing in the five-star section of the San Pedro prison in La Paz.

No, Arce already had plenty to gain from the racetrack. But a money-laundering institution would be icing on the cake. Money could flow into the pari-mutuel system and become untraceable. Even random wagering would fit the purposes of the launderers. They would collect on 80 percent of their input, enough to make it worthwhile. The other 20 percent would go back into their own coffers, minus the tax portion. They could bet on every horse in every race, lose only 20 percent to the track, and then recover most of that 20 percent as owners of the track.

"Arce, there's one thing I don't get. Do you give a shit about horse racing? Do you know anything about managing a track? For me it isn't only the money. I do have this love for racing, and I have my ideas about making a racetrack work."

"Mr. Bosch, what are you insinuating? Did you know that I have bred Arabians? Did you know that it was my money that poured into the failed Cochabamba track? Did you think that Panama Slim would take me seriously if I had no racing credentials? You're just going to have to accept my good faith."

"Then accept mine," I said. "Give me one more week to work on the Marianelas. If I fail to make progress, I'll show up at your door, and you can ship me out. And promise me that Sonia will not be touched."

I had a considerable task awaiting me. How to communicate with Sonia indirectly. I could say nothing of Arce's plan, for she would then become an accomplice, with all the legal consequences that would entail. I would have to provide her with some sort of implied assurance, in advance, in the event of my "disappearance." The question was how to get Sonia to act unconsciously on Arce's behalf, without letting her know that I was Arce's instrument.

I would try all sorts of "what if" questions about the Marianelas. Were they capable of giving in to Arce, in the name of peaceful coexistence? Were they capable of compromising in a commonsense way? Could they convince the peasants to evacuate the land and move to another territory? Could they be made to see that these peasants would have something to gain from the transfer?

There were too many uncertainties, too many necessary "yeses" in the chain of uncontrollable human reactions. Sonia was only the first step, though a crucial one. She would have to trigger the right response in the Marianelas. And then the Marianelas would have to communicate successfully with the uncompromising peasants.

I tried one last argument.

"Arce, how is it not possible for you to find another property for your racetrack? Wouldn't that make everyone a winner?"

"Impossible, my friend. If we go into the nearby jungle, the world ecology movement will be at our throats. If we apply any type of eminent domain, as your Dodgers baseball company did for their stadium, entirely legally, in Chavez Ravine, we would be scorned in the Bolivian media, and masses of protesters would shut down the country. We do not want more attention. We want less of it. Besides, this is my land we're talking about!"

Arce agreed to give me a week. He warned me against talking to Panama Slim. He warned me against coming clean with Sonia. He warned me that some very mean people had learned to be very reasonable for political reasons, but if those political options were no longer on the table, they could regress into predemocracy days.

"I understand that Panama Slim's hundred thousand now seems like very little to you. If you can pull off a solution one way or another, I'll equal it with my own money."

I had acquired a distaste for this money. But it represented the ticket to my betting freedom. How often does one have a chance to earn a good sum of money without hurting a soul? The peasants would get their land, and maybe even jobs with the track.

I turned down Arce's offer of lunch. For someone whose men had accosted me, he was remarkably gracious. But how much consideration would he retain if the balance of power were in his favor? Arce's "friends" were goons in business suits, constrained only by Bolivia's peasant and labor movements.

I had been thinking that the Marianelas were pushing the Arces to their limits. I considered the opposite possibility. If Sonia's missionaries were to abandon the scene, the goon elements among the landowners might have the leeway to crush the peasants without mercy. The Marianelas were acting as human shields.

The Arce business was looking more and more like a very bad bet. A stab at a $100,000 Pick 6 would have offered me better odds.

With a live longshot, however, you never know whether or not it's a bad bet until you take the risk. All too often, I had failed to take the risk and regretted it later. There was enough common sense in this racetrack business to stick with it. If it panned out, I would have that betting bankroll that had eluded me for so long, and the bankroll was just the teaser. I would also have a dream job.

I was reasoning as if I had some sort of choice. I didn't.

FIVE

Katari

With good turf-sire bets becoming a rarity, my identity as a specialist horseplayer was damaged. I needed to literally play my way into a new method, but I had no portal to a good old American racetrack nor the reams of past performances required on a daily basis. (Never would I have imagined that betting online would soon become a viable reality.)

With the paucity of betting action, being kidnapped at a race-betting venue was a surprisingly attractive proposition, especially compared to the violent alternatives.

In fact, I could even imagine a horse-betting "vacation" (as Arce called it) at the expense of Sonia. While I would be away losing myself in the immense universe of the races, Sonia might perceive that I was subject to torture and decapitation. Sonia's soft sweet voice was part of her cool nature. In a moment of crisis, panic was not an option. When faced with tragedy, she conjured up solutions based on practical philosophy that would have made her a guru in the self-help market, were it not for the fact that nothing in her inventiveness was for sale.

She had been married to an ogre. The man had once pointed a gun at her. She had stared him down at high noon, and he had melted away, dissipating onto the horizon.

As a former banking employee, she had been present during bank robberies, and then come home that evening to cook an elegant dinner.

"By the way," she had said, one evening, "they tried to rob the bank today, and they had us with our faces to the floor."

When Deedee had an appendicitis attack, I had zigzagged like a fly around a light bulb while Sonia reminded me that we lived in the late twentieth century and that I should calm down and appreciate modern medicine.

Yes, Sonia could handle the stress of a kidnapping. Her blood pressure, normally 105 over 65, might rise to 110 over 70.

There were other risks involved in a staged kidnapping. If there were ever a hoax investigation, I would be liable for criminal charges. This was a convenient way that Arce could wield eternal control over me. If I were to jump ship at a later date and oppose him in any way, he could have me locked up. In Bolivia's criminal-justice system, the little guy usually pays. I considered telling Arce to discard the "planned" nature of this kidnapping, and make it the real thing. I suffered from the dizziness of juxtaposed images: looking into a pari-mutuel window and looking out from behind a jail cell.

If the Marianelas and the landless peasants refused the propositions for abandoning "their" land, Arce could have me iced, that is, if Panama Slim's evaluation of Arce was correct. Slivers of evidence were emerging that Arce might have been an accomplice in the cocaine dictatorship at the outset of the 1980s, but not enough for me to call it the truth. Even so, Arce had insinuated that bad people in bad times can become good people in good times.

When things get complicated like this, I usually retreat. Call me a coward. Having lived in tempestuous situations, I had become a collector of retreats. Mountain glaciers were a retreat. Horse betting was a retreat. Jazz was a retreat. I would wait for the fax to click on with the next set of past performances and then head out to the Thelonius Bar to hear a group called Bolivian Jazz. Sometimes they would invite me to sit in on a number.

In the meantime, I had planned on presenting the arguments of a win-win situation to Sonia. The peasants could have a bigger and better settlement, and have it legalized. It seemed so clear to me at the time.

"The history of these poor people," Sonia had said, "is of broken promises."

Sonia had her own initiatives. Rolando Katari was a guest speaker at the UMSA university this evening, and I shouldn't miss the chance to meet him. I could sleep off the margaritas with an afternoon nap and accompany her. At this high altitude, one of the pleasures of life is to bury yourself under heavy quilts after lunchtime and sleep for an hour or two, waking up then to a fresh and new part of the day.

KATARI WAS A leader of the Landless Peasants Movement. Sonia gave me his bio. I listened attentively. Knowing one's adversary is the first step to learning how to co-opt him.

Katari was raised near the cold highland city of Potosí, 13,000 feet above sea level. Potosí had been the wealthiest city in the world in the seventeenth century. With the amount of silver extracted from Cerro Rico ("Rich Hill") overlooking Potosí, they could have built a bridge of pure silver all the way across the ocean to Spain. The wealth of Cerro Rico lasted for centuries, with tin and zinc gradually replacing silver as the mother of all lodes.

But those who extracted the wealth did not partake of it. A miner's average lifespan, even at the end of the twentieth century, had only risen to 40 years. During the heyday of silver, black slaves went into the mines, were worked to death, and were replaced by a new wave of Indian slaves.

Katari had worked in the mines, for the Bolivian national mining company, COMIBOL, which was created from the expropriated properties from the three "Mining Barons." But the nationalization of the mines, following the 1952 revolution, took place at a time when world prices for Bolivian minerals had plummeted. Thousands of miners were laid off in the 1980s. Katari was one of them. The miners were promised new jobs if they were willing to relocate. They relocated. They got nothing.

Promise I: broken.

Many of these miners homesteaded in the tropical Chapare region in the Department of Cochabamba. They became coca farmers. Katari was among them. Coca had been chewed by the miners to ward off hunger and summon strength. Coca to the miners was like coffee to modern-day office workers. Coca is a prolific leaf used since ancient times for medicinal and ceremonial purposes. In city offices and restaurants, coca is imbibed as a tea. The miners knew coca, a resilient plant, more than they could know bananas or mangos, whose tropical abundance drove prices to below subsistence level.

Coca was also the raw material that eventually became cocaine after processing in Colombia. Bolivia became a focal point of the War on Drugs. The United States, supported by the UN, used the carrot and stick approach, sending in repressive forces (the Bolivian antidrug army, UMOPAR) and offering attractive bribes: $2,500 in cash if you allow us to eradicate your field and you agree to grow alternative crops. But the War on Drugs failed in its promise of a market for the peasants' alternative crops, and after they witnessed their fruit rot on the trees, they would turn back to growing coca.

Katari took the $2,500. Katari spent the money on machinery and on a cleft-palate operation for the younger of his two sons. Katari was encouraged to grow pineapples and mangos. He grew beautiful pineapples and the sweetest mangos in the world. But the War on Drugs failed to produce the consumer base for these products. Katari could not sell to U.S. markets because Bolivia did not have preferred-nation trading status and other countries could offer lower prices for the same fruit. Katari's children were forced to break with the normal corn-and-potato-based Bolivian diet and eat what was overly abundant: pineapple jam and mango soup, pineapple pie and pork in mango sauce. The rest of the pineapples and mangos rotted in the field. The panacea of alternative produce was dysfunctional. No markets were provided.

Promise II: broken.

An increasingly defiant Katari then joined a squatters movement near Santa Cruz, where the few roads for transport were sturdier, safer, and more within reach of markets for produce. The Landless Peasants Movement, originally from Brazil, and then mainly among Guaraní Indians from Bolivia's Chaco scrubland, soon established contact with Katari's group. By pooling resources, they could increase production and reduce expenses, enabling them to compete with the agribusiness of the region. Katari's group had already been coerced off one settlement, with the promise that they would be given legal title to another area of land. The Bolivian Agrarian Reform bureaucracy then became bogged down in legal complications, and the land was never made available. By now, Katari had become an organizer with a considerable base of followers. The rules of the game favored Arce's oligarchy over Katari's. The mirage of legal titles disappeared on the horizon.

Promise III: broken.

Once Sonia finished the narrative biography, I considered my predicament. Even without Sonia, I had an outside chance of establishing some contact between Katari and Arce. But given his peasant perspective, Katari would have a different impression of landowner Arce than I had. Arce might be a killer. Arce could be a womanizer. Arce was an exploiter. But in the end, I viewed Arce as a man of his word, capable of productive negotiations, while Katari saw him as duplicitous.

Katari's presentation at the university did nothing to ease my apprehension. His high cheekbones and a prominent nose marked him as part of the Quechua multitude. But that was the inevitable initial stereotype. There was an optimistic twinkle in his eyes, which defied the cliché of the taciturn Indian. Katari's picaresque eyes scanned through the audience and met each person in attendance, as if he were speaking to us one-on-one. He had copious notes but did not consult them. He moved off the podium and into the aisles, occasionally asking a question directly to a spectator. He spotted a skeptical look on the face of a man in a business suit.

"You've eaten tomatoes," he said, "but tell me, have you ever picked them?"

In traditional La Paz, the business suit is ubiquitous along the El Prado boulevard on a workday, even among low-level office workers and owners of small shops. Katari broke the custom, remaining in shirt sleeves, but he was not oblivious to fashion. He wore a finely-stitched shirt of indigenous origin. He would have fit side by side with Arce in his designer *guayabera*.

Katari was probably in his late forties or early fifties, but you couldn't tell from his jet-black hair that had never known a curl nor sprouted a gray strand, and there was neither a wrinkle on his bronze face nor the whiskers of a white man. From my vantage point his eyes looked black and opaque, but when he looked directly at me, suddenly those eyes became deep wells opening a channel into centuries of enigmatic history.

He stood taller than most Bolivians, at least 5'10". His Spanish was crisp and resonant, and even when he reached a crescendo, even when arriving at a key slogan, he did not shout. His charisma, spiced with wry irony, suggested an authentic caring for the audience. As he looked at us again and again, one by one, there was a sense of "very pleased to meet you" that reached us as individuals. He sprinkled his discourse with words from Quechua and Aymara in order to embroider his message.

"It is time for a new Agrarian Reform," he said. "Land given to a peasant family in 1952 is now divided among all the offspring. The farms of 1952 are the puny gardens of today. We need more land. The oligarchy in Santa Cruz leaves its land fallow. The land is for he who works it. That's not only the law. That's wise economics. There's a difference between living well, which few people do in Bolivia, and living better, which a few people do at the expense of the many."

Students applauded. Their professors applauded. Sonia applauded. I refrained. Nothing against the speaker. I don't even applaud at concerts. Applause reminds me of mass psychology.

I noted the presence of three stone-faced men in the back of the auditorium. The one to the left wore designer sunglasses. They all wore ties. They were not applauding. They could have been vestiges from the era of dictatorships, but for the fact that they wore business suits instead of olive-green uniforms. Their nonapplause and mine had nothing in common. Katari's warm gaze seemed to purposely avoid that part of the room. I decided to join in and applaud. It was the first time I had clapped my hands since I had heard Chucho Valdez performing in Paris. The opal eyes of the three stone men in the back of the room seemed to be riveted upon me. It was almost as if they had come to see me rather than Katari.

At that moment, Katari spotted a blind man of indigenous features in the second row.

Katari interrupted his text, stepped off the podium, and approached the old man. "I've seen too many blind people during my stay in La Paz. Sir, would you mind telling us what is the cause of your blindness?"

"I cannot say," the man said. "I don't know."

I feared the worst. It had the feel of a revivalist meeting, with Katari as the faith healer.

"And you don't know because . . . ?"

"I could not afford to see a specialist," he said.

Katari turned to the audience. "What if this gentleman has cataracts? That's a curable disease! What kind of country is this, where we have underemployed doctors who are desperate for work and we have a multitude of unattended patients who are desperate for care. Now you tell me. Is that an efficient way to run a society?"

I had my own "what if" question, and suddenly the wording was clarified thanks to Katari's use of the word "efficient":

What if a productive and labor-intensive business were proposed for your land? What if some of you could be given jobs in that business? What if the others were offered a viable alternative settlement? Is that not the most efficient solution?

I refrained. I might have been hooted out of the auditorium. If I proposed the idea to Katari at that moment, he'd probably launch into the classic historical destiny of the Indians when they believed the white man. He had the comprehensive past performances to prove his point. But I had a new angle. I resolved to share my angle with him in private. I resolved to use his own word: *efficient*. As Sonia's husband, I had my ticket to meet with him, if I could find a moment when he was not surrounded by admirers, or by his own entourage, or by stone-faced anachronisms from a repressive past.

I also had some questions for myself. *How objective was my trust in Arce?* Given the fact that I hoped to receive $100,000 from Panama Slim (I had the signed agreement) and another $100,000 from Arce himself (I had a handshake), how capable was I of making a reliable odds line?

The same questions could be asked about Katari. Was he a committed ideologue, a needy farmer, or a political opportunist using demagoguery to become a senator or minister?

Sonia was Miss Objectivity. In matters of human relations, I would discuss with Sonia and then cede to her judgment.

But in this case, I had to keep it all to myself. Sonia and I were on opposite teams.

Temporarily, I hoped.

SIX

Pick 4 and "Two for Ten"

I spent the next day and night in retreat mode. I was planning for a daily double: horse racing in the morning, jazz at night.

The fax machine rumbled. In came the past performances of the seventh race at Arlington. As usual, too many horses qualified by the turf-sire ratings. Six of the nine horses could have been worthy wagers. That should have meant a *pasadena*. No play.

Vince had included the *Daily Racing Form* consensus grid, with the top three choices of six different public handicappers. Vince and I went back many years, but this was the very first time he showed any respect for the guys who make picks for the *Daily Racing Form*.

In the old days of Marge Everett's Hollywood Park, Vince was an L.A. bookie. When a big bet came in, he'd often ask my opinion.

"Tell me the horse can't win, Matt. Am I gonna get killed today?"

Vince had lost three wives because of his failure at personal diplomacy. The D.A. wouldn't let him visit his son from his first marriage because he'd told the judge, "So what if I slept with Barbara's friend! She seduced me, knowing I was Barbara's husband! I saved Barbara from a failed friendship. She should thank me."

"You could have avoided the conflict," Vince's lawyer had told him, "if you'd kept it a secret."

For the same reasons that Vince could not hold down a marriage, he was incapable of sustaining a straight job. He would say things like, "I'm gonna have to leave early today because I have a live one in the third race," instead of conjuring up that he had to be home to open the house for the plumber.

The bookie business was the ideal professional refuge, where Vince answered to no one but himself. But the advent of full-card simulcasting and widespread off-track betting wiped out most of his business. He opened a racing bookstore and just to play it safe, added a porno section in the back.

He opened the store in Orange County, bastion of family values. The neighbors hated him. The local Chamber of Commerce brought charges against him. Evidently he was breaking an 1893 pornography statute that no one had ever heard of. Vince distrusted flashy lawyers. He ended up with a public defender, a young man with unruly hair ending in a ponytail, only recently out of law school.

On the morning of the trial, the overworked public defender had not yet come up with a defense argument. He sat on the courthouse steps, unconcerned about ruffling his cheap polyester suit, fearing that he could be accused of legal malpractice. Surely there was some defense against an obscure century-old law.

Across the street was the Marriot Hotel. He stared at it, the way we stare at the past performances when we're stymied.

Suddenly, he sprinted across the street, dashing into the plush lobby of the Marriot, posing as a potential guest. He asked about their cable TV service. Yes, the rooms had cable. He asked for a program. He was handed the in-house entertainment guide. He noticed a cable TV channel that broadcast porno movies.

Vince had been considering firing his poverty lawyer, but he decided not to postpone his meeting with destiny. The young attorney made a motion asking the judge to dismiss the case. Vince imagined his lawyer was following a worn-out script, just to keep himself on the payroll. Following the same script, the yawning judge asked, "On what grounds?"

"Your Honor, right across the street, the Marriot Hotel is offering a porno menu to its guests. The Marriot belongs to the local Chamber of Commerce, and the neighbors aren't complaining."

The judge took one look at the TV program guide, let out with a cynical and fatigued "Case dismissed," and admonished the Chamber of Commerce to first clean up its own house. Vince was back in business.

The fact that Vince had now sent me the grid of public handicappers suggested that he was giving up on my Tomlinson method. It was a new *Racing Form* with ambitious handicappers who were provided with an expanded database of information, and who actually put their reputations on the line by using their own names rather than classic pseudonyms like Sweep or Hermis.

"When I first began faxing you the PPs," he told me, "from a bookie's standpoint, I would have turned down your action. You were good. But something is changing. Those ratings you use aren't working the way they used to. Now I see a race, and I say to myself, 'I want this guy's action.'"

So Vince was hinting that perhaps there was some better information among the public handicappers. I scanned the grid.

One horse jumped off the page, based on my "informed-minority" method. The *informed minority* refers to the infrequent occasion when a single handicapper has picked a horse that the other experts have ignored. When there are six or fewer experts on the grid, I require that the informed-minority pick must not be chosen even for place or show by any of the other experts. It has worked for most years with the Breeders' Cup, but with so many public pickers for that event, there is no need to apply the place-and-show criteria. It works best at special events like the Breeders' Cup and the Claiming Crown, when the newspaper handicappers are at their maximum intensity. It also seems to function well at the outset of the most prestigious shorter race meets, when public pickers are primed for the maximum intensity, such as Saratoga and Oak Tree Santa Anita, though for this my evidence is only anecdotal.

The informed minority emerged from Vince's handicapper grid. Marcus Hersh was the only public handicapper to choose Chris Block's horse Go for Four on top. No one else had picked Go for Four in the money.

Winning at the races requires contrarian reasoning. Most public pickers wax conventional except for rare moments of inspired discovery. The informed minority cherry-picks the best moments of intuitive reasoning of the experts. Go for Four could have been yet another soaring flight of the Marcus Hersh inspiration. Memory is a strategic tool for handicappers. With my short memory, I committed brain space to things like Hersh informed-minority picks and Matlow first-time starters, at the expense of birthdays and anniversaries. Sonia understood, and she even forgave me for having once forgotten her birthday.

In my long-term statistics in Breeders' Cup races, the informed-minority system yields a 13 percent return on investment, but with only 10 percent winners. The average payoff is sky-high. With Hersh, the win percentage for those times when he was the informed minority was somewhat higher, but the sample was far too small to proclaim 90 percent reliability.

Curiously, Hersh's pick was one of the three horses that did not qualify by the Tomlinson turf-sire ratings. That's the contradictory reality of the past performances. However, Go for Four's damsire was the great Irish turf horse Go and Go, of Belmont fame. I suspected that Hersh might have discovered information on the dam not included in the Tomlinson stats. I am convinced that the dam, with the XX chromosomes, is more influential in determining the career of an offspring. I faxed Vince asking for $20 to win and $20 to place on Go for Four. Had Go for Four been a Tomlinson qualifier I would have raised the wager.

Just before dinner, the fax machine clicked on. The fax paper rolled in with big handwritten letters. Go for Four: $32.60 to win, $14.40 to place!!!

That meant $470 added to my ledger.

At such moments, the horseplayer feels invincible. Only the negative Tomlinson had prevented me from betting more, and for a few seconds, I lamented my lack of killer instinct. Negative statistics, after all, should be seen as low hurdles to vault over in the inevitable rush to victory. I ate Sonia's quinoa-avocado-tomato-cilantro salad with inflated optimism. The Arce business would work out whichever path was chosen. I squelched the voice of experience within, which told me in muffled tones to calm down and be objective.

I brought up the Marianela business in an inoffensive way.

"Sonia, you should be writing a cookbook instead of spending your energy on the Marianelas."

"Don't forget where the avocados come from," she responded. "Without peasants to farm the land, you'd be eating industrial tomatoes and things like cilantro would disappear with the end of biodiversity."

La Paz is ideal for partaking of fruit and vegetables. Things don't rot when there's so little oxygen density. An opened avocado that would turn black in fifteen minutes at sea level remains fresh and green for hours in the highlands.

AT THELONIUS, I was invited by the group called Bolivian Jazz to have a go at "Round Midnight." I thanked their generous keyboard man for giving up the chance to play some classic Monk. We improvised for a good 10 minutes. When playing Monk, it's best not to imitate. He's one of a kind. So I kept a respectful distance, with my romanticized version perhaps a bit sappy to a purist. I got lots of encouragement from the bass and the drummer. This grand moment became the second half of my daily double, a second high at precisely the time my life needed a prolonged rally.

Once leaving the club, I accompanied the musicians, uphill to a dark, adobe-walled apartment building near the Plaza San Pedro prison, where we would participate in a good-bye ceremony for a British sax player. Half the people were Bolivians and the other half expats. We sat on a dusty floor in a circle. The parquet was in desperate need of sanding and varnish. I took care not to get a splinter in my ass.

A plastic bag of coca leaves made the rounds, never touching the floor. Each person reverently plucked out green leaves. In synchronicity with the coca bag, a bottle of hard alcohol, *aguardiente*, passed from mouth to mouth. Leading the ceremony was a Yatiri, an indigenous wise man, a priest-medicine-man-philosopher, wearing a woven poncho of mainly bright red mixed with burnt orange. He invoked the Pachamama, Mother Earth, code-switching between Aymara and Spanish.

The surprise from this ceremony was the physiological reaction, a pervading mellowness, a high-octave harmony, and a deep need to commune with Sonia. I was tempted to chuck all the crisis management, forget about the hundred thou, and just stand behind Sonia, embracing her idealism. At the same time, Arce's contradictions seemed to readjust themselves into a more positive order, one of confidence and trust. The kidnapping hoax seemed like the right idea. Arce was a smooth operator but a straight shooter. I could trust him.

The coca and *aguardiente* had removed the sharp edges from my life. I was experiencing a syndrome diametrically opposed to paranoia. Everybody around me was a good guy. I trusted the policeman. I trusted the alky moaning on the steps of a church. I trusted that the supertrainers were not doping their horses.

With the Yatiri ceremony, my daily double had become a Pick 3. The séance had lifted my emotional bankroll to a higher level. When I left, it was already 1:30 in the morning, but I felt as if there was still time remaining for a fourth good thing to happen. The fourth leg of my Pick 4 would be consummated in bed with Sonia.

I no longer felt the usual biting cold of the La Paz night. I hurried home, anxious to embrace the woman I profoundly loved.

Nearing the front door of the apartment lobby, I felt thick arms grabbing me from behind, a hand squeezing a towel into my mouth. Strangely, my heart was not thumping as it should have been. I empathized with all those snatched prey I had seen on *Animal Kingdom*. My head bumped the upper doorframe of a car where I was planted so hard that the shock absorbers lost their spring.

I wanted to say, "Arce, you were supposed to give me a week. You jumped the gun by three days."

My words were smothered in the towel.

Before I could visualize any more than swirling shades of darkness mixed with stripes of neon, they blindfolded me. Thanks to the Pachamama ceremony, I was soon calm. In my bizarre state of antiparanoia, I trusted these kidnappers. Arce must have realized that a voluntary kidnapping would expose me to hoax accusations and a potential sentence in the San Pedro Prison. You get thrown into San Pedro, and if you have no cash on you to pay the rent for a cell, you sleep outside in the courtyard, on hard cobbles cold as ice cubes. Arce's men were now saving me from doing time. Like the alky on the church steps and the supertrainers, my kidnappers were the good guys.

But these men of Arce were overdoing the theatrics. I felt bruises on my arms and swollen lips where they'd forced the towel in my mouth. My head was still throbbing from having banged against the doorframe. These guys were accomplished actors. This was a very realistic portrayal of a kidnapping.

I sensed we were spiraling up a beanstalk, but I trusted in whatever ogres we'd meet on top, in El Alto. I could tell it was El Alto when feeling the ground flatten out under our wheels. Once out of the city, bumping over a high plain dirt road, my benevolent abductors removed the towel.

"You guys are overdoing it," I said. "Didn't Arce tell you I'd go willingly?"

If Arce had planned to send me to Nevada, he should have given me time to gather my trainer stats. And my backpack.

"We don't take orders from that *maricón* Arce," the driver said. "We don't take orders from your fairy friends."

The acting was so realistic that I began to doubt there would be anything resembling a winning last leg of my Pick 4. This was the final leg that would obliterate the three previous victories.

The gorilla to my right removed the blindfold. It was too dark inside to get a good look at my captors, at least not for catching any detail that would distinguish them from other Bolivians. Except for the driver, who had, if the starlight was not lying, a strange patch of white hair amidst the black hair on the back of his head. The car had passed beyond El Alto. Flat nothingness. Infinite darkness. Except the Milky Way blazing outside my window and Van Gogh's *Starry Night* descending all the way to ground level.

I wanted to ask, "Who are you?" and "What do you want from me?" but I clamped up. No sense in asking stupid questions that would dissipate in the stars.

"This is a helluva long taxi ride," I said. "What's the fare gonna be?"

"We don't charge for one-way trips," the driver said.

Kidnappings are a rarity in Bolivia. But a few weeks earlier, the human-rights activist Waldo Alba had been kidnapped for three days. He returned in battered form. He said it was the police. Was Gandhian Bolivia suddenly "Colombianizing"? If so, Sonia could be in danger. Her face had appeared in the newspaper next to Rolando Katari. In fact, it was she who had introduced Katari to the La Paz public, and that public included the stone men in the back of the room, the ones who did not at all appreciate what Katari had to say.

The Yatiri magic had worn off. The driver had said, "One-way trip." The silent stone faces I'd seen at the Katari conference reminded me of the Chilean torturers in 1973 or the Bolivian torturers in 1981. They lacked a sense of humor. They became enraged by reason.

I groped for a possible identity of my captors. The stone men had seen me shake hands with Katari following his speech. But Mendoza had also seen me conspiring with his partner-rival Arce, while Arce was flirting with Mendoza's wife. They said that Mendoza had his own paramilitary squad. These men could be torturers, Arce rivals, or maybe revolutionaries, suspecting this gringo face of being CIA.

If the stone men were paramilitaries, then I had to be an anarchist revolutionary supporting the Landless Peasants. If Mendoza resented Arce, then I must have been a tool that helped Arce maintain his power. If I had been taken for a CIA spy, then what mercy awaited me at this outer edge of the universe?

I couldn't eliminate the possibility that these guys had been sent by Arce, and that Arce could drive away the Marianelas by killing the husband of their public spokesperson. Or maybe Mendoza was Muñeca's passionate Latin suitor and resented my spending a platonic night with her at Arce's ranch. Mendoza would never believe that there was nothing between Muñeca and me. Even gringos have red blood in their veins.

"He slept on the couch," Muñeca would have told him, "and I slept in the bedroom, alone." That would have infuriated the lover Mendoza. Had she said, "Yeah, I slept with him," Mendoza might have let it go as business-as-usual. But hearing what Mendoza would assume was a lame lie would have provoked the most furious fit of jealousy. "Sure, you slept alone," Mendoza would have said, "and Mary got pregnant alone and Lee Harvey Oswald acted alone."

Then there were the government ministers who stood to gain a kickback from the racetrack deal. If they felt that the Marianelas were in their way, it would be reasonable for them to order the kidnapping of the husband of a prominent Marianela. In fact, Sonia had become the face of the Marianelas. Most of those Marianelas lived with the Landless Peasants and remained anonymous, but Sonia dealt with the public. A sweet female face could not be marred by a gallant Bolivian macho, so they'd have to go after her husband.

My imagination swirled out of control. Arce's partner-rivals, the stone men at the university, Muñeca's wealthy suitors, government ministers: Any one of these power mongers could have wanted me eliminated.

For someone who prefers to lie low, I had certainly exposed myself, stupidly. I grasped for a vine of hope. I clung to the *aguardiente*-coca dream that if these gorillas let me go alive, the scare might prompt Sonia into convincing the Marianelas to take their base community elsewhere.

But as the Yatiri effects had subsided, fear welled up in me. They might connect electrodes to my testicles and then press the button. I might not live to see another Breeders' Cup. In Chile, before electrocuting Jara from the balls up, they had shown their skill at symbolism by cutting off his hands, because he played the guitar. What if, knowing I played keyboard, they went for my hands? In Argentina the paramilitaries took their suspects up in an air force plane and then dropped them thousands of feet into the sea. I had often ranked the ways of dying, from bad to worse. Drowning was in first place. Electrocution was a close second. Little did I know that my abstract exercise would become so vividly imminent.

If these goons had intended to keep me alive, either *they* would be masked or I would. Adding to my fear of pain and agony was the horrendous cowardice that prevented me from fighting back. A few hours ago I was soaring with Monk. Now I was mired in frightful shame.

The car jerked to a halt. I was elbowed out, rebumping my head on the same dumb doorframe in exactly the same place. We were standing on a makeshift runway. They rifle-butted me up the steps of a Piper Cub. The plane took off. We flew toward Sajama, the highest mountain in Bolivia, 22,000 feet, white cone-shaped crown glistening in the moonlight. From behind I could see the patch of whitening hairs on the back of the pilot's head. The same guy who had driven the car was now joyriding the plane.

My heart now thumped for a very good reason. The drop could take place at any moment. If I plopped onto the glacier my body would remain in frozen preservation, for months or years. If they dropped me in this vast desert to a one-thud death, the vultures would quickly render my death entirely anonymous, flesh gone, bones eventually buried in the swirling sand.

I was hardly in a strong negotiating position. In fact, I had nothing to offer. Anything I said would be considered a sign of weakness.

The Sajama glacier shone brilliantly under the Milky Way. The wings of the plane nearly scraped the white robe of Sajama. The pilot circled his toy plane around the volcanic glacier. We began descending, and I knew from my map studies that we had crossed the dusty border and entered Chile. We were descending in the direction of the Pacific coast.

The white powder of Sajama functioned like cocaine up the high-and-mighty pilot's nose.

"Those Chilean fags sucked the British cocks. They used the British to steal our coast. This should be Bolivian territory. Faggot Bolivian politicians sold out to Chile."

Suddenly I knew a surefire way to save my life. I would propose a plan for recovering Bolivia's coastline from Chile, a plan that only I could pull off. I would make myself indispensable.

The pilot continued his rant.

"The Argentines and Chileans knew how to deal with pricks like you. We Bolivian faggots, we didn't have the balls."

The plane began to descend. I begged my heart to stop throbbing. The stupid fear could bust my aorta. They were landing. Perhaps the one-thud Argentine death would have been better than what awaited me. If the Marianelas had asked me at this moment to confess and declare my infinite faith in the Almighty, I would have confessed, repented, and kissed their holy feet. I would have signed away my IRA to their missions.

Perhaps Sonia had phoned the Marianelas when I hadn't arrived. Perhaps they would all pray for me in unison. It was now out of my hands.

The plane landed in the barren Atacama, the most arid desert in the world. It had rained exactly once here in the past 215 years, and that time you could have counted the raindrops.

The three men (now I could see there were three of them) yanked me out of the plane. I saw some resemblance to the stone men at the back of the auditorium, but they were not so different from some of the guests at Arce's ranch, or people I see going in and coming out of government ministries. The Bolivian mestizo has straight black hair, a round face, prominent cheekbones, dark eyes. I had still not learned to distinguish Bolivian faces in daylight, and under the starlight physical appearance was vague.

They walked me to one spot in the desert that looked no different from the rest. I could feel that the man who had me by the left arm was limping. They went into action. Here and there inside my body, sockets became unhinged, as booted feet and gnarled fists came at me from all directions.

I managed to grab one guy's foot before it crushed me. He went down. A fist bounced off the side of my head. Silence was not my best strategy. But these guys were not into verbal logic.

"Welcome to Chile," the pilot said. "Don't you ever go back to Bolivia. We don't want to see your gringo face again. If we had the choice we'd feed you to the vultures."

They gave me a few kicks for the epilogue, as I huddled in the sand. They kicked me in the ass, and tried to kick me in the stomach, but they hit my arms. They tried to kick me in the balls, but they hit my knees. They stomped on my ear and half-buried my other ear in the hard sand. In a hundred years, or a thousand years, someone would find a fossil of my ear imprinted in this lonely desert.

"*Mi jefe*," one of the men said. "Shouldn't we take the man's wallet? He'll have cash, or at least credit cards."

"Haven't I told you, man, that we have principles. What gives you the fucking idea that we could be cheap thieves?"

And they shuffled off. I heard an engine grumble, and then grind, and the gurgling sound subsided into a whirring that died off in the distance. There were no crickets, no leaves blowing in the wind, no cicadas, nothing but silent stones and silent sand, hardened by 215 rainless years. No baby in any womb had experienced a silence deeper than this one. Throbbing pains reverberated from my head, my left arm, and my right thigh. I could hear my pain sizzle, and I could see it in the millions of stars flaring above me.

The act of rising from the desert floor was a prelude to what I would face if I had not been put down before the aging process ran its course. There were too many idiosyncratic aches to catalogue, it seemed, one of them for each star. The ground was too hard to have preserved the footprints of my accosters. I limped back in the vicinity of where the plane had landed, hoping to find some relic from my kidnappers. Gradually my stride evened out. I came upon an empty Marlboro box. I picked it up by the corners and slipped it carefully into my shirt pocket. I prowled around in vain, searching for any other telling sign.

Where to go? If I were to walk in the wrong direction, I would die like a Mexican immigrant in the Arizona desert.

The whole brilliant galaxy settled down not far from the desert floor, as if I were walking directly through a whole universe. I lost my sense of time.

I stumbled for minutes or hours along a jeep track, and it eventually led me to a narrow paved road. A sensation of resuscitation alleviated the physical pain. I decided to hail any car that approached from either direction in the silent universe.

I could not forget that they had declared me persona non grata in Bolivia. I convinced myself that it would not be cowardice but pragmatism if I should end up on the Chilean coast rather than back up in La Paz. It was only 45 minutes on LAN Chile airlines from Iquique to La Paz.

I limped along the road, senselessly, because I was not going to arrive anywhere on foot. The same vehicle that I might find farther up the road would have had to pass by the spot where I was at the moment. I walked, not to go anywhere, but to keep warm.

The stardust swirled around my head, and my thoughts spun into overlapping conjectures as to the identity of my kidnappers. Sonia's beautiful dark eyes, prominent in the media, represented the Marianela threat to the ministers who were lusting for a racetrack kickback, but also to the paramilitaries who could associate me, her husband, with the intransigence of the squatters. Katari's people were not beyond suspicion. There was this knee-jerk image that any white gringo face represented the CIA, a traditional supporter of the landowner status quo. Arce himself could not be entirely excluded. Someone capable of complex strategic thought had ordered the kidnappers to leave me alive, when they could have killed me with impunity.

My immediate guess was that Arce had nothing to do with this, but that he would jump in to take advantage, urging the Marianelas to be reasonable before any more "senseless violence" erupted, stressing that whoever had plucked me off a La Paz street and knocked me around in the desert would have done so because I was Sonia's husband.

The profound silence merged with a vast emptiness to provoke an eerie sense of freedom. If I so desired, I could disappear on my own, everyone would be sure I was dead, and I could reappear as a new person in a remote OTB with no past and an entirely transformed identity. My daughter was just fine without me, and the woman I loved would move deeper into her religious plenitude. I considered the idea for what must have been a couple of kilometers and then eased it out of my mind.

Instead, I resolved to demand a raise from Panama Slim, including a substantial advance. He too would be thrilled about this kidnapping, for the same reasons as Arce.

Just before sunrise I hailed a night trucker. He looked remarkably similar to my kidnappers. He was transporting Bolivian artisanry for export. I expected a barrage of questions about my battered face or about how it was that I was staggering alone in the desert night. There is a certain type of Bolivian who takes things as they come, no questions asked. In the beginning you think these people are remarkably indifferent, like New York taxi drivers. They do not meddle. They are blind to your foreignness. This may partly explain why tourists in Bolivia are not stalked as they would be in other poor countries.

The driver only cared that I had two functional ears. He launched into a diatribe. Bolivia had no sea. He had to use the Chilean seaport on what was formerly Bolivian territory. I listened to his rant about how Chile had stolen Bolivia's coastline in the 1880s. The man's words rhymed with those of the pilot, and for a moment, I was back in the plane, preparing to be dumped over Sajama.

"*Stay out of politics,*" my Aunt Ada would advise me. "Keep your nose clean and go into business."

I had followed her advice. I had gone into business, racetrack business, and it had sucked me directly into politics.

The trucker left me on a street in Iquique. I walked to the beach and fell asleep against a palm tree. I was awakened perhaps hours later by the snarling of a motorbike.

People on the sidewalk were turning the other way as I approached. My battered face must have frightened them.

I found a telephone in a bar. The barman took one look at me and urged me to get to a hospital. I dialed our home phone number. Sonia had forgotten to turn off the blasted fax. One day a sadist composer would write a symphony of fax tones. Either Sonia heard nothing, or she was out looking for me. I wanted to tell her I was all right and definitely to not go to the police.

The image of the brave and petite Sonia triggered contradictory emotions. I was grudgingly proud of her spiritual outlook, but jealous at the same time, that the Marianelas were stealing her from me, at least stealing a part of her heart that had been so tender and protecting. Bolivia should have been a remote land where we could appreciate each other free from outside distractions.

All the facts told me that my kidnappers would not go after Sonia, that they had made their symbolic threat to the Marianelas through me. Clear thinking aside, I still feared for her safety.

I had forgotten Arce's phone number. I fumbled in my wallet, flipping through cards, dropping some of them. The only Bolivian number I came upon was on Muñeca's business card.

I rang her up. It rang four times, eight times, eleven times and she finally answered.

"Sorry I woke you," I said.

"Who are you?"

"It's Matt, the guy you met at Arce's house. You gave me your card, and you said that one day I would need you. You were right."

"Oh yes, how could I forget you? You're the different one. No one plays hard to get with me. You are a memorable man."

I asked Muñeca to phone Arce, and to tell Arce to phone Sonia.

"Just tell them that someone's goons deposited me in Iquique, and that I'm all right. Tell him not to gloat about it."

I would let Arce sort it out. No doubt he would attempt to profit from the disaster. Maybe convert this dumb mess into the successful fourth leg of my Pick 4. The final leg of an exotic wager is always the most anguishing. The Marianelas would fear that the kidnapping was carried out by their enemies. They would see Sonia as the next victim. They would negotiate with Arce. Eventually they would vacate and accept an alternative site. The battering I had suffered would result in a Pick 4 "consolation" of $200,000.

At the moment, a cold beer was worth more than $200,000. I spotted an off-track betting parlor and bar across the avenue. A couple of dried-up whores hung out near the doorway. I needed to collect myself. Gain the courage to return to Bolivia. Back in La Paz I would devise a way to protect myself. A gun was out of the question. I'd get stopped and searched at a police checkpoint, they'd find the gun, and I'd be dumped in San Pedro as a foreign subversive. No way to trust Arce's bodyguards. They were part of the problem. One thing for sure. Muñeca would have contacted Arce, and Arce would be sure to have Sonia protected. He'd stake his goons out below our apartment, and they'd follow her to her office. The Marianelas would also know by now, and they'd protect their accountant and public relations star. Sonia would have been hustled to a safe house. I had time to reflect.

The Chilean OTB was a seductive retreat. I first had to pass through the veteran whores to get in. They took one tired look at me, and I became a vet-scratch from their list of also-eligibles.

The push-open slatted doors reminded me of an Old West saloon. The desert outside added to the effect. The whores adorned the image. Only the sea breeze was out of place. The illusion was obliterated when I saw the modern TV monitors hanging along the walls. The first step was to order a beer. I drained half the glass and then asked for a racing paper. It was published in a slick five-by-eight magazine. Inside were the strange past-performance lines, seemingly new paradigms. But they contained a universal truth. If you learned something different from the crowd, you could make some money. You could do this anonymously. The goons of the world would be eclipsed by the past performances and totally buried from my memory as the horses broke from the gate. If you've ever analyzed a horse race and then bet on it, you will understand how racing represents the ultimate therapeutic refuge from a cruel world. Racing purges. Racing liberates.

I had three hours to first post. With my thirst dissipated, my hunger finally hit me. Across from the OTB was what looked like an old greasy-spoon restaurant, the type you used to see along Route 66 with an EATS sign. I ordered pork with mashed potatoes and hot vegetables. Hardly the right choice for the tourist getting to know the regional specialties. But I did choose a vintage red Chilean wine, Casillera del Diablo.

What a beautiful way to muffle the screams of tortured souls, to filter through the membranes of captivity, to screen out the sinister maneuvering that characterizes a raw struggle for power that includes paramilitaries and poets, politicians and priests. The past performances allowed for the pure exercise of the human mind, the elegant balancing of abstraction and objectivity, undistorted by cultural hang-ups and class consciousness, in a context of a rainbow of pastel silks and magnificent animals in shiny coats barely touching the ground with their ballet-dancer legs as they move forward in rhythmic splendor.

I could have rushed to the airport and caught the first flight to La Paz. But I needed a day of total anonymity. I needed to learn how to think straight all over again. I would not make a move until I could map out a clear path through a maze of literal dead ends.

I ate slowly, savoring the herby taste of the pork. I might be dead tomorrow, so I didn't want to forfeit today. I wouldn't accept that any neurotic fears could hold me hostage. I leafed through the pages and discovered two cards of 16 races with up to 18 horses per field. No one could be crazy enough to play these races.

I studied the past performances, mapped out contenders, paid for the meal, crossed the dusty street, and pushed my way back though the slatted swinging doors of the OTB. I watched the first two races without betting. What I saw triggered an instant handicapping methodology. Each race was marred with serious bumping incidents. Yet there were no stewards' inquiries, no jockey objections.

Nor were there trouble lines in the past performances. I could safely assume that any horse that lost a race had probably gotten into serious trouble. I could assume that every horse was bumped, that every horse either took up on the turn or went eight wide.

The approach was simple. In cases where I found horses that took turns in beating each other, I would play the horse with the highest odds. If Mentiroso had beaten Mafioso in the last race by six lengths, but if Mafioso had defeated Mentiroso six races ago, I would bet on Mafioso, at the higher odds.

I needed to get lost in 32 races in order to expel the pain and neutralize the fear. Handicapping impossible races would prepare me to confront the next step in the great off-track puzzle.

I imagined a racetrack in Bolivia. I imagined that I had my plush office there, and that horses shipped in from Argentina, Brazil, Chile, and maybe even from the USA. I imagined helping to design a state-of-the-art backstretch, watching workouts in the morning with a cup of steaming coffee in my hand, hanging out at the rail during the afternoon, hearing the hoofbeats on the turf, watching the tractor smooth out the dirt on the stretch and around the turns, chatting with trainers, riders, and grooms, listening to a bulging, cheering grandstand muffle out the voice of the race caller as 10 galloping Thoroughbreds rounded into the stretch at a graceful 40 miles per hour.

With no real time to handicap between races, I was able to isolate one of my favorite "horse-futures" methods: the two for ten.

Rule 1. A horse must have been 2-for-10 in its first 10 career races. Reasoning: Horses that win too frequently are overbet while horses that lose 90 percent of the time or more are unreliable. But horses with a 2-for-10 record have won frequently enough to show they have a winning spirit but not often enough to get overplayed by the public.

Rule 2. The horse must have won those two races with double-figure payoffs, indicating that it is an overachiever (performing better than the odds would warrant).

Rule 3. Play the horse in its next five races (career races 11 through 15).

Rule 4. Exclude any trainer with less than a 12 percent overall win rate, unless the trainer shows a positive return on investment in a specific area of expertise.

For the Chilean OTB I made a quick adjustment. Given the larger fields, I required that the horse's most recent win should have been at 6–1 or up. I also did not demand to see the horse's first victory, since it might be buried beneath the bottom running line of the past performances. So if a horse was listed with, say, 12 lifetime races, had won 2 of his first 10, and showed a 6–1 win for his most recent victory, I'd play him back today in career races 13 through 15. Of course, I was not going to hang out in Iquique waiting for a horse's follow-up races, so I'd be playing only a one-race slice of time.

I found a total of six plays for the afternoon, the best of them all at 23–1. He was making a bold move on the inside during the last turn into the stretch when suddenly he was squeezed into the rail after the horse outside of him lugged inwards. The rider nearly went down. The horse took up, fell back, recovered, moved back up on the outside, and nearly won. The stewards' inquiry, that should have been, never materialized.

Another of my horses, Paraiso Val, at 8–1, looking much like Mr. Magoo, moved forward irregularly, causing everything else around him to bounce and bobble. Paraiso Val was the only horse untouched by the traffic problems he had provoked. He inherited first place in deep stretch and held on until the finish line. Thanks to Paraiso Val, I turned a profit for the day. P. V. was also a horse that had taken turns beating and then getting beat by the race favorite, so my original handicapping approach was partially validated with this one piece of anecdotal evidence.

Ever since moving to a racing-starved corner of the world, the horse-futures concept had become increasingly present in my horseplayer consciousness. Today the betting public has become ever more intelligent. Hunch players are now gone from the betting pools, having defected to the ubiquitous slot machines. With the *Daily Racing Form* now providing increasingly sophisticated information, fewer players make misinformed wagers. So the contrarian thinking necessary for profitable play is harder to conceive. With the vast majority of the betting public handicapping on a race-by-race basis, "horse futures" represents a refreshing perspective. A player who projects the "shape" of a horse's career pattern enjoys an unusual edge.

A most intriguing aspect about a horse's career shape is discovered early on if he shows that he is capable of winning or finishing in the money at high odds. When a horse is sent off at longshot odds, the betting public has determined, usually correctly, that this horse's recent past performances do not earn him much of a chance of winning or even coming close. Horses that show that they can "overachieve" or race "better than their odds" on more than one occasion are telling us that on any given day they can reach an unexpected peak and that in the long run they may even yield a positive bottom line for the player who backs them consistently. A horse with a profitable career shape is like a solid mutual fund investment. You're not supposed to watch the performance of your fund on a daily or even monthly basis. You're in it for the long term.

Look at it the other way. When a horse wins at low odds, it means that he was facing inferior competition. Given a choice between two seemingly equal horses, one that was victorious at 7–5 and the other having won at 6–1, the second one gets preference. Sometimes the betting public makes adjustments and bets down an overachiever the next time they see him on the track. But other horses seem to remain under the public radar and go through a large part of their career as overachievers.

It becomes inefficient to spend too much handicapping time on races where the low-odds favorite has a true edge. In the aftermath of my kidnapping, I had become much more aware that my time on earth was an unrenewable natural resource. I had used my handicapping energy inefficiently, as if the resource of time were inexhaustible. Keeping the spigot open for hours a day meant that too much wasteful sludge got caught up in the flow.

Horse futures is like the alternative energy of handicapping. By developing long-term and time-saving automatic bets, I could actually have more time left over for analyzing a truly magnificent race in depth, one that comes up so intriguing and baffling that it might contain a solution that is hidden from the betting public.

I call this "handicapping resource control." In these terms, my involvement in the Bolivian racetrack scheme was looking like one of the most inefficient investments of time and energy in all of history. But what did I know? Back in La Paz, there was now a remote possibility that my kidnapping might have triggered a change in Marianela policy, a change that would bring me closer to my goal.

SEVEN

The Consul

They knew my address. Still, I had no choice but to go home to Sonia. By now, she would have deduced that I was working for Arce, against her beloved Marianelas. I would not be returning to the same relationship.

No doubt Sonia would be harboring conflicting emotions: relief to see me alive but anger that I had been working for her enemy, and that I had been deceptive about it all.

I ducked out of the crammed minibus, entered the high-rise, and took the wood-paneled elevator, pressing 8. Either the mirror inside the elevator was distorted, haunted-house style, or my face was badly messed up.

My key failed to fit the slot. Smart move: Sonia would have changed the lock. I rang the bell, and she responded with a shaky "Who is it?"

After the usual "It's me," I added that I was alone.

Sonia fell into my arms. Normally it would take a lot to make her cry. She didn't cry at weddings. She didn't cry at the movies. She didn't cry at funerals. This time, she was sobbing. Between the sobs there was an "It's all my fault."

"Your fault? You didn't ask me to hook up with Arce, Panama Slim, or who knows what else."

"I see you have some sort of business with Mr. Arce, and I'm worried. I'm beginning to realize what that means."

The bulky sofa was considerably softer than the Atacama Desert's unforgiving crust. Sonia was about to curl up with me, but had second thoughts.

"You must be starved. What can I make you?"

"Just sit here. I had a sandwich on the plane. Whaddaya mean, your fault?"

"Katari told me that the paramilitaries follow him wherever he goes. You shook hands with him. They must have seen you shaking his hand. My God your face is a mess. Let me dress it up."

"Wait!" I said. "Since when does Bolivia have paramilitaries? Bolivia's been clean since '82."

"Katari says that there would be paramilitaries in the USA if the law allowed farmers to occupy unused land. The big landowners can't control the federal courts, so even if they own the local judges, they can't dislodge the peasants. So they say, 'This is my land, I have the title, and I have a right to defend it.'"

"So why me? Why not the Marianelas?"

"They're women, and they're Catholic. But Katari says that's only a temporary truce. The landowners are fuming. They just murdered three Guaraní squatters in El Chaco, and no one will be arrested."

Sonia had not come clean with me about the danger of her work, so she could not hold it over me that I had been less than frank about my own doings.

"Let's forget it all for a while, and we can roll around together," I said. She was cuddled next to me, and the skin on her delicate arm and soft cheek was sweet as a teenager's. "We can sort things out later."

I slipped on a Billie Holiday CD and beckoned her to the bedroom.

"How can you think about sex when they might be coming to kill you at any moment."

Good question, I thought. How quickly I could blot out the cowardly trembling fear I had experienced in the Atacama.

"Let them wait," I said.

"We're now enemies," she fired back. "How can we make love when we've chosen opposite sides of an imminent war?"

"Precisely," I said. "That adds some extra excitement!"

"You might be killed at any moment," she repeated. "If they dropped you in Chile, whoever they are, it must be because they don't want you in Bolivia."

"All the more reason why we should do it now. It might be our last chance."

"You're crude," she bit back.

"And you've become a hard-to-get Calvinist. But that just arouses me more."

We went into the bedroom and, for the first time since moving to this apartment, we closed the door, even knowing that it made no difference.

OVER A COFFEE in the kitchen, with Illimani in the distance, I used a pseudo-Socratic approach to move Sonia in the direction of understanding that Arce and Panama Slim had viewed me as a bargaining chip. Through me they would get directly to Sonia, who would exert influence over the Marianelas. The Marianelas could convince the squatters to come to an agreement with Arce.

On a separate level, my bosses also thought I could have direct influence with the squatters themselves. I spoke fluent Spanish, and they expected that with my Latin American background (my father's side), I could develop rapport with their leaders. I could show them there was a better deal if they dismantled their makeshift settlement.

This was wishful thinking. Panama Slim probably figured that if they dangled all that money before me, I'd be sufficiently motivated to produce a miracle. Sonia explained that the tactics of bargaining through the Marianelas exposed the stupidity of both Arce and Panama Slim. First, the landless peasants were not *led* by the Marianelas. It was the racism of Arce and Panama Slim that made them believe that the Marianelas were manipulating the squatters. The peasants were in the driver's seat all the way. They didn't want charity. They wanted solidarity. The Marianela sisters were only spiritual supporters, public relations tools, and perhaps, human shields. But not decision makers.

Sonia and I had to decide whether or not we should lie low at a friend's house. We quickly concluded that if the paramilitaries wanted to find me, they would. Sonia suggested that I return to the States. But I had unfinished business. I shot back that it was she who should return to the States. But she was now a deeply committed Marianela. So with great irony, our opposite missions caused us to remain together. We decided to postpone Deedee's arrival. School in the Southern Hemisphere did not begin until February, and we were in October.

Through all the conflict, the kidnapping, and the inherent dangers in continuing on the same "career path," my protracted duel with the tote board was never forgotten. Even as I was being kicked in the head by my captors, I wondered whether I would ever again make a wager. The Chilean off-track betting became my "I'm still alive" statement ("Still alive in the daily double," we horseplayers would say). After having eked out a small profit in the Iquique OTB (not bad with a 35 percent take-out), my diminishing professionalism was eroding my horseplayer ego. The Tomlinson turf bets had become a liability. I was collecting less often, and my goal of making a living through horse-race wagering was in limbo.

In a rare moment where I could see myself from afar, I peered in and saw a degenerate. I was more perturbed by the deflation of my horse-betting ego than by threats on my life. I wouldn't dare share this perverse set of values with Sonia. The game had become the foundation of my desired real life, while real life was turning into an unwanted dangerous game.

No matter how much I succeeded in blotting out the memory of my abduction, my intellect warned me that those guys could return. The key was to find out who had sent them.

Meanwhile, Breeders' Cup was looming, and I could not imagine myself remaining aloof from it. I figured that I could travel to the USA for the Breeders' Cup, see Deedee, and perhaps make contact with Panama Slim. Sonia's vulnerability was the only factor keeping me from leaving.

I phoned Marvin James, a consul at the U.S. Embassy. Marv was a sometimes hiking companion. He told me to meet him at 5 P.M., at the athletic field on the Bolivian army base in Irpavi, in the South Zone of the city.

"Why there?" I asked.

"We have a big softball game."

* * *

THE PLAYING FIELD was makeshift. They found rags for the bases. They cleared out stones from the infield. Marv was the lefty first baseman for the U.S. Embassy team, a tall six-foot-three inches. They were playing against the team from the Cuban Embassy. The Cubans had not been accustomed to underhand fast-pitch softball so Kelly, a secretary at the U.S. Embassy, became the Cubans' pitcher. You'd have never known that the United States and Cuba were at international loggerheads. In Bolivia, where baseball and softball were as foreign as apple pie, Americans and Cubans felt a common bond.

When the Americans were at bat, Marv was able to talk to me in the shade of a cough-drop-smelling eucalyptus tree behind first base.

His degree in anthropology meant he was predisposed to empathize with the culture where he served as consul. Not only did he speak fluent Spanish, but he'd learned enough Aymara to handle a conversation with the highlanders, with both Spanish and Aymara dominating in the region of La Paz. Marv was also tinkering with the basics of Quechua, the other main Andean tongue, prevalent in Cochabamba and Potosí, inherited from the Inca Empire that had followed the Aymaras and had lasted a scant 60 years until the Spanish conquest. Some two dozen other languages had survived here and there in small pockets within the dense and isolated valleys.

Marv was aware that Bolivians referred to the American ambassador as "the Viceroy" and that they believed the embassy financed those Bolivian electoral candidates who would most likely serve American interests. But our conversations were coded to skirt around those issues. He knew that Sonia was working for the Marianelas and that there was no love lost between the missionaries and the embassy.

"Marv, I'm gonna be straight with you. I wanna go to the Breeders' Cup, but I'm afraid to leave Sonia alone. She's working with the Marianelas, and they're supporting the squatters. That could blow up one of these days. Can you provide any protection for her? I mean, the paramilitaries are capable of kidnappings and, who knows, rape and torture."

"Matt, there's nothing the embassy can do to protect someone who is voluntarily going out and making enemies. My advice would be for Sonia to call it off and work for a charity or apply for a job at the World Bank."

"You mean the embassy has a position against the Landless Peasants?"

Sentimentally, Marv was rooting for the Landless Peasants. Those were the types of people he studied in his anthropology research. But as a diplomat, he could not take sides in such issues, and the embassy would more likely wish that the Landless Peasants Movement would go away, since stability was their primary concern.

It was Marv's turn to hit. He lined the ball into right field. When the right fielder juggled the ball, Marv rounded first base and tried to make it to second. His slide over the pebbly surface was clumsy, the throw was a bullet, and Marv was tagged out. Two outs. None on. Marv came back to the tree behind first base.

"Matt, you saw how I went for an extra base and I got thrown out. If I decide, for reasons of anthropological interest, to steal a visit with the Landless Peasants, I doubt I'll get any protection from my own embassy, and I'm their employee. Sonia must have received a letter with a list of activities that Americans should not deal with. The Landless Peasants are on the list. Sonia has waived her right to any type of protection."

With the third out, the Americans took the field, and the Cubans came to bat. The La Paz sun was hammering down, and this may have been the reason why Marv could not handle a pop-up in foul ground behind first base. On the next pitch, Gómez, the Cuban cultural atta-ché, drilled the ball between the right and center fielders and ended up on third base. The Cubans scored three runs after two outs, and Marv's dropped ball loomed as the culprit.

By the last half of the seventh inning, the Americans were down 4–2 and needed a miracle. Marv went to bat. Ever the pull hitter, he drove the first pitch down the right-field line. The ball hit one of the crusty areas where there were no tufts of grass, no stray stones, and it skipped over the crusty ground, over a curb, and onto an unused street in the Irpavi military compound. Marv made it home.

But the game ended 4–3.

The Americans and Cubans shook hands cordially and left for their cars. Some of the Cubans lived in the neighborhood, which was not far from their embassy.

Marv apologized for not sticking around. No time for our usual rounds of margaritas.

"In any case, when you're gone at the Breeders' Cup, Sonia can stay with Julie and me."

I shook his hand and thanked him.

"But this is all unofficial," he said. "The embassy cannot protect American citizens who choose to take dumb risks."

I had omitted the fact that I had been kidnapped. I did ask if there was anyone named Panama Slim in the embassy computers.

"Even if there is, if it's classified, you know I cannot give it to you. But I'll have a look."

EIGHT

Breeders' Cup

For the first time since she signed up for a five-year hitch with the Marianelas, Sonia suffered a mild bout with indecisiveness. Tough Sonia, the petite but elegant fighter for justice, expressed her worries, first as a mother and then as a wife.

My initial reaction was jealousy. Hard-to-get Sonia was now softening up, but it wasn't me who triggered the change.

"All the Marianelas are sacrificing something or other," she explained to me over a breakfast of crusty *marraqueta* bread with butter and quince marmalade, along with manzanilla tea. "If I mention Deedee to them, they might wonder why I did not consider the fact that I was a mother *before* joining. The few other married women in the group had their kids in Bolivian schools."

The usual morning frost had seeped through the brick walls of our apartment. We sipped our steaming beverages next to the window where the sun rays converged from their rising position behind Quimsa Cruz Cordillera. No wonder it's so hard to sell an apartment in La Paz if it has no exposure to the sunlight.

"Tell them that your case is different," I suggested, opportunistically. "You have a husband who was kidnapped, and the kidnapping relates to the Landless Peasants."

Anything to nudge them in the direction of seeking alternative acreage for their peasant heroes.

"Matt, let's drop the subject. Let's just be together and make the most of it. You're leaving tomorrow."

"Only for a week," I reminded her. "And you can stay at Marv's house."

The phone rang. Had to be Marv.

"Panama Slim is really Howard Stoner," he said.

"I knew that, Marv. Give me something bigger than that."

"You want bigger? Well he's the founder and president of an organization called GBC."

That sounded okay to me. GBC is Gamblers Book Shop in Las Vegas, the best in-person shop for horse-race titles in the world. But it wasn't *that* GBC. It was *Get Back the Canal.*

"He's a loony," Marv said. "Honest conservatives now realize it was good business to cede the Canal to the Panamanians. This guy is on the fringe."

"What else?" I asked.

"I can say no more. The rest is classified."

"Well, at least tell me where I can look."

"You can find out about his organization in any public library. I have the basic stuff. The GBC subscribes to the belief that Polk's Manifest Destiny covered all of the Americas and not only the West. So the Canal is their example of a foothold in what they believe should be 'our back yard.'"

Given what I had just heard, the Bolivian racetrack might be part of a grander scheme for Panama Slim. But he was certainly a racing enthusiast, so, giving him the benefit of the doubt, the Bolivia racetrack deal seemed more like an attempt to integrate business with pleasure.

"If I told you that Panama Slim was interested in Bolivia, what would you say, Marv?"

"I'd say, *stay clear of him.*"

I PHONED ARCE to catch him before he left for his office in downtown Santa Cruz. Señora Arce picked up the phone. I summoned my knowledge of Spanish social vocabulary and asked her in the most polite way if I could speak to her husband.

"He's out playing in his garden," she said, with sudden friendliness, as if she were happy for me to take her husband away from his all-consuming passion. I held on for at least five minutes before Arce could get to the phone. I thanked him for communicating with Sonia.

"Well, Matt, I am delighted to know that you are back home and well."

"Is that all you know, Manuel? Come on! Let me in on a few secrets about the goon situation. After all, I'm the one who provided their entertainment."

"I wish I could help you, Matt. We need you! But it's a mystery to me."

"Yes, you need me, but you also needed me kidnapped. I'll bet you've already tried to take advantage of what happened."

"And why shouldn't I? It's in your best interest as well as ours. I had the Chamber of Commerce send a letter to the Marianelas here in Santa Cruz, expressing our deep concern about escalating violence, asking them if they had received any threats or demands from the kidnappers, since the victim is the husband of their administrative director."

"You could have saved the postage and asked me. If they'd received any threat, Sonia would have known about it." I had stumbled on my own slow thinking. I picked myself up. "I get it. Your letter *was* the threat, wasn't it?"

"My dear friend, if you had been here you would have drafted the same letter with the same wording. It *is* in your interest, correct?"

"Look, Manuel, I don't think you had anything to do with this, but surely you know about loose cannons, maybe Mendoza has his own paramilitaries."

"I admit that Alberto Mendoza is not the life of the party, but that's the way he is. I'm trying to get him involved in garden therapy."

"What about those three Mendoza look-alikes who follow Katari and his peasants? They must be working for someone."

"We landowners do not talk about each other's defense strategies. Such conversation is taboo. None of us wants to be accused of aiding and abetting what the other does for self-defense."

"So my kidnapping was someone's self-defense?"

I could imagine Arce's usual paternal smile.

"I am against the kind of kidnapping strategy you suffered, but I'm in the minority. You'd better speak with Panama Slim. He knows all these landowners, better than we know each other."

"And how is *that*? You're the president of the fucking Chamber of Commerce."

"Yes, Matt, that's true, but he is their cut-rate supplier."

I wanted to know more. Arce warned me against wild suppositions, reminding me it was dangerous for any of us to talk about paramilitaries.

"Matt, today, we are in a better bargaining position than we were before your kidnapping. That's what's important. I really need to get back to the garden. I need this therapy each morning, or I wouldn't be able to handle what I must do each afternoon."

Sonia and I went out for a stroll and picnic. At the point we crossed the river-become-sewer Choqueyapu, it was vaulted over, and the stink was faint. We then marched up a steep ridge between the two sides of the Hole, each draped with a patchy quilt of earthy red-brick slums. The ridge, called Laikakota, offered a magnificent 360-degree view of the contradictory city with its pastel high-rises below and its red-brick hillside shantytowns above. Beyond the colorful confusion, you could see several of the 500 snow-covered peaks of the Royal Cordillera.

We had picked up some juicy *salteña* meat pies from a street stand, along with a papaya soda.

We snacked at the edge of Laikakota, not far from an immense children's playground. We had resolved to bury all subjects of fear or conflict, and concentrate on our being together in this authentic country.

"Just imagine," I said, attempting to be reasonable. "If neither of us had our missions here, we could get lost together in some small village down from the mountains, in the cloud forest. We could survive on tropical fruit, corn, and potatoes, and we could explore places where we'd have to make our own maps. We could come across undiscovered Quechua ruins and maybe even unknown endemic animal species."

Sonia nudged me playfully. I was often the butt of her sarcastic caricatures.

"You wouldn't survive without your dark chocolate bars and your bordeaux wines."

"Sonia, how can you be so cynical when you're working with hopeless romantics?"

Her dark eyes glistened. Her thin wrists were delicately erotic. "I want everything you mentioned. But are you just dreaming for an hour, or would you take your own words seriously?"

I *was* taking it seriously, and that's why I still held some slim hopes for the racetrack deal, which essentially would lead to my independence. But we had agreed that such subjects were not admissible at Laikakota. Our legs dangled over the edge of the ridge. We finished our snack with the vague hum of the traffic below providing the muffled background music. I held her hand, hoping for some sort of verbal breakthrough, a soaring communion of language that would erase the deep gap in our relationship. Like the condor circling around the same ridge again and again, our discussion hung in one invariable orbit. Eventually we descended back to civilization and saw that nothing had changed.

The Breeders' Cup was going to be held at Churchill Downs, but I had decided to do the races at the plush Albany OTB, with various friends and colleagues, including Nick Kling, Tom, and Art. Vince was flying in for the weekend.

I'd phoned Panama Slim to arrange a meeting. I wasn't sure how it would take place, but I envisioned some sort of confrontation, unless he came clean with his true motives. He wouldn't miss Churchill Downs on Saturday, but he said he'd fly to Albany and meet me at the Albany OTB for a Sunday lunch. This time, I resolved to choose my own menu item and not be touted by Slim. If I couldn't even stand up to him on innocuous things like seafood versus vegetarian, how could I hope to raise the bar of my demands to a significantly higher level?

The plan was to fly to D.C., pick up Deedee in Maryland, and take the train with her to Albany, New York, stopping off in Manhattan for a brief tour. Deedee had never been there. We would then stay with Aunt Ada, who lived in Albany, and be within cycling distance of the OTB. There was room at Ada's to put up Vince as well.

I would need to rein Vince in and avoid references to the porno business and who knows what other gaffes he might commit.

Everything was going smoothly, except that Deedee seemed hardly excited about seeing me. At first I thought she resented our having left her. But in fact, she was so occupied in Maryland with her Aunt Charlotte and Uncle Rob that she didn't have much time to miss us. They were doting relatives, and the school's philosophy of "learning is fun" was hard to beat for a child.

We had decided to put her into an avant-garde private school in September (the end of the previous school year in Bolivia), even if she would eventually have to drop out and restart in La Paz. She was in a Spanish immersion program where the language learning was designed to be exciting enough to compete with computer games. Deedee's high level of self-esteem contained a dose of indifference towards the rest of the world.

I plowed through the multiple-choice test. Deedee's indifference was:

A. a defense mechanism against what she perceived as our own indifference for having left her behind;

B. a product of her immense self-confidence coming from both her independence from her parents and the school system that nurtured the individual above all else;

C. the result of being spoiled by her aunt and uncle.

Our brief stop-off in Manhattan gave us only a few hours. I figured she could see it all from a high place.

The World Trade Center had been the scene of a 1993 terrorist attack. As a handicapper, I analyzed that if the extremists were to come back, they'd go after the Empire State Building because they would assume that all the heavy security apparatus would be concentrated at the WTC. Even knowing that statistics show car accidents to have the far greater probability of untimely death than terrorist attacks, I felt that it would be a tad safer for us to visit the World Trade Center. But aesthetics won out, and I chose the more venerable Empire State Building.

Once up, I pointed down to the George Washington Bridge, explaining to Deedee that one could walk on the Long Path beginning at the bridge and end up in Albany. I asked her if she preferred to walk or take the train.

"Don't be silly, Daddy. It would take too long to walk."

Evidently Deedee had not recovered from the long hikes Sonia and I had subjected her to at Sugarloaf Mountain in Maryland. At 11 years old, she was already into a video view of life, and appreciated being chauffeured around.

The New York-to-Albany Hudson River route is one of the world's great rail trips. Stupidly, I pointed out the beauty of the Palisades to Deedee while she was more interested in listening to her head-phone music. The Edward Hopperesque charm of the old red-brick factories lining the river between Ossining and Poughkeepsie was foreign to her. I wondered whether the consumer society had already stolen her from me.

Vince took his rented car to pick us up at the train station. What they used to call "the Depot" had been banished from the city center and exiled across the river.

I introduced Vince and Deedee. Deedee told Vince that he looked like a soap opera gangster, with his dark glasses, graying sideburns, and crazy beret. Vince told Deedee that she looked like a space cadet with her Walkman and pink sweater.

Ada, now in her eighties, had once believed that racing was immoral, until she collected on my tip on Sunday Silence in the 1989 Derby. Then she became more tolerant, making a bet from time to time.

Since her husband had died, she enjoyed a steady stream of visiting guests, and that's how she had offered to put up my friend Vince, who had arrived the night before.

Ada loved to cook for visitors, but she was not at all skilled at the art of cuisine. I could handle her food, but Deedee and Vince were both picky eaters. I feared that the hostess might be insulted by the guests. Deedee would be understood. She was only 11. But if Ada were to ask Vince if he enjoyed the food, Vince at his diplomatic best would say, "It's okay, but haven't you ever heard of basil and garlic?"

I had warned him in advance to avoid any talk of the food, but with Vince, such warnings were as useful as a CIGARETTES KILL label on a pack of cigarettes in the hands of a chain smoker.

I also warned Vince that Ada might ask him if he had any children, and that he should not respond with a "Yes, a daughter, but the judge won't let me see her."

The food issue was temporarily resolved when Vince explained that he was picking up a pizza for dinner. But Ada would be preparing a salad, and she would often slice apples into the salad, which might trigger the type of discussion I wanted to avoid.

Dinner went well enough. Deedee left the apple slices at the side of her salad, and I gobbled them up while Ada wasn't looking. Vince gulfed everything down and even thanked Ada for putting apples in the salad.

"My girlfriend tells me I don't eat enough fruit," Vince explained. "She shoulda thought about sticking apples in the salad."

I should have been thrilled, but if Ada followed up with the wrong question, we would all be hearing that Vince was 46, while his girlfriend was only 23 and she looked 16.

Seeing that Deedee had been unimpressed by the Long Path or the Hudson River kitsch, I suspected that the Albany OTB would not enter into her dreams of romance. Following dinner, Vince plucked out an extra *Daily Racing Form*, handing it to Deedee. He flashed $14 and then pointed to the past performances.

"Deedee, if you study the *Racing Form*, then you can use this money to make a two-dollar bet in each Breeders' Cup race. If you don't study, you can't bet, and you'll have to return the money to me."

Vince smiled.

"Do you like puzzles, Deedee?"

"I love puzzles."

"Do you love difficult puzzles? Because this is one of the most difficult ever invented, but if you solve the puzzle, you win money."

I was surprised by Deedee's positive response to Vince's proposal. All I'd gotten for every rabbit I'd tried to pull out of the hat, from Maryland to Albany, was determined indifference. The one time that I failed to tell her, "Take a look at this!" she took a look. That was on Fifth Avenue. She was gawking at the boutique windows, wanting to buy this or that item of haute-couture clothing, none of which came marked with a price.

Here was the utmost irony. Suddenly the antimaterialistic Marianelas seemed like the only ones who could save my daughter from the onslaught of consumerism. Otherwise, she might grow up like her dad and do business with the first nutcase who dangled a hundred thousand in front of her.

The Albany OTB has two sections. One has free admission, but the player is charged the extra 5 percent takeout on wagers, a system that has plagued the whole New York OTB. It's dumpy in that section. But if you pay the $3 admission, you get into a player-friendly restaurant-racing theater. You don't have to consume anything, as there are sections beyond the restaurant with comfortable tables to deck out the *Form* and well-placed monitors beaming in the races from various tracks. Thus, it's cheaper to pay the admission than to pay the extra 5 percent takeout, but so many players don't get it. In one way they have a point. Gambling is more titillating in a seedy environment.

Nick and Tom got us a special room with our own betting windows.

I passed the first two races. They were baby races, and I had no notion. Deedee asked what she should do. I said that she could pass and bet more money in the other races, or she could study the *Form* and pick a horse in those races.

She passed the first race and picked Baffert's Silverbulletday in the second. She was disappointed to collect only $3.60 for her two bucks. Not enough for a sweater on Fifth Avenue. I reminded her that she would now have an extra buck and change to add to a later race.

"You have a choice with the extra money," I explained. "You could bet a second horse, you could back up your top horse to place, or you could play an exacta, which means you pick two horses and you need them to finish in order. It's more risk but the payoff is much higher."

"Daddy, I think I wanna try an exacta."

"Fine," I said. "Maybe we could combine your horse and mine in a later race."

In the next race, the Sprint, I picked Richter Scale at 29–1 and Deedee chose Reraise. Reraise won and paid $9.60. My bet finished 12 horses back.

I had arrived in Albany with a wounded horseplayer ego. That ego was not bolstered when an 11-year-old girl could pick them better than I could, even if that girl was my own daughter.

"Be thankful," Vince said. "Deedee's probably inherited your handi-capping genes."

In the next race, the Mile, I struggled to pick out the best foreign horse on the turf. Deedee picked out Hawksley Hill, trained by Neil Drysdale, at 15–1.

Suddenly I noticed the *Pink Sheet*, the local racing rag that displays the selections of eight different public handicappers. Nick was one of them. Nick was the only one to pick Da Hoss, the Michael Dickinson horse that had won this same race two years ago. Sometime after the race he suffered an injury. Dickinson had nursed him back to good health with infinite patience. Da Hoss had only had one snail-pace prep race, hardly enough to prepare for such a big event following such a long absence.

But this was Nick Kling, the informed minority. No need to ask Nick why he picked Da Hoss. Yes, it was his pick, but it was *my* system. I was obligated to back the horse. Why handicap?

Da Hoss came from midpack to win the race. I was thrilled to collect a $25.20 payoff. But before savoring the moment, my vulnerable racing persona suffered a major setback. Hawksley Hill, the horse chosen by Deedee, had finished second. The $2 exacta had paid $377. I had forgot-ten about our plan to combine our two horses in an exacta.

The money could be recovered at a later date. But this would have been *her* money, and she would have earned it.

But for Da Hoss, I had lost every single race. It came down to the final leg of the Breeders' Cup, the Classic. Here I had an opinion. In racing, if you can go against a favorite, then you can make money, even if you don't have one particular horse to play.

I had decided to take a stand against the favorite, Skip Away. Skip Away had won this and other top races. He was the star. But for me he was washed up. In his previous race, he looked to me like an unmotivated athlete, one that still has skills but has lost interest.

I liked three horses. Swain, an Irish horse, was my top pick, at nearly 7–1. I also liked Awesome Again, who was the up-and-coming dominant classic horse with a near-perfect record. My third choice was the 5–2 second favorite, Silver Charm. I felt that Silver Charm, also a former champion, had lost a few steps and was nearing a less glorious finale of a brilliant career. I felt that newcomers Swain and Awesome Again were both peaking.

Racing is not much different from the stock market. You can have a hyped company that is entering a business slump. Investors get caught in the hype and keep buying when they should be selling. Such was the stock of Skip Away.

"Throwing out" Skip Away meant inflated exacta and trifecta payouts, even though the horses I liked were not longshots à la Da Hoss. I boxed my three horses in a trifecta and boxed my two highest odds, Swain and Awesome Again, in the exacta.

It was a memorable race for one particular reason. The jockey on Swain, the flamboyant Frankie Dettori, perhaps the best in the world, made a grave error. As they entered the stretch, with all of my three horses battling for the win, Dettori whipped Swain left-handed. Swain bore out to the right, as if he were galloping to the grandstand instead of the finish line. And yet Dettori kept whipping him left-handed.

To this very day, even with Dettori as one of the most dominant riders in history, I believe he cost me the win on Swain, and the exacta with Swain and Awesome Again.

Not a pretty picture. As they neared the finish line, it looked to me like the wide Swain would fade to fourth place and cost me the trifecta as well. Awesome Again was moving so powerfully that you could see he would be the winner. The win bet would only be a consolation, though, if Swain self-destructed into fourth place. I would calculate that by boring out, he probably ran an extra fifteen yards compared to the other horses.

Still, when they crossed the finish line, from the TV angle it looked as if Swain had held on for third place, a neck behind Silver Charm.

The photo sign flashed on the screen. The stewards would determine whether Swain or Victory Gallop had gotten third place. The gap between Victory Gallop near the inside and Swain, parked way out where the railbirds could smell him, meant a longer inspection from the stewards.

The OFFICIAL sign went up. A whole eternity could be compressed into the nanosecond between my perceiving the flash of tote lights and then distinguishing the numbers they represented. Swain's number 2 reverberated in third place. I had won a $247 trifecta mainly by having been able to eliminate the falsely favored publicity horse.

I told Deedee that we would share the profits. But that made no impact on her. She had picked Swain to win, after having seen all the 1's in his finishes.

Her Fifth Avenue dream had ended.

Vince asked her how she liked the idea of handicapping in order to make money.

"It was fun for one day," she said, "but I think this is really hard work. I wouldn't have time for school if I wanted to do this well."

That was a valid intellectual finding, one that many horseplayers should make for themselves. If they can't invest the time and learn the artistic intricacies, they should not expect to win. Luck can erupt in the short run, but in the long run, skill, the mixture of analytical prowess and artistic intuition, will rule, and then only if accompanied by a rigorous work ethic.

As always happens on a good day, the studious horseplayer discovers something that could have made things much better. After the fact, I noticed that all seven of the Breeders' Cup winners had either won or finished second as first-time starters. Four of them had been debut winners, including the 6-year-old Da Hoss. A quick perusal of previous Breeders' Cups showed me that first-time or second-time-out winners of their maiden race won far more than their fair share of Breeders' Cup races, based on "impact-value" statistics.

A hypothesis had been formulated: yet another "horse-futures" method based on the precociousness factor. Thoroughbreds are athletes, but some are more "natural" than others. The natural ones win early in their careers, and this natural competitiveness makes a difference even later in their career evolution. I suspect that it would work for human beings as well. The more talented and more aggressive kids in the school yard have a greater chance to make it in pro sports. If they are aggressive but not talented, they might turn into a Panama Slim. If they are talented but not aggressive, they could turn into a Katari, who uses words as his weapon (Arce calls it demagogy). Katari would gain followers by taking off his jacket and joining the masses on the soccer field for a scrimmage, where he could put the ball in the net with an acrobatic bicycle kick, but he could not handle the elbowing as the corner kick arced in front of the net.

In order to win races, horses needed a naturally athletic stride coupled with a dominant herding instinct, both of which contribute to debut wins. That was my hypothesis for horse-futures betting.

For my next kidnapping, I would have to request that my captors supply me with a stack of *Racing Forms*, good Portuguese coffee, and a work desk, and that they should not allow the outside world to interrupt me. In this way, I would come up with a system for betting debut winners automatically in a later segment of their career.

On the way out of our special room, Tom gave me a pile of old *Racing Forms* he'd collected from his OTB work. While Ada, Vince, and Deedee watched *Jeopardy!* and *Wheel of Fortune*, I raced through the PPs with pen-and-paper tallying. I used one of Ada's antique desks for added inspiration. Whenever they appeared in any past performances, I isolated career races 6 through 10. I compared the returns for horses that won their debut race, compared to second-, third-, fourth-, and fifth-career-race maiden breakers.

By the time I'd finished, everyone was asleep. They may have said good-night to me but I'd blotted everything else but the past performances from my consciousness, even my own daughter. I checked the clock in the living room. It was already 3:10 A.M.

Final tally for career races 6 through 10:

Horse was debut winner: 117 wins from 484 races (a tad above 24%)

Horse broke maiden in second career race: 142 wins from 606 races (slightly above 24%)

Horse broke maiden in third career race: 99 wins from 572 starts (17%)

Horse broke maiden in fourth career race: 74 wins in 468 starts (16%)

Horse broke maiden in fifth career race: 57 wins out of 389 starts (15%)

My hypothesis had become a legitimate theory. Horses that break their maiden early in their career, either winners of their debut or second career race, are better bets later on than the slow developers. Could be that they are simply gifted athletes or that they have been born with a competitive streak in the realm of their herding instinct.

(I later checked with an animal-behavior prof at USC, who corroborated the logic of my theory, based on his research of the fighting fish of Thailand.) This was good news. The more I could discover in the way of automatic bets, the easier it would be to return to racing-deprived Bolivia. The next morning I was already on the phone with a mathematics prof/horseman colleague at Hastings Park. He agreed to follow up on my research.

NINE

Panama Slim

What I had lost in hours of sleep I made up for in the depth of restfulness, as if I had condensed a whole winter of hibernation into five hours.

It was a brisk, sunny autumn morning. I decided to bicycle to the OTB. Vince would catch up to me in his car, and perhaps arrive before I did. I had been preparing for my food fight with Panama Slim. I had decided to probe him on the Get Back the Canal group, hoping to trigger some telltale reaction that would clue me in to his real motivation for the Bolivia enterprise. If this cat-and-mouse approach failed, I would go as far as to ruin my dessert by being blunt and demanding an advance on my contract.

I had chocolate cake in mind for dessert. But for me, chocolate is to be consumed only in moments of total calm. Chocolate should be a mantra for meditation, and each bite should be independent of all outside static. Eating while doing business is an aspect of our culture that needs a serious overhaul. A moderate compromise would be to talk business during the salad or starter and gradually work toward excluding all thoughtful verbal exchange by the time the main course was set on the table.

Bicycling through Albany to the Western Avenue OTB had its emotional ups and downs as well as the literal ones. Some of the old Albany had survived. Here and there were two- and three-story red-brick and brownstone walkups whose style dated back to the colonial period. There were ornate Victorian houses with wrap-around porches, some of them sparkling bright with subtle yuppie colors thanks to the modern paint industry, and others seeming ready to wobble in the first wind.

Albany's attempt at modernism was not a total failure. The style of the newer government buildings was attractive, with sweeping angles and a gothic-like grasp for the sky. The problem was at street level. The streets were rendered dead by an absence of ground-floor commerce or street-level windows. Through their standoffish style, these structures announced that access was for cars and not people.

Passing through downtown, I came upon the Western Avenue strip, and little by little, slums appeared, and used-car lots, and sprawling shopping mall parking lots. There was nothing appreciable to distract the eyes.

Drivers failed to respect the rights of two-wheelers, even though we were not the ones sending carbon emissions into the ozone layer or provoking drastically rising health care costs as a result of a car-induced sloth culture. Regional public transport administrators provided friendly bus service, but in the Albany region the buses were too slow to draw people out of their cars.

I saw Panama Slim's rented Lincoln in the OTB parking lot. Once more, there were no railings for my bike lock. I resorted to the trash bin system behind the kitchen, and the OTB cuisine workers promised that my bicycle would be safe. The bicycle is a perfect tool for working off the frustrations of a losing day at the races, while a winning day serves as natural doping for pedal power.

Slim and I shook hands or, I should say, Slim shook my hand and my whole body with it. I reminded myself to not feel intimidated, but my intellect could not keep up with my beating heart. We were escorted to a booth. The young waitress plopped down two menus. I put my hand on my benefactor's menu and decided that the inevitable confrontation would best begin now, long before the main dish.

"Slim, you know damn well that the signature you sent me for was already a done deal. Why the fuck didn't you tell me I was being set up as your bargaining chip?"

"Whoa, Matt, calm down. Recall my words. I said, 'You know Spanish, you know Bolivia, and you know racing.' That's a whole lot more than a blasted signature."

"That's not enough, Slim."

"I'm an optimist. I told you, 'I know you can handle anything.' I said the word *anything*. You're a jazz musician. You shoulda had the imagination to understand me. I was betting on your improvising skills."

"Or you knew that, just by being there, as Sonia's husband, I'd turn into a bargaining tool."

"Hey Matt, what's coming over you? Calm down, and let's have a good lunch. It's on me."

The waitress, a freshman at Albany State, from her accent a local girl, probably a farm girl, told us her name was Marina, and she could take our order.

There was nothing unusual on the menu, no aubergines, no tofu, nothing I was used to with Sonia. I asked for the pork in mushroom sauce with mashed potatoes.

"Wait," Panama Slim said to the waitress. "He's not gonna have t-h-a-t."

I looked at Slim. It was a replay from Saratoga.

"Now why don't you tell me what's wrong with the pork, Slim? Surely you don't believe that trichinosis . . ."

Slim butted in.

"Honey, what ya say your name was? Marina, please give us another five minutes.

"Matt, you can order anything on this fucking menu, but not the pork. I hate mushrooms."

"But you're not gonna eat the mushrooms."

"Did you know that mushrooms are a fungus? They're not plants. They're invaders. They don't come from seeds. They just settle in, like athlete's foot."

"You don't have to look at them, Slim. You can look at your own plate."

"*I'm* inviting, Matt. There's a certain order in my life that I like to keep intact. I've successfully excluded mushrooms for all my 54 years, and I'm not gonna let a funky jazz musician suddenly improvise my own existence."

Whew. I had resolved to not allow Slim to control the menu. But for
the second time, I had no options. Sonia would tell me to pick my battles.
I could hear her voice, in her pre-Marianela days: *Matt, just be objective.
Which would you consider more important? Mushrooms today or a check for a
hundred thousand tomorrow?*

I began connecting the dispersed dots. Slim had a one-track mentality, and not only at the dinner table, where he would never mix any two
things in his mouth at the same time, not even his drink. He was obsessed
with the Panama Canal after the rest of the world had forgotten the issue.
Strangely, he was not at all detail oriented about his dress. There was an
edge of informality, a tie slightly loosened, his thick and bushy hair purposely haywire, an occasional gray strand shining under the booth lamp.
He was so much bigger than his appearance that he didn't need any damn
façade to assert his authority.

In the end, things had to be his way, little things and big things. It was
some sort of syndrome, though the name for it escaped me. He talked at
people but not with them.

In the end, Slim ordered fish, but it wasn't so easy. Marina had to go
back to the kitchen to find the exact ingredients in the white sauce, and Slim
wasn't convinced that the runts in the kitchen knew what they were talking
about, so when she came back he had changed his order to grilled fish.

The charcoal aromas were pleasing so I looked for something grilled
and ended up with the fish myself. Hardly a rebellious move, but with the
food out of the way as an issue, I could concentrate on the more essential
points of conflict.

I decided against beating around the bush.

"You know very well," I said, "that your edge increases proportionally
to the level of my anguish."

I stopped short of mentioning that my death might be the final straw
that could cause the Marianelas to abandon their squat. Why give him
ideas? I did insist that using me as a bargaining chip could only go so far.
The squatters did not depend on the Marianelas, and were far less sus-
ceptible to strong-arm methods. Slim nearly knocked over the table, with
an arm-waving response.

"You do-gooders think those squatters are some sort of noble savages with an unbreakable philosophy," he said. "They can be *convinced* like anyone else. I'm bringing those fuckers real progress, and they will have to understand this one way or another."

"How can I be sure this is not just a piece of your Panama Canal puzzle?" I asked.

"Well, hot dog! You're discovering the world is round! Bolivia is our backyard. If they want progress, they're gonna have to accept our terms. The fucking Indians are not going to bring Bolivia out of the Middle Ages by farming with fucking oxen."

I knew the argument. But if Arce was being straight with me, and why shouldn't he be, I also knew that Slim had some obscure interests in South America. There comes a point when you have to distinguish between abstract economic arguments and concrete interests.

The word *interests* flashed through my mind. I was getting away from the issue of my own existence. I resolved to bypass the political discussion and get to the point. If I was a human bargaining chip, exposing myself to all kinds of very mean people, I would at least need an advance, and also an insurance policy that, in case of my death, would get the balance of the hundred thou into Sonia's hands.

It was time for dessert, but this time it was I who asked Marina to hold off for a while. I saw people standing at the entrance waiting for seating. But with Panama Slim at my table, not even the owner was going to ask us to hurry up.

Surprisingly, Slim agreed to both the advance and the insurance policy. The advance was only seven thousand, but that amount served as a symbolic gesture that motivated me to work on.

Sonia and I had discussed the theme of insurance over the years, and I can't say we agreed. I figured that life insurance was a bad bet because the only way to win was to die. Sonia spoke of security. Her father had died when she was three years old. Her mother had become wasted and fatigued from raising children. Sonia was an unwanted child, because her father denied her mother the right to an abortion. She responded by having Sonia but losing her interest as a mother.

Circumstances led to Sonia having to deal with her own self-sufficiency as soon as she was a schoolgirl, even though her food and housing was assured by a relatively affluent middle-class background.

Sonia had argued that if her father had had life insurance, her struggle for survival would have been lightened. This was one more argument that I could not win against Sonia, and I made the bad bet and bought a life insurance policy. There were no clauses in it about death from kidnapping, a loophole that the insurance merchants would certainly take advantage of.

In a way, the insurance policy that Slim would have to dish out was not the classic bad-bet life insurance. It would truly insure my life. In case Slim had the idea of contacting his paramilitary customers and having them wipe me off the map, he would now have to part with $200,000 according to the policy I required. Therefore, at least he'd think twice before considering that I would be more valuable to him dead than alive.

Slim opened his leather briefcase and took out a receipt pad. Without a word, he scribbled a promise for the advance and the insurance. He would draw up the official documents on his computer at his hotel and have them for me in the morning.

As dessert was set on the table, I savored the idea of intensely concentrating on each bite of my tiramisu. Business was done, and I had a few minutes to withdraw into the subtle world of chocolate and cream.

At that moment, Vince walked in carrying a *Racing Form* in one arm and guiding Deedee with the other. I wished I could have returned the tiramisu to whence it came. Knowing Vince, he would introduce Deedee to Panama Slim. The plan had been for Deedee to stay with my aunt, and maybe go shopping. Within a few seconds, Panama Slim would be aware that I had a daughter: a potential bargaining chip. I was too upset for dessert.

Vince introduced Deedee. Panama Slim eyed Deedee as if she were the fine print in a contract.

"Well, I didn't realize you had such a beautiful daughter, Matt. I'm hoping you will protect her like a good father."

What did he mean? *Protect her!* From what? He could have said,

"What grade are you in?" or "Has your daddy taught you to read the *Racing Form*?"

I offered my tiramisu to Deedee, and she was thrilled to dig the spoon into it. I would save dessert for a moment when I could appreciate it.

Deedee, Vince, and I spent the rest of the afternoon watching the races. I made two bets and lost both of them. Deedee ignored the race monitors and read her teenage novel. I felt as if I were losing her. In three days we would take the train back to Maryland, I would deposit her at Uncle Rob's house, and be off to Bolivia.

And those days swept by predictably. No superfecta score, Slim's promises sucking me into a deeper hole, Vince charming everyone until they got to know him, Deedee moving inexorably to her teens, and the lonesome beauty of the Hudson River, until it came time to say good-bye. Deedee hugged me, just sweetly enough, and then skipped to the TV room as if I were merely going out to buy cigarettes. I embraced Charlotte and her two daughters, Rob drove me to Baltimore International Airport. Having grown up in rough New York streets, playing with other kids, unsupervised, I was startled by my last words to Rob.

"Sorry to badger, Rob, but I seem to remember you telling me that Deedee's always supervised when she plays in the street?"

"What has become of us?" Rob asked. "We move to the suburbs to escape crime, find an ultrasafe development, and then behave as if we were living in Sarajevo during a civil war. We have Neighborhood Watch, cameras all over the place, and no-thru streets so that strangers don't come roaring through. And yet we all watch our kids like hawks."

I boarded the plane for Miami echoing the same question. Was I, once a critic of sheltered childhoods, now becoming an advocate for Gated America?

TEN

The Strike

It was as if my trip were sandwiched between two slices of indifference. First there was Deedee, who had no regrets about her dad flying off to another continent. Then it was Sonia, whose initial hug and kiss were constrained by a distant protocol.

It happened on the minibus winding down from the El Alto airport into La Paz. It happened after I told Sonia about the advance. (I had kept the insurance policy a secret.)

"I imagined you were going to tell Panama Slim that you wanted out!" she lamented.

"I weighed the alternatives, Sonia. If I jump off the moving train, I might get killed."

"You know that your racetrack will displace hundreds of poor farmers. Where are your principles?"

I struggled for the right words and ended up with a dumb cliché.

"It's a win-win situation. With the racetrack, I win a long-term consulting position doing what I love the most. Your peasants win jobs that will put them in a much better situation than they are right now. For a moment we're on opposite sides. But the deal can only go through after the racetrack management makes some very concrete offers to your people."

Sonia raised her delicate arms in a show of exasperation.

"They've been lied to for 500 years!"

"Look Sonia, I got a business plan. I've got figures. You like figures. Do your banking analysis of my figures."

"I don't want your figures. They doctor books all the time. When are job promises ever upheld in Bolivia? Either you're naive about your benefactors or you're a cynic. When I married you, you were not a cynic."

"I wish you could meet Arce. He's straight."

"I trust him less than the other goons," Sonia responded, probably echoing the sentiments of her squatter friends.

"Even if I wanted out," I said with emotive flair, "once I got off, someone would find a reason to use me as a bargaining chip, keeping my function alive. They can go after me because I'm the husband of an agitator. As long as I stay with Arce, I have a chance to help both sides."

With the details of my dysfunctional argument, I thought I could reach her through her heart. But she held her ground, without even raising her voice.

"Melodramatics don't convince me," she said. "There's a big issue here, and you and I are on opposite sides of it."

Sonia had a way of inspiring doubt. Did I sincerely believe in this great enterprise, or was I simply rationalizing, blinded by self-interest? I repeated my questioned mantra: *Subsistence farming was not an answer for starving peasants.*

Once we got back into the apartment, I suggested that things would work themselves out and that we should bury the contradiction and just enjoy a moment of togetherness. Normally, upon my return from the horse race wars, we would move directly into the bedroom and go at it with passion. Ever since Sonia had joined the Marianelas, a part of her passion had been displaced. I had been willing to share her. After all, she shared me with horse racing.

But now it went beyond hard to get. She withdrew. Before I could even say the magic word, *why*, she lectured me from her status of near nunhood.

"Matt, you need to understand me. For me, sex is a spiritual thing. Two lovers sharing the same bed need to share the same values. But now we're on very opposite sides."

"You're talking about mere ideas, Sonia. Who's to say whether your squatter friends will be better off scratching the land or working for a racetrack with a dependable salary?"

"That's their decision, not yours!"

I made a valiant effort to bridge the widening gap.

"But we're tossing around abstractions. You and I, we are prisoners of ideas. *Spiritual* is something higher and deeper than simplistic worldly ideas."

I could have used the word *transcend*, but I would have set myself up for a dressing-down.

"I'm sorry, Matt. Please don't expect me to feel pleasure with you for one morning, knowing that you will be out there in the afternoon working against what I stand for."

"What if I dropped this right now? What if I returned the check to Slim and told him I'm out."

"You flatter me. You're capable of forgetting your own ideals for a moment of sex, but that doesn't mean you really want to commune with me. Physical pleasure is momentary unless it's accompanied by true solidarity."

Whew! Without saying it, Sonia had declared a strike. Her demands were steep. Not only did she require me to give in to the material part, but she wanted me to suddenly change my whole belief system, something that one cannot do mechanically.

"You need a glass of orange juice," she said. "Your defenses are always weak after a trip. Let's drink something together."

I resolved to wait and think. She still had this need to take care of me. I hadn't lost her yet. I considered organizing the Clueless Husbands Movement. Surely she would then find a way to identify with me. I groped for a way to win her back, knowing she wouldn't accept any phony tactics.

I had slept for a total of eight minutes on the all-night flight from Miami. I knew the precise time because I had dozed off following an elevator arrangement of "Falling Leaves," missing Keith Jarrett's version of "My Funny Valentine," the only song on the American Airlines jazz audio that I had yearned to hear.

After the juice, I went into the bedroom and got under the mounds of blankets that you need in La Paz to stop the shivering. I resolved to let my subconscious take over, hoping that I would wake up with a solution.

ELEVEN

Rolando Katari on the Front Page

With the exception of an interview in *La Razón*, the Bolivian press was generally hostile to Katari. Radio Panamericana was the only station that gave him a chance to express himself. The Catholic station, Radio Fides, considered Katari an agitator against Bolivia's newly-won democracy. PAT TV scorned Katari's methods while purporting to understand the legitimate sentiments of the peasants.

Why would it be otherwise? The media was owned by the oligarchy, according to Katari, according to the miners, according to the teachers union, and according to Sonia. Yet there were voids in the media apparatus, investigative reporters still existed, community radio was thriving. It would only take a few reports from the international media to trigger a change that would favor the Landless Peasants.

First it was Radio France International, which had established a station called Radio La Paz. A Radio La Paz reporter had traveled to Santa Cruz to interview the peasant squatters. These interviews could only inspire sympathy within the small radio audience.

Then it was the BBC World Service, whose reporting was translated to Spanish in a morning broadcast. The BBC featured an interview with Katari himself. From the interview we learned that his father had died of silicosis at the age of 38. Katari and his brothers and sisters had scrounged for a living working outside the mines. When the mining industry plunged into despair, the Kataris had set off for the Cochabamba tropics and eventually the region of Santa Cruz, learning agriculture along the way.

In his rural schools, Katari had already displayed signs of organizing talent, uniting the children to oppose a particularly violent teacher, and then to demand school breakfasts. When Katari ascended to the leadership of the peasants union, his meager salary barely covered living expenses. He continued to work the land of others, for a pittance.

The British and French reports seemed to catalyze a transformation in Bolivian coverage. The drama of migrant farmers morphed into ongoing reality TV.

I figured that with Katari's new stature, any hopes for a racetrack would be dashed. This is what I told Arce one morning over a cup of coffee at the five-star Radisson Hotel in La Paz, where he was staying for a meeting of the National Chambers of Commerce.

"On the contrary," Arce tutored me, "before, we had to deal with thousands of angry peasants. Now, with Katari's new prestige, we only have to deal with one man. Our task is infinitely easier. We now can make an offer to one person."

"When will this be?" I asked. "And what will you offer?"

"Not me," Arce explained like a sermonizing priest. "Not any of us. To the peasants, we are the oligarchy. They do not trust us."

Too bad, I thought. Arce had a way with people. He would have been an ideal conveyor of offers. But smooth talk might not be enough to erase his questionable past during the late 1970s and early 1980s dictatorships. These civilized landowners who love their children, are tender and caring with their dogs, and nurture their flower gardens may also have paramilitaries at their service. Arce might have had his own men, but I had not been able to extract this information. I let it drop from my mind.

"Then who can talk with him?" I asked.

"Why, you, of course."

"I'm a foreigner and a gringo. Surely that disqualifies me on two accounts."

"On the contrary, you are the husband of a Marianela. You do not represent a company or a government. You are the most innocuous of any possible contacts."

I mulled over this whole deal. Not only would I be directly undermining Sonia's activities, but I would be doing it in her name. My marriage would be headed for a crash landing.

On the other hand, if I could pull off an agreement, something that would make the peasants happy, and, to use Sonia's word, "enfranchise" them, then I might be able to win her back.

I let Arce know that I would need a list of specific offers.

"What specifics, Matt? You don't want to box yourself in. You're the jazz musician. Improvise."

Mornings were cold in the apartment. I'd drift from window to window, wherever the sun was strongest. Faxes with past performances were not streaming in, and I had heard from Vince that he had another problem with his porn store, potentially more threatening.

"Those fundamentalists in SUVs are out to get me," he said over the phone. "They're gonna lynch me."

"Serves you right for putting your shop in the middle of suburbia. Why didn't you stay in L.A.?"

"And why didn't you stay in the USA, and why did you get involved with Panama Slim?"

With Vince's store shut down temporarily, he was hanging around his house, where he referred to himself as "a caged panther." Vince was a master of clichés.

"I've got time on my hands," he explained. "With the store shut, I think I'm gonna go out to Nevada and play the ponies. In Nevada, once you get outside of Vegas and Reno, you can have all the pussy that money can buy."

Vince was into brothel collectibles. When the Mustang Ranch brothel outside of Reno was shut down for tax fraud, he had purchased some of its auctioned-off furniture, which he kept in his store.

"I'll find me a town with a race book and just stay there, somewhere in the vicinity of the night action. In my shop I sell this travel guide called *The Best Cathouses in Nevada*. I'm gonna pick me out a race-book town that's in striking distance of a few of them."

Vince offered to put in my daily action. This was my chance to get out of the betting rut. I didn't need a *Racing Form* in my own hands because I had researched a winning system, but I did need a dependable agent to scan the past performances of as many tracks as possible every day. Several of my racing friends lamented that they had to hold down a straight job, and could not help me on a daily basis. They longed for the day when they could quit and play the races full-time. I needed a full-time agent for my system. Vince was the only one available.

I still needed more research on the horse futures, so I outlined a more classical system for Vince to play and told him I'd send him a check for a thousand for my bankroll. The rules were simple for what I called the "maiden-comeback method." You want a horse that has raced no more than twice in the maiden special weight class, and is still a maiden. You want to see this horse laid off at least 45 days and then coming back after the layoff. (With today's public increasing its willingness to play layoff horses, I subsequently raised the minimum layoff period to two months.) You want to see that the trainer keeps him at the same class level. That's a must, implying the horse is in a healthier and wiser state. It's an indicator of positive intention. And you want a trainer whose intentions fit with his results, so for this method, you exclude all trainers with less than 12 percent winners.

And that's it. It's amazing, but these horses usually improve their speed rating, having matured during their time off. This is especially true when you have a maiden that lost one or two races as a 2-year-old and is now coming back at 3. For this reason, one colleague suggested I call this the February-March Madness method. The horse will have grown, and his speed will increase. The public measures his slower 2-year-old speed figs against the 3-year-old figures of the horses that had not been laid off for a vacation: unfair comparison. A 45 Beyer Speed Figure for a 2-year-old is worth a 60 or more for a 3-year-old horse.

This went along with another research project of mine, which showed that the average winning horse, racing at the same surface and same distance as its previous race, improves his speed figure by between eight and nine Beyer points.

A horseplayer who can project improved speed gets a much better average payoff than one who predicts continuity. It's the same truth for stock market investors. The big winners are those who project change, not continuity.

I had researched this particular method on my own, and with such promising results that I had submitted it to a skeptical Las Vegas research company. With a separate database, they came up with an 8 percent profit. There were 18.5 percent winners, and according to those guys, that was 4.5 percent higher than what could normally be expected.

In order to boost the average mutuel, I instructed Vince to demand at least a two-month layoff. I dutifully entered this change in the crib sheet I carried around with me.

"Where do I mail the check?" I asked Vince over the phone.

"I'll fax you my address in Nevada," he said. "You don't have to wait till I get the check. You got good credit."

I reflected on Vince. Here was a misfit, once a petty criminal with his bookie business, now hardly a pillar of society with his porno store, and yet I felt I could trust him. If my horses won, he would not pocket the money for himself. Sonia called me naive. She had now become convinced that anything outside the realm of faith was not trustworthy. She felt that if people were not constrained by a set of religious principles, they would go astray, and that this was human nature.

I noted that people within the realm of faith were involved in the lynch-Vince plot, hardly constrained by their faith, but Sonia differentiated between fundamentalists and what she called "profound believers."

I couldn't get past an intrinsic contradiction. Here was Sonia, moving gradually in the direction of nunhood, and yet she had no trust for human nature. And then here I was, kidnapped, beaten, and hanging out with low-lifes, and yet I had this trust in fragile human beings like Vince, a porn-store owner, and Muñeca, a call girl, the only person in Bolivia I was able to phone when I had been kidnapped.

I groped for a bridge that could bring Sonia and me back together. I reflected on John Coltrane. A church in San Francisco, perhaps an offshoot of Catholicism, worshipped to the music of Coltrane, using it as a backdrop for their masses. Coltrane was their bridge between frail humans and the almighty spirit.

I ground some coffee beans I'd brought from a health food store in

Albany and brewed myself a coffee, anything to warm up the morning. I could have gone out jogging around the dusty soccer field, but I was waiting for a call from whoever was arranging for my meeting with Katari.

My mind jumped on its own from one scenario to another, and almost every one of them contained paramilitaries. I was working on my own, with no support from any organizations. Freelancers like me were the ones that got killed first. That's what happened in Chile with Teruggi. He was on the loose, and should have joined any type of group that would have offered an escape network in '73.

I reflected on my contacts. Arce was too close to the landowners. The musicians in La Paz only wanted to jam and chew coca leaves. They were on another fringe.

There was only one person whom I could talk to, and that was Muñeca. As an escort, she met people with power, and she contained them in their most vulnerable positions. Some of them might even say things to Muñeca that I would like to know. Who knows, Panama Slim's arms couriers could very well have ended up in Muñeca's arms. She would personally know, in every sense of the word, some of the landowners who paid the paramilitaries.

And I had not even thanked her for passing on the message to Arce about my kidnapping. She must have done exactly as I'd asked, for Arce had then telephoned Sonia, and managed to break the news to her in an unthreatening way.

It was 10:30, probably too early for Muñeca to be out of bed, but I dialed her number anyway. She answered after the third ring.

"*Alo?*"

"This is Matt. I just wanted to thank you for taking my message."

"You haven't been kidnapped again?"

"Why do you ask? Do you think they'll do it again?"

"You take too many risks. You do business with people you do not even know."

"Look who's talking," I said.

"I know how to control my clients, Matt. You're the only one I have not handled."

"How about other gringos, there must be others like me."

"I can melt them like butter," she said. "They're the easiest. They don't bargain over price. The Latin ones bargain."

"I can imagine," I said, "knowing how beautiful you are, that you disarm them. I bet they even talk about things they shouldn't talk about."

"If you want information, you won't get it here. Check my card. It says, TOTAL CONFIDENTIALITY."

"I don't expect any secrets, Muñeca. But let me ask you one question, just a yes or no. If someone mentioned me in a negative way, in a way that suggested he might want to do me harm, would you call me and tell me to be careful? I'm not asking for information, am I?"

"I met you only once, Matt, and we didn't even do any business. Do I owe you anything?"

"Nothing," I responded, trying to hide my disappointment. "But you did give me your card, and you said, 'Don't lose my card, you will find that you need me.'"

"What makes you think you can trust me? Why should I be helping you at the possible expense of my paying clients? What if I told *them* about *you* and not the other way around. Aren't you taking a big risk?"

"They can find out about me anywhere. I'm playing a longshot. If I lose, I go on to the next bet."

"Matt, I will talk to you, but not over the phone. Next time you come to Santa Cruz, call me. Or when I go to La Paz, do you want me to call you?"

"Sure. It's important to me."

"Okay. I'll probably be accompanied, but we'll find a way to talk."

TWELVE

The Two Little Pigs

I once lived on a ranch in the California high desert, near Palmdale. I had fruit trees, mainly apricot and peach. I sold fruit to Korean groceries in L.A. I also produced eggs, but mainly for home consumption. Instead of a bottle of wine, I would take a dozen eggs to offer the host of a dinner engagement. I had white eggs, brown eggs, and some smaller blue eggs from a few Araucana hens. Those critters were flighty explorers who could make it over the fence, and eventually they were killed, one by one, by coyotes.

I also had two pigs, a female red roan and a pink castrated male. Pinky and the red roan were rivals, lusting for each other's mudhole, and even eating out of each other's troughs. It was usually the red roan who headswiped Pinky away from his own food. She was the good-looker, and the neighbors told me I had a possible prize winner. No one wanted to know anything about Pinky the gelding.

The point is that these two critters were matched against each other day after day. On winter nights, when the high-desert heat had quickly dissipated, it would drop below freezing. Pinky and the red roan would make a temporary truce and curl up together in order to keep each other warm.

La Paz nights are much like the California high desert. There's nothing to hold in the heat once the sun vanishes and the night takes over.

Temperatures plunge. None of the houses have central heating, and electric space heaters fail to permeate the room with warmth.

So everyone sleeps with heavy blankets. I keep my down jacket next to the bed, in case I have to wake up during the night. Sleeping with wooly pajamas and thick blankets is uncomfortable. The weight of so much cloth upon the body is a nightmare-inducing burden. There are dreams of asphyxia.

So Sonia and I reduce the burden of blankets by keeping each other warm. Lately, since Sonia's strike, the touch of her soft skin upon mine has been leading nowhere. It's been a very practical togetherness, just like that of the red roan and Pinky.

Unlike the gelding Pinky, I wake up aroused in the mornings, but it's too damned frigid for a cold shower. I get up, step into my running suit, do some stretching, and go out running around the dusty soccer pitch, enjoying a splendid view of the two white peaks of Illimani Mountain. I hold a stone to ward off the stray dogs. I gain energy thinking that any day now Sonia could call off her Calvinistic strike. Sometimes I think of Muñeca.

If Vince had been here in La Paz, he'd have become a regular at El Tropezón, a lively bar with willing women. At this point, another woman would be the equivalent of a strikebreaker. I considered myself the offended party, but from the point of view of the striker herself, any woman I would hook up with would be considered a scab.

By playing hard to get, Sonia was setting off all kinds of new passion connections in my neurons. Every time I glimpsed at her agile movements, her flowing walk, her café-crème skin only slightly exposed, my sexual maturity receded another notch until I became the starved eighth grader who lusts for the smart girl in the first row, the one who, after class, is surrounded by football heroes. The erotic image of Muñeca would slip into my mind without asking, and I would do my best to nudge it out of the way.

I hoped that these adolescent lapses would not interfere with the image I would be projecting at the other side of the table from Rolando Katari.

THIRTEEN

"Positive Expectation"

The enabler was baby-face Joe Nuñez, head of the politically power-
ful but financially impoverished Rural Teachers' Union. Joe was the
chief negotiator between the union confederation (the COB) and government, one of the few people in this world who can be inoffensive to all
factions. The baby face was his emblem of trust.

Arce and Katari could not be seen together, nor could they fraternize.
Both peasants and landowners would have reason to become suspicious
if Katari and Arce shared a restaurant booth to drink coca tea. But Arce
could contact Joe Nuñez, and Joe could talk to Katari. This is how the
interview was set up.

The site was not far from my apartment. I walked a few blocks up the
minivan-infested 6 de Agosto Avenue, across the Nudo de Villazón bridge,
past the peeling posters on the façade of the high-rise university, and past
the downtown boulevard El Prado, the hangout of young businessmen,
women money-changers, masked shoeshine boys, retirees on benches
reading newspapers, and street vendors at makeshift wooden stands
bursting with versatile arrays of products: alternative remedies, batteries,
candy bars, herbal teas, quinoa bars, pirated cassettes, umbrellas, wallets.
From El Prado I turned right, up a side street, past a row of outdoor card
tables occupied by men with old Remington typewriters who helped the
most humble of citizens fill out forms for the bureaucracy. I entered a

dingy gray building with a mazelike interior whose oddly arranged corridors and angular staircases quickly caused the first-time visitor to lose all sense of direction, as if in a Skinneresque plan of social engineering to throw arriving negotiators into a tizzy of insecurity.

A man in a faded alpaca sweater seated me in an armchair in a windowless reception room that also served as a temporary office. Old newspapers and magazines, piled in no particular order on a coffee table, presented a chaotic history of recent Bolivia. A former minister, charged with corruption, escapes to Argentina and undergoes plastic surgery to gain anonymity. Etcheverry leads Bolivia's national soccer team to a 2–0 defeat of Brazil. Women coca growers arrive in La Paz on a rainy morning after a one-month, 500-kilometer protest march, some of them limping, others carrying infants, as citizens emerge from their houses and apartments with oranges, crackers, and hastily-concocted sandwiches to offer the trekker-martyrs.

The bare walls of the office encouraged my inner imagination, and from a blank slate, I decided that, with the blatantly honest Katari, it was best to lay my cards on the table.

Within 10 minutes, go-between baby-face Joe Nuñez brought Katari in, and we were introduced. I reminded the peasant leader that this was the second time we had shaken hands.

Our discussion began at 10:15. Katari seized control.

"I'm not sure what I can do for you."

"My wife won't give me the time of day," I said. "Ever since she discovered that I was working in favor of a racetrack. She is a true believer in your cause."

"Rightfully so," Katari shot back. "Our people have been exploited for more than 500 years by the oligarchy. They have promised us this, and they have promised us that, and they have never kept a promise. Why would they suddenly change their ways?"

"But I'm not the Bolivian oligarchy," I said. "I've done a little farming myself. I once had apricot trees, hens, and pigs."

"Arce has gardens. That doesn't make him identify with the peasants."

I had prepared for this interview. I knew that Katari's outer boldness masked a legendary shyness that bordered on humility. He had once admitted, in a *La Razón* interview, that even if he had read about the theory of probability, he had never studied algebra or trigonometry. He could tell you everything about Hobsbawm and Galeano but had never read Marx or Thomas Paine.

"In fact," he added, "you should not expect anything from this talk of ours. I cannot make any decisions on my own. They put me in front of a camera because I've read a few books and can think quickly when I'm bombarded with questions. But that's it."

"What if I convinced you that a racetrack could be in the interest of your community?"

"It's not me you have to convince. There are thousands of peasants out there. What do you have to say to them? They know farming. They produce food. As far as I know, horses are unproductive animals. If you talked about llamas or hogs, they would listen to you."

Arce had told me that negotiating would be easier now that we could isolate a single decision-making man. But this one leader came tethered to thousands. By referring to his people, he was letting me know that he could not be bought off.

"I've heard you speak," I responded, "and I've read your interviews. I don't doubt you for a second. But what if, thanks to a racetrack, each and every person in your community was given either a job with a steady income or a fertile plot of land?"

"Mr. Bosch, surely you are not so naive. Do you realize how often in the past we have been promised jobs? Do you realize that those who promised us never made good, not even once. Why would it be different this time around?"

At that moment, Joe Nuñez came in with a tray of *salteñas* (juicy meat pies) and soft drinks. He asked me to clear the coffee table and put the magazines on an empty chair. Among the soft drinks was Coca-Cola. Katari began his usual lecture on how Coca-Cola induces diabetes among his people and siphons precious water away from Bolivian farmers. People drink poison cola when the traditional fruit drinks are much more nutritious.

"How many Bolivian fruit growers are eliminated from the market," he added, "because their product is replaced by Coca-Cola."

He noted that Coca-Cola uses coca in its formula, while the American Embassy demonizes Bolivian coca growers.

"We cannot export our coca tea," Katari lamented, "because the coca leaf is considered evil. So how is it that Coca-Cola is free to massively poison Americans, Bolivians, and people in every other remote corner of the world?"

"Mr. Katari," I responded, holding my *salteña* in suspension, "you'd be surprised that we have much more in common than you would guess. There's a significant American environmental movement that thinks the way you do. But let me give you some specifics about the racetrack industry that you may not be aware of."

"Mr. Bosch, you probably know that I am self-educated. I was expelled from secondary school for having organized the students. Even if I had stayed in school, the conditions were frightful. But I am always learning something new. Tell me about your racetrack industry."

"Most important," I proudly explained, "it is labor intensive. There is no mechanical way to train horses and prepare them to race. You need people. Same thing for maintaining the track itself, the stables, and the grandstand. You need hundreds of people. A racetrack employs people."

"For what, Mr. Bosch? You are talking about gambling. I find it difficult to believe that anything connected to gambling can be sustainable economically. I would prefer to know something about you. I don't mean to be distrustful, you know. What is there about you that places you on the side of the gambling industry?"

Just as ideology had built a barrier between Sonia and me, it was now preventing any real communication with Katari. I decided to drop the whole polemic, and use his question on gambling to communicate on a different level.

I launched into an explanation of the maiden-comeback method, as an example of the intellectual challenge that racing presents. Katari was a most intense listener. You can tell when someone is losing patience or concentration. Katari, an example of independent learning, had never been trained to filter out so-called irrelevant information. Anything that could be learned was important. He could have been fascinated by analyzing the construction of the Brooklyn Bridge, the game of baseball, or quantum mechanics. So now, I launched into a step-by-step explanation of how a studious horseplayer could make money by gambling on a positive expectation.

I carried around a notebook, just in case I was struck by a new research idea. I looked down at the crib sheet and reread my notes, looking for a simplified way to show Katari that betting on horses was a great mental test that had nothing to do with casino gambling. I used the maiden-comeback method as an illustration of the concept of positive expectation.

Unlike horseplayers of the 1990s, he was not preconditioned to believe that a layoff is bad. He was not like the old railbird who eliminated layoff horses while exclaiming that he had 30 years experience in this game and knew what he was doing. For too many players, those 30 years are simply one year of experience repeated 30 times. Katari was not tainted with "experience."

I was sensing a collegiality that I had never felt in the halls of academia, where knowledge is nothing but power. Here with Katari, knowledge was stripped of its opportunistic functionality, and we were delving into the beautiful logic of a conceptual breakthrough: the notion of positive expectation.

When I finished with the maiden-comeback method and showed him how I had compiled the statistics, he was visibly impressed. In a difficult negotiation there are various layers that you need to pass through, one by one, patiently. With Katari the first layer was the differentiation between intelligent horse betting and mindless casino games.

I suppose that I should have then turned back to the racetrack issue. But why ruin a moment of authentic intellectual communication? I had made my point. Losing at the races is mainly due to flawed anecdotal evidence that is not supported by the history of the past performances. To win, one extracts knowledge from the past performances and adds the element of calculated risk.

There was a roguish twinkle in Katari's eyes.

"So now you must understand, Matt Bosch. We have 500 years of past performances telling us so clearly that oligarchs like Arce will not make good on their promises. Yes, we are surely willing to gamble, but we need to have the probabilities on our side."

Baby-face Joe Nuñez reentered the room.

"Rolando, you've gone way past schedule. You're already late for the next meeting."

"Next week," Katari said, "we can make another appointment with Mr. Bosch. He already knows that there's not much I can do for him. But we do have more things to discuss. That is, Mr. Bosch, if that would be okay with you."

Even the most honest among us will be co-opted when drawn into the political game. But Katari was a most authentic soul. For a moment, his faced looked less angular, cheekbones less pointed, dark eyes more transparent.

The red and purple pattern woven into Katari's backpack undulated as he searched for something within.

"Please wait one moment, Mr. Bosch."

He drew out a small plastic bag of coca leaves.

"Take this. It is a very simple but symbolic gift with a millennium of past performances behind it."

WHEN SONIA GOT back home from the Marianela office, I yearned to tell her of the common chord I'd struck with Katari. But I feared that she would view me as a crass opportunist attempting to taint her idol, an ugly American distorting the culture of the noble savage. I merely let her know that Katari was not at all interested in any racetrack for Santa Cruz.

She was not surprised.

It was late-afternoon teatime. She invited me across the street to a small shop where they served tea with *cuñapés*, a native pastry that mixes yucca flour and cheese. We sat in the rustic booth in cold shadows, where we were able to get beyond our differences by simply restricting the encounter to small talk. She was shining with fulfillment, and I could see that her work was rejuvenating. She was a deceptively beautiful woman: "so near and yet so far," as Mel Allen used to remark.

I felt as if I were looking in on a human-interest story, vicariously enjoying a moment of great discovery experienced by a truly decent but naively romantic woman.

FOURTEEN

Thelonius

The old Steinway looked as if it had made its way up to La Paz from the Chilean coastal port with the help of Laurel and Hardy. They had asked me to sit in on a version of "My Funny Valentine" with a group that featured Chris Hogan on sax. Hogan had the first solo, and he was taking the romantic classic on a new, enriching trip. I tried to pick up on what he was doing in order to make my own solo responsive. Amidst the moaning melancholy we carved our way into a darker side of love, unintended by the original composers.

Normally I do not notice the audience in the middle of a solo, but Muñeca had come in and taken a table under the light in front of me. She was not a back-of-the-room personality. In retrospect, her presence may have affected my solo in some way. Already, Sonia's prolonged strike had pulled a haze over the whole concept of romantic love and my way of portraying it. Sonia was now excluding not only sex from our household, but red meat and even chocolate, which she said was a symbol of exploitation of the peasants in the Ivory Coast.

Normally I would have blended the harmony of "My Funny Valentine" with the mystical "A Love Supreme." But Coltrane's vault into religiosity reminded me all too much of Sonia, so instead I found a way to integrate this classic romantic harmony with Monk's cynical "Well You Needn't."

Later, Hogan would applaud me on my discordant harmonies. I would have preferred if Muñeca had caught it. Not a chance.

After ceding to the regular keyboard man, I left the stand. Muñeca got up, took my hand, and guided me to her table, as if I were emerging from a classroom at the Braille Institute. The man accompanying her was an American geologist named Rudy. I perceived a West Side Chicago accent. Following the set, she invited me to accompany them back to the Radisson, where Rudy had forked out $150 for the room with a view, in La Paz's most modern and fashionable hotel.

During the short, downhill walk over irregular sidewalks and cobbled outdoor staircases, I could perceive in Rudy's nice-guy tone of voice a swelling disappointment, that I ("an old friend," Muñeca had explained) would be interrupting his tryst.

Once in the high-ceilinged modern-gothic lobby, Muñeca explained to Rudy that she needed to talk to me alone.

"Matt and I need a moment of privacy. He's an old friend. He and I will go up to the room. Please be patient, Rudy, and wait for me at the bar. I promise I will not disappoint you in any way."

Rudy's jowls sagged a few inches, but he accepted the deal meekly and shuffled off to the bar, where a beautiful young trainee would serve him a Singani. The unpaid trainee would probably be fired after her probation period, and the Radisson would hire another trainee for three months and repeat the process. Nothing from Rudy's $150 would find its way into the trainee-barmaid's pocketbook.

Once in the elegant room, with Illimani's shining twin glaciers intruding through the picture window of the 26th floor, Muñeca explained that she had some news for me.

"I'm not giving you this information out of any loyalty," she explained. "My parents are mestizo peasants. This is just my way of honoring them."

"You certainly do get to the point, don't you?"

"Rudy is waiting downstairs."

"Go for it."

"There's a loose cannon among the landowners," she explained. "He's planning to have Katari wiped off the map of Bolivia."

"You mean, exiled?"

"I should have said 'the map of the world.'"

"Shit. Should I tell Arce?"

She flinched.

"I doubt that Arce's involved, but don't take any chances. Find another way to stop this from happening. If my source is honest, and men usually are after a good lay, this event will take place at Katari's next public meeting, while he is speaking."

"Why?" I asked, trying not to sound naive. "Why not disappear him. No one would ever find the body, and no one would be caught."

"They want to kill a whole movement, not just one man. They want to frighten all of Bolivia."

I looked back at my spotty knowledge of history. They had murdered Archbishop Romero during his sermon, after weeks in which he had been calling for a halt to the flow of arms into El Salvador, insisting on the need for a just peace. Malcolm X was also gunned down in an auditorium. It's the hard-sell methodology of public relations.

"I guess I'd better get going," I said. "I'd hate to be shot by Rudy in the lobby."

"On the contrary, you need to be calmed down. You're the only person I can trust. Rudy will wait like a good boy."

She took my hand, and such a simple gesture sent me swirling back some three-and-a-half decades, to my teenage days, when I had first felt the touch of a girl's soft skin in front of my locker. I was melting down, and I had no control over what is known as common sense.

Soon we were on the sofa. "Not the bed," Muñeca had explained. She wanted Rudy to see the bed made solidly, army style, so that he would be the first one to rip open the quilt.

I melted into Muñeca. My experience with meditation allowed me to expel virtually all else from my mind. It's the same technique I use when eating chocolate in the dark. Considering Sonia's long strike, I was conditioned for a Santa Anita sprint, but as we moved about on the sofa, it developed into a slow-paced Auteuil steeplechase, the Grand Steeplechase, with all 23 hurdles. During the uphill stretch drive, we lugged in and lugged out, in a rhythm whose lyrics might

have been, *I got him where I want him. I got him where I want him.* And
then the finish line.

Within minutes, I was unable to retrace the steps of this encounter.
A haze drifted over the white peaks of Illimani and little by little, the joy
subsided. It had not been Coltrane's "A Love Supreme," but rather Max
Roach's obscure riff called "A Blip on the Screen."

It was as if I had divulged myself to my source, and my source was
no good anymore. Now that I was just like the rest of them, why should
Muñeca feel the need to feed me more vital information? Was Rudy a
gunrunner? Who had sent him? Was Muñeca Mendoza's mistress? Was
that why Mendoza had been so royally pissed off about my presence at
Arce's ranch? Because Muñeca had been hired for me, and he, Mendoza,
could do nothing about it?

"I don't give away anything for free," Muñeca said, flashing a nuanced
smile that I was unable to interpret. "Please be there when it is going to
happen, and stop them. *Y Dios mío, no digas nada a la policía!*"

I got into my pants and fumbled to tie my shoes.

Muñeca smiled. "We could be lovers. But you would be the jealous
type."

We went down to the lobby together. Rudy was at the bar. He hadn't
noticed us. At the revolving door, Muñeca and I shook hands, and I kissed
her cheek, Bolivian-style.

"Be there early," she said, "before Katari arrives. You can stop it."

"I can be there, for sure, but I can't guarantee I can stop it."

"Who knows? They could be the same ones who kidnapped you.
You'll find a way."

My apartment was only three uphill blocks above the Radisson.
As I climbed the winding, ankle-busting cobblestone staircase from
Avenida Arce to 6 de Agosto, I worked out my most immediate strategy. Usually, following a night at Thelonius, I would accompany the
musicians in a coca leaf séance. Arriving home, I would go straight
to the shower. Sonia hated the smell of coca leaves. It was the only
indigenous thing she could not identify with. So I would shower it
away.

Now I would also be showering away Muñeca's expensive Chanel.

Sonia would not ask where I had been. She never asked, not even before her determined strike.

I yearned for Sonia. The blip on the screen had faded away like Halley's Comet. It had been a brief and brilliant flash, with an unknown orbit.

I could not tell her where I had learned about the planned erasure of Rolando Katari, but I could find out exactly when and where the icing was supposed to take place, and tell her I would be attending.

Sonia had been drawn away from me by ideology. I had been marginalized from her by mere circumstance. Now, mere circumstance might hurl me back into Sonia's orbit.

The loose cannon, whoever he was, illustrated how pure stupidity causes needless violence. If they put down Katari, my racetrack project would be packed in ice forever. The peasants would erupt in a larger movement, guided by anger. The stupid warmonger would have provoked a response that was the precise opposite of his intention, and that would be the death sentence for the racetrack. I had to stop the thing from happening, but I had no idea how. I was not known for my bravery, and for years I had been a master of avoiding violent conflict.

Decision making involves a complex set of variables. Saving the racetrack was somewhere among them. So was my loyalty to Muñeca. And winning back Sonia could become the immediate result if I could pull it off.

If I had been phony about it, I would have simply adopted Sonia's ideology and then had her back in my arms. But I couldn't force myself to see things the way she did. Something in my formation, something in my material conditioning, was preventing me from identifying with masses of Indians who were applying the tactics of Thoreau.

But here was something I could do to win back Sonia, something either opportune or opportunistic depending on how you judged a man's intentions. There was also a more visceral factor. I now knew Katari. He had asked me, in all earnestness, to explain the horseplayer notion of positive expectation, and I now saw him not as a peasant leader but as a fellow human being.

If the goons were allowed to erase Katari, the inevitable peasant uprising would destroy all hopes for a racetrack, including my share of the business, and an ideal gig would vanish from my horizon.

FIFTEEN

The Mexicans at the Pool Table

Katari's bodyguards were too ideological to be competent. That's what I inferred from Sonia's glowing description of their restraint. They believed that the unarmed masses would triumph over tanks and machine guns. They allowed Katari to mix with "the people." It was not in their culture to use firearms, though their miner allies, when marching, would detonate small explosives as symbolic reminders of their presence. It was mainly thunder, though, with little or no lightning. Given the inherent pacifism of Katari's men, I might have to act alone if I spotted a threat. I had spent my whole life successfully avoiding such confrontation, and even if I were bold enough to act, and I had my doubts, I lacked the experience that would allow me to play the precise chords of combat.

I mulled over my potential as Katari's ad hoc bodyguard. A gun in my hand would probably knock out the chandeliers or kill an innocent bystander. Physically I'm strong but at 5'7" and 150 pounds, I'd be no match for the three or four goons I expected to encounter. I had been in a brawl once or twice and emerged relatively unscathed, but that could be attributed to luck more than skill. In a hole-in-the-wall bar on Centinela Boulevard in Culver City I had had an unfriendly encounter with a 6'4" heavyweight on PCP, and had managed to hold him off until the Mexicans from the pool table had grabbed him and heaved him out of the bar. My survival strategy had depended entirely on the Mexicans at the pool table.

You don't see too many six-foot Bolivians and I'd have a fair chance against any one of the goons of my own size, but what were my odds against two or three of them? I was forced to admit the unthinkable: I was genuinely frightened. Memories of helplessness during the recent kidnapping did nothing to boost my morale.

The assassins would be armed with handguns. I replayed the wording of Muñeca's negotiated plea. She had not even asked me to stay alive, only to stop the murder of Katari. If I were to take the bullet meant for Katari, our contract would be honored, and I'd become her eternal hero.

The queen bee example was all too real to be a metaphor. In exchange for 20-some minutes in Muñeca's arms, I should now be willing to meet an honorable death. Of course, I had other reasons for wanting to keep the peasant leader alive. The murder of Katari would inspire a major peasant revolt. Arce would lose all hope of negotiating for his land. The same bullet that would kill Katari would penetrate the heart of my racetrack paradise.

Katari's handler, Nuñez, should be informed of the plot so that his boss would be more adequately protected. But if I were to approach the veteran labor activist, he would immediately suspect me of dubious contacts with their enemies. I could read his mind: how else could Matt Bosch be privy to information unless he was a CIA mole?

Over a breakfast of a crusty *marraqueta* bread with butter and home-made pineapple jam, I jabbed away at the subject with Sonia.

"The last time Katari spoke, there were three creeps in the back of the room. They could have killed him!"

"Everyone in the audience would have stopped them," Sonia said. "The paramilitaries know that thousands of peasants are ready to defend the movement."

"Don't be naïve. One lone loony filtered in between a team of body-guards and shot down RFK."

"Robert Kennedy did not have an entire population ready to die for him."

Reasonable discourse was getting me nowhere with Sonia. She har-bored a romantic view of "the people." I knew that the people could lynch an innocent suspect, the people could vote for Hitler, the people could line up to get royally screwed.

"That's Marianela pacifist garbage, Sonia. Every black man in the USA would have defended Malcolm X, but they still found another black man to shoot him, smack dab in the middle of a public auditorium. They nailed Archbishop Romero right in the church while he preached his sermon, with all his loyal followers in the audience."

"Matt, these are different times. The Bolivian aristocracy knows it can't get what it wants through violence. They know there would be a big backlash. They will refrain."

"There are loose cannons among them. You're in denial if you don't see more and more paramilitary groups sprouting up."

"I'll let Rolando Katari know about those three men you speak of, and I know he'll warn his bodyguards."

We changed the subject, went over our possible plans for Deedee. Sonia then relapsed into small talk: not her usual style. I searched for a way to trigger her old pre-Marianela sweetness that would prompt her to cuddle up with me at any possible moment. I tried playing the romantic ballads of Luis Miguel, her old favorite, and she asked me to switch it to the protest music of Soledad Bravo. If I could only become an activist for social justice, she would embrace me and welcome me back into her heart. That's the way I understood it. But if I tried, I'd come off as a phony, and the strategy would flop. For me it was pure foolishness to march behind a revolutionary leader, knowing he would eventually be bought off, and if not, would unleash a new formula for the old oppression.

Following breakfast, I paced around the apartment, groping to conjure up a few "Mexicans from the pool table" to accompany me to the UMSA university auditorium at 6:30 on Wednesday evening, in preparation for the 7:00 talk by Katari that would probably not begin until 7:30 or 7:45. The pro-Katari people I knew were not up to the task. The poets and artists I would meet and drink with in the cobblestone colonial courtyard of the Hotel Torino were lost in clouds of their own making. For my jazz companions, social revolution meant sitting around in a circle and chewing coca leaves.

Marv, the consul, might have an idea or two. Surely the American Embassy would not want to see Katari assassinated. Even if the ambassador himself was apparently on the side of the oligarchy, most career diplomats felt sympathy for the Landless Peasants Movement, as long as it was run by a pacifist leader who could guarantee stability. As an ethnologist, Marv held a romantic view of the Inca civilization, but today's descendants and their political movements were out of bounds for any diplomat. Too bad for me. I was on my own.

I had to deal with two more nights of intermittent insomnia, tossing and turning over anticipated scenarios for preventing a murder. I tried to convince myself that nothing was going to happen on Wednesday evening at 7:45. But then I would relive the past performances: Gandhi, Martin Luther King, and innumerable other pacifist leaders would inevitably be gunned down. This time, there was no avoiding a confrontation.

At 3:00 in the morning of Tuesday, I woke up with the idea. Search each person entering the auditorium. I nudged Sonia. I asked her if the bodyguards would do a full body search of each person at the door.

"You could have asked me in the morning."

"I wanted you to sleep on it."

"You're really concerned for Katari, aren't you."

She cuddled up close to me, pulling my arms around her before drifting off. I was aroused, but no way would I ruin this moment of closeness by advances that would be met with certain rejection from a woman who was bent on sustaining her strike. I was still working for her enemy.

Closing my eyes did not help. More images glided by: Romero, shot down on the pulpit, Malcolm X, eliminated in front of an audience, and it was as if I had been there at these events, seated in the front row, doing nothing. Then there was the image of the bar on Centinela Boulevard. I was doing my best to hold my own against the crazy giant when I suddenly noticed that there were no Mexicans at the pool table.

If there had been a way of crawling back into a womb, I'd have welcomed a return to oblivion.

There's one thing worse than being a coward, and that's having everyone else witness your cowardice. Surely I could walk away from the Wednesday evening event and do nothing. If I did nothing, Sonia would know, Muñeca would know, and Marv would eventually find out. And worst of all, I would know.

Faced with the anguish of humbling insomnia, I resorted to my usual tactic: immersion into numerical abstraction. I tossed around the various horse-future patterns: 2 for 10 lifetime with double-figure wins, play next 5 races; broke maiden in debut, play career races 6 through 10.

SIXTEEN

Queen Bees and Early Bloomers

O n Tuesday morning, Sonia was off to work. I sat in my down jacket by the one window that collected the most morning sunlight, waiting for a fax from Vince. No use tossing around the Katari event in my mind. I would be there with the bodyguards at the door. Sonia would introduce me to them. I would watch each person approaching the door. At the slightest suspicion, I would alert the guards to do a careful body search. From then on, I'd improvise.

I collected a pile of old *Racing Form*s on the table at the window. The past performances blazed under the unfiltered sunlight. I began a new round of research with the "early-bloomer method." Horses that win their debut or second career races are perceived as natural athletes and have an edge over horses that have taken longer to break their maiden. I would look at career races 6 through 10, and calculate the return on investment of automatic wagers on each and every horse that broke its maiden in career race 1 or 2. The method had shown a flat-bet profit for three straight seasons at Hastings Park, and was also profitable in another research sample that included racetracks across the country.

Now I had a fresh new package of *DRF*s, courtesy of Vince, who mailed the package to my PO box at the post office on El Prado. The research is nearly as thrilling as betting. Here I had the chance to vali-date or confirm my previous tallies. This could emerge as one more automatic bet, another way I could continue to invest on the races from afar.

The phone rang. I expected it would be Sonia, calling from the office, maybe with some information about the bodyguards. I had asked her to set up an appointment with them prior to the Katari meeting.

It was Muñeca.

"I'm in La Paz. Can we get together?"

I jumped to attention. Suddenly the room was not so frigid anymore. I would explain to Muñeca that I had come up with a method for protecting Katari.

"Where are you?"

"Meet me in the lobby of Hotel Presidente. I'll be there waiting for you. My client won't arrive until this evening."

Her voice remained soft and resonant, but it had the sound and rhythm of a business call. If I had not known her, I would have guessed office manager, or even CEO.

The Hotel Presidente was 15 minutes away on foot and maybe 20 minutes by taxi, given the bumper-to-bumper traffic on El Prado: mainly belching public buses (old American school buses), swarms of taxis, and here and there a private car. I decided to walk.

I crossed the Nudo deVillazón bridge to the brick UMSA high-rise, where Katari would be speaking in some 30 hours. Up El Prado's central boulevard I passed some shoeshine boys with thick cloth facemasks, Potosina women beggars dressed in drab brown ponchos and floppy hats, *cholo* men in business suits (typical La Paz formality), and a couple of Bolívar professional soccer players coming out of a hotel.

Muñeca was seated on a couch in the lobby, leafing through a copy of *Elle*. The leather couch was soft and low, forcing her knees upward. Thanks to the awkward position of her tight cream-colored skirt, I could look up her legs. Her magnificent upper torso was hidden under a burnt orange sweater that in turn was partly covered by a business vest that matched her skirt. She got up, flashing more leg as she did. We shook hands, and she took my kiss on the left cheek.

She was still the firm leaf in a violent wind. Steady Muñeca could have walked right past the guards at Windsor Castle. There was no time to have a drink at the bar, and anyway, it was too early, and we needed the privacy of her room. Ever since our last encounter, I had fantasized that she'd been longing for the next sofa where we could roll around together, but she was driven by an entirely different need.

I have enjoyed collecting images of five-star hotel rooms. This one was less spacious than the Radisson's, and the view was less superlative: rooftops that alternated between orange colonial tile and tin *réalité*. My favorite five-star room is in the Hotel Paris on the Plaza Murillo, imitation Versailles, in a restored 1890 building. The Hotel Presidente could hardly compare. We sat on the practical Danish sofa, each with our own individual cushion.

"Matt, I need to make sure you will be there Wednesday night and stop the mess they've planned."

"You don't trust me, do you? What do you care about Katari, anyway? You're not in his movement. You have your own business."

"My father wasn't even involved in the movement. He's an independent grower. It just so happened that we were living in the wrong place at the wrong time, and they suspected he was a leader because his features were more creole than indigenous. They broke into our house, turned things upside down looking for papers. At that particular moment, my brother Enrique was the oldest male present, so he got macho brave and tried to defend the family. Too bad I was not there. I was like his surrogate mother. My mom had too many kids to watch over each one of them. Maybe I could have taught him to keep his cool.

"They shot him dead. He was only 15."

"I'm sorry."

"I don't want your pity. You asked me a question, and I gave you the answer."

"And you have my commitment that I'll do everything possible on Wednesday."

"You sound like a politician."

"Look at it from my point of view. We made love once, and because of that one moment of pleasure, I am now about to do something that could get me killed. It reminds me of the male bee. He makes love with the queen and then he dies."

"If you don't think it was worth it," Muñeca said, "we could do it again, this time there's no Rudy waiting downstairs. My client doesn't arrive until about 3 P.M."

"But then what else could I do for you beyond dying?"

"Don't be silly. I need you alive. You could find out who these people are."

"Muñeca, surely you could get the goods from Arce."

"He may not know, and even if he does, there's a pact of honor between landowners, even if they hate each other's guts. They can have it out between each other, but never would they allow an outsider to intervene."

I explained my plans to Muñeca, that Katari's bodyguards would arrive early and search each person entering the room. I could ask them to check for IDs as well. Muñeca explained that whoever was going in there to make trouble would be carrying a false ID. In Muñeca's presence I felt a swelling confidence that I would fear nothing and confront whatever I had to confront. But I knew that once she was gone, the "fight or flight" instinct would take hold. I represented the "flight" side of the equation.

The client to be escorted by Muñeca was an arms trafficker. I asked her how it was she ended up doing business with lowlifes, maybe the same ones who supplied the weapons that killed her brother. She explained that her business was by word of mouth, that she had begun at the very top of the pyramid, with CEOs and ambassadors, but that little by little, one client would recommend another, and from time to time she had to deal with an unsavory character.

"The one who's arriving today, I could have told him I was busy, you know. It's in my interest to let everyone know I'm hard to get. But this guy's a trafficker, and I want to find out who's sending the goods and who's receiving them."

"Well, you can send him to have a drink with me, and then you can rifle through his papers," I offered, hopelessly under her spell.

"I was looking at it the other way around. I thought I could give *you* the key, and when you saw us leave, you could come up to the room and search through his papers."

"For you it's no risk," I said. "Your name is on the register. In my case, I would be considered a burglar."

"True," she said. "But you're faster at reading English than I am. There might be something in there for you. I need to know who's receiving the goods, and you want to know about the sender."

I told her I needed time to reflect on the best strategy. She suggested that we reflect in bed. I asked her who was going to make the bed. She reminded me there was maid service. We enjoyed a preliminary round, she produced a joint, we shared the joint, she talked about how men were jealous and that she didn't think I would be any different, I asked her if she was jealous of my wife, she said she admired my wife, I said I'm not sure Sonia would be so honored, she said that people who have a true mission are beyond jealousy, I asked her what her mission was, she said it was to support her family and kill the men who killed her brother.

I was too stoned to understand the significance of her words. They seemed so natural at the time. We put out the joint, and went back under the covers for the main round. She had me where she wanted me. I found it so easy to say yes to each and every one of her propositions. The more dangerous the proposition, the more willing I became. As the passion neared its breaking point, my bravery reached record new heights. As the softness of her skin neared infinity, my courage entered the realm of insanity.

Even after the physical part of the equation came to its rousing finish, my insane invulnerability continued its process of fatal inflation.

On the way back home, the bubble of bravery had still not burst. I stopped off at Sonia's office. She was sixties elegant, indigenous chic, sitting behind the desk not as a clerical worker but as one who could move the whole world with passionate ideals. I suspected that the men in the office would hit on her. I was jealous that she was the center of attention, and I particularly watched the male employees and couriers going in and out of the office, checking to see if their eyes wandered. Sonia had her mission, and nothing could stop her. Her mission made more sense than Muñeca's mission. But Muñeca was now the queen bee.

"I gotta miss dinner," I said.

"I'll miss you. Where will you be?"

The question was pure protocol. She didn't really seem to care.

"You don't want to know where I'll be."

"I assume you have your reasons. Just don't get kidnapped again."

I was on my way out when she got up from her desk and met me at the door. She took my hand.

"I still love you, you know. I only wish we were on the same team."

"Maybe we are," I said.

She pecked me on the lips.

Back at the apartment, I took a bag of Arabica coffee from the refrigerator, brewed it up, and then dug into my research: my only calm in the turbulence. In comparison to the world around me, racing is so secure. I mean horse betting. I was searching for the elusive automatic bet. My dream was to sit in the park, smoke a Cohiba, and know that my horses were getting the job done for me at the track. I would smoke half the cigar. The other half would be my prize if I happened to make a profit that afternoon. But even if my horses lost during one afternoon, or two, or three, I would be in possession of the automatic bet, and it would be better than any mutual fund, with a positive bottom line at the end of the year.

I already had the maiden-comeback method. I had the informed-minority method. The 2-for-10 method did not yet count, looking bright but needing further research. And now I was on to a third automatic play, the early-bloomer method. I reminded myself of how the theory had come about, when I had done research at Ada's house following the Breeders' Cup. If you bet all Breeders' Cup entrants that had broken their maiden in their debut or second career race and excluded all others (all the late bloomers), you came out with a flat-bet profit. This was unbelievable: that 5-year-old turf horses that had won their debut races at 3 on the dirt would outperform other 5-year-old turf horses that had been slow to break their maidens.

I looked for a universal reason. Any random factor, say "post position 5," could conceivably show profit for a period of time, only to collapse when the sample got larger. My conceptual foundation was based on research in human and animal behavior, evidence that early behavior traits in both children and young animals are often indicators of future behavior as adults. This was not a question of determinism and merely referred to probabilities.

I gently nudged the early-bloomer theme back into the more comfortable horse racing arena. If these automatic bets could work for me, I could say "screw you" to Panama Slim and Arce, and I could forget about hustling for gigs. I could play "My Funny Valentine" for free, and I suspected that if the automatic bets became reality, my music career would also be liberated from the constraints of needing to get paid. When you don't need the money, the money comes in by itself. I'd play the piano wherever I went, and without any apparent connection, I'd receive just compensation.

The on-paper idea had been to tally all horses that had won their debut or second career start, focusing on races 6 through 10 of their careers. I had churned through the tally. Result: In career races 6 through 10, horses that won their debut race won 24 percent of the time. Horses that broke their maiden in career race 2 became winners of 23 percent of their races in career races 6 through 10.

Then the stat fell off a cliff. Horses breaking their maiden in career races 3, 4, or 5 ended up with between 15 and 17 percent wins during career races 6 through 10.

But since then I had come up with a refinement, with the valuable help of a horse-owner mathematician, John Samber. The new rules were kept within the spirit of the law but altered the letter:

Early-Bloomer Method
1. Horse won career race 1 or 2.
2. Play horses back in third to sixth races following their maiden win. Specifically, a first-time-starter winner would be bet back in his career races 4 through 7 while a horse that broke its maiden in his second try would be bet back in his career races 5 through 8.

Percentage of winners: 22.86 percent
Return on investment: plus 17 cents on the dollar.

Once again, manually tallying the early-bloomer method, I was coming up with a flat-bet profit. As the devil's advocate, I excluded one big longshot from the mix, as if it had been a fluke. The bottom line was still clearly profitable. A researcher friend had suggested that only by excluding the top two longshot winners from the sample could I be sure of the sustainability of the system being researched. "For the on-paper results to be dependable," he said, "they need to reflect the worst-case scenario."

I excluded the second-highest longshot winner from the sample and the results, though still profitable, were less cause for long-run certainty. I looked back at the tallies. By excluding trainers with less than *an 18* percent win record, which was becoming my "standard exclusion," the results went back up, but the sample got smaller. The 90 percent certainty calculation was not certain enough for me to confidently walk away from the tempting scheme of spiraling risk that was emanating from Panama Slim, Arce, and now Muñeca.

SEVENTEEN

The Trafficker

S he was in the lobby of Hotel Presidente, just as planned. The hotel could have paid her for hanging around in the lobby as a piece of elegant décor. Her trafficker friend was nowhere to be seen.

"What if I told you," I said, "that I could offer you security for the rest of your life, on one piece of paper. All you had to do is scratch these crazy plans of yours."

"I think I've heard this story before. If it's attached to a man, I don't want it."

"Not what you imagine. You have a bankroll, and you make these automatic bets, and then you do whatever you please during the day while these horses are making your income."

"I'm intrigued Matt, for sure. But don't minimize my feelings. I have a family's honor to defend."

She had blended a potent brew: family values with revenge murder. She had her dependable livelihood, which supported a father, a mother, and seven remaining brothers and sisters. The revenge factor could ruin it all for her. She was seriously contemplating homicide, and the way things were working out, it would be premeditated.

"Take the key, wait at the other side of the lobby, and when you see us leave, count five minutes, just to make sure Greg hasn't forgotten something. Then go up there, and give yourself an hour. I'll make sure we're gone for two hours. I chose a restaurant where the service is slow, and I'll make sure it's slower. But you get out of there after one hour. That's enough time for you to leave everything exactly the way you found it. We'll talk tomorrow morning, but don't phone me."

I only had to wait for a few minutes. Greg showed up. The arms trafficker description didn't match. He could have been a suburban husband who mowed the lawn on Saturday mornings and chauffeured the boys to their karate lesson. But for a day or two, he would become Muñeca's lapdog. They left through the side door. I fidgeted on the lobby sofa for six minutes, got up, then waited another minute until the uniformed receptionist was distracted with guests. It was another 30 seconds to get into an elevator.

I unlocked the door, then experienced a heart throb, which I attributed to an irrational fear that someone would be in the room. It looked empty.

Greg had made things easy. His briefcase was right on top of the desk. But Muñeca was no pro. She should have made sure that the briefcase was unlocked. I had an hour to whisk the briefcase out of the hotel room, find a nearby locksmith, and pay him handsomely for opening the damn thing, then get back to the room to sift through the papers.

I found a locksmith on Calle Comercio. I explained the problem, that I was a tourist here on business, and asked him how much it would cost to get the blasted thing open. He stared me up and down to make sure I was telling the truth. I knew that the tourist line would cost me more. But if I'd said anything else, he'd suspect I was a thief, and that would have raised the price above the tin rooftops. The locksmith got it opened in three minutes. The locksmith was rewarded, and I was back up in the room 10 minutes later.

Here and there in the papers, whose stack order I attempted to memorize, there were eight names that might have had some sort of meaning, including Muñeca's. I jotted down the seven other names, none of which rang a bell. On a separate paper in his notebook, there were American names, first names only. I recognized business coming from California and Nevada. The names meant nothing to me: Paul from Reno and Richie and Howard from Los Angeles. Another page contained what seemed like codes, letters and numbers. I jotted them all down in the same order, without taking time to reflect on what they could mean.

I was at the 45-minute mark, and I could have stayed for another 15, checked drawers and maybe tried to get into his laptop. I should have had a hacker with me. There were plenty of good ones in La Paz who'd have accompanied me for a small fee. I was a near dud at the search profession.

But I was getting out of there safely, and everything was left precisely where it had come from. My sense of relief did not last long. There was a sudden plunge in my heart cavity, as if an elevator from the hundredth floor had disengaged into free fall. Muñeca had not told me where to leave the key. I could leave it under the door, or take it with me. My heart began thumping once again, as it had when I'd entered the room for the first time. Then there was a second thump, potentially more dangerous. It was the door. Someone was rapping at the door. Hiding was no use. If they didn't have a key, they'd just walk away.

The knocking continued. I approached the door, looked through the eyehole. Something blocked my view. I imagined it might have been cleaning staff, but cleaning is done about noon. Hotel security had no reason to check in there, as no one had seen me, unless Greg had hired someone to check.

I began to panic. I panned around the room. The window was of no use, nor was the closet. I was not going to be foolish enough to hide under the bed. I tried again to see through the eyehole, but it was still blocked.

Then there was a hushed voice:

"It's me, Muñeca. Let me in."

I opened.

"Are you done?" she asked.

"Hell, you scared my pants off."

"Don't be dramatic. Are you done?"

"I got it. No one will ever know I was here."

"I left Greg at the table. I came for the key. You should have asked me where to leave the key."

"It's your key. You should have told me what to do with it."

"Keep your voice down," she whispered energetically.

I handed her the key, she locked the door, and we walked down the hall to the elevators.

"We can take different elevators," I told her. "Just in case Greg comes back."

"He won't be back. He knows I'm returning for dessert. Let's go out and make photocopies for me."

"Forget photocopies," I said. "He could catch you with the notes."

"Let me see what you got."

I flashed the documents. She scanned the seven Spanish names.

"I recognize three of these names. We'll talk tomorrow."

Spurred by the adrenaline, my walk in the direction of the apartment was effortless. The thumping had subsided. I had recovered my hunger. Sonia would have something ready to warm up. I stopped off at Mongo's for a beer. I needed to scrutinize my findings before getting home. I didn't want Sonia to see me studying strange notes.

I took a table near the door and far from the bar. I took out my prize and re-inspected the three names in English. Paul meant nothing. Richie failed to remind me of anything. But Howard told me something. I went back over everything I'd done and everyone I'd met during the past months. Marv, the consul, had mentioned a Howard. Sure, it was a Howard Stoner, and that was the real name of Panama Slim. With hundreds of thousands of Howards in the English-speaking world, it was a stretch to think that this Howard was indeed Panama Slim, except for the fact that Slim was reputed to be an arms trafficker.

On the notes with the initials and numbers, one set of initials popped off the page. It was GBC. Get Back the Canal. Panama Slim's organization. At first, I thought I was on to something. Panama Slim, supplier to the paramilitaries. But I had already suspected as much. I would need to connect him to the names in Spanish.

Muñeca and I were bound by fate. She and I both needed to discover a formula. I had half the solution, and she would have the other half. But knowing the answer might not bring us the happiness we sought. Muñeca could end up in prison, and I could end up dead. For a brief moment, I was in awe over the fact that my destiny was tethered to an exotic call girl from Santa Cruz with long flowing hair and Okinawan eyes. A few months back, such a destiny was unimaginable. Then the awe swirled into a feeling of pure stupidity. I was in deep shit, and a thousand things had to happen in synchronicity in order for me to get out of it.

Sonia had prepared *sajta de pollo* with a juicy chili sauce that included just the right hint of cumin. As I soaked up the sauce with *marraqueta* bread, I found myself in an aggressive mood.

"Just because we might not see things eye to eye," I said, "doesn't mean we can't form a tactical alliance. I don't want anything happening to Katari but you don't seem to care."

"You only began to appreciate Katari when he became interested in your horse race systems. You're not very lofty these days."

"And you're not very down to earth. I'm telling you right now that you'd better make sure Katari's guards are there at least an hour early, and that they search everyone entering the auditorium."

"You sound like you know something that I don't know."

"I know that every social movement will eventually run up against a deranged fanatic who believes in assassination, and the more successful the movement becomes, the greater danger its leaders will encounter. Protect Katari, and you make up for what happened to King."

"Matt, I promise that the guards will be there and that no gun will enter the auditorium."

That night Sonia edged a tad closer to me. Any man who had been with the smooth Muñeca that afternoon could have accepted death as a fair exchange. But my willingness to volunteer for human sacrifice had now subsided. If Sonia hadn't been on strike, if we'd had the usual banal marriage, perhaps I would have established some sort of hierarchy, maybe even with Muñeca as the higher prize. But in a world where what is scarce is what is most valuable, my scarce Sonia had become the epitome of secret eroticism hidden behind a veil of activist sainthood.

In the night coldness under the heavy La Paz blankets, Sonia nudged close to me. Muñeca or no Muñeca, I was once again aroused and very tempted to try to break her resistance. But she was playing a serious game, and I had to make my moves carefully. The way I saw it, inevitably her strike would end. My best strategy was supreme patience.

EIGHTEEN

Revenge

In La Paz people eat *salteña* meat pies for a midmorning snack. The crust is slightly sweet, and the meat is garnished with other goodies inside along with a juicy sauce. In a match race between the Bolivian *salteña* and the Argentine *empanada*, the *salteña* wins by several lengths, and it's the sauce that makes the difference. The *salteña* is often accompanied by a soft drink, but even at 10:30 or 11 A.M., I prefer a beer. Otherwise the combination is too sweet.

Muñeca agreed about the beer, and she also agreed that we needed to find a place with a booth, in some hidden nook, somewhere near the Radisson, for she had to meet up there with Greg. I still had a key to Greg's briefcase, and wondered if it could again come in handy. We found Nelsy's just across from the university where Katari would be speaking that evening. You step downstairs into the underground Nelsy's, and there are booths in the back where no one will ever notice you. We were near Sonia's office. There was a faint probability that she and her office mates could stray into Nelsy's for their morning snack. But the geometry of our relationships had nothing to do with a triangle. Sonia had moved me out of a certain space in her life, which was filled by the Marianelas. This created a void, which was occupied by Muñeca. If anyone should be jealous it would be me. Sonia's passion for the Marianela cause was broad and deep and voluntary. My passion for Muñeca was turned on and off by Muñeca herself, and I was simply a tool in her life, willing, yes, but involuntary.

Before combining notes, I tried once more to dissuade Muñeca from the ultimate revenge.

"You're too cool to ditch everything you've worked for," I said. She was a firm and beautiful leaf remaining cleverly resilient in a summer of storms. Her only weakness was a desire for combat against one of the ill winds. "Okay," I said, "let's prove who killed your brother and find some other more subtle way to punish him."

"Don't idealize me. And by all means do not consider contacting the police."

"I don't believe in the cops any more than you do. But I do know one thing. In American movies, women like you are usually dished up for the ultimate sacrifice, with their partners ending up as the heroes."

"I have no partners. Only temporary allies. One day you'll be gone. I don't let illusions interfere with my thinking."

"Just promise to let me know when you're ready to do something stupid. Give me one more chance to convince you otherwise."

I would come to regret having made such a plea.

I expected Muñeca to rush into comparing our notes, but as usual, she was patient and calculating. I did some calculating of my own. I delved back to the images of my kidnapping and conjured up the most sensible question.

"Of the names you recognized on the list, did any of them have a limp, or did anyone flash a weird patch of graying hair on the back of his head?"

"Contreras. Rafael Contreras."

"Which? The limp or the gray patch?"

"Both."

I thought back. I had noticed the limp when we were on the Atacama Desert, and the gray patch when I sat behind the man who drove the car and then flew the plane. Those were separate moments. It hadn't occurred to me that the guy who grasped me by the left arm and hauled me over the sand could have been the same one who had driven the car and piloted the plane. No way to forget him: He was the one who called the Bolivians faggots because they gave up the seacoast to the Chileans and took orders from foreigners.

Digesting this information was too engrossing for me to savor the bites of *salteña*.

"Have you ever entertained men by the names of Paul, Richard, or Howard?"

"I have my ledger back in Santa Cruz. I'll check."

"Have you ever heard of an organization called GBC? It means Get Back the Canal?"

"I may have heard something, but I forget such things. I hear too many names, usually at moments when I don't have a pen and paper handy."

"Well, if Contreras shows up tonight, I'll recognize him."

"And then? You can't haul him off to the police!"

She was right. I would recognize him, and then what? Collapse under the weight of my own impotence? I would have to improvise. It was odds on that Contreras was one of the three stone men I'd noticed in the back of the room the first time I saw Katari speak: the only ones who had not applauded Katari.

Muñeca was meeting Greg at the Radisson. They'd have lunch, and then he was taking a taxi up to the airport. She was to accompany him. Her flight was descending to Santa Cruz and his to Chicago. Somewhere along the way, Greg would pay her a wad of bills, and once in Santa Cruz, she would deposit most of the money in a bank account held by her father. With some of the rest, she'd go shopping for accessories that would make her even more "presentable" for her next stint of duty, or she'd play a round of golf with one of the local would-be professionals, a game she intended to master. The game of golf fit her well. If she made a mistake it would not come from any loss of cool, only inexperience.

"Why don't you ask Greg if he ever heard of Howard Stoner, also known as Panama Slim. If he asks why, tell him that a friend wants to say hello. See if Greg hints at any link between Stoner and the paramilitaries. You can phone me from Santa Cruz."

Muñeca asked me once again to assure her that I'd handle the situation in the auditorium.

"You'd never make a good business manager," I said. "You gotta learn to delegate tasks. You can fly to Santa Cruz, and I will make sure nothing happens to Katari."

There was a bombastic tone in my voice that could have told her that I was not at all so sure about things. I did everything I could to mask my fright. At the moment we parted, she seemed hesitant. There were sensors in her embrace, intended to pick out any vibes within me of insecurity or fear. I did my best to allow the electro-erotic joy from her touch to ease out the impending paralysis of my fear.

I was soon on my way home for a last attempt at sleeping for a few hours before it was time to show up for the Katari event. I tossed and turned, realizing I had no planned solution, that I would have to improvise right from the get-go. This was no "My Funny Valentine." One bad note and my music would be silenced forever.

I got there at 6 p.m., an hour early. With no living beings present, the dark, unheated halls were frigid. I could not tell if my shiver came from the cold or the fright. I went back downstairs to the courtyard of the university, bought a cup of coffee from a *chola* woman with a percolator on a makeshift charcoal grill, and stood at an angle where I would capture the last rays of sun. I watched the students milling around, most of them well aware that if they were lucky enough to graduate, there would be no jobs waiting for them. Some would eventually apply for a visa for the USA, and I hoped that Marv would sympathize with their plight and give it to them. If so, they would be siphoned into the brain drain.

Marv was still my source at the embassy. He might have learned more about Panama Slim. Surely the embassy chiefs did not want Katari killed, even if they opposed his movement. The rank-and-file diplomats most likely identified with Katari's indigeneity. I made a mental note to phone Marv and pry a few more items from him.

A moment of relief set in when I caught a glimpse of Sonia approaching from the overpass, agile as always in her tight jeans and jet-black sweater, swaying with youthful confidence. If she'd added just one extra layer of syncopation to her movements, she'd have launched into the flow of a *cueca* dance. She could have been one of the students, even if she was 15 or 20 years older, except that she carried a briefcase instead of a backpack.

We embraced. I offered her a coffee, forgetting that caffeine was one of the enemies on her Calvinistic diet hit list. Her voice was steady, with the understated sweetness, faint yet firm, of the great jazz singer Blossom Dearie. We got up to the second-floor auditorium. No one had arrived. The university attendant showed up and unlocked the door to the auditorium. I asked him if there was any other way of entering. He assured me we were standing at the only entrance.

Everything looked so simple until a half hour before the listed time of the event, when none of the bodyguards had shown up. Perhaps they were with Katari. I needed them at the door. Another half hour passed, and still no one had arrived.

"Stop pacing around. This is Bolivia," Sonia reminded me. "Nothing begins on time."

If any hit men were to show up, they'd wait and filter their way in with "interference" from the crowd. The first to arrive was the baby-face labor activist Nuñez, Katari's "manager." Before he reached us, I whispered to Sonia that she should remind him about the door guards. He remembered me from the Katari meeting and shook hands, greeting me in broken English. He kissed Sonia on the cheek, shaking her hand simultaneously.

"If the guards don't show, can *you* search people at the entrance?" Sonia asked Nuñez.

"They'll be here."

And sure enough, three of them showed up. Sonia and I stood and watched as they dutifully began searching each and every person arriving. They searched old women as if they were potential terrorists. They searched young women to cop a feel. They searched peasants. They searched student activists. They searched professors.

I recognized some of the usual faces in the crowd, colleagues from Sonia's office, local activists, and a young TV reporter, Channel 11's pretty face, Linda Gutierrez. Every man in the line envied the guard who got to search Linda Gutierrez. The crowd thickened, and it was then that I saw the same three stone men approaching the guards. One of them was dragging his left leg.

I thought they'd try to wind around the crowd and escape the attention of the guards. Instead, they stayed in line and dutifully approached the guards. When the leg-dragger turned away, I noticed a patch of graying hair on the back of his head amidst the jet black hair. I had been watching the hands of the guards during each search. Their hands pressed upon Linda Gutierrez and squeezed the old ladies. But their hands barely grazed the three stone men.

I sensed the same thumping I'd felt when entering Greg's hotel room.

"Sonia," I said, desperately, "are you sure these guards are working for us and not for them? They're not even searching those three monoliths."

We watched the monoliths enter the auditorium.

Sonia and I went up to the guards.

"Shouldn't you have searched those three men?" Sonia asked.

"We did," one of the guards responded, looking and sounding like Stan Laurel.

"Not like the way you searched Linda Gutierrez," I said. "If you don't search them, I will."

"And who are you?" the head guard asked. "We haven't searched *you*."

"He's my husband," Sonia said.

"Husband or no, we have to search him."

"You should have been more earnest with those three."

"Señora Bosch. Those men have been attending these events every week. We know them well. Please instruct your husband to show us some respect."

The three men took seats back to back along the right side of the center aisle. If they'd been mere friends, they'd have sat side by side. But all three of them were on the aisle, as if to have their escape route assured. I pulled Sonia aside.

"The one who dragged his feet, that guy was one of the guys who kidnapped me. Sonia, I don't want him to see me yet. He's the one sitting behind the other two, the one with the patch of gray hair. Get behind him and tell him, I mean, before he sees you, as if you knew each other, tell him, 'Excuse me, Mr. Contreras, can I borrow a pen?'"

"Matt, are you sure you know what you're doing?"

"Damn right I do."

Sonia approached him, catching him off guard from behind. He acknowledged the "Mr. Contreras." My first duty was to protect Katari, but I had a score to settle as well. I drew up a plan quicker than it took to create a new riff for "Straight, No Chaser." With the adrenaline now freely flowing, anger was surging through my chest cavity and pushing out the fear.

"Contreras," I said, flashing my face, "why don't you come with me, and we can talk about the good old days."

"Who the fuck are you?"

"You mean you don't recognize me? We traveled to Chile together. You were a fine pilot. Remember Sajama?"

Before he could get up, I jumped him. I shouted, "Assassin!" It was a gamble. I needed the crowd's attention. I had to separate him from his friends, and then hope to find a gun on him. I had his neck against the rim of the chair, and he was too twisted out of position to defend himself. His partners were not long in jumping me, but there was not much they could do from behind. I had Contreras immobile and searched for the lump that would validate my strange behavior. I found it around his left leg, the one he dragged.

One of his partners had grabbed me from the neck. My neck was bending and twisting as if I were a chicken at a rural slaughter. My body was pushing down upon Contreras, and my head and neck were bending up. Only the neck of a right tackle on the Chicago Bears could have resisted the pressure. My neck, in its present position, would have landed me a part in *Swan Lake*. My brains were now concentrated in my grip, and if they had completely severed my neck from behind, my hands, those same hands that play "My Funny Valentine," could have continued to crush Contreras. But the pain in my neck was now throbbing, and I also knew that at any moment I could be shot from behind by one of the other two monoliths.

Where were the damned guards? To the students around us, I looked more like the aggressor than the victim. I shouted, "HE HAS A GUN!"

I was about to relinquish my grip on Contreras when my neck whipped back into place. Someone in the crowd must have grabbed the stone men behind me. I imagined 100 pool-shooting Mexicans coming to my rescue, and I regained my grip on Contreras.

The guards, embarrassed into action, were upon us, and Contreras had no way to undo the leg holster. The whole auditorium was looking on. Katari's so-called guards had no choice but to do their job. I took advantage of the rugby-like pile-up to dig my right knee into Contreras's groin. They found handguns on all three of the stone men. I can only imagine that the other two refrained from shooting me in the back for fear of hitting their boss.

In Bolivia, the city and national police are not allowed on the autonomous university campus. Someone pushed an alarm for the campus cops. Katari's "guards" removed the two monoliths from the grasp of the students, held them, and announced that they were taking the men across Avenida Arce to the PTJ (the police). It took them a long time to pull me off Contreras. Later Sonia told me that it looked as if I were trying to choke him to death. I had now evened the score from the first round on the Atacama Desert. The odds were pointing to a potential third round of a three-game series.

The audience was prepared to defend Katari in any way necessary, but they had been paralyzed by the confusion. I shouted:

"These three goons entered the auditorium without being searched. These guards were paid off!"

The guards held their captives tight, trying desperately to avoid being exposed.

I yelled again. "If you let these guards take the goons, the goons will be released once they are out of your sight."

My shirt was untucked, my brown leather jacket had been torn from the back, and my neck was throbbing in pain, but otherwise I felt high and mighty. At that moment, Rolando Katari came in. Sonia explained to him what had happened. He assigned new guards on the spot. They took over for the false guards. There was a question of what to do with the captive monoliths but also the phony guards.

When Katari's new guards took over, I feared I would lose my chance to grill Contreras. Only Contreras could tell us who had sent him, not only to kill Katari but also to kidnap me.

Katari had no choice but to send the captives to the police. Before he phoned the cops, though, he asked Linda Gutierrez to carefully observe the leg holsters on the three monoliths and have her cameraman take pictures. The cops would learn that the media had exposed the guilty parties. The cops would have a difficult public relations job to justify releasing their new captives, and even the payoff system would be put on hold.

Sonia was sobbing. She thanked me for intervening, she pardoned my twisted ideology, and, practical as ever, she promised with deep emotion to mend my leather jacket.

I tried to improvise a way to corner Contreras, alone, but I was the cornered one. Linda Gutierrez had thrust a microphone in my face.

"Mr. Matt Bosch, you are at the center of an unlikely incident. An American foiling an assassination of a Bolivian farm worker activist. Can you explain how an American could have developed this unlikely allegiance?"

I'd always imagined that Channel 11's Linda Gutierrez was just a pretty face for selling the 8:20 news. But on her own, she showed a willingness to pry beneath the surface. I didn't relish the attention. But I had it. I recalled the old public relations advice: If you're interviewed, get your message across even if the question does not call for it. I saw the possibility of boosting my music career.

"As an American jazz pianist," I corrected her, "my allegiance is to my music."

"But you *were* present this evening."

"Mere curiosity."

"But you, an American, caught the alleged assassin."

"Only because Bolivians pointed him out to me and because Bolivians were around to make sure I wasn't outnumbered. Believe me. I don't go out on a limb."

"Can you give us your opinion on the position of Rolando Katari. You said you were curious. You must have followed the issue in the media. Surely you have some point of view."

"My opinion makes no difference. I don't believe in American intervention. This is a Bolivian issue. If folks want to know how I feel, they can listen to my music."

"Thank you, Matt Bosch. This is Linda Gutierrez for Channel 11."

Once the mike was off, and before she could pick out anyone else from the crowd, I gave her a business card and urged her to call me about the racetrack issue. She could be a potential ally.

In all the confusion, I had not noticed the most unexpected image of the evening. Muñeca had been hanging around at the back of the auditorium. For how long I did not know. I walked back up the aisle.

"You didn't trust me, Muñeca, did you?" I said. "You're a control freak."

"Matt, don't underestimate my ability to understand human nature. I trusted you. But at the airport, I realized that there would be some unfinished business."

I was not satisfied with her explanation. Why had I been summoned to stop the assassination? Muñeca could have done the job herself. She was fearless, and probably cooler and more calculating than I was. She was an expert at bending and melting men into a submissive position.

Muñeca followed the group of Katari supporters who were hauling the three monoliths off to the lock-up two blocks away. Sonia was signaling me. I had to stay.

"Don't do anything stupid," I said to Muñeca.

"I'll only do what's in our best interest, Matt." She said "our" so I supposed that her homicidal instinct was under wraps.

The Katari conference was a smooth after-statement to the night's events. As he spoke, little by little the peasant leader's supporters returned to the auditorium from the lock-up. He repeated his philosophical slogan, "Live well but not live better," adding that "you saw tonight that *living better* can be the excuse of some people to crush others, as the big growers tried to do tonight with their hired thugs." Following the conference, Katari thanked me for having "stuck my neck out" for him. I would have explained that I had done this act "literally," but it was not a Monty Python moment.

I measured my words. I hadn't given up on the racetrack enterprise.

"You wanted me to show you more about horse betting," I responded. "I didn't want to stop the course mid-semester."

He promised to call me for another session with the past performances. We shook hands. In his embrace I sensed a wave of solidarity. I hoped that this vague fraternalism would cross over into the racing issue. I was now in a negotiating position that should have thrilled Arce and Panama Slim, as if they had themselves staged the assassination attempt.

That night, Sonia called a moratorium on her strike. But she warned me that she would "walk off" again if the gap between us widened once more. I asked her if the only way I could have it was by thwarting murders. She reminded me, playfully, that we were still on the opposite sides of a grand issue and that my side was hopeless materialism. Her words were clear and simple, but her voice was a sweet *adagio* flute, now descending into a lower, jazzier level.

"I suppose I've been a bit too judgmental," she said.

Anyone listening to Sonia would have commented on her talent for understatement. But Sonia did not believe in understatement. She is the most literal person I have ever known. "A bit too judgmental" meant exactly what it said.

When we'd met, I was down and out, living in my car, and she was a bank administrator. I was ruined by exorbitant child-support requirements and my ex-wife's mortgage payments that Judge Mary Doyle had tacked on to my responsibilities because she thought horseplayers were degenerate and that jazz pianists were cokeheads. Sonia had basked in a certain noblesse oblige.

"You don't want to see me wealthy," I had noted at the beginning of her walkout, referring to her opposition to my racetrack plans.

Sonia was too dainty to smirk. She smiled maternally. "When I hear you dreaming aloud about your newest get-rich scheme, you remind me of fat old Ralph Kramden, even if you're thin and sinewy."

Rolling around in bed with Muñeca had conjured up the behind-the-beat, contralto sound of Carmen McRae, earthy and ironic. Sonia's feel demanded Blossom Dearie in the background, girlish but masterfully controlled, high-pitched but never squeaky, ethereal but playful.

Sonia had grown up in reverse. As a young girl, father dead from an ulcer, mother drained from various childbirths, Sonia had to fend for herself and was forced to mature at an early age. Gradually she had regained some of the natural childishness that had long been suppressed. With it came romanticism. Most people become cynical as they age. Sonia discarded the more brutal aspects of realism, and naïve idealism filtered in.

With Blossom Dearie's version of "Once Upon a Summertime" in the background, I groped for our pre-Marianela days in Paris, when Sonia and I could invent our own tropical canopy and nestle for days on end in our dumpy apartment, then hold hands on a bench at Square des Batignolles, with apartment window shutters looking down coarsely upon us through the tall oaks, and then again at the outdoor café on a cobblestone street that served as our living room.

Sonia knew my past performances by heart, that following a long layoff, I was usually on edge and prone to quit after five-and-a-half furlongs. She mentioned that she hadn't expected the marathon after I'd been starved for so long. I responded that the recent events had probably taken off some of the edge, without noting that Muñeca had been one of those main events.

The next morning, I was back with my *Racing Forms*, Sonia was back at work, and I wore the same down jacket, my super-robe, to protect against the gnawing La Paz cold. I leaned like a houseplant toward the same sunlit window that provided faint heat until 11 A.M.

The phone rang. It was Muñeca. She asked me to meet her at 46 Capitán Ravelo, second floor, to the right of the elevator. It was urgent.

"Will my life be in danger?" I asked.

"I told you, I need you alive."

NINETEEN

Contreras and the REC

I got there, saw that the elevator wasn't working, and went up a cold dank adobe-walled staircase. The stone steps were shorter than normal so that I had to use the balls of my feet to avoid slipping. The staircase smelled of urine. By the time it had spiraled up, I'd lost my sense of direction. The hall was dark except for dim light coming from under doors. I knocked, and Muñeca opened. I got no kiss, and her head was turned away from me. She was looking down on Contreras, who was sitting on an old torn sofa. She had a gun pointed in his direction. Her delicate hand was firm and steady.

The other man in the room, I learned, was her distinguished lawyer friend, the very attorney who had sprung Contreras on a temporary "bail." She called him Bernardo, but I imagined him as "My Attorney Bernie." Bernardo and I shook hands.

"I got him out," she explained. "You had some questions for him, didn't you?"

Bolivian law didn't contain the same bail formalities that Americans are used to. There were ways to extract a man from custody, most of them having to do with influence and money. Not so essentially different from the USA, except there was no bail bondsman as an intermediary. If Contreras didn't talk, Bernie—I mean, Bernardo—promised a legal fate that was worse than prison.

Contreras didn't seem to mind the prospect of a sentence in San Pedro. His paramilitary bosses would pay for a miniapartment in the five-star section of the prison, and he'd have his own TV, a kitchenette, and a toilet that really worked.

I whispered to Muñeca, trying not to sound neurotic, that I wanted nothing to do with kidnapping.

"We paid for this one, honey," she said. "Kidnappers don't pay for their captives."

I was supposed to interrogate Contreras. A straight line of questioning would get me nowhere. I tried to think in a circular way.

"Contreras, why didn't you kill me?" I asked in Spanish.

Standing above Contreras allowed me to compensate for the nagging limitations of my 5'7" frame. Contreras was no taller than I was, but he was chubby and sported the beginnings of a beer belly. He had straight black hair and a thin mustache. He shaved his sideburns into a thin line that went down his jaw and then twisted around to his mustache. His dark eyebrows were bent in angular meanness. They tilted as he spoke, as if graphing the sound of his voice on a monitor.

"I was *overwhelmed* with pity," he answered in perfect English.

"You said that the Bolivians were queers because they let the Brits and the Chileans walk over them. You take money from Americans. Does that make you a queer?"

"I won't suck your American dick, if that's what you wanted. But I'll make you happier. I'll lick your daughter's cunt."

Was this simply an example of gangsterese rhetorical flair, or had he been told about Deedee?

Even within my limited sense of values, I harbored a deep opposition to torture. But I understood that those who engage in torture might be our next-door neighbors, and that we ourselves could get drawn in. I was tempted to give Contreras another knee in the balls. I would have found it entirely permissible to strap electrodes to the man's testicles and then press the button and hold it down past the time recommended by the School of the Americas. Contreras had a way of bringing out my humanity.

Muñeca intervened.

"I know lots of people!" She spoke slowly, with no threatening tone in her voice, with dry syncopation. "Important people believe me when I talk. I can tell them that you sang, and they will think that you sang. But if you sing now to us, right now, no one will know about it. Consider the alternative. If you don't open up now, I mean just between you and me, then I'll make sure your lowlife partners learn that you named names. Then I won't need to ice you myself, Contreras. I can press buttons and the job will be done, with no blood on my hands, and not even the need to give the order."

Contreras was mute. She let him roll it over in his mind.

"You see," she added, "we can also let you go now. If we do, your colleagues in Santa Cruz will wonder how it is that *you* walked while your two partners remain behind bars."

Muñeca's attorney Bernie took out a pack of Marlboros.

"Relax, Contreras. Have a smoke. I'm sure you can come up with some sort of solution."

Contreras accepted the smoke. Bernie flicked the lighter. The paramilitary code of honor was no small issue. They abided by their own law. If Contreras walked, then they'd imagine he talked.

Bernie trotted out a bottle of Singani from an old closet.

"Drink for anyone? Muñeca? Matt? Contreras?"

Contreras nodded. Bernie took out two glasses, one for him and one for Contreras.

"Mixed or straight? I'm having mine mixed."

Bernie held up a bottle of tropical juice, a mixture of squeezed tangerine, *tumbo*, and pineapple. Contreras nodded again, pointing to the juice. Bernie served, Contreras took a swig, and Bernie added a refill.

"I have my principles," Contreras explained. "You ignore history. The landowners are our first line of defense against the encroachment of the Brazilians, the Argentines, and the Chileans. The Bolivian army is useless. I'm sure Katari gets funded by foreigners."

Geopolitically he was not far afield. Brazil, Paraguay, Argentina, and Chile had all chipped away at Bolivian territory during the centuries, and mostly it happened when lands were not sufficiently colonized by Bolivian settlers or capital interests. For an organization like Slim's GBC, it made sense to bolster the right-wing landowners, but for a different reason. The landed aristocracy was always willing to eat out of the hands of Americans and Europeans. They saw the Americans as sources of capital, buyers of raw materials, and protection against both neighboring countries and rebels from within. The Marianelas were Americans, but not viewed as such. With their support of primitive farmers, the Marianelas were seen as a force that would weaken the grip of the landed aristocracy. So it made sense that they would kidnap me as threat against the Marianelas. Had I not been married to Sonia, no one would put the slightest dent in my anonymity.

After a few drinks, Contreras seemed to soften up.

"Believe me, whoever gave me orders is an underling. We don't know who's calling the shots. And that's on purpose. By keeping it a secret from us, we can't talk."

"But you must have heard names flung about," Muñeca said. Recalling the GBC, I was about to add the word "initials," but Muñeca stepped on my toe, as a warning for me to hold off. My presence seemed to stimulate rebelliousness in Contreras. Muñeca wanted to continue the softening process. While Bernie served Contreras another drink, I nudged Muñeca, whispering, "Ask him about the GBC."

"What about initials?" Muñeca asked him. "Things like USA, FBI, CIA, GBC."

"None of that. We all understand that our support comes from the REC."

I'd never heard of anything resembling REC. Bernie looked puzzled. Muñeca asked him to spell out the meaning of the REC.

"We have no idea. We know that they have money and guns."

"Come on, Contreras. Give us a name. Any name. You say you have principles. Why would they have murdered my brother? He was only 15. Why him?"

"It had to be a fucking mistake," Contreras explained. "They send their men in to frighten. They kill only when they know it's a leader."

For the first time since I'd known her, Muñeca flashed the face of raw anger. One of her soft rouged cheeks seemed to extend a tad longer than the other. Her usually sensual lips hardened and bent. Her big playful eyes were now boiling, and her eyelashes lost their beckoning wink.

"Bullshit," Muñeca said. "To punish the leader, they'll kill the leader's son and rape the leader's daughter."

"I gotta take a piss. Where's the shithole?"

"Just follow the stink," Muñeca said. He got up, she followed him. She clutched the pistol. "Keep the door open," she said.

Contreras pissed loud and hard. Once back at the torn sofa, he sank in and relaxed.

"I have nothing else to say. Hell, you probably know the man who killed your brother. I sure don't."

"Who gave you the orders to kidnap Bosch?"

"If you want to hear the same story again and again, feed me a good lunch. Give me a menu."

Muñeca's face turned gray. I caught a glimpse of what she'd be looking like maybe 15 years from now. Contreras was wearing her down. I decided to add my two cents. They'd soon be taking him back to the lockup. I had nothing to lose by stepping back. My speaking to him in English was tacit recognition that he was educated and deserved some respect.

"Contreras, you're no dummy. Goons like you must hear rumors. Your organization doesn't keep you in solitary confinement."

"If the man who sends us orders was a motherfucking ogre, we'd have found out who he is. We have heard that he's quite respectable. The word from the grapevine is that he's a good man, someone who deserves our allegiance. And that's about as wordy as I can get. Give me something to eat and take me back to jail."

Muñeca suggested that I leave, promising that she and Bernie would do nothing foolish, and that they'd dump Contreras back at the PTJ.

I had my hand on the doorknob when Contreras called out.

"Bosch, I have my work, and you have yours. You're no pillar of the community, are you? I could have killed you, and no one would have ever known. That was my dumb mistake. That's why I'm here. Maybe we'll meet again."

"Drop it, Matt," Muñeca whispered, grasping my hand with more than simple formality, as if to assure me that she had everything firmly under control, and that I should not respond verbally to the threat.

Once I found my way out of the drab labyrinth that they called an apartment building, I wove through the belching traffic in the streets around El Prado. The word *REC* throbbed in my head. It was not the type of name Contreras could have invented. I memorized the name by associating it with the word *recreation*.

I tried to make my way through the heavy people traffic on the sidewalk of 6 de Agosto Avenue, but with each step forward I was stopped by men, women, and even teenagers who offered to shake hands. Some of them sported Katari tee shirts. The underground pirate tee-shirt business had already sprung into operation, in makeshift factories near the outdoor Huyustus market area, where Katari decals were being ironed onto blank tee-shirts. Katari wouldn't make a penny from the sales. A Katari groupie, a young woman with highland indigenous features, came out from a pizza stand to embrace me. She asked me to autograph her copy of *El Diario*, which I discovered had my picture on the front page. I held my head down like a fit racehorse and slithered through the hordes in front of the film development shop, the clothing store that was always empty, and then the La Paz Conservatory of Music, where I often went to practice the piano. It would only take one bad guy in the crowd to ruin my day.

Back home, I was grinding some coffee beans when the phone rang. It was Marv.

"Well Matt, now that you're a star, we need to talk. I'm concerned."

"You saw what happened on Channel 11."

"Channel 11 and in *El Diario* and *La Razon*. I need to speak with you before it's too late. Now that this is out in the open, I don't have to be so tight-lipped. Can we have a quick lunch? Can you meet me in front of the embassy at 12:30?"

I was about to fire a few hot questions at him, like what's the REC?, but I caught myself in time. His phone calls would be monitored.

Marv was punctual. He had made last-minute reservations at a nearby Mexican restaurant on Avenida Arce, where the food was too bland but the needed private booth was available.

I ordered a simple plate of enchiladas and asked for a double margarita. Marv didn't even consult the menu. He asked for number 3, which turned out to be *mole poblano*, chicken and beans in an ancient Aztec sauce of 16 different chilis and spices that included a hint of chocolate.

"Matt, you should have kept out of the limelight."

"Fat chance, Marv."

"You know I sympathize with the peasants. You may think that our embassy is full of jingoist extremists, but I can assure you that most of us are simply career diplomats, and we identify with the country where we're stationed. The ambassador is beyond us, and there are a couple of nefarious offices, but most of us are not ideologues."

"Why are you telling me this, Marv? I never asked you for justification."

"Because I'm going to give you some information, and I don't want anyone to know where you got it from."

My first sip of the margarita went down brilliantly, and I resolved to order a second double when I finished this one, and that wouldn't be long.

"Before you tell me anything, tell me what the hell is the REC."

"I thought you already knew. I thought we'd discussed it!"

"Shit, I don't remember you ever mentioning the REC."

"Of course I did. Remember the GBC? Well that's the REC. REC is the Spanish name for GBC. *Recuperemos El Canal.*"

One more example of what a slow thinker I was. I'd have needed a week or so to discover the correlation.

"I found the name 'Howard' in an arms trafficker's notes. Would that be Howard Stoner?"

"Most likely."

"I never told you I was kidnapped, did I."

"We found out."

"Was Panama Slim behind it?"

"Logic says yes, but I have no validation."

I recalled how Slim had met Deedee at the Albany OTB. There was only one way Contreras could have learned I had a daughter, but most likely he was simply improvising upon a classic underworld insult.

"Marv, tell me why Slim would fuck over a man who is working for him."

"He'd consider it part of your job. You should have him figured by now. He would assume that you're getting paid, so you'd be ready to handle a few discomforts."

"He could have told me."

"It's all quid pro quo. That's the business. But that's not the reason I called you."

I took a long swig. Marv removed his glasses, and set them carefully on the table, brushed back his long, wavy hair, borderline hippie hair or embassy chic.

"Matt, I think you'd better call off your racetrack business. Get wise. We have reason to suspect that it's a tool for money laundering and for advancing the agenda of the GBC. The track would be their foothold on the continent. The people involved are not nice guys."

"The people you work for are not necessarily nice guys, either. They put in Pinochet, didn't they?"

"That was another era. Believe me, they've learned their lessons."

I held up my empty glass and brandished it high enough so the waitress would catch a glimpse. Marv savored his food, tearing his tortilla in a smaller piece and using the natural corn-flour utensil to scoop up the *mole* sauce. He had been stationed in Mexico City and had adopted their eating customs.

He wiped his hands with the large cloth napkin, and then loosened his tie. He was wearing a neat but ordinary suit, probably to fulfill the minimum embassy requirements. He'd once mentioned that he envied my lifestyle because I was not tied down with formalities.

"The real reason I called you is to tell you to back off and lay low. The people who are involved with the racetrack will have seen your mug on TV. They might associate you with Katari, and conclude that you're a turncoat."

"That's fine," I said, thanking the waitress for the big round glass of margarita with shiny salt on the rim. I stared into the margarita, recalling how Sonia and I, just getting to know each other, would hang out in a Mexican restaurant on Lankershim in North Hollywood and sip margaritas. "So the racetrack people are gonna give me flak for supporting Katari, and I'm in Sonia's doghouse for supporting the racetrack."

"You're gonna get calls from the media. Tell them you are not available for interviews."

"I was considering using the publicity to advance my jazz career. A concert here and there could maybe generate some business."

"Matt, this is a miserable market. Don't risk your life for a small market. And Sonia should not risk hers, either. If I knew her better, I'd tell her directly."

Marv scooped up the last traces of *mole* sauce with a corner of a tortilla, I downed the last drops of the second double margarita, hardly remembering what I'd eaten, and Marv took his credit card and grabbed the bill. He invited me to the next softball game at Irpavi against the Cubans.

"Marv, when the money laundering thing is more than just a suspicion, I'd appreciate some sort of written document, especially if it has the name Howard Stoner on it."

"I've already stepped beyond the line of diplomacy with you, but I'll see what I can do. At the moment it's pure hypothesis."

That night I phoned Deedee in Maryland. I told her never to talk to "Stranger Danger" and that if she had no ride to and from school, she shouldn't go. I then spoke with her Uncle Rob, asking for all of Deedee's play to be supervised.

"Since when have you become paranoid, Matt? Next you'll ask us to move to a gated community."

Rob was right. I was overreacting. Contreras was much too smart to risk problems in a new setting where he had no protection. Slim had too much at stake to blow it with such an indirect strategy, and a dumb one to boot! Sonia was a more likely target than Deedee, but she'd be protected to a certain extent in the Bolivian cultural context, just by being a woman. That left me, the husband of the Marianela spokesperson. Some great confrontation seemed inevitable, but I had no idea when, how, where, or with whom it would happen.

TWENTY

Sonia's Ultimatum

The weekend was nearing, and Sonia suggested we give ourselves a break from the stress and the altitude and travel down to the warm hillside town of Coroico in the dense gorge region known as Los Yungas. I'd received a call from Thelonius. For that Saturday they had already booked their acts, but they asked me to do a solo piano set each night of the following week, beginning on Tuesday, to take advantage of my sudden celebrity tag. I was skeptical. They were not dealing with a crossover audience, I explained. They assured me the place would be packed, and tips would be gushing in. I had already experimented with the haunting major-minor chord swings of indigenous Andean music, so I'd come up with a happy fusion that might alarm the purists. Inevitably, Sonia would argue that I'd owe half the tips to Katari.

I needed the change of venue in order to reflect on which way to take my vanishing illusions. Following the Contreras capture, the racetrack business had looked nearer than ever to becoming a reality, with a more malleable Katari negotiating. But then there was lunch with Marv and his exhortation for me to call the whole thing off. To minimize the Marv effect, I had walked up to the Conservatory, taken a piano room, and worked on an arrangement of "Let's Call the Whole Thing Off," with a mocking stride rhythm.

I contemplated our getaway. From La Paz, at 11,000 feet, the minibus winds up to La Cumbre at 16,000, and then descends over what is known as the World's Most Dangerous Road to Yolosa, at 3,000 feet, where people swim or wash clothing in an Amazonian tributary. The road practically bathes in the river before it winds back up around switchbacks lined with banana trees and lianas. Suddenly Coroico appears, pastel façades clinging to the slopes, nestled at 4,000 feet above sea level.

Three blocks up from the town square, the cozy Hotel Esmeralda occupies the idyllic spot with a swimming pool and a mountainside view that takes the eye all the way up to the peaks on the north side of La Paz. We'd probably have a clear view of the flat-top Mount Mururata some 50 miles away, glowing white under the sun.

Sonia promised to provide me with an airtight reason for dumping my racetrack project. Except for her deep flirtation with the Marianelas, she was quite the matter-of-fact woman, a realist who spelled out what she had to say in easy literal English. She did not enjoy metaphors, nor did she appreciate my "torturing" the melody of "Autumn Leaves." "If it's a beautiful melody, why change it?" she would say.

If there was anything dramatic about Sonia, it was the fact that she would hold back from saying things, the type of things we'd usually want to get off our chests, until she had chosen the right time and place to maximize her message. She felt that the deep gorges along the hairpin turns of the World's Most Dangerous Road offered the right setting for her to unveil her conclusive argument for ditching the racetrack project. When Sonia decides to keep me in suspense, she usually has something dramatic to offer.

We chose the most reputable minibus company, leaving from the northern hillside suburb-slum of Villa Fátima. Before Sonia would begin her promised diatribe, we eavesdropped on the other passengers, making sure there were no potential English speakers who might understand our sensitive subject. As the minibus rocked and rolled above the tree line and reached the La Cumbre pass, it became apparent that the passengers knew only Aymara or Spanish.

We sat on the left side, which would eventually avail us the best view of the 1,000 foot drop-offs lining the road. (I'd once viewed this road from across the gorge. It looked as if a giant fingernail had scratched a thin line through the tropical vegetation that hung profusely on a vertical limestone wall. A precarious ledge had been carved out of the wall and someone decided to call it a road.)

The icy cold around La Cumbre would soon be a thing of the past as the minibus began its descent through a canyon lined by slick unclimbable glaciers that stand jaggedly tall and nearly perpendicular to the road. Past the police checkpoint at Unduavi, what remained of the cold was gradually losing its nip. The asphalt section of the highway was soon replaced by a dusty road. We heard, and felt in our butts, the stones thumping up against the muffler and exhaust pipes of our tortured vehicle.

At this juncture, the road passed onto the infamous ledge on the side of a cliff, and two vehicles could no longer fit side by side. As soon as our driver spotted an approaching truck, he would turn left onto whatever natural lookout was available. It was a complex maneuver that allowed the climbing vehicle to pass on the cliff side, to our right as if we were driving in England. One mistake by our driver, and we would tumble into the misty abyss of the cloud forest and join other forlorn wrecks. On one of the sharpest bends, where vehicles moving in either direction would be blocked from each other's view by the mountainside, we encountered a human traffic light: a man standing with green and red flags to wave us on or motion us to wait for an approaching vehicle to pass.

From my window seat I could look downward into the apparent infinity of the cloud forest, as if the sky were below us. It was here that Sonia sprung it on me. A few weeks back, she explained, the peasants squatting on Arce's land had been digging to prepare a foundation for a health clinic that was to be paid for by the Marianelas. The dig had stopped because they'd come across a human skeleton.

Sister Gabrielle had taken a bone from the skeleton, hidden it under her habit, and then driven a four-wheel drive back to La Paz, filtering through the police checkpoint at Unduavi, and then on to La Paz. She went directly to the office of ASOFAMD, the organization of the mothers of the disappeared (families that had lost their sons or daughters during the period of dictatorships). These women stage monthly protests, calling for the government to investigate the fate of their offspring. They have connections with doctors and laboratories that can perform DNA tests.

A DNA test was performed on the bone sample Sister Gabrielle had taken from Arce's property. The DNA matched that of María Calderón, the daughter of one of the mothers. María had been a student at the UMSA. She'd been disappeared during the cocaine dictatorship of 1981. The Marianelas planned to hand the results over to the police.

"The point is," Sonia said, "these bones were found on Arce's property! I'd like to visit his garden, the one you talk about so fondly. I wouldn't be surprised if we found more skeletons."

I grasped at the last straws of my racetrack illusion. "Anyone could have used his property."

"You're a man of probabilities, Matt. What is the probability that it was someone else, other than Arce?"

With the caressing warmth of the cloud forest, I stripped down to my Julie Krone tee shirt. Sonia removed her sweater, leaving only a tight top that displayed more of her curves than I thought appropriate for the traditional indigenous population of the minibus. Suddenly, the driver slowed down. He instructed everyone to close their windows. He steered the bus through a stretch of puddles over the dirt road, under a stone ledge. The bus was bathed by a waterfall catapulting down from the overhead ledge. The waterfall continued off the road and down into a gorge. Looking down, I saw what appeared to be the rusty steel frame of an old bus.

"Matt, you could end up in one of those deep ravines, and no one would ever find you. You have a wife and a daughter. I'm pleading with you to call it off."

"Sonia, you think you're exempt from paramilitary reprisal? They know your face as well as mine. You're a walking logo for the Marianelas. Many of them actually think you're the leader. I'll call it off if you call it off."

"I'm fighting for a cause, and you're fighting for quick money. Can you see a difference?"

"Cut the rhetorical questions. I'm not your child."

"Speaking of children," she said, "I think we can agree that it won't be safe for Deedee to join us."

I watched the banana leaves on my left that mercifully blocked the view of the gorge and the ferns on my right in the shade of the vertical cliff, growing profusely in perpetual shade. We agreed to continue the debate in the calm of Hotel Esmeralda and enjoy the rest of the Most Dangerous Road. At one point, the driver pulled out over a ledge to wait for an approaching truck to pass us. From the ledge I looked across the gorge at distant bulldozers on a scarred landscape that was on its way to becoming the new road to Coroico. The road we were traveling was destined to become a haven for hikers and "gravity-assisted" bicyclers going from La Cumbre to Coroico.

Once we got to Hotel Esmeralda, we dumped our backpacks in the room, changed into shorts, and went down to the pool, passing through the rustic dining room to grab drinks. I chose a Singani with freshly squeezed tangerine juice, Singani being Bolivia's version of what they call Pisco in Peru. Sonia, true to her health food fundamentalism, chose a *tumbo* juice.

The place was deserted. The backpacking visitors would be hiking in the nearby mountains. We sat in beach chairs side by side. For some people, the pool at Hotel Esmeralda is a refuge. For me it was the OK Corral. It was confrontation time, and following my second drink, I decided to place my cards on the beach table. I let Sonia know that I hadn't been ignoring other women during her strike. She said it was not important because she imagined my relationships would be purely sexual. On the other hand, she had a more nuanced foreign relations conflict.

"Yours is sexual, but mine is spiritual," she explained. "I admire people like Rolando Katari more than I admire you. Even after you saved his life, you didn't even consider why his life was so important to save."

"His life is no more important than anyone else's," I said. "He's not a god. He's a politician. He has his price like all the others."

"Don't you think you were saving much more than a human being?"

"There you go again with your rhetorical questions. Is that the Marianela preaching style?"

"They don't preach. They enfranchise, and they share spirituality along the way. If I'm still with you, it's because I believe you still have your principles and you're just too damned cynical to want to admit it."

I thought I saw an uncharacteristic tear in her right eye. I wanted to tell her that she was in this for her own self-enrichment, that spirituality is just one more commodity, like designer clothing, though probably of higher quality. But that would have gone too far. She'd walk away from me.

Muñeca's corner of this bizarre quadrangle remained in a fog. Now there was Sonia, there was a lofty ideal in the person of a farm worker named Katari, and there was me.

"Should I be jealous of Katari?"

"Why should you be? It would be so easy for you to defend the cause of the less fortunate. You've never gawked at aristocrats or plutocrats."

"No, but that might be because I haven't yet become one of them."

"Christ, Matt. Don't put up a cynical façade!"

Sonia harbored this image that represented what I should be more than what I really was. She'd often noted that if I hadn't identified with the underdog, I wouldn't have become a longshot player. I had to reckon with her words. Even as a child, I was rooting for the misfit New York Mets and their antiheroes like Marv Throneberry against the ruling-class Yankees. I'd read my baseball history. I knew that the old Brooklyn "Bums" had abandoned their fans for the money and become the designer Dodgers for the Hollywood crowd. In racing, I identified with unfortunate geldings like John Henry, and I enjoyed the Claiming Crown more than the Breeders' Cup.

The sun was hiding behind the hills, and the usual backpackers were now filtering back to the hotel. I heard them speaking German, French, and British English. I also picked out an American accent among them. For the moment, they were all rooting for the underdog. But it was virtually inevitable that they'd get a job, marry, have kids, and change sides.

Sonia got up from her beach chair and sat down on the edge of mine. I squeezed over for her. She cuddled up with me.

"Matt, maybe I love you because you're so hopeless."

"It's your noblesse oblige, Sonia."

I wasn't kidding. She now belonged to the spiritual nobility.

She looked into my mind, and I stared at her smooth, soft legs and felt her mellow heartbeat.

I preferred to stop thinking altogether and to simply feel her next to me. But as happens all too frequently, we had weighty practical matters to discuss, like what we were going to do with Deedee. For the first time, Sonia considered quitting the Marianelas. They would understand if it came down to a case of the safety of our daughter. By quitting, we'd return to the States, and she'd be saving me from what she called "the Arce mob." I'd be able to play the races every day and not depend on a fax from Vince.

At dinner that evening, at a pastel-façade, hole-in-the-wall, ma-and-pa restaurant on a cobblestone street in Coroico, Sonia began considering the possibility of giving the Marianelas a month's notice. I supposed it was the equivalent of leaving a cult. She'd be harboring the guilt feelings associated with tearing oneself away from a sect. For Sonia, though, *sect* was not the word. It was a *movement*.

There were practical matters that involved her responsibility. The Landless Peasants were gaining momentum, and the paperwork of the Marianela support had multiplied accordingly. She would have to be on hand to train a new volunteer to take her place. Eventually, the Marianelas would have to remove themselves from the peasant context. They were not indispensable. They were a mere support.

Sonia suggested that I leave Bolivia immediately and that she would catch up with me. For me it was out of the question. With the new success of the squatter movement, the losers in the equation would be scapegoating the Marianelas, and Sonia's visibility made her vulnerable to attacks of people on the edge of defeat, which are the most brutal of all attacks.

Like many restaurants in the warmer tropics, this dive in Coroico opened out onto the street. Passersby could look down and see that we'd not finished our potatoes or that we had chosen trout instead of beef. Our most meaningless habits were exposed to the outside world.

Meanwhile, back in La Paz and Santa Cruz, bizarre mechanisms were clicking into place, and we had no control over them.

TWENTY-ONE

The Underground Economy

O n the bus back from Coroico we sat on the sheltered side, visibly removed from the abyss. We continued our brainstorming and finalized a deadline for returning to Maryland. I was overwhelmed by a grand nostalgia for the races at Laurel. Most horseplayers consider Laurel a holy dump, but I preferred playing the ponies in a setting without glitz or distractions. Laurel had been a pioneer in full-card simulcasting. I relished buying the *Racing Form*, taking a whiff of the print, and then confronting tracks across the country, scanning the past performances from Laurel, Aqueduct, Hawthorne, and Santa Anita. Even the winter Big A inner dirt track now warmed my heart more than the sensual tropics.

The Bolivia racetrack scheme, Sonia asserted, was a shambles, given its attachment to murder and dictatorship. I delved for a mellow way to explain that the discovery of a dead body on Arce's property was hardly worth a blink of the eye. I had heard a rumor that the body of a murdered Teamster was found in the excavation of the Meadowlands Racetrack. Mafia connections with casinos and race books were well known and did not dissuade anyone from patronizing those places. Even when governments were responsible for human rights abuses, people still paid their taxes. The initial shock of the dead body on Arce's property had subsided, and I saw no reason to abandon the project now that I had Katari's attentive ear.

I decided to play a defensive strategy, to communicate with Arce and let him know that I was still on the side of the racetrack, but that I preferred political strategies over assassination.

Arce would apologize and repeat his mantra: *We do our best to rein in the loose cannons.* I wanted very much to believe that the circumstantial evidence surrounding Arce was misleading, even if details were piling up. First Marv had warned me about the probability of the track as a money laundering institution, and now Sonia had brandished the evidence of murder. I'd meet with Katari and get a feel for where he stood. If his whole movement won, then he could more easily afford to give up on holding the acreage that would house the racetrack.

Since when are racetrack owners nice guys? I repeated to myself. I'd do everything possible to get the racetrack contract money to fall into my lap within the allotted month. Otherwise, my policy was simply to neutralize Arce until we could get out of the country.

I decided to keep all this to myself. Without combativeness, I dropped little hints from history about thriving racetracks whose owners were not pillars of the community.

My solo gig at Thelonius was a greater success than I had suspected. For a week I could imagine I was Keith Jarrett, knowing all the while that I was a temporary big fish in a small and quickly evaporating pond, and that my new-found popularity had more to do with an extraneous event in an auditorium at the UMSA than with the quality of my music. The human ego needs to be massaged, and I accepted my musical glory the way a pig takes to a mudhole.

The management made a real event out of it. Each person entering the bar was searched by ear-pierced, tattooed guards who looked very much like professional wrestlers. Public relations firms would have to admire the imagination that went into it. By being searched, incoming spectators were given the vicarious feeling that they were actors in the Katari drama. By Thursday night, with word of the picturesque door search operation, curiosity seekers added to the already bulging bar. Of course, peasants couldn't afford to pay $3.50 for a drink, but the event gave middle-class Paceños a chance to feel part of the movement.

The tip money was not inconsequential, but sustainable it wasn't.

Purely as a concession to Sonia, I donated half of it to Katari, indirectly through Sonia so that I would not be marked as a supporter of the movement. But on the third night of my gig, the management requested that I wear one of those underground-economy Rolando Katari tee shirts during the set. At first I said no, but they begged me. So I negotiated a no-camera clause. The bar faced the audience from one side, and Carla, the bartender, promised to monitor the situation, to stop all cameras before they could be raised in the air. If any flash went off, she'd go over and confiscate the film, with the help of the door guards. I thought I had everything under control.

The word got around so effectively that even Marv went to hear me. Clubs in La Paz don't get going until past 10:30 P.M. Sonia, who usually goes to bed by that time, made an exception and showed up on Thursday and Saturday. The week gig ended on Saturday night. When the dust settled, I wondered how many people actually appreciated my music. I had to recognize the truth. I was light-years from ever reaching the intense beauty of Keith Jarrett, and it wasn't in me to sustain the element of exquisite surprise that you'd hear with Monk or Mayburn. But I could extract the flavor of a song, and I hoped my music would be appreciated. The applause was generous, but how much of it was for me, and how much for Katari? At one moment I'd seen Sonia applaud, and even with my own wife I could not tell if her enthusiasm was for my music or its indirect Katari symbolism.

On Sunday afternoon, Sonia went shopping at the Huyustus with her office companions. I had stayed in to sleep off the week of late gigs. The Huyustus is a vast outdoor agora on the undulating foothills of the northeast quadrant of La Paz. The informal economy dominates profusely. One finds contraband appliances from Chile, illegal pesticides, pirated software, the ubiquitous silver and alpaca artisan products, black-market clothing, functional furniture from small factories, and everything else that you cannot imagine. There's even one street that specializes in selling sundry stolen goods.

The Bolivian government often embarks on crusades against the underground economy, which is anything but underground. However, reality always sets in, and everyone soon realizes that if you suppress underground commerce, Bolivia's unemployment rate would jump from 10 to 60 percent. The informal economy is tolerated. The people in power know that without it, half the population would either resort to crime or join a revolution.

I was looking forward to Sonia's return so that we could go out to dinner. I had been sleeping in my jeans, on the couch, with heavy wool blankets pulled up over my chin to ward off the humid cold of the La Paz rainy season. The doorbell rang. Before opening I followed our safety rules and asked, "Who is it?"—not that paramilitaries would be stopped from breaking down the door if they should decide to pay a visit.

"It's me," she said, and those two universal words soared with joy. Perhaps she had found some sort of collectors' item at the Huyustus, or the right size shoes, which was not easy for her since she had tiny feet.

I opened the door. She jumped on me and hugged me.

"Congratulations! Why did you keep it a secret?"

My only secrets from Sonia concerned the details of my relationship with Muñeca and my persisting attempts to pull off a racetrack deal. I doubted she'd be so thrilled by such secrets. I asked the only dumb question available.

"What secret?"

"Your new CD!"

I had never recorded a CD, so she must have been talking about a gift for me. Perhaps she'd found a *Keith Jarrett at Carnegie Hall*.

She fumbled in her handbag and took out a CD. I looked at the cover. It read, *Matt Lessons*. The subtitle was "A Matt Bosch tribute to Rolando Katari."

Carla had promised to stop all photos. She'd done her job. But we hadn't considered tape recorders. Someone had smuggled recording equipment into the bar. I had no illusions about the sound quality. As with the Katari tee shirts, the counterfeiters were fast operators. I would never get paid.

I hoped that the distribution of my unfortunate new work of art would be limited to the Huyustus and not spread to Santa Cruz. Fat chance! Soon Arce would have his copy. I had the choice of preemptive damage control in the form of an awkward conversation with Arce or simply remaining silent and waiting for Arce to sort it all out on his own.

Bolivia's underground economy was an ongoing triumph against adversity, worthy of great appreciation, if only I had not become a part of it.

TWENTY-TWO

Chasing a Bad Bet

Whatever control I had over the events surrounding my professional aspirations (racetrack manager, jazz musician) had vanished. Normally when things bend in the direction of the irrational, I get myself to a racetrack and fix my attention on the tote board, a symbol of fair play and equal opportunity. In the absence of a track, I phoned Vince at his Nevada apartment. I received a recorded message. The number was out of service.

I called him on his cell phone. This time he answered. He had moved back to Southern California, to a Venice Beach studio. He'd gotten into some sort of "hot water," he said, in Nevada.

"But don't worry, Matt. I only lost a few days with your maiden-comeback method. You're up by 717 bucks."

"Should we raise the bet?" I asked.

"You want the truth, Matt? I fear the well is drying up. The average mutuel is lower than what your research said it would be, and you got lucky by inheriting the win on two disqualifications."

"So what do ya mean '*drying up*'?"

"Two reasons. The *DRF* now publishes layoff trainer stats. That knocks off a point or two from your average mutuel. Then, trainers are now openly declaring that they *like* laying off their horses. They're aware of the bounce factor, the public is seizing on the idea that recency is no longer the positive factor it used to be."

I had no doubt this was all true, especially coming from Vince. In the perverse world of a horseplayer, this news came down more heavily upon me than the discovery of the dead body on Arce's ranch. I realized that my racetrack ambitions paled in comparison to my goal of discovering an automatic bet. This news was especially hard to take because the maiden-comeback method had been validated by the most reputable racing research companies only a couple of years back.

"I'd say, Matt, that this method has legs for a year or two max, before it's completely eroded by the new public awareness."

The amount of my profit on this particular part of my bankroll would seem meager to professional horseplayers. But I consider racing on the basis of dollars per hour. By using an automatic bet, I'm investing far less time than a comprehensive player who needs to handicap each and every race individually, each race with its own decision-making process. With the automatic bet, the player reduces the type of decision-making complications that can result in major fuck-ups. So for the time being, I could afford to continue with the maiden-comeback method, and I'd wait for further validation on what Vince had identified as a declining average mutuel.

"Don't call me again on the cell phone," Vince said, "or it'll eat away at your bankroll."

I jotted down his new fixed phone number. He was on his way out to Hollywood Park. We resolved to catch up on each other's lives in a few days.

At noon the next day, the phone rang. It was Muñeca.

"Matt, I've made a big mistake."

I perceived an uncharacteristic shakiness in her voice.

"You haven't . . ." I stammered. "I told you not to . . ."

"Matt, save the lectures. I need your help. I found the man who was responsible for killing my brother."

"And you want me to help you . . ." I choked on my words.

"Some of the names you got from Greg's notebook were good ones. I followed the leads, and now I have him."

"Whaddaya mean you *have* him."

"Here in my apartment."

Dozens of responses swirled around in my throbbing head. I couldn't establish the right hierarchy. "Don't kill him" could have been my initial response or "Don't do anything stupid." But my curiosity won out.

"Who is this man?"

"Matt, you won't believe me if I tell you."

"Just spit it out."

"Matt, it's Arce!"

"You better be damn sure about this."

"Believe me, we're talking about the scum of the earth."

It was Arce who had catalyzed Muñeca's career. In Bolivia it would have been unimaginable that the daughter of farmers could become a beauty queen. One afternoon, Arce had been driving through downtown Santa Cruz. He stopped at a red light. He saw Muñeca at an outdoor café. He pulled over.

She was the most exotic thing he'd ever seen. He desired her for himself. The beauty pageant was a pretext. Her smooth mestizo complexion came from a mixture of Spanish and lowland indigenous, or even Croatian, as she'd led me to believe. I suspected there might be some Okinawan genes in the mix, but that hypothesis didn't jibe chronologically with the time of the Okinawan immigration to Santa Cruz.

Arce had offered to finance her entry in the Miss Santa Cruz pageant. She was in a dead-end clerical job at the time, harassed by her boss, and looking for an out. She accepted the pageant backing and probably paid Arce for it with a few erotic liaisons. Sex is casual in Santa Cruz, so Muñeca would not have considered that she was being used. Sorry, feminists. That's reality in Santa Cruz. She could have won first prize at the pageant on her own merits, but Arce's political influence certainly played a role in her victory. Most of the judges had been on his payroll at one time or another. From a business standpoint, you could argue that he owned the pageant, since he controlled the collateral businesses that profited from it.

For Muñeca to suspect Arce of murder, she'd have to get past years of trust and respect for him. She had a collegial business friendship to overcome, so she must have had resounding evidence. Sometimes you try to pin it on someone because you suspect him subjectively. Subjectively,

Muñeca had considered Arce as not guilty. She had scoured every document and grilled every possible witness just to prove that the man who ordered the paramilitaries to her parents' house was someone other than Arce. Arce had once assured Muñeca that her brother's death was the responsibility of an unhinged lone ranger, beyond his control, so Muñeca had to explore all the free radical leads.

My quixotic urge to save a damsel in distress was neutralized by my need to not get involved. I was in my countdown to Laurel, and each and every act in my life was directed toward making sure that in three weeks Sonia and I would be on the plane back to Maryland. I would visualize myself at the rail at Laurel on a gray winter day. There would be patches of snow in the infield, and the cold wind would be blowing the pages of my *Form*. After my tribulations in Bolivia, Laurel would be my tropical island retreat.

"I lured him here with the intention of shooting him," Muñeca explained. "But I haven't been able to pull the trigger."

"That's a good step," I said. "You're on the right track."

"For such a long time I've been longing for revenge. Now that I have my big chance, I can't pull the trigger. But if I let him go, he'll have me killed. Matt you've got to help me."

Ever since her brother's death, Muñeca had envisioned revenge, and the great day of retaliation had blossomed during her daydreams and night musings into an imminent reality that could not be contained.

"Why don't you put him on the phone," I said, not having the slightest idea what I could say. I would soon be on Arce's hit list, as soon as he learned of my unintended CD tribute to Katari. But I also knew that if Muñeca murdered Arce, the shockwaves could blow me down. They would check her phone bill and note that she'd called me just before she killed him. I resolved, too late, perhaps, to control my telephone vocabulary.

An unexpected witness might step forward and claim to have seen Muñeca and me together. The fact that many Bolivians were now identifying me with Katari would create a legitimate motivation in the eyes of the police, since Arce was Katari's rival. The police would be thrilled to nail a foreigner as the scapegoat. These were only a few imagined connections between me and the potential dead man. There would be unimagined shockwaves, and no computer simulation can anticipate the unforeseeable.

"Matt, there's nothing you can do on the phone. I need you here! Please!"

"Muñeca, that sounds so easy to you. I just hop on a plane and fly to Santa Cruz."

"You once told me it took you an hour and a half to get to Santa Anita, and that you did it every day. The flight from La Paz to Santa Cruz is half that time. I can call a driver to pick you up at the airport."

"Think for a moment of other possibilities."

"At the moment I have only two options . . ."

I interrupted her. I knew all too well. Shoot him, or let him go and wait for him to kill her. Either way, I would suffer unforeseeable consequences. I was sucked in.

"Let's talk in person. You're right."

It made no sense to scold her at this point. I might provoke a desperate reaction. There were flights every two hours to Santa Cruz. If I left immediately for the airport, I could be at her apartment in less than three hours. I'd have three hours to come up with a third way.

"Muñeca, you've got friends in Santa Cruz who could help you. Why me?"

"Everyone in Santa Cruz is tied in some way to Arce. And besides, you have a special relationship with him."

"Special my eye! He might have been the one who ordered my kidnapping."

"Well, now you can find out."

"Promise me," I pleaded. "Don't do the unthinkable. But don't let him go, either. I'll be there."

I phoned Lloyd Airlines and reserved a seat on the 2 P.M. flight. They told me that if I missed the flight, they could fit me on the next one at 3:30. Muñeca called back. She'd have a driver waiting for me at 2:50, right outside the front entrance of the Santa Cruz airport.

I jotted down a note to Sonia. It said that I had to take care of some urgent business, not to worry, and that I would probably not return until the next day. I added that she should have someone from the office stay at our apartment that night for security, and if that could not be arranged, she should go to Marv's and sleep there for the night. I reminded her that it was urgent for Sister Gabrielle to first take the DNA evidence implicating Arce to the Bolivian government ombudsman, Maria Campos, and have Campos send it to the police.

I stuffed a few odds and ends in my backpack, a change of clothes, toiletries, and my calendar with important phone numbers. In La Paz it's easy to find a taxi. In fact, the cabbies find you. Just stand on a corner, and a taxi driver will pull over and ask you if you need a lift. It would take us a half hour via winding freeway up to "JFK" at 13,000 feet in altitude. On the way up I realized that it was a dumb move for Muñeca to have a driver pick me up. The driver would be a witness. I resolved to phone her from the airport and have her call off the driver.

I had obstinately resisted acquiring a cell phone. It was an intrusion on my privacy and meant that a man would be on call, from employers, from the ex-wife, from messengers of bad news. Muñeca could be featured in a "why you need a cell phone" advertisement.

I bought some special phone tokens from an ambulant vender at the airport and called Muñeca from a booth. I told her to cancel my ride, and to not call anyone else for help, that we didn't want any witnesses. I asked her how she had Arce under control. She said that Arce was locked in the bathroom. She assured me there was no escape window in the bathroom.

"He must be shitting bricks," I said.

"On the contrary, he doesn't seem at all frightened. He challenges me to come in and shoot him."

I couldn't resist the old cliché: "You really have gotten yourself in a holy mess!" and then knew it would boomerang back to yours truly.

I was besieged by a deluge of reasons why murdering Arce would come back to haunt me. He had business papers with my name on them. Any police investigation would require my testimony, and they'd probably order me to stay in the country as a future witness, pending trial. Yet a dead Arce might be less threatening to me than a live one. If Arce were allowed to walk out of Muñeca's apartment, I would hear from him. I recalled how roughly his guards had dealt with me when they'd extracted me from the street and taken me to meet him in the South Zone of La Paz, and that was considered a friendly pick-up. That was back in the good old days when Arce and I were entirely on the same team. Part of me hoped that a *surazo* storm would hang over Santa Cruz and that all flights would be cancelled.

"Matt, you're good at improvising. You'll find a solution, right?"

"Sure," I said, masking the sarcasm.

I'd slept with the queen bee, but the inevitable death of the suitor was being prolonged into agonizing torture.

It's all downhill from La Paz to Santa Cruz. You take off over the Cordillera Quimsa Cruz, catch a long and impressive view into the glaciers of Illimani, and then, already, the descent begins before the flight attendants can bring out the drinks. It was past lunch hour, and the flight was shorter than Flushing to the Bronx via subway, but Lloyd Airlines served drinks and sandwiches. For practical reasons, I ate the ham sandwich and downed an orange juice. I wasn't going to Muñeca's house for a candlelight dinner.

It was hot and humid in Santa Cruz. I had the taxi driver drop me off at the Hotel Felimar on Calle Ayacucho so that he could not associate my arrival with Muñeca's apartment, which was three blocks to the east, cattycornered with the main Plaza 24 de Mayo, not far from the basilica. Her apartment was on the sixth floor, above a pizzeria. The streets were occupied by hordes of strollers. In thick humidity, many people would hang outdoors all night to escape the infernal heat of their apartments. I noted that if there were a dead body to deal with, Muñeca and I would have no privacy for its disposal, and decomposition of a corpse would accelerate in the tropical humidity.

I knocked on the door. She checked through the hole, saw it was me, opened. I felt a gush of air-conditioning. She embraced me, as if the ultimate answer to her life had just materialized. I was quick to remind her that I had come with no reliable solution. I scanned around her apartment. The design was modern, the furnishing trim and stylish, the area rugs indigenous chic over parquet floors, and the kitchen appliances state-of-the-art. There was one valuable painting on the wall, a colorful

Mamani Mamani that depicted two indigenous women. Such paintings go for at least two thousand dollars. There were a few original Edgar Arandia drawings, in neo-Goya style. If there hadn't been a captive in the bathroom, it would have been an artful setting for having a few drinks and then making love on the sofa.

"I had it all planned, Matt. The music from the Plaza is so loud that no one would hear the shot."

"Don't tell me you didn't consider how to dispose of the body. I had you pegged as cool and calculating."

She pointed out to an alley behind her building.

"That's my car parked below. No one ever uses the back stairway."

"Still, you wouldn't think of dragging a body down those stairs. You'd scrape DNA all over the place."

She took me to her bedroom. There was a body bag on the soft bedspread of the king-size bed.

"So, you went and bought a body bag. Don't you know that the purchase will be traced by the cops?"

"I got this bag right after my brother was buried. I've been planning for this moment for years."

"But you can't pull the trigger."

"I've visualized pulling the trigger. Each time it seemed easier. I've dreamt of myself doing it, with no effort. But now that the moment of truth has arrived, something has come over me."

"Something they call common sense," I said.

"Can I serve you a drink? You need to loosen up."

"Coffee would be much better. I need to sharpen my mind, not dull it."

"I'll offer Arce a cup of coffee," I said. "Sooner or later he's gonna know I'm here. Maybe he'll say something that will lead to an idea."

I knocked on the bathroom door.

"Arce, it's Bosch."

"Get me out of here, Matt. Call off this wicked woman."

"Can't do it, Arce. If she lets you go, you'll kill her."

"I'm a diplomat, Matt. I find other ways to work things out."

"I don't believe you anymore. You ordered my kidnapping."

"It wasn't me. It was Panama Slim."

"You disappeared people during the dictatorship."

"You give me too much credit. I had no control over all the hatred that was going around."

"You were the godfather of it all, weren't you!"

"I'm just a gardener who happens to be a businessman in order to support my garden. I'm not responsible for all the villains in the world."

"If Muñeca shoots you, she'll bury you in your garden, and you will be reborn as a beautiful rose."

"Bosch, you know that if she kills me, you're aiding and abetting. You'll rot to death in a Bolivian prison."

"And if we let you go, you'll have us killed."

"Bosch, we're partners. We have a potential business together."

"Why didn't you tell me about the money laundering? I was a very silent partner, wasn't I? A passive partner, I should say. Just another naïve gringo."

"You hear rumors, Matt, and then you go over to the other side. What do you call it in English? Flaky?"

"I simply stopped your goons from committing a stupid murder. Couldn't you see that Katari was our only chance to negotiate for the racetrack? If he's gone, everything erupts. If he's around, and especially if he wins, he becomes more flexible to our offers. How could you miss it, Arce?"

"Bosch, I hear you. I'm flexible. Let's not give up. We can still pull it off."

Muñeca brought the coffee. I set mine down on a nearby coffee table. She opened the bathroom door, directing her gun at Arce, who, I discovered, was stark naked.

Muñeca flashed a playful smile. "I made him take off his clothes to prevent him from fleeing."

I handed Arce his coffee. He was not at all muscular, but quite fit for his age, probably about 60. For the first time since I'd known him, he looked vulnerable in his hairy nakedness.

Muñeca bolted the door. As I sipped the coffee, she showed me a few documents that indirectly implicated Arce, and mainly repeated the hearsay evidence she'd obtained from her sex-doped sources. Together with Marv's assertions and the human bones from Arce's property, there was now an overwhelming body of circumstantial evidence that Arce was the warlord.

Both Muñeca and Sonia were convinced that Arce called the shots. Muñeca suspected that I was not entirely convinced. She sat down with her drink. For the briefest moment, I was distracted by her sleek outfit, an earthy ocher combination of top and shorts that blended with her smooth bronze skin. I knew that I could not postpone a decision for long. Arce would be reported missing, and a kidnapping investigation would be unleashed.

"Pablo Rivera was one of the names on Greg's list," Muñeca explained. "He told me that the other landowners looked upon Arce as their hero. Rivera worked for one of them, and he had always assumed that all the paramilitary decisions were controlled by Arce. But the most damaging evidence came from Mendoza."

"Mendoza has an axe to grind, Muñeca. I think Arce was sleeping with his wife."

"You think wrong. Mendoza's burning rage comes from his hatred of violence. I had a long session with Mendoza, and trust me, I can tell sincerity when I see it. The phony one is Arce."

Muñeca grabbed a book from her shelf: *Bolivia: From Dictatorships to Democracy*, by the great historian Pablo Salon. She flipped to page 73, and pointed to a paragraph with her manicured index nail, painted a burnt orange.

Santa Cruz landowner Manuel Arce worked closely with the Bolivian Ministry of the Interior, coordinating the deportation of Argentines who had sought refuge in Bolivia to escape the Argentine military dictatorship. It was understood within Operation Condor that the deported Argentines would arrive to a military reception and would be tortured and disappeared.

"You see, Matt. You can murder without pulling the trigger."

"You realize," I said, "that we now find ourselves in a position where it's easier to kill him than to let him go. We'd have more time to leave the country, that is, if it took them a long time to find the body."

"Matt, are you saying we should shoot him?"

"Whatdaya mean 'we.' I don't have the balls to shoot a man in cold blood. It's not the same as slaughtering a chicken. If it were a war and we were in the trenches, it would be different."

"It is a war. Arce has been waging war on the Bolivian people. My brother was the Bolivian people."

The next time I began to tremble before placing a large wager, I would remember this moment, and understand that no wagering decision could compare with a decision to execute another human being. Arce was clever, playing passive so that whatever we did would have to be in cold blood. In theory I favored the death penalty. I opposed it in practice: All too frequently it involved some criminals passing judgment upon others. Sometimes the ones who ordered a death penalty were themselves guilty of crimes against humanity.

Sonia had once told me of rumors that Arce had been Bolivia's contact with the Argentine Dirty War. But ideological arguments were useless. This was a simple binary dilemma: him or us.

TWENTY-THREE

Bridgejumping

Muñeca dozed off with her head on my shoulder. She hadn't been asleep for more than five minutes when she trembled. Her head straightened abruptly, untangling her flowing dark hair. I was right there, able to hear her vivid dream sequence before it dissipated into oblivion. I combed the story for a subliminal hint of what we should do or not do, reworking it into my own narrative to gain some degree of control over it, as if by navigating through her dream we could discover a way out

It was dark. We escorted Arce down the back staircase of Muñeca's building, promising him that we would release him in the middle of nowhere. I drove Muñeca's Suzuki four-wheel drive. Muñeca sat directly behind me, her gun hidden under a loose pink blouse, with Arce, now dressed in his designer jeans and white cotton guayabera shirt, inclined against the right window of the backseat. We arrived at the Most Dangerous Road in the World, and I drove the car up the hairpin turns in the direction of La Paz. As is always the case, there was no night traffic. Muñeca signaled me to stop on a ledge to the right. She ordered Arce out of the vehicle. We had him cornered on the ledge. Suddenly, without warning, Muñeca employed self-defense training and let loose a swift karate kick. Arce went flying over the vertical ledge. For a few seconds he was visible under the full moon, until he plunged into the cloud forest canopy. Rumors that the gorge was bottomless were confirmed when there was no sound from Arce hitting bottom.

"It always seems so easy when I dream of doing it," she explained. "This time I didn't even have to use the gun."

Her story was geographically invalid. The highway she spoke of was a whole day's drive from Santa Cruz. In order to get into that highway at Yolosa, we would have had to pass through a police checkpoint, and even if we got through, night traffic was usually prohibited up the old road. Even drivers who had done the route on a daily basis had never appreciated the frightening beauty of the setting under a full moon.

The dream had left Muñeca with the inclination to extinguish Arce from the face of the earth. "It's him or us," she repeated. "What choice do we have?"

I delved into her dream for a morally justifiable option. Committing a "perfect" murder was equivalent to bridgejumping. In race betting there is a strange character nicknamed the bridgejumper. A bridgejumper, sometimes called "the phantom plunger," looks for a horse that cannot fail to finish in the money: a sure bet. Often he finds his bet in a five- or six-horse field, betting a super-favorite to show. The payoff will be the minimum $2.10 for two bucks, so the bridgejumper will only make 5 percent on his investment. He reasons that this is 5 percent in less than two minutes. For any kind of financial benefit, he needs to wager enormous amounts of money. This creates what is called a "minus pool." Imagine if, in the show pool, $55,000 of the $60,000 has come from the bridgejumper's wager. That means that the track should be returning less than $2.05 rather than the $2.10 minimum legal return: The track loses money since it is obligated to return the $2.10 minimum.

I have found that in cases where we identify a bridgejumper in the pool, it would be better to bet $2 to show on all the other horses. In a five-horse field, that means an $8 investment. If the super-favorite happens to flop, even rarely, the show payoffs will be enormous enough to compensate for all the times when the favorite wins and we lose. Imagine, for example, that if the 3–5 favorite is off the board, with bridgejumper amounts of money in the show pool, the 5–2 second favorite might pay more than $20 to show. A longer shot could return $60 or $70 to show, even if it would only return $20 or $25 to win. It only takes one or two failures of a super-favorite in bridgejumping situations to make up for the many losing plays when we bet against the bridgejumper favorite.

The bridgejumper decides to engage in such a monumental investment for such a small return because he thinks that his horse is "the perfect bet" (like the perfect crime), and most probably because he has this great desire to stick it to the track. He has read all the information on this horse and has found no flaws whatsoever.

Bridgejumpers end up losing. They need 19 horses out of 20 in the money just to break even. To me, icing Arce was a bridgejumping situation. Even with all the evidence pointing to his guilt, killing him would require an enormous investment (the risk of getting caught) for a meager return (the fleeting satisfaction of power and revenge). I handicapped all the past performances on Arce. The evidence was overwhelming that he was at least one of the men who gave orders to the murderous paramilitaries. First I reviewed the words of Panama Slim:

"After you meet Arce, you'll appreciate me as the nice guy."

Second was the information from Marv, a very reliable source. Arce was a leader of the Santa Cruz mafia and would be using the racetrack as a money laundering instrument.

Then came Sonia's contention that Arce was behind the death squads during the dictatorships, plus DNA evidence showing that one of the disappeared had been buried on Arce's property.

Point 4 came from Muñeca. Granted, her lowlife source Rivera was a mere henchman, but his assertion that Arce's orders were behind the paramilitaries was extracted by Muñeca, who had a known talent for making men talk and sing.

The fact that Arce's name was even found in books by reputable historians, as Bolivia's link to the torture and disappearances of the Argentine Dirty War, was icing on the cake.

My handicapping of Arce's past performances was based on circumstantial or hearsay evidence. A bridgejumper needs 99 percent certainty. I felt that it was no more than 90 percent probable that Arce had sent the paramilitaries to Muñeca's house, leading to the death of her brother. It was difficult enough for us to kill the right man, but there was a slight chance that we might be killing the wrong one.

Bridgejumpers bet for a very temporary feeling of power against the supposedly invincible house, more than for the certainty of long-term profit. The mere idea of killing Arce stemmed from a visceral need for a "regular player," Muñeca, to crush the man who had stacked the odds against her. This triumph would certainly be temporary, and the long-term odds did not look good.

As we sat on the sofa, Los Van Van syncopations were thumping in the background, which in combination with the hum of the air-conditioner would eliminate the possibility that Muñeca's 76-year-old 8th-floor neighbor, Señora Flores, could perceive any shouts coming from Arce. Arce knew that shouting was useless and preferred to maintain his long-nurtured dignity by remaining as silent as the plants in his garden.

Muñeca and I were leaning into each other on the sofa. It would have been a perfect scene if there had been no naked man in the bathroom. But then again, with no Arce in the bathroom, what would bring a beauty-pageant winner with an Hermès handbag into the life of a struggling jazz musician who would not qualify on the basis of looks for a role in *Days of Our Lives*. I had the man in the bathroom to thank for bringing us together, which meant that Muñeca and I really had nothing else in common. Whatever we had of a relationship was tethered to the man who had probably been responsible for our torment.

Muñeca got up from the sofa and stood resolutely by the living room window, where you could see the sun setting behind the plaza.

"I'm sure I can pull it off," she insisted.

"Which would make me an accomplice."

I replayed Muñeca's dream in search of an alternative solution. We did not have to let Arce out the front door. It was getting dark. We could drive him outside of Santa Cruz and deposit him in the middle of nowhere. That would give me a chance to find a temporary hiding place for Muñeca. If the courageous Bolivian ombudsman acted quickly, as she normally did, there would be murder charges against Arce, and he would be arrested. Since Bolivia had been able to imprison its most recent dictator, the system's political momentum would kick in and punish one of the dictator's henchmen: Arce. Once Arce was arrested, Muñeca's thirst for revenge would be satisfied.

"Arce will be arrested, and your safety will be assured."

"Not so," she said. "He could still give orders from prison."

"If he did, he'd have other bigger targets than you, like the people who got him arrested. You'd become a very small fish. Look at it the other way. If you kill Arce, eventually you'll be discovered and put out of circulation. How will you support your family from prison?"

Our discussion could not be entirely logical. Arce had been like a father to Muñeca. He was twice her age. He had pulled her out of a café, taught her how to behave in the highest circles of society, taught her how to handle businessmen and criminals, and led her to victory in the Miss Santa Cruz pageant. Once or twice this father figure had slept with her, resulting in a nagging metaphor of incest that perturbed her view of him. I felt that if we could make him come clean, a type of "truth and reconciliation" session, her lust for revenge might be eased.

For her it would be truth and reconciliation, but for me he would be plea bargaining. With Muñeca's grudging approval, that's the way I would present it to him. But first, before we went through the process, I had to back up my part of the bargain and find a temporary hiding place for Muñeca.

My plan was messy and flawed, but it offered a viable alternative.

First I asked Muñeca if she had a valid passport. She did. I promised to explain my plan after I rushed through some errands.

"Where can I make some phone calls?" I asked her. "Not from your phone. I don't want these calls on any record."

She told me that I could call from the pizzeria below. The man behind the bar was fat but agile, with a thin mustache. He was Rodrigo. I borrowed Rodrigo's phone and called Marv on his cell phone. "Marv," I said, "I have a friend who needs to leave the country temporarily so they don't kill her. She has money, she doesn't look like someone who's going to work illegally, and I can vouch for her. Sorry to hit you with this one, but it's a question of life and death."

Normally it took days or weeks for a Bolivian citizen to get a U.S. visa. Muñeca needed one for tomorrow.

"Does she have a criminal record, Matt? I need to know."

"She's clean, Marv."

"Send her here to the embassy tomorrow. She'll need to show a bank account with enough money for a short stay, something objective that I can write into the records. Does she have employment?"

"She works in the informal economy, so there are no records."

"Then we'll have to depend on the bank account. I hope no one suspects laundering. Can you furnish me with an address where she'll arrive, and a letter from someone who's inviting her?"

"Yes, I can."

"Well, it looks like it can be done, but make sure she has a round-trip ticket. One-way tickets are automatic eliminations from the tourist visa process."

I thanked Marv and then phoned Vince. I handed Rodrigo a $20 bill, and told him he could keep the change. I instructed Vince to send a fax to my address directed to Muñeca Molina, inviting her to stay with him for two weeks and wishing her family well.

"Hey, Matt, I'm living in a two-room. This person will have to sleep on the sofa."

"No problem, though I'm afraid you may want her in bed with you. If she doesn't feel up to it, promise me you won't insist."

"Matt, you're intriguing me. I'll send the fax."

Next, I phoned Sonia. It was dinnertime. No doubt she wondered where I was. I told her to expect a fax from Vince with an invitation. I told her to guard it with her life, and not to doubt me.

"Matt, you might want to tell me where you are and what is happening. I am your wife, you know."

"I'm following up on some business," I said. "I don't want to say any more over our phone. You gotta trust me."

"Please don't get yourself killed over a racetrack," she said. "I'm afraid that when I'm not around, you can lose your common sense."

I went back up the stairs three by three. I told Muñeca to prepare a suitcase with at least a week's change of clothing, including a jacket in case it cooled down in L.A. I added that she should carry her passport and her bank card, with an account book showing as much savings as possible, plus a bunch of recent electric bills for reference.

"Matt, you sure we can't kill him?"

"I don't have the balls. Do you?"

"I've been gathering courage."

"I just explained to you that every human rights organization in Bolivia is going to have DNA evidence about a disappearance on Arce's ranch. If they follow through on it, Arce could very well end up in jail."

"But we can't let him walk out of here. He'll turn around and have us stalked."

"Precisely. Think of your dream. We could take him to an unpopulated area outside of Santa Cruz and dump him there, and then drive to the airport and get out of here. It would take him hours to get to a telephone. Before anyone comes after you, you could be on a flight to L.A."

"Would you go with me to Los Angeles?"

"Muñeca, I'd love to go with you. But it's more complicated than that."

"Arce will tail you until he finds you and buries you in his garden."

"I think I can deal with Arce. I'll be getting out of Bolivia in a matter of weeks."

I ran downstairs one more time to the pizza place, phoned American Airlines, and made reservations for Muñeca on the 6 A.M. flight from La Paz to Los Angeles, via Miami, for Thursday morning. Luckily it was midweek and off-season. It was Tuesday. We'd fly to La Paz, stay at my apartment, and go to the embassy early Wednesday morning. Then we'd hide Muñeca on Wednesday night and get her to the airport at sunrise on Thursday morning.

I wanted to be with her on that flight, for my own safety. But I couldn't imagine leaving Sonia alone. There were empty seats on that Thursday flight. If I could convince Sonia to drop everything, all three of us could be on the flight to Miami.

For Muñeca to smother the urge for the ultimate revenge, I needed to get Arce to open up. Muñeca passed him his clothes through the bathroom door. He came out. She ordered him to sit on the sofa. We stood over him.

"I hope you've had a change of heart," he said, his distinguished tone of aristocracy unruffled.

I looked at him in the eyes.

"We'll let you go, Arce, in exchange for some information. Tell me about the GBC, what you call the REC."

"GBC is Panama Slim's strategy of establishing footholds throughout Latin America, which he considers his backyard. The racetrack would be one of those beachheads."

"It's a crazy scheme, Arce. In today's world you no longer have to occupy territory in order to control a country's economy and politics."

"Panama Slim's mind operates in the realm of old-fashioned geopolitics. He's still in the Theodore Roosevelt era."

"So the racetrack was just a scheme, and I was a tool. If I hadn't been married to a Marianela, I'd have been worthless to you. I was more valuable as a bargaining chip than a negotiator."

"Not so fast, Bosch! We've been serious about the track, even if it had a double function for Panama Slim. Labor-intensive racetracks in America cannot compete any longer with capital-intensive casino games, but here in Bolivia, labor is cheap. Racing here could be beamed electronically to American race books. And breeders like me would have a chance to engage in the sport."

Arce was not talking like a death-squad *patron*. "You gave me time to reflect in that bathroom. I have come to see, as you insisted, that if Katari wins, he's more likely to be flexible in negotiating with us. If we can cool tempers, we still have a chance to pull it off."

"You're telling me that you needed to be kidnapped and held naked in a bathroom in order to suddenly see things logically? Your sudden enlightenment doesn't jibe."

I read him the lines from the Pablo Salon book, that Arce had been linked to the Argentine Dirty War, adding a coda of my own. "You were working directly on the Dirty War. Muñeca has all the right in the world to consider you responsible for her brother's death."

"Hold it, Bosch. The Dirty War was fought with the approval and support of your government. At that time, we were given a free hand to stop the communists. I'm not happy today about our tactics back then, but I was a minor player. Everybody felt at the time that it was them or us, and they were the bad guys."

"Why was I kidnapped? Who ordered it?"

"You remember that we had arranged your safe kidnapping. You were going to be a bargaining chip to force the Marianelas to back off. Panama Slim knew about our plan, but he became impatient and wanted something closer to reality. So he had it done himself."

"Are you saying that he knows the paramilitaries and deals with them directly?"

"He sells them their weapons. In the past, they could get weapons from the Bolivian army. But today the Bolivian army is on the other side."

"So what he's doing is illegal, by both American and Bolivian law."

"You might say that, but that's business. If you want to do business in this world, you can't be a pussycat. If you bow out of the racetrack deal, then you don't have the balls to do business in this real world. It's your choice: live on tips at bars or own the bar and everything around it."

For the first time since I'd known her, Muñeca was furious with me.

"Matt, this man is too slick for you."

"I don't have the same weapons that you have."

It was true. Muñeca had her way of melting a hardboiled criminal. She could have been hired as a truth serum. Even if I were to pull off the racetrack deal, I had no insurance that Panama Slim would pay me the balance of what he owed me. He had manipulated me before, and he could do it again. Working with criminals was causing me more grief than financial gain.

Holding her Hermès leather carry-on, Muñeca ordered Arce to follow her toward the back door. She tossed me the keys and told me to follow Arce and lock the door on the way out. No one could have seen us go down the outdoor staircase.

"You drive, Matt."

She opened the back right door for Arce, and then shut it. I stood outside Arce's door until Muñeca had gotten into the backseat on the left side. She warned Arce that if he tried to escape, she'd send a bullet through his head, and another one, for good measure, into his heart. I got into the driver's seat and began driving north according to Muñeca's instructions. We passed a few outdoor nightclubs with lean-to roofing. I observed people swaying to *cumbias*. In another life, I would have joined them.

Arce began to speak. Muñeca told him to shut up.

Gradually, the buildings got smaller and more dispersed as we passed out of ring one, through ring two, and eventually rolled through ring three. We were headed towards the Viru Viru Airport when Muñeca instructed me to turn left on a dirt road. Within a tortured 30 minutes from the main road, the dirt road had left the farmlands behind and entered a mini-rainforest. The road ended on a red-dirt incline that leveled off on a thin beach of the Piray River. No way to swat at so many mosquitoes coming from all sides.

"We don't have to leave him alive," Muñeca said. Her gun was aimed at Arce's chest.

"We gave our word," I said.

Arce remained silent, as if I were his attorney.

"He's a clever liar in his own right," she said. "He certainly has you bamboozled."

Muñeca was the loose cannon of the moment. Whatever she decided to do could have repercussions. I didn't dare try to force her, for fear of riling her into killing Arce. Muñeca had me get out of the car and block Arce's door. She got out and ordered Arce to slide over and out on her side.

We stood next to the car. Arce finally spoke.

"Muñeca. I'm truly sorry."

Muñeca waved the gun like a pointing finger. "I won't be manipulated by you any more."

Suddenly, Muñeca unleashed a karate kick. This time it was real. She grazed Arce's chin. He tumbled, not so much from the force of the kick, which mainly served to confuse the mosquitoes, but from the surprise that Muñeca had unleashed. It was a mild incline, and Arce ended up on the red sandy bank of the swift river, apparently unharmed. He got up slowly, brushing off his pants.

"You got off easy, Arce," she shouted down to him. "We're still not even. But I'll leave it at that. I'm done for now. But if you try anything against me, I'll finish the job."

We rushed to the car, and she took the wheel. I questioned her judgment, suggesting that she was inspiring his revenge.

"On the contrary, this creep goes after the ones he thinks are the most vulnerable. I had to show him I won't bend."

On the way to the airport, Muñeca called a friend named Gustavo, asking him to pick up her car at Viru Viru. She stopped off at a Dumpster, removed the bullets from her pistol, wiped it clean of prints, and placed the gun in the Dumpster, making sure that it was out of sight beneath the refuse. She dropped the bullets in a separate trash can. When we arrived at the Viru Viru Airport, she stopped the car at a parking attendant's booth, gave the keys to the attendant, and told him that a Gustavo Flores would be picking it up. We hustled into to the airport and eventually caught the 9:20 P.M. flight to La Paz.

TWENTY-FOUR

The Short-Form Betting Method

No way I could enjoy the flight to La Paz. Muñeca was lamenting that she had not had the courage to pull the trigger. I consoled her, suggesting that Panama Slim was probably as much to blame for her brother's death as Arce. She was not at all surprised at my improvised suspicion, as if it had been her idea in the first place.

It was always like this with Muñeca. I would imagine I was finally guiding her somewhere when in fact the reverse was true. She knew how to lead from behind.

I was uneasy about arriving home to Sonia with Muñeca by my side. Throughout the episodes with Muñeca, Sonia had remained at worse indifferent and at best philosophical. Though I'd stopped short of admitting an affair, I'd passed on hints here and there: Muñeca receiving my first phone call from Iquique following my kidnapping; Muñeca drawing me suddenly to Santa Cruz for an unexplained emergency. Surely Sonia must have realized that I was moving in orbit around this dangerous woman.

Even mellow Sonia had her breaking point. Prior to her stint with the Marianelas, she had once been capable of minor bouts of worldly jealousy. But now she'd left all human weakness in her wake. She was committed to a higher cause.

Individualism was the primary trigger in my life as it was for Muñeca.

We both saw things from a personal point of view and went at it from there. Sonia was the odd one out. She had transcended petty personal frailties, and now even her daily habits were linked to her communion with collective justice. She drank a cup of coffee not for the rich taste but because it was a Fair Trade brand in which the growers were paid their legitimate wages and she was even willing to take pleasure in the boost, now that it came from "fair" caffeine. To combat carbon emissions she bought locally produced products, and it was a no-no to eat a strawberry or apple out of season.

Muñeca and I got upset about individuals who'd done us wrong. We took things personally. We were both trying to make a living by cavorting with dubious characters. Sonia was surrounding herself with idealists, and she was convinced that Katari was one of them.

Of course, I recognized that Sonia and I were complementary. I needed her moral stamina, and she needed (though she didn't realize it) my realism.

These were the thoughts sifting through my mind as Muñeca and I ducked into a taxi at the La Paz airport. If I'd been with Sonia, we'd have boarded a minivan for a half a buck, which would get us home just as fast as a taxi. Muñeca demanded her comforts. On the way out of the airport and onto a street of the El Alto shanty-city, we saw the great Illimani shining (seemingly at the end of the avenue) under the full moon, like a white-robed Buddha. Finished El Alto dwellings were far and few between. You saw red-brick walls everywhere. Sometimes a roof was missing. Sometimes window frames were absent. Sometimes the brick edges were crumbling. Inside, few of the dwellings had any sort of heating. It was bitter cold at 13,000 feet above sea level. No wonder so many poor folk would forgo a morning shower.

The cabbie noted my American accent and erupted into conversation. It began with small-talk stream of consciousness, transitioning each anecdote with a "you see?" and eventually reaching the level of probing questions. Finally, he felt comfortable enough to volunteer his latest political theory.

"I'll bet you didn't know that the American Embassy is supporting the Landless Peasants."

I was used to hearing taxi-driver conspiracy theories, but this one outdid all the rest. I resorted to irony in order to brush aside such odd-ball nonsense.

"You must have a special contact inside the embassy," I said.

"That's not necessary," he rebutted. "The United States sends wheat shipments to Bolivia to subsidize their farmers in Kansas. The big farmers in Santa Cruz were planning on growing enough wheat to make Bolivia self-sufficient. That would have cut out the wheat shipments. You see? No more subsidies to the Kansas farmers. So you see why the embassy wants the peasants to hold these lands. The peasants wouldn't have the means to grow wheat on a large scale. They'd stick to corn and fruit and potatoes and fava beans. Then your farm subsidy industry would continue to thrive. Can't you see it?"

"You must have studied economics at the UMSA," I said.

"No way," he said. "You learn more economics driving a taxi than sitting in a classroom. I talk to all kinds of insiders."

"Then you should have learned," Muñeca said, "that the big growers are using their land to produce soy for animal feed in Europe instead of wheat for people in Bolivia."

The cabbie had run up against a formidable obstacle and lapsed into silence.

Muñeca took advantage of the break to shift gears.

"You sure you don't want me to stay in a hotel, Matt?" she whispered.

The taxi passed through the toll-gate and began the winding descent from what they call "the Eyelid": the edge of the Hole, into the sparkling La Paz night. If you blinked, you'd think you were seeing an inverted sky.

"If something happened to you," I whispered close to her silver earring, "I wouldn't forgive myself. In two days you'll be safe in L.A. at Vince's apartment."

I would have wanted to use Muñeca's pink cell phone to call Sonia and let her know I had a guest, but the intrigue would have developed into a new cabbie conspiracy.

We arrived at my building, took the lift up to the eighth floor, and I knocked. I heard Sonia's "Who is it?" and I said, "It's me, and I have someone with me. It's okay to open."

Sonia hugged me and buried her head in my chest.

"Things have been happening a little beyond my control," I said. "I hope it's okay for Muñeca to stay here. Arce will be after her."

Any enemy of Arce was a friend of Sonia, even if this friend might have slept with her husband. While we ate and drank, I explained our adventure, sanitizing certain parts of it that would have highlighted my irresponsibility. Sonia felt vindicated, having been one of the first to point out that Arce was no model citizen. Sonia was a strategic thinker. At this moment the positives of my split with Arce weighed more meaningfully than the negatives of the bizarre link with Muñeca. Indirectly, Muñeca had fulfilled a vital role: force Matt to scrub the racetrack insanity.

Sonia's apparent serenity suggested that she was already aware that Muñeca and I had certain events in common, which other wives would have interpreted as unfaithfulness. To say the least, it was an uncomfortable situation. Famished as I was, I'd lost my appetite and had begun a countdown for Muñeca's departure.

Muñeca, on the other hand, seemed genuinely interested in getting to know Sonia. She did not view Sonia as a rival, for sure, and that highlighted the fact that whatever liaisons she and I had consummated were composed of isolated slices of time that remained independent from her life and mine but for their tactical value.

At the dinner table, Sonia's deep and proud eyes sparkled with confidence. Muñeca could not have missed it. Sonia's delicate self-assurance was a sign of class. She punctuated each syllable in *adagio* rhythm. Muñeca's style was *allegro*, and like an authentic lowlander, she omitted final syllables, which meant that one word would flow into another in a steady stream.

If there were a hidden pecking order among women, Sonia would be the dominant leader, even if others in the herd were more rambunctious or aggressive. Sonia's beef with me had nothing to do with something as mundane as extracurricular sexual encounters. My ideals, or lack of them, were the point of contention. For Sonia, sex, gambling, and other vices were irrelevant when it came to morality. For her, solidarity between man and woman concerned the sharing of higher values of justice and equality.

Muñeca slept on the couch, not before an elaborate change into a silk robe that would have come from a Fifth Avenue boutique, via one of her clients. Once in our bedroom, Sonia donned one of her sexier negligees, an act which I mistakenly interpreted as female rivalry.

Within 30 seconds she had turned away from me and fallen asleep. Even at the height of her strike, I still got a "good-night" from her. The ease with which she drifted off was sharper than a dagger. I imagined a double-edged weapon of indifference and resentment, but then again, it may have been pure exhaustion. It left me groping to define what ill feelings she was protecting in her invisible shell. I would have preferred to have it out. Now, overwhelmingly fatigued as I was, there was no way I could rein in the anxieties that were racing through my head like a flock of ravens.

Normally, if I found myself stifled by a potentially sleepless night, I would slip out and relax on the sofa. On this very particular night, it was out of the question. I was condemned to listen to the serene breathing of Sonia, guessing whether her dreams were of disappointment, resentment, or simple fatigue.

Breakfast between the three of us was happily uneventful. We all left at the same time, Sonia uphill to her office, and Muñeca and I downhill to the American Embassy. Against my best wishes, Muñeca stopped off at a fancy boutique to purchase some beauty creams and bath liquids, replacing the ones she'd left behind in Santa Cruz. Once through the fortress doors of the embassy and uneventfully past the electronic checkpoint, we entered the consulate waiting room, where Muñeca drew number 46. The number post read 38.

Marv came out from behind the counter, shook hands with me, and guessed that the stunning woman at my side was Muñeca. He asked her to accompany him. It took them 17 minutes. She came out nonchalantly, as if anyone in Bolivia could have been granted a visa, when in reality, anyone without high pedigree ratings would be turned away, and even presidents and cabinet ministers were sometimes rejected. Her passport with stamped visa would be soon ready at Window 3.

"So, do I have to wait until my name is called?"

"Muñeca, you don't realize how quick this has been. Even former president Paz Zamora couldn't get a visa!"

Marv came out again, motioning me to go back with him.

"Matt, I've got a special present for you."

He opened a drawer of his oak desk and handed me a document. It looked like what we'd get when we petitioned documents through the Freedom of Information Act. Some words and phrases were blackened out. But one thing was notably free of censorship. *Howard Stoner, aka Panama Slim, engaged in ilg weapons tfk to Bolivian P.M.s.* The "ilg" was "illegal," the "tfk" I assumed was "trafficking," and the " P.M.s" were "paramilitaries."

"Use this as you wish, Matt. You have my blessings."

"Hey Marv, since when does the embassy give out free candy?"

"Consider this a leaked document. No mention of my name, got that? Both liberals and conservatives agree on this one. We consider GBC as harmful to American interests. Our country does just fine defending its interests through the marketplace. We don't need any retrograde geopolitical nut to resuscitate Manifest Destiny. If GBC gets anywhere, it will stain our country, and it won't be good for stability in Bolivia. There's a quid pro quo on this document. I have no express permission, but between the lines, I know that this is the right move."

"Marv, I've never heard you wax so eloquently. But before I head off with this paper, what if I used it to blackmail Panama Slim?"

"Holy shit, Matt, you'd be playing with fire. Panama Slim is an old bull. He'll run all over you. And he doesn't care if the police are watching. He'll kill you."

"Or what if I want to pursue the racetrack deal? Say that Katari wins his struggle, the landless peasants are granted a new agrarian reform, and so they can now sacrifice this one parcel where they're squatting. Katari owes me one. I can deliver the racetrack."

"You just got through an ordeal with Arce, and you wanna go back for more?"

"I got him where I want him. He knows that only I can get through to Katari. I've made myself indispensable. I'm the only person on earth who has any chance to get Katari to cede the land for the racetrack."

"Matt, you're insane. Sooner or later, the money laundering will be discovered, and then your name will be caught up in it."

"Hell, Marv, if upright behavior were required of racing officials, they'd have imprisoned more than a few over the last century."

"This is Bolivia. They lock you up first, and then maybe they get around to having a trial."

Marv was right. I was in my last grasp of a big score that was not meant to be. Who was I to control the super-goons? It was like continuing to wager on a system that no longer functioned, chasing a bad investment with more money. And yet, I had never been so close to the prize.

"And besides, Matt, even if you pulled it off, do you really want to be tethered to an animal like Panama Slim?"

The quid pro quo was simple. Marv was sending me on a mission. The only weapon he gave me was a piece of paper. I promised him I'd make him proud of me. Saving Katari's life was nothing compared to what Marv wanted me to do. If I followed through as he wished, I might even be acting in the name of Sonia-esque idealism, though Muñeca-style revenge could not be eliminated from my inner menu.

My apartment was within walking distance from the embassy, but to improve our probabilities, I hailed a taxi. Once we'd arrived and deposited our coats, we confronted a scene of discomfort. Neither Muñeca nor I could even consider the unthinkable. Sonia's absence was only physical. She had left her Trappist aura in the air. I opened a window and looked out on the glacier of Illimani 26 miles away.

Had we been in a hotel, perhaps we'd have had the chance at one more gallop around the track. Of course, I wasn't even in control. Muñeca decided when and with whom she'd be willing. She wasn't exactly pawing at me.

Muñeca was on her way to L.A., and no doubt Vince would be taking her to play the horses at Hollywood Park. We had nothing to do but wait, and in our tight-security mode, the street was off limits. I'd once suggested, stupidly, that the races offered better money-making opportunities than her profession. Following that moment, she had nagged me from time to time about when I was going to show her the secret. Now, knowing she'd be in racing country, she nudged me to give her the goods. I trotted out a few old *Racing Form*s and decided to show her the "short-form method," one of my dearest inventions. People like Steve Fierro use it. Steve does odds lines for several tracks each day and then bets all of them, playing only those horses that are going to post above their fair odds. Steve has explained that his own variation of my short-form method enables him to handicap several tracks in a short time.

Muñeca had never seen a *Racing Form*. Deedee had picked it up in a short time when we were in Saratoga. If a player has a good automatic bet, it should be something that can be explained to a seven-year-old kid.

I explained to her that my short-form method is for claiming races and that claiming races are easily identified in the past performances. The claiming price is equivalent to the class level of the horse. Any registered owner (usually through a trainer) can "claim" or buy the horse from the race. In other words, a claiming race is a market in horseflesh.

"The method for eliminating horses is really simple," I continued. "Any horse that has lost two or more races at today's claiming price or lower, becomes an automatic toss-out. We only want horses that can win at today's level or that have been racing at a higher level and are dropping in class."

Next, I pointed to the jockey and trainer statistics above the running lines. Eliminate any horse whose trainer has less than a 12 percent win record. If a rider has less than 8 percent wins, you can also eliminate the horse. The method was now looking better than ever. I couldn't wait to go into action myself.

Arriving at such simplicity required first passing through complexity. No need to explain to Muñeca. She just wanted to know how to get the job done. I reminisced to myself at how this method was born directly from the proud union of two beautifully-conceived research projects.

The first research result shows that higher-percentage trainers win with more than their fair share of longshots. You'd have thought that high-percentage trainers would be overbet but this is not often the case once you move into the higher odds levels. Trainer Carla Gaines was one of many examples of how certain trainers get flat-bet profits in certain specialties, mainly by avoiding the public spotlight. By lying low they don't attract public action, and their odds remain in the profit zone. Not only was Gaines profitable within most specialty categories but the stat for all her races read 20 percent wins and a return of $1.27 for each dollar wagered. As long as Carla Gaines remained out of the limelight, she'd probably keep up with the relatively high average payoff that allowed for this profit even while winning only once every five times.

If you had nothing else to go on and just limited your play to trainers whose horses return a profit, you'd survive.

Considering that random wagering produces about a 24 percent loss, much more than the track takeout, for the reason that a random bettor will play more underlays (poor-value horses) than overlays (horses that return more than their fair price in the market), Carla Gaines horses actually returned 50 percent better than random betting. I hoped that C.G. would steer clear of high-profile events like the Santa Anita Handicap and any Breeders' Cup race, for success in those events could remake her name into a magnet for action.

My longshot trainer research had been corroborated by Mike, a skeptical colleague. Using what we call impact value, Mike checked out a large sample of starters at 10–1 and above. He found that 12-percent-and-above trainers accounted for 55.6 percent starters and 65.5 percent winners, while 9-percent-and-below trainers provided 28.8 percent of the starters but only 19.9 percent of the winners. The higher the trainer's win percentage gets, the better the impact value, and once you move up to the 20-percent-win level, these trainers record a profitable bottom line for one who plays all their longshots, though the percentage of winners is quite low.

The companion research showed something that should have been obvious to most players: that class droppers win more of their fair share of races compared to horses staying at the same class level or rising in class from their previous race. I had kept out stray variables from the class research by only analyzing same-distance and same-surface scenarios, so, for example, a class drop win could not be attributed to a switch to the turf or a stretchout in distance. Players had inflated the value of speed figures, and when you overbet in one area (like speed) another area gets underbet. Hence, class drops were underplayed by the betting public.

I had done four separate research samples, and in all of them, class droppers outperformed risers or those staying at the same class level. The win percentage was only slightly higher for the droppers, amounting to

17 percent, but the average payoff was considerably stronger. One sample of 409 class droppers, randomly chosen, showed a profitable bottom line, to the tune of 3 percent. Class risers are usually coming from good performances while the past performances of droppers, for the most part, are much less impressive: hence, the higher average mutuel for droppers.

The point was that if trainer win percentage and the class-drop factor are both underbet by the players, and if you combined the two as elimination factors, you could come up with a quick method for selecting a horse.

So the short form is derived from complex dynamics. You'd think we'd need more, but in fact, nowadays, with information overload, people win by extracting essential things and bypassing the rest.

Muñeca's head was bobbing from exhaustion. For the non-initiated, the *Racing Form* was certainly more sleep-inducing than *Elle* magazine or *National Geographic*, and perhaps that's another advantage of the short-form method in the age of the short attention span.

As a back-up for Muñeca, I jotted down the rules on a piece of paper, simplifying the method into a more cautious formula, based on evolving research.

The Short Form:
1. Eliminate all horses that have lost twice or more at today's claiming or allowance level or less.
2. Eliminate all horses whose trainers show less than 12 percent wins for the current year.
3. If three or more qualifiers, pass the race.

Trainer filter: Play only if (a) trainer has an 18 percent win record for the year and/or (b) in the trainer-specialty stats beneath the past performances, trainer shows a profitable return on investment in at least one category ($2.01 or better) with at least 18 percent wins.

Surely Vince would take her to the races, so I left a "P.S. for Vince": *Eliminate horses going from statebred into open company.*
She took the note, put it in her off-green, off-pink handbag, and settled on the sofa where she caved into deep sleep within seconds, not

before I had warned her to stay put and not leave the apartment, not even for a two-minute stroll.

I had two options. Sit and stare at Muñeca in my private sculpture museum or pick up Sonia at her office and invite her to have a drink. I chose the second. I needed to reach some semblance of peace of mind, and only Sonia's words could get me there. She'd been torturing me in a most crafty way by having hidden her feelings about Muñeca.

I picked her up, and we headed down the noisy Avenida 20 de Octubre. Amid the symphonic belching of wobbling trucks and broken-down buses, Sonia talked about the weather, about food, nutrition, fair trade, cinema, dance, Deedee, organic agriculture, Bolivian textiles, and even human relations, though this last subject was entirely abstract. Not a word about the strange affair between Muñeca and me, even though I was sure the subject was implanted in her mind. If she'd just have it out, we could find the eye of the storm.

I was impatient to let her know that the racetrack deal was dead, though I was still willing to improvise its resuscitation if the right conditions presented themselves, such as if Arce were found not guilty. Not wanting to give ground on my original racetrack premise, I resolved to use Marv's arguments, which were not at all the same as Sonia's. I still believed that a racetrack was a winning idea. Much of Bolivia's industry involved exporting raw materials, following the neocolonial model. A racetrack would churn the revenue into new value-added uses at home, and spin-off employment would result. It would provide labor-intensive jobs, where rural people could easily adapt. The problem was the management. Next to Arce and Panama Slim, even the New York Racing Association seemed like a crew of enlightened visionaries.

Sonia agreed to a drink or two at the Mexican restaurant near the embassy. After I'd downed two double margaritas, I resolved to ban the subjects of dance and cinema and Deedee and organic agriculture, and I blurted out the word *Muñeca*. I resolved to not blame Sonia for her strike and to not present any excuses. I wanted to get this over with as quickly as possible.

I waved my arms theatrically. "You can attach electrodes to my balls and then press the button. There's a hardware store on Calle Comercio where you can buy a set of electrodes. You can keep your finger on the button as long as you like."

"That would be too easy for you," Sonia said. She had that look of hers where she's cool on the outside and there's a serene smile within. She was torturing softly.

"You could push me off Suicide Bridge into the smelly Choqueyapu River," I said.

"That's not sustainable, Matt. I would prefer doing something that I can do a second and third time."

"So what do you propose," I said, as if I were negotiating.

"I propose doing nothing, Matt. I just don't care."

"What about revenge? Haven't you ever wanted revenge?"

"There's enough revenge in you for the two of us. And if you add Muñeca, that would be two to the tenth power. I hope you can handle it."

"Maybe with one more margarita."

TWENTY-FIVE

The Trifecta as Show Bet

Once Muñeca had left for L.A., Sonia and I got down to preparing our departure. Had it not been for the fact that both of us had chosen precarious activities, we could have brought Deedee to study a year abroad. We could have hiked in the cordilleras, explored for indigenous ruins, and bicycled down the World's Most Dangerous Road. I could have played piano with a good mix of Bolivian and expat jazz musicians. But now that it was virtually over, I longed for the rail at Laurel on a grim December afternoon. As for Deedee, I was not the fatherly type, nor did I appreciate the chores that accompanied fatherhood: shopping, theme parks, helping with homework. But I did miss the companionship with our contrarian daughter. I hoped she'd be anxious to tag along with me at Laurel.

We would be leaving a different country from the one we had arrived in. There would be charges against Arce, the Landless Peasants were on the verge of getting their agrarian reform law, and the ever humble Katari was cleverly resisting the temptations that came with his new celebrity status. I still harbored the hope that, at some time in the future, American racing would see the advantage in outsourcing some of its surplus product to adventurous lands, where I might have some role to play. I felt that the U.S. racing industry would be better served allying itself with racing abroad than with slots and casinos at home and the quasi-legal Caribbean bookies.

Just when I had cleared the unpredictable Muñeca from my mind and was digging in for an attempt to win back Sonia's heart, I received two distressing phone calls from L.A., one from Vince and the other from Muñeca. I was hardly the source of wisdom that my callers had hoped for.

With Sonia at the office, I bundled up in a down jacket at the table near the window that brought in the beloved Inti, the sun god of the trembling Incas. I tried to piece together the two versions. Vince claimed that Muñeca had led him on. "She was flashing cleavage, and I could see all the way up her legs when she was curled in the sofa to watch her soap opera."

Muñeca would later give me her side. "At the dinner table, Vince says things like 'I'd rather eat your boobs than the pizza we just ordered.'"

I clenched the phone. "Lay off, Vince."

He snarled. "What does Matt Bosch have that I don't have?"

So, Vince had done it again. To avoid further inflaming the situation, I refrained from telling him that Muñeca was not a rodeo animal that you roped in. Vince had still not learned to hide certain feelings that were socially unacceptable. He'd let his raw guts spill out. He was still a pathological truth teller, exposing his own human frailties, such as the obscene jealousy that most of us have learned to cover up.

One of Vince's proverbs was "Never take a woman to the track, or you'll lose your pants." But he took Muñeca to the track and instead of seriously playing the horses, he tried to wow her, pressing for a big score that never materialized. He dumped five hundred bucks.

"You sent her to humiliate me," Vince said. "I lost my shirt at the track. But that ain't the end of it."

Piecing the information together from both Vince's and Muñeca's accounts, I learned what had happened. Muñeca was dutifully using my short-form method, and in a particular claiming race she had found that only two horses had qualified. One of them was trained by Carla Gaines. She was considering playing both qualifiers to win. I had not explained anything to her about exotic betting, nor about multiple win bets on overlays.

At that moment, Vince had come across a friend in the clubhouse: Dick Mitchell. Mitchell was a mathematician with a penchant for playing heavily in the exotics pool. He was also an author of racing books and thrived on sharing money-management advice. He was a star of the racing seminar circuit. Vince introduced Mitchell to Muñeca at the moment she was mulling over the short-form bet.

"By all means play them both to win," Mitchell said. "At 9–2 and 8–1 it's worth playing two overlays to win in the same race. But you can also put them in trifectas, wheeling them in all positions with everything that can walk!"

Dick Mitchell marked out the permutations for playing the two short-form horses every which way in trifectas with the only four other horses that he said "can walk."

He explained that when you bet two value horses in a race to win, a back-up bet is called "the trifecta as show bet": use your two overlays in the place and show spots, with the other contenders in the win spot of the trifecta. The idea came from my own "exacta as place bet," where you've played your longshot to win and you back it up by using the longshot in the place hole with the favorite and any other worthy contender in the win slot of the exacta.

"I was so disappointed," Muñeca had explained. "The Carla Gaines horse *almost* won, but in the end he was passed by another horse so he finished second, and my other horse finished third. When the race was over, Dick Mitchell hugged me, and I thought he was hitting on me, and he's a big man and he was squeezing tight, so I wriggled out, but in fact he hugged me to tell me that a longshot finished first, the trifecta would be big, and I had it."

"She collected $495," Vince griped, "and I didn't play it. There was a full moon that night, and I felt romantic. After a steak dinner at Norm's and back at the apartment, I thought she'd be in a better mood, so I made my move, and she went and grabbed my balls. I thought she was encouraging me. You know, letting me know that she wanted it. I figured, maybe she was one of those people who respond to the full moon."

Muñeca's version was purely on the dark side of the moon.

"I couldn't shake off this friend of yours so I squeezed his balls, hard. I tried to hurt him so that he'd shy away. The technique has always worked for me, even with gangsters and lowlifes. I squeeze their balls real tight, and then they back off like scared puppies. But your friend Vince is a phenomenon. He considered it an invitation!"

With Muñeca reneging, Vince resorted to extreme measures. He'd taken out his gun, the one he had bought for the protection he claimed he needed during his bookie days. He'd argued that it would only take one disturbed client to pack him in ice if he did not have protection. I'd told him, to no avail, that he was more likely to be shot by his own gun than to be protected by it.

"You gotta understand," Vince pleaded with me. "This woman is irresistible. So I got my gun and pointed it to the side of my head, and I told her, 'If you scorn me anymore I'll kill myself.' At the moment I really meant it, Matt. So you know what she says?"

"No . . . what?"

"You know what she says to me, Matt?"

"Cut the suspense, Vince. Just tell me."

"I say, 'If you scorn me I'll kill myself,' and she says, 'Go ahead, I dare you.' Imagine, she says, 'Go ahead, I dare you.' Then she asks me to give her the gun and meekly I give it to her, and she goes and hides it. Now what am I gonna do?"

Phone marketing, telephone employment searches, and even phone sex are all easier than phone refereeing. I had tried to cool down Muñeca, and now I was hoping I could get Vince to retreat. I figured I'd have to find another place for Muñeca.

"Now I feel like a scumbag," Vince said.

"How's that, Vince? Did you kick her out?" I groaned. "Don't tell me you kicked her out. You promised me . . ."

"I didn't kick *her* out. She kicked *me* out . . . out of my own apartment!"

I told Vince to knock on the door, shout an apology and promise to be a good boy, and Muñeca would let him back. Knowing Muñeca, sooner or later she would snare a yachtsman from Marina del Rey or a business leader from the Santa Monica Chamber of Commerce. I warned her that if she planned on going to the beach in her bikini, she should choose Marina del Rey, but avoid Venice Beach. Otherwise she'd be hounded by hoods.

And that was just the unimportant news from Southern California! A much bigger story was brewing. An investigative journalist in L.A. named Gary Webster had written a series of articles for the *So-Cal Sentinel* on the illegal arms trade in Latin America and its California dealers. He was now being excoriated for having kept so many of his sources a secret. Various special-interest groups were calling for him to be fired. Marv faxed me the articles, and I could not help but notice what was absent from Webster's articles. He had missed the Bolivian connection, and there was nothing on Panama Slim. Marv egged me on.

"Matt, you got the missing piece to Webster's puzzle," he said. "Why don't you contact him and give him a hand?"

"You have the missing piece, too, Marv. Why don't *you* help him?"

"Shit, Matt, you know damned well that a State Department employee deals under the cloak of diplomacy. That's why I leaked the story to you."

"Yeah, and you seem to want me to get killed by Panama Slim. Didn't you tell me that he was a bull in a china shop and would stop at nothing? Why should I get involved?"

"If you appease Panama Slim," Marv warned, "he'll still want to crush you, especially after what you did to Arce, and what you've done for Katari. Think of it. You saved Katari, maybe even from Slim's own men, and then you go and humiliate Arce. Your *Homage to Katari* CD doesn't help you any in the eyes of Panama Slim. That's equivalent to treason. You might as well nail him before he nails you. All you have to do is stick your neck out for Webster."

"What's in it for you, Marv?"

Marv reminded me of his background in anthropology. "I'd like to take advantage of this great country, travel into the hinterlands, and get to know some of the ethnic groups. But I can't hop around until there's some degree of stability. Believe me, this crazy GBC is a big headache."

Marv explained that Bolivians were wary of the U.S. Embassy after what had happened with Operation Condor, and the diplomatic corps, at least at the lower levels, was trying to make amends. If the GBC flared up, it would be a public relations disaster for the embassy. Most Bolivians would erroneously suspect that the embassy was behind the harebrained scheme of Panama Slim.

Marv urged me to fly to L.A. and meet with Webster. I told him that leaving Sonia alone was out of the question. Marv had all the answers. At the moment of my departure, he would have Sonia move in with his family, and he'd have an embassy guard accompany her wherever she went, up to the moment when she boarded the plane that would take her to Maryland. Sonia's final tasks for the Marianelas could be done electronically, to minimize visits to the office. She was already training the computer-illiterate Sister Gabrielle to take her place.

That afternoon, I picked up Sonia at her office and insisted we walk to the top of Laikakota, that sharp ridge in the center of La Paz. This had been our spot for dreaming together and searching for miracles. We stepped down carefully over the ankle-bending surface that passed for a sidewalk, down into the Choqueyapu Ravine, where you could still smell the former-river-turned-sewer, then up past the concert stadium, scaling a winding sidewalk flanked by eucalyptus trees (foreign invaders that were rugged enough to survive above the tree line but which choked off other vegetation). One by one, stray dogs joined a trailing caravan. I grabbed a stone in my right hand, but the strays were more streetwise than house pets and were unlikely to lunge at us.

We reached a pass. Straight ahead was the Miraflores neighborhood and the modern soccer stadium that seated 50,000 but amazingly had no parking lot. As we neared the top, the landscape evolved into a juxtaposition of rising and descending cubist angles, as the view of the contradictory city opened up on four sides. From the top we could see directly into the glaciers of Illimani, some 30 miles away. On either side, we looked down upon modern high-rises, most of them in various shades of pastel. Farther up were middle-class residential neighborhoods. The rest of the mountainsides in either direction, the *laderas* or "hillsides," were made up of vast slums of partly finished red-brick structures. If you squinted, here and there you could see open sewers that trickled down into the various underground tributaries of the Choqueyapu. Beyond this scene was the magnificent Royal Cordillera.

When Sonia and I would face a major decision, we would find some neutral spot removed from our living quarters in order to sort things out. The advantage of Laikakota was that no one could have followed us without being seen. The expanded view seemed to open up our minds. As usual, we sat on an exposed ledge.

In moments of leisure, Sonia was capable of getting sentimental and excluding reality from her thoughts. But when faced with a dilemma or conflict, she turned into a thinking machine. The issue, of course, was whether or not I should go to L.A. and once and for all stand up to Panama Slim. If I met with Gary Webster, I would have to do it in the open. Slim would know. He was a mean bull who, when cornered, would abandon all tactical sense and engage in frontal battle even if it meant exposing himself to consequences. He had a talent for intimidating away the consequences, and he seemed to have the perfect chromosome combinations for police immunity.

Sonia knew that if I went, I'd stay with Vince and Muñeca.

"I've never cared about the details of your friendship with Muñeca, but I do have the right to intervene when the relationship becomes dangerous."

She knew that Muñeca could go to extremes, sucking me into her crises, as had happened when she'd held Arce captive.

"Let's put it this way," I responded. "She has a knack for pushing the right buttons and gaining control of the people around her."

The exception had been Arce, but she had partly rectified the inconsistency.

Sonia was tough in a completely different way. She'd simply look me straight in the eyes and speak with authority.

"I would much prefer that you stayed, but Marv makes sense. I don't think that this Panama Slim will ever leave us in peace. And besides, this is the right thing to do. It's strange, but I feel as if you'd handle everything perfectly, except I worry about the presence of Muñeca."

Not the slightest hint of jealousy: Sonia was coldly clinical in her analysis. That didn't stop her from shining beautifully in the high-altitude luminosity. No matter how firm her words, her voice remained mellow, and her soft cheeks and delicate jaw-line never sharpened. No cold reasoning could shut off the warm transparency in her dark brown eyes. Her hair was up in a bun, which had the effect of highlighting her large eyes and long eyelashes. I longed for the day when she'd let her hair down and forget about making important decisions.

I recalled the riveting fear leading up to my confrontation with the would-be assassins of Katari, and then my great relief when it was done and over. A confrontation with Panama Slim was even more inescapable. I resolved to use my Mexican-pool-table technique and make sure that whenever and wherever my confrontation with Slim took place, members of the human race would be present. With the help of Gary Webster, I resolved to have the bull wounded before confronting him.

Sonia and I agreed that I'd return to La Paz so that we could fly together to Maryland. She prodded me about my intervention with Katari and about the confrontation with Arce.

"If I didn't know you better, Matt, I'd think that you were becoming principled."

"I'm just a victim of circumstances. Confronting Panama Slim has nothing to do with ideals."

"I'm not so sure. At first there are isolated incidents, but when they come together, you see a pattern."

"The only pattern," I said, "is legitimate self-defense." Grudgingly, I had to admit admiring her for her sense of values. "But so much energy is wasted fighting for ideals that have no chance of becoming reality."

"In this case, Matt, you could be wrong. Arce may end up going to jail, and hundreds of thousands of poor farming people may finally have a new life."

"I'd rather think about you and me in Maryland. I'd go to Laurel in the day, come home, invite you out to dinner, you'd insist on cooking, I'd uncork a bottle of Menetou-Salon, and later that night, we'd roll around together."

"Only if Deedee goes to sleep on time," she said. "And I don't drink anymore. You'll have to serve me grape juice."

TWENTY-SIX

Le Tour de L.A.

I n advance of my trip to L.A., I spoke several times with Gary Webster.
I sent the document about Panama Slim to his private fax, and kept the
original for myself. Separately, I mailed a copy to his apartment address.

At the ripe age of 32, Webster was one of the few remaining investigative journalists in the USA. Tall, blond, and clean-cut, he had the
potential for becoming a star TV reporter, but the mainstream net-
works considered him too hot to handle. I suggested that he really
didn't need me there in person, but Webster insisted. Not only did he
want me to speak with his publisher, who was under pressure to discon-
tinue the series of articles, but he felt that without visible support and
a human accompaniment to the proof I was supplying, he might get
fired. Major interest groups were pouring on the pressure, and even his
fellow journalists were beginning to publish articles in places like the
L.A. Times and *Washington Post*, questioning the reliability of Webster's
sources. In the world of Webster, my role was that of Mexican at the
pool table.

For me, Gary Webster was a simple medium for carrying out the
plan to neutralize Panama Slim. I provoked Marv by insinuating that his
enthusiasm for exposing Panama Slim was simply a small detail in the
rivalry between the State Department and the Department of Defense:
diplomats versus the military-industrial complex.

"On the contrary," Marv argued. "Surely the Department of Defense cannot be comfortable about freelance military operations."

At the baggage carrousel at LAX, Vince and Muñeca were waiting like silent stones. In the parking structure, outside Vince's Opel, Muñeca and I briefly debated as to which one of us would be voluntarily banished to the backseat. Muñeca won out, reformatting herself at an angle where passing truck drivers could look down between her legs from their cabins. Truck drivers would be rear-ending Hondas and flying off overpasses.

The next debate took place in silence between Vince and me, as to which one of us would have the right to stare at Muñeca through the rearview mirror. She wore a subdued pink pleated skirt and a matching top that suggested without confirming. Her long black hair flowed in all the right directions.

The sleeping arrangements were not clear. Vince had a double bed in his bedroom, and then there was the sofa. One of us would have to sleep on the sofa. An ugly triangular dispute could have reared up, were it not for Muñeca, who decided that she would take the sofa and that Vince and I would have to find some way of sleeping in the double.

Vince's Venice apartment, a typical L.A. Spanish-style three-story deal, a motel look-alike, was only two blocks from the beach. The descent from 12,000 feet to sea level left me the extra energy that comes with an immense army of hundreds of thousands red blood cells reinforcing my body's oxygen reserves. Even with a heavy backpack and suitcase weighted down with binoculars, gift boxes of quinoa, and a bottle of Singani, I floated effortlessly up the two flights of Vince's outdoor staircase. For about two or three days, I'd have all this pent-up energy with few ways to use it. Moving around in bed with Muñeca would have been a fine release, but this possibility was promptly scratched from the program. Vince would not tolerate such behavior under his roof. It was already enough to ask him, a sex addict, to lay off Muñeca. He would have erupted in jealous rage if I shared his bed or his sofa with the woman he was hopelessly fixated on.

Vince shrugged.

"It's bad enough that this voluptuous princess is off limits, but with her here, I can't even bring up other women to my place."

"Of course you can! Muñeca wouldn't mind at all."

"Sure, but how do you think my lady friends would react if I take them up here and they walk in the door and they see this sexy feline curled up on my sofa?"

It was late afternoon. We found a bar on the boardwalk and downed a beer. On the way back, I came upon a bicycle rental shop. Here was the answer for my bursting energy. I negotiated a week rental, but the price was too steep, so finally I just bought one of their used bikes. It was basic, but had six speeds on the right handle and three on the left, which added up to 18 speeds, enough to get me up to Gary Webster's newspaper office in downtown L.A. the following morning.

The annual winter rain clouds had not yet emerged over the Pacific horizon, and the jasmine-spiced warmth of L.A. was a welcome contrast to the inhumane cold of La Paz. The next morning, I left for the *Sentinel* office at 7:45. I pedaled up along Venice Boulevard. At La Cienega, I decided to try the L.A. bus-bike system, placing my bike on a rack of the 33 bus, below the front window. I stayed on the bus until the top of the hill at Crenshaw, got off and continued cycling. Venice Boulevard narrowed after Hoover, passing through gangland. I arrived at Olive, as if I'd passed through a portal and come out on the other side in Mexico City. I swung left on Olive for a few blocks. I spotted a parking lot right in front of the Sentinel Building. I usually negotiate with parking attendants for a safe spot for my bike near their cabin.

I never got that far. On the street in front of the *Sentinel*, in a No Parking zone, a big dark Buick monopolized the scene. It was Panama Slim's. Slim was bulging in the front seat. He would have fit better on a tractor. No time to consider how he found out I'd be showing up at the *Sentinel*. He might have been waiting for Webster, planning a preemptive strike. Webster's previous article had announced, with fanfare, an upcoming piece about the L.A.-Bolivia arms-trafficking connection.

I got back on the saddle, hoping that Slim had not seen me. My plan had been to confront him after he'd been softened up by Webster. My plan also involved having a friendly audience when facing off against Slim. Olive Street, in this parking-lot-office-building district, was deserted.

Surely he would immediately associate the man in the brand-new counterfeit Huyustus jeans and the azure Bolívar soccer jersey as Matt Bosch. Had I been wearing something more generic, I might not have caught his attention. His bulging eyes went from the jersey to the man in it, and he saw it was me. He opened the car door and got out.

The swelling urge to have it out once and for all was rapidly replaced by intelligent cowardice. He'd likely be toting a gun, and even if he wasn't, our relative sizes were the difference between his Buick and my bicycle.

"Traitor, we have an account to settle!"

"Yeah, you owe me," I shouted.

I wasn't hanging around for a response, but thanks to his boom box voice, I heard it anyway.

"Bosch, you fucking rodent, I'm gonna churn you into dog food."

I wheeled down Olive against traffic on a one-way street. From behind me I could hear Slim's door open and slam shut. The Buick revved up and blasted out behind me.

My plan of self-preservation was simple. Get caught by a cop going the wrong way on a one-way street. I'd explain to the cop afterwards. Let him take me in. It was the only safe option.

In my days of car commuting, on these same streets near the garment district, whenever I made an illegal move, there was always a cop waiting around the corner. Now no cop could be seen. Slim's Buick morphed into a panther in pursuit. The old bull had no scruples about driving the wrong way on a one-way street. If I played my cards right, the cops would let me roll by and stop Slim. I turned right on Venice. Traffic was backed up, and Slim would have to brake. I slipped through the space between the line of traffic and the parked cars, hoping a door from a parked car would not suddenly jerk open in front of me. Cyclers call it "getting doored." I left Slim way behind and increased the odds in my favor by passing through a red light.

I turned right at Normandie, and then swooped left into another one-way street lined with tall leaning palm trees, against the traffic, parallel to Venice Boulevard. I was heading in the direction of Vince's apartment, but I expected to be stopped by a patrol car long before my arrival. I heard a revving motor behind me, also against traffic. Hadda be Slim.

Who else would disrespect the strict L.A. traffic laws, the Holy Scriptures of this city that was built for the automobile!

Where were all the squad cars? No matter how hard and fast I pumped the pedals, the potent blend of flowing adrenaline mixed with a mighty reserve army of red blood cells prevented fatigue from setting in. Having been a bicycle commuter, I knew the ins and outs of the most complex traffic jams. The streets of L.A. had become the extension of my own veins and arteries.

Luckily, a car came at me head on. I flowed to the side and glided on. Slim would have no room to pass. I turned left on Crenshaw, back to Venice Boulevard. A 33 bus was on its way to Venice Beach and Santa Monica. At this downhill stretch where the road widened and traffic thinned out, Slim's Buick would have an advantage over my bike. Slim's car was still out of sight. I slipped my bike on the rack in the front of the bus and hopped on. Slim would not expect me to be on the bus. I'd advance partway in the bus, wait until traffic was backed up and then hop off.

The backup came at the freeway underpass between Fairfax and Centinela, where the bus had stopped for what I knew was the longest red light in all of L.A. I gladly passed through the red, increasing my chances of being stopped by a patrol car. I would have been honored to hear the sirens coming upon me from behind. Where was the LAPD when you needed it? I barreled through the intersection. A semi that had just come off the freeway was turning right in front of me. I swerved and nearly went down. I could hear the driver's "Hey, cocksucking idiot" dissipating in the sweet jasmine air.

We were two miles south of Hollywood. Had this been the L.A. of Hollywood cinema, Slim's Buick would have barreled into the semi. I continued cycling along Venice Boulevard, passing faded carbon copies of generic mini-malls, approaching Culver City, trying to conjure up the location of the Culver City police station. I knew it was near, and in fact, I had once been there to report a stolen bicycle, but evidently premature senility had set in, enriched by panic. I could not place the police station in my mind. It made no sense to ride around in circles looking for it, nor to stop and waste time asking someone who might not even know.

L.A. gangland should have been swarming with police. I saw *cholos* with red bandanas, I saw Salvadoran cleaning ladies. I saw illegal workers hanging out on a corner waiting to be picked up for an under-the-table day job. With the total absence of the cops, everything seemed so quiet and calm that the silent hordes could have heard my heart thumping.

I wheeled through Culver City, by the Versailles Cuban restaurant to my right, and finally located a through side street in Mar Vista with the ubiquitous rows of palms, trying to outfox my pursuer. This time I went with the traffic. No time to go sideways in search of another one-way street. My side street ended in a T-junction at Sepulveda so I had to swing left. There was no gap in the onrushing traffic, but I cut through anyway, causing brakes to screech and enraged curses to flow freely, and then hung another right back onto Venice Boulevard.

Bad move! I had turned right precisely in front of Slim's Buick. He must have made up ground by passing every red light on Venice Boulevard, while I was trying to finesse it on the side street. He gained on me until I could see the shadow of his Buick stretching from behind.

A shot rang out. I knew it had missed me because I kept rolling. I swung right past a row of garages, hoping that I could follow the between-block alleys as far as I could take them until Slim's Buick would be blocked by a garbage truck or a street-soccer game or a moving van. I got lucky. College kids with UCLA tee shirts had parked in the center of the alley, in the process of moving boxes from the trunk. I zipped by them, nearly scraping a garage. I could imagine that Slim would brandish his gun and frighten them into the car and out of his way, or if not, he'd simply bang into the car as if it were a bowling pin.

I took nothing for granted. I vaguely remembered a police station on Lincoln Boulevard, but I couldn't recall *left* or *right* so I got back onto Venice. I thanked the Sun God that there was a traffic backup and gained the distance of two football fields from Slim. Eventually he barreled through the jam, but I was already turning onto the street of Vince's apartment. My stupid reflex was to stop and lock the bicycle, but I caught myself in the act, dumped the bike on the grass, and sprinted up the stairs. Until I got to the door, I hadn't realized how much energy I'd expended. I had been saved by traffic jams, one-way streets, students parked in alleys, and a reserve army of red blood cells, imported from the Andes.

Once inside I bolted the door shut. Muñeca was on the couch, watching a quiz show.

"She watches these dumb programs, Matt," Vince said.

"It's good for practicing my English," an outraged Muñeca responded.

"Hey, Matt, you look perturbed. Your face is all flushed. Are you okay?"

"Panama Slim," I blurted out. "He . . ."

We heard a heavy hand thumping on the door. The whole building shook. The neighbors were absent. Either they were at work, or they were gripped by fear and sat tight behind locked doors.

"Don't open, Vince," I hollered.

Slim was the Big Bad Wolf. He demanded that we open the door. No diplomacy. I told Vince to call 911. Muñeca was up and tugging at my sweaty Bolívar jersey, asking what was going on. I was too hyper to enjoy the brush of her body.

Slim banged on the door.

"You better split," Vince shouted. "I called the cops."

"Split? I'm gonna split this door open."

Muñeca disappeared into the hall. Vince shouted at Slim to get the fuck out of there. Knowing that Slim had a gun, I pushed Vince away from the door. We heard the crack of a gunshot, the bolt snapped, and the door boomed open. I saw Slim's Hawaiian shirt, his bushy eyebrows, his furious eyes that had turned livid green, and then I heard what sounded like an elephant fart.

Slim collapsed.

I turned around. Muñeca was standing behind us, Vince's gun in her hand.

"Shit, Muñeca, you pulled the fucking trigger. You saved my life!"

Defiance never looked so profoundly beautiful as it did in the dark eyes of Muñeca.

Slim was now a whale washed ashore.

"That wasn't for you, Matt. It was for my brother."

The cops arrived within minutes, but too late to save Panama Slim. The rest was a long bout of interrogation followed by rounds of paperwork. Paperwork determined that Muñeca had shot in legitimate self-defense. The break-in theory was supported by ample material evidence: the door and the shot-out bolt and the gunpowder on the hands of the man who had broken and entered. Muñeca was clean. It wasn't even her gun that shot Slim. One of the two cops had instantly fallen in love with Muñeca. That quickened the process.

Muñeca sat in the backseat of the squad car. My bicycle was still there on the front lawn. I ran it upstairs and into the apartment. We followed in Vince's car. This time I located the police station. Had I found it before arriving at Vince's apartment, Slim would still be alive, and Muñeca would still be thirsting for revenge.

Muñeca put in two hours of court-ready deposition, rendering redundant the Spanish-English interpreter, since she was thrilled to flaunt her English skills before a court stenographer and tape recorder. Vince and I were also witnesses. Muñeca was given two days to depart for Bolivia. We could have fought it. Clearly the police were cutting costs, sparing themselves an elaborate paperwork process with the Department of Immigration and Naturalization. Muñeca was ordered to not say a word in public about the event.

On the way out of the police station we were politely accosted by a smart-looking woman in a corporate business suit. She said she represented the National Rifle Association. She invited Muñeca to appear in an ad (the beginning of her USA career as a model?). I spotted a twinkle in Muñeca's eyes, and she was up on her toes, looking agile and ready to act. Vince grimaced, his clean-cut face morphing into a grotesque expressionist portrait, like the silently screaming figure on the bridge. Before she could conjure up her response, I intervened, acting as if I were her lawyer, thanking the woman and explaining that there was a police gag order. Needless to say, the extra publicity and an extended stay for Muñeca would mean big-time trouble for the three of us.

Paperwork also determined that my information on Panama Slim and his illegal support of paramilitaries was run in the next Gary Webster article. The shooting of Slim gave Webster's article extra pizzazz. Muñeca became an unnamed lady tourist from South America.

Paperwork also determined the fate of Gary Webster. Slim had not been a lone ranger. There were forces around him that wielded influence on the media. They faxed and phoned the newspapers and TV channels. They threatened the *Sentinel*. The already besieged Webster was down on the canvas. Channel 7's *Eye on L.A.* went so far as to allege that Webster's investigation had led to the death of one of L.A.'s prominent citizens. Webster took the count of 10 and was fired. An elaborate set of documents, drawn up painstakingly by corporate lawyers, showed that Webster was guilty of libel against Howard Stoner, aka Panama Slim, and other favorite sons of the Southland.

I phoned Channel 7 and offered a rebuttal. They connected me from one office to another until one of the editors finally told me that my documents were of no use because their programming required visual content.

What better visual than Muñeca? She was a walking, swaying, reverberating document. She was the real visual thing. But a TV appearance on *Eye on L.A.* would break the gag order and reopen the case, not at all in Muñeca's interest.

The following morning, the four of us (Webster was the new member of our gang) sat on Vince's balcony, overlooking a swimming pool with leaves and debris floating on its surface. I had brewed the coffee. Vince had brought croissants from a nearby bakery. You'd never know we were in the desert. There were magnolia trees, maple trees, jasmine, and noisy Japanese gardeners arranging an array of flowers, trimming hedges, cutting grass, using water that was piped in 400 miles from Mono Lake.

I vetoed any idea of Muñeca risking her safe passage. But what say did I have? She was toying with the idea of speaking about Slim to the media. If you saw her, you'd imagine that she had just climbed Everest without the aid of an oxygen bottle, that she'd piloted a glider over the Grand Canyon, that she'd won a gold medal.

"When I return to Bolivia," she said, "I will not return to the same life. I no longer have to do things out of necessity. I have choices I've never before had."

Webster backed me up. "If you talk to the media, Muñeca, they'll eat you alive. My job cannot be salvaged, no matter how you present the story."

"But they're whitewashing Panama Slim," she said.

"Slim's finished," Vince said. "He's a nonfactor."

Back inside, the phone rang. Vince went through the open glass door and picked it up. The call was for Muñeca, in Spanish. From her side of the dialogue I gleaned that it had to do with her legal status. If she did not leave the country, as agreed, the police could change their minds and press charges.

We went back to the balcony, and she filled in details.

"It's a threat," I explained.

Webster spoke with authority. "The arms traffickers don't want a trial where they might be exposed. It's business as usual. Strange, I have all this hot information, and no one wants to publish it."

For me, the solution was brilliantly clear.

"Gary, I think your best interest is to find a new job in Iowa or Kansas covering high school basketball and tornadoes."

For Muñeca, I had a whole encyclopedia of evidence that she should abandon any idea of breaking her promise to the cops. I had worked in the L.A. courts as an interpreter and paralegal. I dealt with the same courts when I was my own lawyer in my divorce proceedings. It was easier to predict the result of a horse race at Hollywood Park than a court case on Hill Street.

Two days later, Vince and I drove Muñeca to LAX. Muñeca and I embraced before she entered the checkpoint. For the first time as long as I'd known her, she cried. Muñeca didn't just sob. She broke down. She let out a strange "I'm sorry, Matt" between the heaving. She hugged me tighter than she'd ever done before, even during the most intense love-making. I felt strength in her arms and soaring self-confidence. *Sorry for something she did or sorry for something she was going to do or sorry for something she had not done?* It was too late to sit down with her and hash it out.

It was a very different Muñeca who boarded that plane, a person I would have loved to get to know better. So long as Arce put his dignity above his raw ego and let her be, Muñeca would be safe and free to enter so many open doors that were waiting for a fearless woman with a level of mellow serenity that would make a Buddhist envious.

TWENTY-SEVEN

The Ultimate Exotic

I needed to recover from the dizzying days of Muñeca and Slim and Arce and Katari, to recapture my balance. The place to go for this therapy was Hollywood Park. We went in Vince's old Opel, arriving in Inglewood in time for a late breakfast/early lunch in a dumpy but authentic Mexican restaurant. It was my choice. Slick Mexican restaurants offer a bland, sanitized version of the real thing. Back in Bolivia, a Latin American country, authentic Mexican food was hard to come by. Missing the USA involved missing the races, missing friends, missing the Baltimore Orioles, jazz at the Blue Note, the Albany Public Library, Los Angeles City College, *The Simpsons* in English, and Mexican food.

The plan was for Vince and me to go over the *Racing Form*, with Gary, the now freelance journalist, getting a feel for our own special form of investigative journalism: deciphering the past performances. A potential new series on "the oval stock exchange" would be less aggravating for Webster than the one on illegal arms trafficking. He would have to decide whether regular players were marginal misfits or men (and renegade women) on a meaningful mission.

Gary's presence altered the usual dynamics, with Gary and Vince shifting from the racing pages to the past performances of Panama Slim. We still hadn't recovered from the dramatic shock of Slim's sudden demise. Gary had done his research. He had years of contextual clues that would help him piece things together. Slim ran the guns to fuel the paramilitaries, Gary explained, and the gun that killed Muñeca's brother most likely came from Slim, as did the brazenness of the armed goons.

Vince ordered *huevos con chorizo*. He was lean and wiry, and his muscle was impervious to the loads of fat in his preferred foods. A fresh salad couldn't even make Vince's also-eligible list. "You can have the rabbit food," he'd say to me. Gary asked for the most American-looking thing on the menu, a burger with fries, just wishing to survive the meal. I scanned for what I had missed the most, which turned out to be enchiladas in mole (pronounced *moleh*). *Mole*, the Mexican curry with 18 different spices, contained a hint of chocolate, which would fit well with my newfound peace of mind. The word *chocolate* came from the Aztec Nahuatl word *chocolatl*.

The conversation shifted to the day's races, and Vince and I explained the menu of betting alternatives, ending with the Pick 6, the "ultimate exotic" because 877 things had to happen in synchronicity in order for a player to hit this type of bet (which requires picking six winners in six consecutive races, and which can pay off in six figures on a longshot day). You could have 876 things figured out, and be on your way to a big score. Yet, one apparently isolated event, such as a horse that should have been a come-from-behinder challenging for the early lead against what should have been *your* lone front-runner, could burst your bubble. The unexpected front-runner would eventually fade, but not before he dueled your horse, thus preventing a walk-away victory, with the end result being that you have five winners instead of six.

I knew people who'd hit it for six figures. But I knew of no one who'd performed the feat twice. Barry Meadow was mathematically correct in warning smaller players that it would be better for even the best handicapper in the world to buy in on a piece of someone else's $4,800 ticket than to go it alone for $48. I had once collected on a Breeders' Cup Pick 6 by being part of a syndicate that did all the right permutations and cost-saving devices, including primary tickets, secondary tickets, A horses, B horses, and C horses. In the end, the investment was so large that each of us got back only 5–2 for our investment.

And then there was the time at Santa Anita with an extended carryover and hundreds of thousands in the betting pool when all the big syndicates struck out, and one of the two winning tickets had been bought by an old woman visiting from Oklahoma who had used her social security number.

Gary Webster sipped his coffee and listened like an earnest graduate student. He must have been out of journalism school for at least a decade.

"Why of course!" he said. The apple had just plopped on Newton's head. "I've studied this event thoroughly, and I think you have experienced the ultimate exotic."

He stared into my eyes as if he were my therapist.

"Brace yourself, Matt," he said. "Everything fits. All 877 pieces!"

Gary had not spent more than a few minutes scanning the past performances, and in his mind they still must have seemed like the façade of a Mayan temple. For Gary, this ultimate exotic went beyond the day's races.

"This is one find that I will never be able to write about!" There was a childlike sense of wonderment in his voice. "Matt, I can tell you that it's Muñeca who's scored what you call the ultimate exotic. Can't you see? She saw in you a chance to savor her sweetest revenge. She met you, and she began toying with a vast set of probabilities, ever since she gave you her business card at Arce's ranch.

"In the beginning I'm sure she was improvising, the way you do when you begin to read the horses' past performances. At some moment she knew that she had to make a difficult choice as to who was most responsible for the killing of her brother. She had long ago eliminated the guy who pulled the trigger from consideration. She knew where the real power lay. Arce and Slim were the main contenders, what you call the co-favorites. She decided in the end, not without hesitation, and nearly betting on the other candidate, that it was Slim. But even before that decision, she figured that you were the one who could help her carry through with her project. She didn't trust any other Bolivian. Bolivians were either too forgiving to seek revenge or too complicit with the system to let her get away with it. From then on, she softened you up and molded you through a complex series of steps, where hundreds of events, macro and micro, needed to fall into place."

I challenged Gary Webster. I felt that Muñeca had first slept with me because I had inadvertently played hard to get. Webster disagreed. He felt that she had "selected" me for a different reason, that I was the type of man who was soft enough to be manipulated but loyal enough to hang tough through a long commitment. But she also needed a perfect context, where even if she would not be in control of all the details, she'd be in a position to bend reality when it came upon her.

"When she got you to go to Santa Cruz and you became her accomplice, she felt you would be her enabler and her protector. Her big exotic revenge was supposed to be killing Arce. If in the end she didn't do it, don't think it was a lack of guts. Her indecision did not stem from fear but rather from uncertainties as to whether or not Arce was the main man. She weighed the factors. Arce was just as mean as Slim and maybe worse. But he was also slicker than Slim, more aware of his image. He was that type of Latin descending from the seventeenth century who was dominated by the image others had of him. If only for public relations or his image among his people, he couldn't have been associated with anyone who killed a young teenager for a nebulous strategy of terror. Arce was too meticulous to throw out the baby with the bath water. I could see this in the way you describe his gardens, Matt."

I tried to interrupt Gary's monologue. He flashed the palm of his right hand, explaining that I was too close to the story to see it objectively, that he was a trained investigative reporter, and that I should hear him out. He continued.

"Slim, on the other hand, wasn't big on nuance. He wasn't concerned about consequences. So he was entirely capable of planting the seeds of anarchy by pouring those rifles into Bolivia, knowing they'd fall into the hands of vicious criminals. Muñeca could have very well hesitated about eliminating Arce simply because she felt she'd lose her chance at getting her revenge at the source, which she felt was Slim."

"She couldn't have planned her trip to L.A.," I said. "It was *my* idea all along to slip her out of Bolivia."

"Matt, don't underestimate her ability to connive, and to do so with great patience. She knew Slim was in L.A. She knew that if you went there, he'd find you. She knew that he'd be fuming about your having saved Katari and recorded a CD in his honor. Wasn't it she who had you save Katari, when she could have done it herself?"

I objected. "I had nothing to do with making that CD, nor with labeling it in homage to Katari. That was the Bolivian underground economy."

"Or it could have been Muñeca! Makes no difference. You saved Katari. That's what counts. Slim was too broad-brush in his thinking to realize that his project had a better chance with a live Katari. That was the difference between Slim and Arce. Arce's strategy was to use people. Slim preferred eliminating those he considered an obstacle, even if that created greater obstacles down the line. That's why he was incapable of understanding that his country could control the canal better once it came into Panamanian ownership.

"Muñeca knew that Slim had the mentality of a steamroller. Muñeca knew he'd hunt you down. She knew you could bring him to her."

"Wait a minute," Vince said. "She didn't find out I had that gun, Gary, until after this so-called plan you've discovered. There's too many things she didn't know."

"If I understood what you've explained," Gary said, "when you win a Pick 6, you don't know everything that's going to happen. You try to position yourself in a way that the breaks will fall in your favor. And you need unanticipated breaks in order to cash. It's not entirely deterministic. Not the way you've explained it to me.

"If you didn't have the gun, Vince," Gary Webster continued, "she would have found another way. She'd have gone for a kitchen knife."

When you hear everyone around you speaking in Spanish, you figure none of them know English. Both servers and diners all looked like recent immigrants who hadn't studied English in high school. But just in case someone could hear us, unlikely with the jukebox blaring *norteña* polkas, and just in case they could understand our words, I decided to bring everything down to a whisper.

"Gary, are you telling me that the killing of Slim was premeditated?"

"The Arce kidnapping was premeditated," Webster said. "So why not Muñeca's final step?"

"I think we better change the subject," Vince said. "It happened in my apartment. I don't wanna hear any of this stuff. I might get questioned by the police, and I don't want these crazy ideas in my mind."

Vince was right. If Gary convinced him that the whole thing was premeditated, he'd have to sing it all to whoever questioned him. Vince needed to be shielded from sensitive information that might work against him. He had never outgrown his mania for telling the truth.

I took Gary aside, with the pretext of showing him a Mexican plate at the buffet.

"Gary, you better tell Vince that this is just a fictional plot in your mind. Tell him that Muñeca had no way to plan it, that this story of premeditation was just some wild speculation."

"Matt, you couldn't prove my theory in a court of law, so there's no reason to be concerned."

"Yes there is. Eventually we'll have to answer questions at a deposition. Vince has a syndrome that prevents him from dissimulating. He sings the truth the way a patient's knee pops up when the doctor taps it with a hammer."

"Okay, Matt, I'll drop it. But it makes sense. Muñeca manipulated you to serve her plans for sweet revenge."

I tossed it around. Most human beings manipulate. Even a perfect marriage involves some manipulation between husband and wife. Sonia manipulated me to go to Bolivia. I manipulated her to live in Maryland. Gandhi manipulated the masses, and he was a saintly man. Even Mother Teresa manipulated the world media. Some people manipulate in a coarse way, with public relations and false statistics. Muñeca manipulated with style and with artistic subtlety. I felt no shame for having succumbed. Good for her if she pulled off "the ultimate exotic." So long as I finally had my peace of mind.

Gary and I filed away the dangerous story, and went back to the Hollywood Park past performances. Just when I had been about to embark on a rare flight of tranquility, I had to harbor the potential of Vince spilling the truth, no truth serum needed. But Gary Webster had agreed to self-censor the truth he'd discovered. After a few minutes of eyeing the first-race past performances, my concerns had dissipated, and my mind was liberated for a day at the races.

It was a memorable day, not because of any ultimate exotic, but thanks to the sense of great refuge, which allowed me to make a few good decisions. If my past performance kicked in, I would lose more bets than I'd win, but I would cash in on automatic plays based on the trainer stats. There were horses trained by Richard Matlow and Carla Gaines on the card, and the short-form method allowed me a safe and efficient operating structure. If there had been any epiphany during this soothing afternoon in 70 degree balm at Hollywood Park, it was the culmination of a great discovery. Even before the horses went to post for the first race, I no longer doubted it. Trainer statistics now outweighed speed, pace, form, or class as the primary factor in horse race handicapping.

I had yet another batch of research stats to prove my point, thanks to Kevin Maki, a Ph.D. and professional medical researcher. Maki and I had shared trainer research before, and I had his new findings as a confidence booster. He used a mechanical method to isolate contenders. His mechanical computer method normally came up with 25 percent winners over thousands of races, without considering the trainer stat. He then subjected all his contenders to the trainer win percentage for the 365 days prior to the race.

Cɪ Tʀ%	#Rᴀᴄᴇꜱ	#Wɪɴɴᴇʀꜱ	%Wɪɴ	Pᴀʏ, $	ROI ᴘᴇʀ $
All	22611	5814	25.7	$37,115.20	0.821
<=9	3356	660	19.7	$5,354.90	0.798
>=14	14351	4094	28.5	$23,855.80	0.831
>=16	11898	3474	29.2	$19,794.80	0.832
>=18	9284	2827	30.5	$15,667.30	0.844
>=20	7528	2376	31.6	$12,871.30	0.855
>=22	5375	1780	33.1	$9,262.30	0.862
>=24	3512	1214	34.6	$6,127.20	0.872
>=26	2175	778	35.8	$3,720.60	0.855

You could say, with these stats, that even with *identically qualified horses*, 16 percent trainers win nearly 10 percent more than 9 percent trainers. Once you get above a 25 percent trainer win rate, the return on investment declines somewhat because of a lower average payout (probably due to the fact that at a certain level, trainer-win percentage begins to have a greater impact on pari-mutuel consciousness). What I liked about these foundation stats was that they came before being refined by more specialized statistics, such as layoff, stretchout, or first-time starter. A good trainer-specialty stat would bring the return on investment into the profit range.

It had to be that way. The other factors all depended on relations of chaos between multiple variables. But the trainer factor was crafty manipulation. Muñeca's ultimate exotic was a metaphor for a human being manipulating the multiple factors around her. It was not pure determinism, but it did reflect the greatest possible control over unpredictable circumstances. A victory for a Matlow first-time starter required the type of long-term patience that culminated in a blip of time lasting a minute and 12 seconds. A Carla Gaines horse that won when stretching out for the first time required careful attention to detail, new leg bandages every day, patient gallops, monitoring of eating and drinking habits, over a period of weeks and sometimes months.

The race card unfolded slowly, as if I had successfully frozen time. But before I could entirely savor the afternoon, it had melted into the ninth and final race. I was up for the day, thanks to a wire-to-wire route win of a Carla Gaines horse and a class dropper in a maiden claiming race facing proven losers at the level. I'd lost all my other bets, but in racing, a winning bottom line depends on the average mutuel more than the percentage of winners.

I hoped that the Richard Matlow horse, Determinist, would end up as the perfect example of my trainer findings. All the right signs popped up. First-time starter, maiden claiming race, slow workouts, and low-percentage rider, Barahona: all the needed circumstances that would discourage betting action on this horse. This was my last race before flying back to La Paz the next day. Win or lose, it would be a fitting end to a week of supreme anguish. The ultimate epiphany was the discovery of a truth and not necessarily the winning of one particular horse race.

I played Determinist to win and place, at 9–1. If Dick Mitchell had been there, I might have explored the exotics, but my red blood cell reserve had dissipated, the adrenaline was used up, and my power of concentration drained. In the absence of maximum mental intensity, the horseplayer should keep it simple.

Determinist got off smoothly and cruised to a length lead. By the turn for home he was three lengths ahead. He changed leads seamlessly and appeared to be drawing off. At that very moment an airplane was following its flight path over Hollywood Park for its landing at nearby LAX. Normally Hollywood Park regulars are immune to the roar of the engines, but it seemed as if Determinist had gotten distracted. One horse left the pack from behind and made his way closer and closer to Determinist.

My psychological time expanded like the universe after the Big Bang. During the near-eternity of the stretch, the challenging horse moved boldly, managing to draw side by side with Determinist. When the wire came up, the rival's nose was three inches ahead. The photo sign flashed, but I knew that Determinist had been caught. The rest of the field was nine lengths back.

Matlow had done his job. The horse had fulfilled his contract. When you finish second by a nose, nine lengths better than the rest of the field, you've run the equivalent of a winning race, even in defeat. I'll never know if the airplane had distracted Determinist or if he'd simply been defeated by a new superstar. There are always unanticipated variables.

But a more ominous sign emerged from this race. Just as my Tomlinson turf-pedigree method was a successful automatic investment but not a permanent one, Matlow's apparent determinism would eventually come to an end, maybe now, maybe a few years down the road. If I saw him snatch more defeats from the jaws of victory, I would have to consider getting off.

Trainer specialty bets should be seen in a choice portfolio, like a mutual fund. At any given time, two-thirds of the profitable trainers might continue in the right direction while a third would be past their prime, with some of those on the down escalator. My research of automatic bets on trainers with hit rates of 30 percent within profitable specialty categories resulted in a subsequent collective win rate of 21 percent, enough to sustain a positive return on investment but not enough to literally reproduce the past performance of those trainers.

Through this research I could learn, or at least infer, that Matlow's star would probably stop shining one day. It had taken him many months of patience to sharpen Determinist for his debut race. The plan was to win. Ninety-nine percent of the plan had been effective. Matlow had been through this before. In the past he would not lose a night's sleep over the day's misfortune, but that could change.

For the time being he would collect his consolation purse, and I would collect my place bet. He would have other debut horses in future months and years, while working with his small stable 24 hours a day, seven days a week, 365 days a year. At that moment, his first-time starters showed a positive return on investment of 17 cents on the dollar for a period of nearly two decades. That was better than the Dow-Jones Industrial Index, but with considerably less fanfare. And yet, as I had learned with the eventual decline of my turf-pedigree bets, automatic betting does not mean a permanent system. This was my great research realization, and I was relieved by it. As happens in all financial markets with even the best of automatic investments, one day things change. Was Determinist's performance validation of the continuity of the Matlow method or the very first sign of an eventual flat-bet loss? Now I no longer would fret about it.

Matlow's feats surmounted steeper obstacles and fulfilled greater challenges than those of blockbuster actors or hack politicians, but we lived in a celebrity culture and he would remain virtually anonymous. I felt privileged to live a life that could appreciate the Richard Matlows and Carla Gaineses.

It was unimaginable that whole countries and cultures could exist without horse racing. The next day I would be traveling to one of them. The racing culture would have fit beautifully in the warm lowlands of Bolivia, but the adventure of a new track in the hinterlands looked finished. It was as if I were traveling to the funeral of a dead dream.

TWENTY-EIGHT

Five-Star Prison

Once back in Bolivia, I needed to meet with two people, just to straighten things out. Both meetings were sensitive. I chose the easiest one first, with Marv.

Marv made no effort to hide his joy at the news of Slim's death. For many an embassy employee, at least those working directly with the State Department, Slim had been a dangerous free radical and potential diplomatic embarrassment.

Marv and I sipped margaritas in the South Zone at a restaurant with tropical decor advertised as "Mexican Bar" in English. The food was bordering on tasteless. But these were the best margaritas in town.

My friendship with Marv encountered one great obstacle: the truth. The version he had heard, and the same one that I was reinforcing, was that of a killing in self-defense. It was entirely plausible.

"I have this strange feeling as if I had been an accomplice," Marv said. "I was the one who granted her the visa. If it had been a murder, my superiors would be checking into how the visa had been issued."

In a Pick 6, there's an average of 48 horses spanning the six races, and all 48 have to fit perfectly within the scheme of things for a player to win the bet. Even losing horses have to run a certain way so as to not affect the dynamics of a race, or to affect it in the right way for the benefit of the winning horse. In Muñeca's complex permutation that led to the death of

Panama Slim, Marv was one of those 48 pieces, and probably one of the most important ones, even though he had not figured directly in the outcome. Muñeca's ultimate exotic could not have come to fruition had Marv not been willing to bend procedural rules and grant her the quick visa.

"Could be the most important visa I ever approved," he said, following his third margarita. "Now I can indulge in my passion for field studies in ethnology without the fear of an 'ugly American' incident connected with Panama Slim."

The Margarita Effect was in full force, prompting me to be more loose-tongued than usual. I managed to resist the temptation of letting Marv in on the truth. And besides, that was Gary Webster's truth. I wasn't obligated to accept it.

Once outside the restaurant, Marv and I resolved to get together for a Baltimore Orioles game. With diplomatic immunity, he could drive his car back to upper La Paz with four margaritas under his belt with no threat from the police. He dangled the keys, asking if I'd prefer to drive. I was no less tipsy than he was. It would have been a sorry bit of irony, after having confronted so much danger and emerging unscathed, if I had succumbed to a mundane automobile accident. Year after year, motor vehicle deaths outnumber war deaths. Statistically, trains and subways are the safest transportation wagers while automobiles show a horrendous flat-bet loss. And yet our municipal leaders continue to make bad bets on cars.

Standing outdoors at night in La Paz, I could not help but recall my kidnapping. My reflex reaction was to scan 360 degrees, across the boulevard, behind trees, into dark windows of parked cars, groping to make sure that a new band of thugs was not present.

"Long live the Pachamama," Marv said. "Let's go back in there and order some stiff coffee."

SONIA WAS BUBBLING with good news. Arce had been arrested and jailed on suspicion of murder, related to the body that was dug up on his ranch. A new political party had been formed among former miners, small farmers, and school teachers, and Katari was being proposed as one of its congressional candidates. The Landless Peasants had received temporary legal papers and were building infrastructure, with the spirited support of the Marianela Sisters cheerleaders.

At the same time, large landowners were bracing for a desperate defense of their rights. Two landless peasants were murdered in the Chaco, a remote region where local police are totally under the control of the landed oligarchy.

This bad news only served to magnify Sonia's frustration with me. "You can't remain neutral on a moving train," she said to me, quoting the title of an American author. In the shower she would hum the song "Which Side Are You On?" and when she came out wrapped in a Bolivian towel depicting a llama, I would tell her that she had lost her capacity for subtle communication. Then, without much of a thought, I blurted it out.

"Hey, Sonia, today's visiting day at the San Pedro Prison. What do you say we go visit Arce?"

I felt that if Sonia got to know him, she might see that the world was more complex than the good guys against the bad guys. In that way, she might be more tolerant of what she perceived as my waffling.

"Do you mean to say you're still harboring the hope for your race-track? I can't believe it!"

"Please remember what Muñeca did to Arce! I think I owe it to her to go and urge Arce to not take revenge. And besides, you might learn something."

"You don't even know if he'll want to see you."

"I suspect he will."

Like most places in upper La Paz, the San Pedro Prison was in walking distance. We carried our passports as identification. On the way over to Plaza San Pedro, I detoured to El Prado where I stopped at a cigar stand and bought a five-pack of Cohibas for Arce.

There are two entrances to the San Pedro Prison. The gate that faces the park is for the common prisoners. Around the northeast corner was an arch that led into the five-star section of the prison. There's quite an array of celebrities in there, from high-profile drug traffickers to bank officials accused of corruption: anyone who can pay their way into a more comfortable cell. The guards took our passports as collateral and led us into a yard, where Sonia ducked to avoid a flying soccer ball. Several young boys along with a skinny girl were kicking the ball around. Makeshift goals had been marked by rags at both ends of the prison yard. No doubt these were children or nephews of prisoners.

Arce came out on a tottering balcony from his second-floor apartment.

"Are you sure you wanna see us?" I asked.

"By all means, as long as you're not coming to lynch me."

We entered at ground level and scaled a cramped and creaking spiral staircase, taking care to not bump our heads on the cracking adobe ceiling.

A tiny sitting room faced the cement yard, with a small pressed-wood table and three folded beach chairs leaning against it. Up two steps from the sitting room, split-level style, was a narrow kitchen with a waist-high refrigerator and a hotplate on a linoleum counter. The staircase continued upwards to Arce's sleeping room. In the window of the sitting room was a flower pot with two plants: chili pepper and cilantro.

I introduced Arce to Sonia. He recognized her from a TV interview. They shook hands.

"If you want to know about the body they dug up, I can't talk about it. Lawyer's instructions."

"I didn't come here as a judge," I said.

"But your beautiful wife has certainly already judged me."

Sonia didn't blink. "What excuse can there be, Arce, for torture and murder?"

"In the 1970s and '80s, your School of the Americas encouraged South American military people to do *everything* within our power to fight the communists. There was a communist threat, if you have not forgotten. I'm not saying that the extremes were right, and I'm not even saying that I participated, but please do not put all the blame upon our leaders of that period."

"Don't tell me you're trying to shift responsibility to the Americans. I know of no citizen in my country," Sonia said, "who would agree with mutilating people and disappearing them."

"You have a comfortable life over there," Arce rebutted. "If your people's fantasy existence were suddenly threatened, I'll bet suddenly you'd find yourself debating about the usefulness of torture and targeted assassinations."

Sonia's dark hair was up again in a bun, which made her eyes enlarge like a Japanese cartoon character. I could see a line on her forehead that only appeared in moments of conflict. Then I saw through her into overlapping images of Rosa Parks, Helen Keller, Norma Rae.

"Arce, you feel no remorse. Matt, let's get out of here."

"Please don't go," Arce said. "Let me prepare you a cup of coffee, or would you prefer tea? I'm sorry I only have instant Nescafé or any of our usual Bolivian teas."

Arce served two cups of Nescafé and a mint tea for Sonia. He added a square of dark chocolate next to each cup. He continued his monologue.

"I am a much changed person today compared to what I was 20 years ago. People believe they have universal traits, but in fact most of us are products of our times. In the world you have saintly people, and you have devils. Those account for maybe 2 or 3 percent of the population. The rest can be swayed in any direction according to their self-interests. By all means judge me for the way I was 20 years ago. But rest assured I had nothing to do with your kidnapping, and you have my promise that I have no hard feelings against Muñeca."

I was relieved that it had come from Arce. I didn't want to find myself in a pleading position, and especially not in front of Sonia.

"If you really were in a repenting mood," Sonia said, "then you'd give us whatever information you have about the death squads. They just killed two peasants in Chaco."

"I have been giving whatever information I have to my lawyers. The only information that is useful to the two of you is that I fear you should leave Bolivia as soon as possible."

"Whoa, Arce," I said. "Is that a . . ."

"It's not a threat," Arce interrupted. "Both of you have had your pictures in the papers. The squatters have won their battle. It's reasonable to assume that among the landowners there are a lot of furious folk. If I weren't locked up, I might be able to calm them down. I say *might*. I'm not the Godfather you think I am."

"We're leaving in two days, Arce. Can I bring you anything?" Sonia nudged my leg with her foot. We had perfect nonverbal communication. She was warning me to not be so forthcoming with Arce about our plans. At this moment I trusted his sincerity.

"Just do me a favor," he said. "Between now and then, don't stay alone, and don't go out into the streets. And, Matt, please understand me. I was committed to the racetrack, and I continue to believe that it would be a great asset for Bolivia."

On the way out of the five-star prison yard, I wished I could step through the portal and find myself on the rail at Laurel. The prison guard handed us our passports. I opted for intelligent cowardice and waved down a taxi for only a six-block ride. We got to the apartment, phoned Marv and packed our bags. Sonia phoned the Marianelas, who would be taking back their apartment. We would leave the keys with the guardian on the first floor.

I had discovered a way to stretch out my time on earth, almost to eternity: put myself in a situation of urgent escape, and then try counting down the minutes or hours until the escape vehicle arrives. Sonia seemed to harbor entirely different emotions. She stared blankly into shadows and scanned empty walls.

"You're already feeling nostalgia," I said.

"I'm feeling as if I were leaving these good people in a very dangerous situation."

"I'm sure they're aware of the risks. That's their calling."

"They're heroes, Matt. Why can't you see it?"

"Look, Sonia. You did a good job. It was *your* face that was in the newspapers. At this moment, you're the most vulnerable. Don't feel guilty for leaving. Look at everything you've accomplished."

It was no use. She was sinking into an uncharacteristic depression.

The entire expanse of our two divergent worlds was now compressed into this nearly barren apartment. Considering the packing, the eating of leftovers, the back-and-forth debating, the long silences, an uncomfortable sleep on a sheetless mattress, and finally the freshening up and dressing in the biting pre-dawn cold, we had been waiting in this barren cubicle for 39 straight hours when Marv knocked on the door.

Sonia perked up with Marv's joke about his rescuing her from a cult. If I had used precisely the same words, Sonia's reaction would have been entirely different. Marv did his best to reconstruct my image in her eyes.

At 4:45 A.M. on the morning of our flight, we were now rolling up El Prado and then "taking off" onto the uphill hairpin freeway. We approached the full moon while passing hillside shantytowns. Marv parked his car at "JFK" and saw us all the way through the checkpoint.

Soon our American Airlines plane was skimming the dense Quimsa Cruz mountains, wings nearly touching the glacier of Illimani. We had hardly taken off and we were already on the descent. The flight out of La Paz is a downward experience wherever you go. We would refuel at Santa Cruz and depart for Miami.

Sonia and I had eight hours to talk things over. We paid no attention to the Disney-approved movies, nor did I listen to a sanitized jazz track.

During our time in Bolivia, she had been the Don Quixote and I the Sancho Panza. Now we decided to terminate the Yin-Yang relationship and try for a new, yet-to-be-defined merger. The only turbulence on this flight was our own thumping discourse. She had the philosopher-economist E. F. Schumacher as a reference, from his *Small Is Beautiful: Economics as if People Mattered*. The only philosopher I could quote was Andrew Beyer.

Sonia's dark eyes were welling with joy, in anticipation of renewing her role of mother. I had still not learned to be a good father. I was already thinking of how to get Deedee off to sleep so that I could share a moment of carnal pleasure with a liberated Sonia.

It didn't quite happen that way. After our first dinner back home, Sonia and I went to the bedroom with Deedee following. I turned on WPFW, the local jazz station. Deedee was sitting in bed with us when the inner lights suddenly went out for both Sonia and me. The prolonged dose of adrenaline had suddenly dissipated after the months of tension, agony, conflict, and juxtaposed highs and lows.

Charlie Rouse was soloing on "Bolivar Blues" when we woke up. It was 10:38, Saturday morning. Deedee offered to bring toast and orange juice to our bed.

That afternoon, I cycled out to Laurel. On the street just outside the parking lot I made my way through a group of six or seven people handing out leaflets. They resembled the Grey Panthers, except for one young man wearing farmer's overalls. The student-farmer made eye contact with me, and I felt a vague responsibility to grab a leaflet, fold it, and stash it in my back pocket. Once in the lot, I parked the bicycle against a tilting iron railing that connected to nothing, a few yards from the walking tunnel that led to the grandstand entrance.

I went out to the rail, passing wooden picnic benches until I was as near as possible to the far turn. From that angle you can tell which horses have any gas left in the tank as they glide home. It was 20 minutes to the second post time of a six-furlong sprint for $16,000 maiden claimers. I used the short-form method, eliminating no-win trainers and tossing out every other horse that had lost at least twice at the same maiden claiming level or lower.

I was left with only two horses, the 6, second favorite, and the 8 at 16–1. I bet them both to win and boxed them in the exacta. The stretch duel saw three horses with a chance: the 6, the 8, and the odds-on 2 horse, now outside of them. From my position at the rail you could hear the cracking of the whips. The sound diminished, and the muffled roar of the crowd took over as the three battlers merged with the dusty sunlight. At the moment they hit the finish line, I could pick out three asses neatly lined up in a dead heat. But from in front, it was the 2 horse who had the head advantage. My two horses were second and third. I was rusty, or at least I was lacking the rhythm involved in daily play. I had failed to use my two horses in a "trifecta as show bet" with the favorite on top.

I started to tell myself, "Good method, bad result," but that was just an invented cliché. Something was missing. With no warning, unintentionally, I saw a vision of what I needed. In a flash I recalled the past performances of two particular short-form longshot winners and realized that both also qualified by the early-bloomer method. Why not superimpose the template of the short-form method upon the early-bloomer method, thus focusing on lightly-raced horses.

It seemed like a potent combination. I couldn't wait to get back home to churn out the research. How could it have taken me so long to connect the dots?

Following the race, I took the leaflet out of my back pocket and began speed-reading it, expecting it was from one of various local antigambling groups. It wasn't. It was a group called the Maryland Coalition for Economic Justice (MCEJ). The text railed against the oppressive working conditions of the grooms and backstretch employees, most of whom had been farming people from south of the border, forced off their meager lands by what was termed as "the economic steamroller of intensive agriculture."

Sonia would enjoy reading the leaflet. That was my first reaction. Since landing back in Maryland, I had become a slow thinker, and it took me at least five minutes to realize that the refolded leaflet, now crumpled in my back pocket, was a potential time bomb, set to go off in my own bedroom.

I envisioned Sonia joining the MCEJ and helping the group grow. If I opposed her idealism, Sonia and I would be back to square one. Today I owned a whole section of the apron in front of the rail. I had found my eye of a storm. None of the hum and bustle from the agitated grandstand reached my way. I was still exhausted from the preceding months of tension. The silence resembled my favorite glacier retreat in the Andes. My head bobbed for a moment, nodding off into a dreamy catnap.

I rolled up one afternoon to the Laurel entrance and encountered an extended MCEJ picket line, with Sonia among the chanters. If I crossed the pickets and played my longshot, Gated Community, in the third race, he'd probably lose. But if for some reason I decided not to cross, in order to avoid a dinnertime debate, Gated Community would win by nine lengths at 25–1, without my money on him.

I mustn't have napped for more than a minute and 11 seconds. The dream was a warning. It was too soon for an eternal return to kick in. Sonia and I had learned too much from our Bolivia relationship to start all over again as thesis and antithesis. It was 17 minutes until the next pari-mutuel adventure. Things would work out.

POSTSCRIPT ON BOLIVIA

The background for the story in *Tropical Downs* demanded that I handicap the past performances of Bolivian history. As I turned in the manuscript, Bolivia's first ever indigenous president, Evo Morales, had won a landslide recall election with 67 percent of the vote, unprecedented in a country where candidates would become president with less than 30 percent of the popular vote, and only after scratching around to build coalitions.

The president's platform has included an agrarian reform. Thus, it seemed inevitable to me that some large landowners, opposed to the agrarian reform and having lost control of the state and its army, would resort to hiring paramilitaries.

I had done lengthy interviews of several of the lowland oligarchs a decade ago for articles related to agriculture and banking. Some of them have been accused of receiving illegal land grants from dictators. One of these was the then-governor of Pando, Leopoldo Fernández, who owns or controls through associates more than half the territory of an entire state. The gracious Mr. Fernández was generous with his time, and even invited me to an all-expenses-paid tour of his Pando region. I respectfully declined the offer, explaining to him that my newspaper would pay for such a trip if it was necessary. I referred to interviews such as this one to develop the character of Manuel Arce.

The reason for this postscript is that Prefect (Governor) Fernandez was arrested on September 16, 2008, on charges of acts against the state of emergency. Additionally, other charges for "genocide" are expected for allegedly organizing an ambush in which dozens of peasants were killed, wounded, or unaccounted for at El Provenir on September 11, 2008, according to the Associated Press. Tragically, my handicapping of Bolivian history turned out to be accurate. (This was also the 35th anniversary of the Pinochet coup d'etat against the democratically elected government of Salvador Allende in Chile.)

According to Amnesty International, "Discrimination and racism against the indigenous population of Bolivia has been an underlying feature of these tensions."

POSTSCRIPT ON THE SEARCH
FOR THE AUTOMATIC BET

In reflecting on the research contained in *Tropical Downs*, I have embarked on a real money test by combining templates for the "short-form method" and the "early-bloomer method." By analyzing this research race by race, it has become apparent that if we pile on too many positive factors, then we will lower the average odds and average mutuel, shaving away the higher payoffs. More is not necessarily better.

The power of the short-form method seems to reside in the dynamics between elimination factors and selection factors. We eliminate horses that are proven losers at "today's" class level (two or more losses) and/or whose trainers show less than 12 percent wins for the year.

At this point, horses remain as qualifiers because they are not proven losers at the class level. Then we apply filters that enhance the positives, avoiding the primary factors used by the betting public in order to minimize any erosion of the average mutuel.

The most obvious filter is to require that the trainer have at least an 18 percent win record for the calendar year. A more elegant filter is requiring the horse to qualify by the early-bloomer method, where it must have broken its maiden in its debut or second career race. Bet back the debut winner in career races 4 through 7. Bet back the second-time-out maiden winner in career races 5 through 8. Another possible filter is requiring that the trainer of the qualifying horse show a positive return on investment within one of the pertinent trainer-specialty statistics listed beneath the past performances in *Daily Racing Form*, and including a minimum 18 percent win rate within that specialty. The research process is long and tedious and involves poring over race-day past performances. By researching in such an intimate way, the horseplayer will discover nuances that will help to refine the rules.

About the Author

Beth Rutzebeck/Canterbury Park

M ark Cramer has authored numerous books on horse racing handicapping and adventure (or misadventure) travel. When he's not
betting horses, he's bicycling to jazz concerts, to the French countryside,
and to his job as university professor. He lives in Paris with his wife and son.